Divergent Chill

Battle of Nesma

A Novel by Brian Fontenot

Divergent Chill, 1st edition, published digitally 2010
Divergent Chill: Battle of Nesma, 2nd edition, published digitally and
print-on-demand 2015

Divergent Chill
Copyright ©2010 by Brian Fontenot

Divergent Chill: Battle of Nesma
Copyright ©2015 by Brian Fontenot

Cover art by David Williams and Jerry Shaffer
DrawnWorks Graphics, LLC
www.DrawnWorks.com

Edit done by Raim McIntosh, CEO of Increditus Productions
increditusproductions@outlook.com

ISBN-13: 978-0692466834 (Brian Fontenot)
ISBN-10: 0692466835

Dedication

This novel is dedicated to the memory of Laurie Fontenot.

Acknowledgements

I am indebted to Chris Scarnati, Samantha Morgan, and Barbara L. Fontenot for their editorial assistance. Special thanks to all the friends, family, and teachers who have encouraged me through the years.

Divergent Chill: Battle of Nesma

Contents

Prologue   1

Divergent Chilali   2

Strife's Journal: 302nd Day, 4058, Southern Wilds   17

Failure   18

Recovery   29

Waking Up   41

Strife's Journal: 221st Day, 4057, Northern Hills   49

Sore Legs   50

Born from Fire   55

Aphephobia   61

Strife's Journal: 289th Day, 4056, Silver Sun Capital   78

The Ribbon   80

Strife's Journal: 395th Day, 4058, South Capital Road   88

Just a Walk   89

Past Mistakes   96

The Plantation   102

Strife's Journal: 255th Day, 4057, North Master's Enclave   109

Insomnia   110

The Road to the Capital   115

Strife's Journal: 327th Day, 4056, Northern Hills   124

The Amos Manor   125

The Vineyard   133

Strife's Journal: 2nd Day, 4058, Silver Sun Capital   151

Minnie   153

In His Wisdom   163

All Manner of Help   178

Dealings and Preparations   184

Disguises, Expectations, and Beriszl   193

Strife's Journal: 261st Day, 4057, North Master's Enclave   203

The March   204

Shade   208

Bad News   212

Strife's Journal: 252nd Day, 4056, Blackland Mountains   219

One More Night   220

The Asael   235

Strife's Journal: 260th Day, 4057, North Master's Enclave   247

Orsa in Ruins   249

Peace Offering   267

Strife's Journal: 355th Day, 4058, Burning Sea   270

The Edge of the Abyss   272

The Southern Wilds   282

Strife's Journal: 385th Day, 4058, Ivory (Bone) Cliffs   291

Motivating Factor   293

None Could Console Her   306

Blood-Soaked Boots   311

The Cost of Victory   340

Strife's Journal: 11th Day, 4059, The Northeast Line   353

Reward   354

Divergent Chill   365

Epilogue   372

Prologue

283rd Day, 4254, Orsa

I still see the image of Emma's corpse in my sleep. And thoughts of her will not leave me even during my waking hours. Tomorrow, we will venture into the Divergent Forest to hunt her killer. Perhaps when he is dead, I will find some reprieve.

Dawn will come soon. I pen this by lantern light at a wobbly table in a room on the second floor of Marcus' inn. I've been reading through the journals of General Strife that I copied during my last visit to the capital's archives. Many are missing (removed more than likely), but at least these seem to be unedited and unabridged entries. Those without access to the archives only know of the Order's representation of the journals, but not the actual source.

My interest in the legendary general peaked when I was a boy sitting on my father's knee and listening to him recount tales (fabrications) of Strife. It waned since becoming a man, but in recent days this has changed. Knowing I would soon enter the sacred forest and risk an encounter with a Divergent, I thought to learn as much about them as I could. Strife's journals remain the best source for such information.

I intend to copy selected entries from Strife into my own journal to take with me into the forest. They may be of use should the worst happen.

—Alden Amos

Divergent Chilali

Alden mashed the root between his molars, making some headway toward successfully masticating it. Its sour taste stung the spots just under each of his ears at the back of his jaw. Even though his mouth was sore from chewing, he enjoyed the sensation almost as much as he enjoyed the root's medicinal properties. Ingesting it, as difficult as that could be, reduced the irritation caused by the rashes covering his body—one of the signs the crimson, poisonous plants poking out of the forest floor were killing him.

The plants shot out in long pole-like chutes, usually near the bases of the otherworldly trees in this supposed sacred forest. The longer ones folded under their own weight, forming sharp triangles with the ground. These plants, which seemed to grow everywhere, were dangerous to men. Worse yet, the bark, which was all the plant seemed to be, flaked off, like a scab. And those flakes crumbled into a fine powder covering the forest floor in a layer resembling dry blood.

Even with the medicinal root prepared by Teth, the local tracker he had hired, prolonged exposure to the plants would eventually cause his lungs to bleed, drowning him in his own blood. A man regularly eating the root could last a week or possibly less if he overexerted himself in the forest. Without it, his second day would be short lived.

Men were not supposed to come to this forest, the Divergent Forest. The law of the Silver Sun Empire generally forbade it. But it was more than law or even the danger of running across a wild Divergent. This place was alien to all men.

He knew this as he let his eyes lose focus on any particular object. All the trees in this forest were the same. They sprayed their branches from their black trunks and their willowy branches fell in long curtains of fine cerulean leaves. The color of these leaves made him feel walking beneath these trees was like traversing the sky.

Teth grabbed Alden's shoulder to get his attention. A Blackland Nation soldier sliced off the tip of the old tracker's nose years ago during the skirmishes along the Silver Sun Empire's northwest border. The wound may have left Teth hideously disfigured, but it didn't bother Alden. He had seen far uglier things.

"We're ready to go check the traps, sir," Teth said.

Alden nodded and hopped off the rock he had been resting on and began buckling on his sword and scabbard.

Lea, an assassin on loan to him from the Silver Talon Guild, grunted loudly as she leaned heavily on her bow to string it.

"If you ask me, Shank's too smart for your traps. A Divergent's more likely to get him than your traps," she harped.

Alden regarded the woman. She was about as attractive as a mushroom covered log but could put an arrow through the kneecap of a fleeing man at two hundred paces. His best friend and knight of the Empire, Falcon, answered her before he could.

"Shank has gone feral, Lea. He's no smarter than a rabbit, now, and will be just as easy to trap."

Olin, a Sitaran Priest, rose from his morning meditation with a sigh. A ring, formed with silver tattoos of archaic runes, circled his shaven head just above his brow. When word spread someone was actually going to track Shank into the Divergent Forest and do away with the monster, the Order of Sitara protested, as it always protested any entry into the sacred forest for any reason. Olin was the result of the compromise made between Alden and the Order to gain passage. He was a mere local priest sent along to be a minder.

"I've finished my meditations," said Olin with ridiculous solemnity. "I am prepared to move on."

Alden stomped out the campfire's last few burning

embers.

"I hope you prayed the traps caught Shank," Alden said, not hiding his irritation with the priest. "We can perhaps survive another day in this forest, but I'd rather not try."

Olin gave a nod and waved Alden to lead him onward. Teth carried a sword sheathed at his waist, but he hefted a woodsman's axe onto his shoulder.

Falcon came up to Alden's side as they headed out and spoke so the others could not hear.

"Will you be all right this time?" the knight asked.

In the capital, Falcon was revered for his abilities with his sword and his mind. And he was the youngest squire to ever be knighted. But even as a knight, he often served as Alden's bodyguard at the request of Alden's late father, a merchant widely known and respected in the Empire. This time he joined Alden to aid him in his hunt.

"I think so," Alden said, rubbing the back of his neck.

"I must admit I fear the child-eating monster will escape us this time," Falcon mused. "If only we had more time or more men."

"Or more root."

"Indeed."

"Whatever it takes, Falcon, I will stop him."

They continued to march through the forest in silence. Despite the poisonous plants, the foliage was thin. He found no need to unsheathe his sword to remove an interceding branch or vine, which was a fortunate thing, as Olin demanded they disrupt the foliage as little as possible. The priest was determined not to let the forest be defiled and Alden didn't want to have another argument.

Alden watched the priest at the edge of his vision. He bore his rashes better than everyone else and seemed to quietly revel in the entire experience, as if the discomfort were a blessed penance.

The priest always seemed to know when Alden was watching him and returned a polite smile.

"Last night, did you dream of Emma, again?"

Alden's mind snapped back to all the things he had been trying not to think about for the past few weeks. Shank's bounty was not a new one. The monster plagued the surrounding villages for years. And while the bounty placed on him grew with his terrifying reputation as a child-eater, Alden always calculated the risk of hunting the beast did not outweigh the reward.

Shank was one of the Lesser Races, a Rageborne, and possessed physical prowess beyond any man.

Three and a half weeks ago while traveling between the Chain, the villages dangling south from the capital, Alden discovered one of Shank's victims discarded in the tall grass. Her name was Emma. Shank had gutted her with his bare, clawed hands and eaten the thin bits of meat on her arms, legs, ribs, and buttocks.

What remained reminded Alden of a fish picked clean by a cat; only the tail and head were intact. The discovery altered Alden's risk versus reward assessment. Someone had to stop the beast.

"I barely slept," Alden said with a sigh and an angry glare directed at Olin.

He picked his pace up, the itching he felt with each breath be damned.

Falcon caught up to him.

"Light overcomes all darkness, my friend," Falcon soothed. "Draw peace from knowing that."

"You sound like Olin, except you're about as half as condescending," Alden whispered.

"Given I wish to become a True Silver knight, I'll take that as a compliment."

"There's the marker for the first trap," Alden pointed.

Ahead, gray mold covered a boulder like a coat of fur. The trap, a re-designed spring powered mantrap, still lay buried just below the red dust, completely undisturbed nearby. Even though they were a fair distance away, Alden got a nostril full of the scent coming from the bait. He tried to fight his disgust, but it overwhelmed him immediately. He fell to his knees panting and heaving.

"It's not really such a bad odor," Lea smirked.

Falcon shook his head at Lea, as he helped Alden stand.

Olin just shifted his crossed arms inside his gray robe.

"At least we know the enchantments I placed on the bait are still active."

Alden knew Olin just took another shot at him, but he felt he deserved it for asking the priest to prepare the bait. Pink chunks of it littered the ground over the trap's perimeter.

A boy—Alden chose not to learn his name—died when a startled horse kick him in the chest. Since he was an orphan, it was easy enough to barter for his corpse. It was far more difficult to find a willing butcher. But Alden managed to locate one who lost his niece to Shank and was more than willing to go to the extremes Alden was.

The Order had assigned Olin to the expedition by that point. With Falcon's help and the promise of a larger share of the bounty, Alden was able to convince the priest to place the necessary enchantments on the meat to keep it fresh and warm, nearly alive. Olin, perhaps to punish Alden or just to enhance the bait's effectiveness or both, went a step further and increased the strength of the scent the meat produced.

It sickened Alden then, and it sickened him even more now.

"Good, next trap," Alden said as he held the back of his hand to his nose.

He quickly led them away. Teth, Falcon's elder, still looked up to Falcon. The two traded war stories, as they had since setting out. It was a rare opportunity for someone of Teth's class to be able to speak so freely and openly with a noble and a knight. Teth had just been a militiaman. The worn leather armor he wore now was likely the same suit he had worn in battle years ago.

Falcon, on the other hand, adorned a fresh suit of studded leather, protecting his torso and upper thighs. His brilliant silver kite shield, which marked him as a knight, hung against his back, wrapped in dingy cloth. And behind his shield, he strapped his silver long sword, a masterwork engraved with the three virtues of knighthood, victory, sacrifice, and law, on the gold hilt.

Lea kept an ever-watchful eye. Alden didn't know if she was always so careful or just paranoid. Her eyes flitted about all the shadows in the forest as they walked, while she held an arrow on her bow, ready to be drawn back at any moment.

Her wariness drew Olin's attention, as he sought tranquility in all things, because anything less irritated him.

"Lea, this forest is expansive and the Divergents are few," the priest snapped. "We are also at the edge. So, you need not fear an encounter with one."

"You're just saying that, so I don't put an arrow through her pretty eye if I see her sneaking up on us," Lea returned.

"That would be very regrettable."

"A Divergent would kill us on sight for sport."

"But perhaps it is the price we should pay for invading their sacred realm. Sitara did give them to us to protect us from the Lessers. Our trespass not only insults Sitara, but it insults the Divergents, our guardians."

"No one's noble enough to get eaten alive, priest. Not even you."

Lea sped up, leaving Olin behind. Alden noticed the trim of the priest's robe was stained red from dragging on the ground.

"It is unfortunate, good merchant, but know my robes can be cleaned or replaced," Olin declared. "Unlike this forest if we do not take care."

Alden hated the ability of those from the Order to glean another's thoughts. The more experienced and devoted they became in Sitara's service, the more that particular ability developed. The limits of which were secret, known only to the arch priests and arch priestesses, however.

He picked out the marker for the second trap, a log. The actual trap was hidden some distance away from the marker along the direction of a string of trees. His eyes followed the line of trees, made noticeable by their young age. A mound in the forest floor blocked his vision at his current vantage point.

Falcon reached over his shoulder for his sword.

"Something doesn't feel right to me, Alden," the knight paused. "Can you see the trap?"

"Not yet," Alden replied. "We need to walk a little further. It's behind the mound out there."

Alden pointed and wondered why he hadn't used the mound as a marker. Lea drew her bowstring back.

"That's no mound. It's the butt-end of an uprooted tree," Lea harped.

Alden drew his short sword, which was low quality compared to Falcon's gear.

"There was no uprooted tree here, yesterday," he said, his tone full of concern.

Falcon looked Teth in the eye, telling the man all he needed to know. The tracker dropped his axe and drew his worn, but well-cared for, broadsword.

"Teth will go with you, Alden," the knight commanded. "I'll go around behind. Olin, Lea keep your distance. The more time it takes Shank to spot you, the better."

Falcon sprinted off on his roundabout route to the uprooted tree. Teth followed behind Alden as he jogged for the uprooted tree, feeling a burning sensation in his lungs for the first time. It startled him and made him want to slow down, but the thought this could be the moment for revenge for all those Shank killed pushed him forward with rejuvenating rage.

He charged the uprooted tree and warily circled around

when he got close enough. Teth was barely able to keep pace. It dawned on him he should not have secured the trap to this tree. He even remembered thinking this particular tree was too young and thin to successfully restrict Shank. It was only about as thick as his leg. No, to hold a monster like Shank in place, even if he were wounded by the trap, he should have used a tree five times thicker.

He cursed himself for his stupidity as a keen sense of futility drained him of all his energy. Those emotions dissipated in an instant, however. He skidded to a stop as he witnessed what he had done.

Shank did not spring the trap. No, its roundly serrated steel jaws clasped a Divergent, biting deeply into her shins and calves. She had been barely saved from dismemberment by her bones. The jaws were twice the diameter and thickness of a regular mantrap. So, for her to be caught in such a way, she must have tried to leap clear. Alden recalled just how difficult it was to even crank the jaws open to set it, requiring the combined effort of Falcon, Teth, and himself. The reflexes and speed necessary to accomplish such a feat, to even attempt to leap clear of the springing jaws, astonished Alden.

Once trapped, the Divergent had fought against the powerful jaws, trying to force them open. But Alden had the teeth hardened and reinforced and he added a mechanism to lock the jaws shut once the pressure plate had been triggered. Still, some of the teeth were bent and the jaws were noticeably warped. As a result, perhaps, the Divergent's hands were gashed.

And when she failed to force the jaws open, she tried to take the trap with her, he surmised. But he had chained it to the tree by driving a stake deep into the trunk at its base. Its blood-smeared bark bore claw and teeth marks. And her blood also painted a nearby tree, which was slightly uprooted, meaning she had pulled on it to uproot the other.

He dropped his sword. The Divergent, a naked mess of

red hair, wearily held herself up on her hands and knees. Her emerald eyes locked on his. If she were able to stand, the top of her head would only reach his waist. She was a Divergent, even though her form was that of a girl, even though she resembled Emma, he kept thinking.

Teth came up behind him and froze. The Divergent's eyes darted to him then back to Alden, who stood the closest to her. Falcon came around next. She whipped around, dragging the metal trap with her pinned legs, squeezing out fresh blood.

Falcon saw her and leaped away as if he had come too close to a poisonous snake.

"By Sitara!" the knight exclaimed.

When she turned, Alden noticed claw marks, deep serrations in her back revealing bone at places. It occurred to Alden he didn't smell the bait. He searched for it. None of the pink chunks lay about. Shank, he thought.

Olin, his hands reaching for the sky, rushed past Teth to stand in front of Alden.

"What have we done? Sitara forgive us," the priest whined.

Olin took a step toward her, and she rushed to face him, ready to attack. Olin quickly stepped back out of her range and lowered his hands defensively.

"What are we to do? Sitara, what are we to do?" the priest continued to grieve.

Lea kept her distance, fearful and ready to launch an arrow.

"Give the word. It'll only take one shot," she said, absolutely serious.

Olin kept silent.

"I think Lea may be right," Falcon said, as he slowly circled around to join Alden. "You have to use the key to release the trap. She'll never let us close enough to use it. And even still, her wounds …"

"Perhaps, together, we could restrain her long enough,"

Teth said with a hard swallow, as he came to Alden's side.

"No, she would tear us to pieces, even as small and wounded as she is," Falcon said, shaking his head. "We could maybe let her wounds rend her unconscious, then-"

"That would take much longer than we have in this forest," Olin spat.

"Then use your enchantment."

"To what end, knight?"

"Make her fall asleep."

"It would take an arch priest to enchant a Divergent in such a way. No, I believe it is only right that the one who had the idea to set that damnable trap in this forest be responsible for remedying this."

Falcon grabbed Olin by the front of his robes.

"Enough," Alden shouted, turning on both of them.

He grabbed the key hanging from his belt pouch.

"What do you think you're doing, Alden?" the knight questioned, putting his hand on Alden's chest.

"Take everyone back to camp and prepare to leave," Alden ordered with a woeful distance in his voice. "If I'm not back by dusk, go without me. I'm going to unlock the trap."

"She's wounded and wild and will never let you get close enough," Falcon said.

"I did this," Alden said, swatting Falcon's hand away. "It was my plan."

"I know, but it's not what you intended."

"What does it matter what I intended, Falcon?"

"Even if you somehow free her, what then? Look at her wounds? Do you think she'll let you treat them, too?"

"Follow my orders, knight."

"So be it. Lea, Olin, Teth, let's go," Falcon said, sheathing his sword.

"Orders or not, I'll not be letting you commit suicide, sir," Teth stood his ground.

Alden whirled around to face Teth.

"This is my responsibility! Get out of here, damn you!"

"Fine," Teth nodded angrily. "But we'll be coming back for you or your corpse before we leave."

Falcon seconded Teth with an agreeing glance.

"Or whatever is left of your corpse," Lea said under her breath.

Teth shot her a stern look and motioned for her to go. She went without a word.

Olin, still not persuaded enough to leave, continued to stand and watch the Divergent with reverence.

"Olin, go now," Alden snapped at the priest.

"If this Divergent dies by your hand-"

"I know. Now get out of here!"

Olin stormed away.

Alone, Alden believed he had a chance. Little was known about Divergents beyond folktales and the mythology developed over the centuries around the legendary General Strife in the Nameless War against the Lessers.

Strife was an oddity and a miracle. He was a male Divergent, the first ever known to come from the god-born race of females. And he was an elemental user, which made him doubly rare. Divergents were Sitara's chosen people, but elemental powers came from her ancient enemies, the Elemental Kings. Elemental powers were rare among even his people with maybe one in a thousand possessing such a power. Those who wielded the Fire King's power, as Strife did, were one in ten thousand. Even two hundred years later, Strife's elemental power was the subject of intense debate among the Order.

Alden, however, was far more impressed with the tactics Strife brought to the battlefield. He possessed a keen mind, given more to instinct than thought, but still producing victory after victory with acceptable losses. And he picked up language with remarkable ease.

Now, Alden hoped a fragment of that intelligence

existed in the Divergent before him. He believed he could see a glimmer of it in her eyes. He hoped it would be possible to communicate with her if he could establish trust.

Squeezing the key in his right hand, he tossed his sword and went down to his knees in front of her. He grabbed his water skin and held it out. Methodically, he opened it and poured out a short stream of water. He then offered the skin to her.

It took a moment, a desperately long moment, but she began cautiously moving toward him, dragging the trap behind her. The red dust stained her body as much as her own blood had, but her skin showed no rashes. Cerulean leaves littered her hair. And her face showed no emotion as she steadily approached, disconcerting him.

He gauged he was close enough for her to be able to take the skin from him, but also far enough away the chain would keep her from reaching him. So, he faced three risks. He could have incorrectly estimated the length of the chain. She could be able to drag the tree forward. Or she could grab for his hand instead of the skin. If either of the three occurred, he would be dead.

She stretched her hand out to reach for the skin. This close, he noticed an oddly shaped birthmark on the small of her back. But he couldn't make out its shape with the gashes and dry blood. As her hand drew closer, he forced himself to take slow deep breaths and to not look her directly in the eyes while she was so close. Divergents were predators and he assumed such an action would universally be perceived as a challenge.

She gently took the skin from him, and he wondered if she was just as wary of him as he was of her, given her current predicament. She pushed herself backward then tilted the skin upside down. She sucked on it, rather than letting it pour into her mouth. Her thirst must have been overwhelming he thought, as she finished the skin and tossed it aside.

Next, he reached into his rations pouch and removed a piece of jerky. He showed it to her with a wave of his hand, took a bite, and then extended it in the same fashion as he had his water skin, while he chewed. She crawled forward, stopping short of her arm's length to smell it. Then she rushed forward to grab it. The action was so quick he almost choked on his jerky.

Still, she took the meat without taking him, and this time, she had not forced herself backward before eating it. She crammed as much of the strip as she could into her mouth, leaving some of it sticking out while she chewed. He had appealed to the animal in her, but he still sensed if he moved any closer, she would react defensively.

Divergents were intelligent. They were just born wild and were destined to live wild, unless summoned by the Silver Goddess Sitara to aid mankind. This Divergent before him looked so much like an ordinary child, he wondered if she possessed a child's curiosity. But no one knew or had ever reported such knowing, as to whether Divergents were so similar to children. He would find out.

A jeweled amulet rested beneath his tunic. It was a gift from his mother many years ago before she passed. He reached into his tunic and pulled out the amulet. A multi-faceted, sapphire jewel dangled from a polished silver chain, spinning one way and then the other.

The sunlight, as dim as it was beneath the cerulean leaves, still glittered off the jewel. He watched her eyes as she swallowed down her mouthful of jerky in one hard gulp. They grew wide.

He unclasped the chain from his neck as she pushed her way closer to him, daring to use the trap biting into her legs for traction while dragging the tree half a pace. Her strength, no, her ability to withstand pain shocked him, as he heard branches snap when the tree dragged.

He pushed his fear as far down as he could by focusing on the situation at hand. Her odor was pungent like that of any wild animal, so he transitioned to mouth breathing. Her face hovered inches from the jewel he dangled in front of his face. She could grab his neck, now, if she chose to do so.

She reached for the jewel and grasped it. Without thinking, perhaps reacting to the sentimental value he placed on the amulet, he held on, mildly resisting her attempt to seize the jewel. He felt the smooth power of her tug. It jerked his arm down but didn't wrench the chain from his hand.

She didn't persist in taking it, though. She reared up on her knees, staring at him, confused, her tiny forehead wrinkled. He looked down at her hand still holding the jewel and reached for her hand. She tensed for a second when his skin made contact with hers, but she let him gently unclasp her hand from the jewel.

He then held both ends of the chain out with the jewel dangling in the middle and reached for her. He held his breath through the entire process, even when she flinched repeatedly. After silently cursing himself for fumbling with the clasp, he hooked it.

He pulled back as she toyed with the jewel hanging down to her belly. She tasted the chain as she inspected the jewel. She held it out to him, inviting him to see it, he assumed. He leaned in closely to examine his jewel. He had seen it a thousand times before, but that didn't matter.

What did matter was he made his first mistake in dealing with her. She was intelligent, much more so than he ever expected. Much of what he remembered was blurred with motion and vertigo, but when he landed face first on the ground several paces away, he was certain of a couple things. She hadn't tried to kill him, and she took the key from his hand.

He wiped the red powder from his face. Some dusted into his left eye, irritating it greatly. He pinched it shut and covered it hard with his palm. His other eye watered, blurring his vision. When he rolled over and looked back, she was gone. Somehow, she either knew or discovered by watching him the only way to release the trap was the key.

He sucked wind as he pushed himself up to his feet and began stumbling in the direction of camp, holding his eye. She, the little fiend, even stole his amulet. He slapped aside a red chute. He had tossed his sword this way and now he couldn't find it. Perhaps, she stole it as well. Divergents were clearly predators, but he would make sure to warn others that they were also thieves.

Strife's Journal: 302nd Day, 4058, Southern Wilds

It rained for a third day.

As of the last battle, I command 3,458 men and 3 women. 325 men remain wounded. 158 of them will likely be incapable of fighting again. 2 of the women are now with child. Still burning our dead: 2,348.

The rain slows the process. The wind from the northwest grows frigid.

Scouts continue to report nothing of interest. General Aiden suspects the Talarians and the Ragebourne are still retreating further into Talarian territory. I disagree. I will conduct my own reconnaissance when night falls.

Divergent mothers birth their ruby-haired, emerald-eyed daughters nameless and leave them as soon as they are able to walk. I do not begrudge my mother, nor do I regret her leaving. This is for the best.

As a people we have no people. We view each other only as potential threats, for we are rightly arrogant to believe only another Divergent could possibly threaten one of us, as every other living creature is just food.

We are strange cowards indeed to fear ourselves and only ourselves. It is when I meditate upon this tragedy of our race that I am reminded of both our purity and sanctity.

We are the chosen children of the Silver Goddess Sitara—our true mother. She deigns to only gift few of us with the strength to overcome our failing and awaken our minds to the kind of civility the Lessers so foolishly took for granted (to their ongoing detriment).

It is with this gift Sitara calls me to protect man and by this responsibility I am honored. I am grateful for her light, always.

—General Strife Ashwake

Failure

By the time Alden reached camp, he walked regularly, but still covered his left eye; it itched terribly. Falcon and Olin dashed toward him, their expressions full of questions.

"The Divergent's free," Alden said, defeated.

Falcon grabbed him to try to look at his eye.

"Your eye? Did she take it? Let me see."

"I got some of the damnable dust in it. I'm fine," Alden said, pushing Falcon aside.

Olin forced his way between them and grabbed his shoulders.

"The Divergent will survive, yes?"

"The little fiend is more than fine, priest. Now let me go."

"Little fiend?"

"Never mind, let us leave this forsaken forest."

Olin let him go as Teth walked up to them.

"Falcon led us on to the next one, sir. The bait was taken without setting off the trap."

Alden glanced at Falcon with his good eye for verification.

"When we discovered the third trap had been picked clean, I told Lea to trip it with an arrow," Falcon shrugged. "We then went back to the first and tripped it, too. I could not, in good conscience, leave those contraptions out here live, especially when they've proven themselves useless for our purpose."

"Told you Shank was too smart for your traps," Lea unstrung her bow with a grunt. "He's no rabbit."

Frustration threatened to overwhelm him. He took a moment, swallowing hard even though his mouth had gone dry. After only a long deep breath and some careful thought, he spoke aloud.

"It seems I've gone about this the wrong way. For that I apologize. But understand, I've not given up on hunting this monster. I will find a way. I swear."

"Whatever way you devise, know it will not involve returning to this forest," Olin stabbed at Alden through the air with a slightly curled finger. "You've done enough damage, I think."

Falcon stepped in front of Olin and gave him a hard stare.

"I believe he has more than atoned for his mistake by risking his life to free the Divergent."

"So, it seems."

Lea slid her bow back into its case, which was a thick staff.

"Well now that this job is over, I'm heading back. I tired of these rashes almost as long ago as I tired of your company. Expect a bill from my employer, merchant."

Lea began walking away.

Teth rolled his eyes.

"It's been our pleasure, bark face."

Falcon grinned for a tiny moment.

"Name calling is not necessary, Teth."

"Yes, sir knight."

Lea paused then turned around as if she had something more to say. But nothing came from her mouth. It just dropped open as she ripped her bow from its case.

Shank, falling through the blue canopy, attacked Teth first. All five of the curled, obsidian claws, extending from the fingers and thumb of his right hand, raked into the side of Teth's ribs from behind. The claws, which were sharp, were not designed to sheer bone. But they were strong enough to match the power of their master. The raking motion snagged Teth's rib cage and sent him whirling through the air many paces. He landed as a jumble of limbs with numerous dull cracking sounds all at once, making Alden cringe.

Falcon managed to get his sword unsheathed in time to block Shank's next swipe. It took all the knight's strength to toss the blow wayward without losing his sword in the process. He quickly hopped backwards out of Shank's immediate range, hoping to center himself, Alden thought, as he eyed the beast.

Shank looked, aside from the snarling madness, much like any other Rageborne. He stood a-man-and-a-half in height. His arms hung almost as long. His toes bore the same claws as his hands, except they were shorter, flatter. Bristled gray fur matted his back and the rest was tough, dark gray hide. Beneath that were rolls of quivering muscle.

Shank shifted his attention from Falcon to Alden. His face reminded Alden of a wolf's, but the snout was shorter and more wrinkled at the top. And his eyes, narrow bright red beads, penetrated him. Alden knew a Ragebourne's sense of smell was sharp, so he was certain Shank could smell his fear building, as it escaped with his sudden perspiration.

Even if he still had his weapon, it would do him little good. Ten well-armed, well-trained men would be fortunate to survive such an encounter. Or, one or two of them would be.

The Rageborne were very hardy creatures. Their chests held two hearts; a secret Strife learned. The larger worked the same as any other beating heart. But their other heart, the smaller one, would only begin beating when the Rageborne wanted it to do so. And when it did, their strength, speed, and ability to endure pain and injury would greatly increase as a blinding rage overtook them. They were virtually invincible in this state, which had become the namesake of their race.

The surest way to kill a Rageborne in this state was to pierce its small heart, another secret Strife discovered.

Alden took a step backward. Lea was nowhere close to having an arrow notched or even her bow strung. Olin ran to Teth to attend to his injuries. Falcon raised his sword back in preparation to strike. He swung down and across, preparing to reverse his grip and lash out backhanded, but Shank spun aside and grabbed Falcon's sword arm at his elbow.

Shank whipped the knight at Lea, bowling her over. Alden saw her catch Falcon's hip with her face. He figured any injury her face sustained would be an improvement and quickly turned his attention back to his imminent death. He took another step back, as Shank lumbered toward him.

"You've been enjoying the meat I left for you, haven't you, Shank?" Alden dared to ask.

Shank paused. Alden now had a moment to think. Teth's axe lay on the ground a few paces away. He casually sidestepped toward it.

"Fresh, wasn't it?"

Shank's flat, pink tongue lapped his snout. Alden got another step closer to the axe.

"There's more, much more."

He took another step toward the axe. Shank moved too, stepping onto the axe's handle. He chuckled with a coarse barking sound then spoke with a smooth, eerily pleasant voice.

"You think I'm an animal, that I am less than you. This is why I tear your children to pieces and nourish myself with their meat."

Alden stood his ground, facing the behemoth before him.

"You kill innocent children to punish us?"

"Not innocent!" roared Shank.

Shank reared his hand back, preparing to turn Alden into a pile of skin strips and bone. Alden stepped forward, getting as close to face-to-face as he could with Shank. He hissed with all the disgust that had welled up in his gut since he first discovered Emma.

"Coward."

Shank lowered his hand and lurched back as if Alden had buried a sword in his chest. Alden pressed him.

"Your people and the others began the Nameless War," Alden fumed. "And you lost. But we, the Silver Sun Empire, chose to allow you to live. And murdering defenseless children is how you repay the mercy we showed you? Coward!"

Shank growled and shoved Alden backward. His intent wasn't to take Alden off his feet, but to just put some distance between them.

"Your people let us live forever in slavery!"

Alden swung his arm across his body dismissively.

"How dare you claim you deserve better than to be our slaves. You began the war. And the Blackland Nation chose to slaughter your people, your children, while our nation gave you your lives!"

"We have been your slaves long enough! We deserve to be free now!"

"So, you make these claims by sneaking out of the forest to murder children?"

"No, I do it to strike at your race! If I kill enough of your children, your race will dwindle and die as mine does!"

Shank grabbed Alden by his neck; his thumb and forefinger were nearly long enough to ring it, but his claws overlapped. He hoisted Alden from the ground while Alden kicked and struggled. He pulled Alden close to his snout and turned him to speak into his ear.

"Murder children? It matters not. You are just as defenseless, but your taste is not as savory."

Alden felt Shank's hand tighten around his neck. He felt his eyes bulge and his tongue poke out as the undeniable force squeezed his throat shut. His entire head throbbed, surely close to exploding from the pressure building inside it.

Dying out here meant his body would never be recovered. His family would never know his true fate and would live with black uncertainty. Emma would never be avenged, and this monster would continue killing until another fool tried to hunt it in this sacred forest. Utter failure swelled inside his heart, drowning out his will to live, causing his body to go limp and just endure his fate.

Before the end could come, a tangle of red hair, a glimmer of sapphire, and steel fell onto Shank's shoulders. The Divergent twisted Shank's head aside as her legs bled and the amulet swung wildly in the air. Shank had no time to react as she pushed Alden's sword downward into his torso from just behind his collarbone. Only the hilt stopped her from forcing the sword deeper. Alden saw its tip burst out of the upper side of Shanks stomach.

Shank bit his own tongue off from the pain as he dropped Alden. He grabbed the Divergent as she struggled to tear the sword out of his chest. His curled claws dug into her torso, puncturing the dirty, pale skin. He slammed her headfirst into the ground over and over, splattering his black and her bright red blood.

Some of their hot blood spattered Alden. He coughed and gagged. His eyes began to burn. Shank's blood exuded an acrid vapor and Alden realized the monster's second heart was beating. In this fearful state the monster would not even feel his wounds, not even the sword sheathed in his chest.

An arrow whistled past Alden, followed by another and another. One struck Shank in the snout. Another pierced his neck. And the third struck the Divergent in the back when Shank raised her up as a shield. Falcon recovered, rolled low, and came up with a powerful two-handed slash, freeing both the Divergent and one of Shank's hands.

Her body thumped on the ground as Falcon twisted around to slash Shank's head. Even as enraged as he was, Shank knew this was a losing battle, now. He ripped the sword out of his chest, cleaving through his own collar bone, to block Falcon's strike. The swords clanged off each other violently. The shock stunned Falcon, nearly breaking his hand and giving Shank more than enough time to kick the knight solidly in the chest.

Falcon sailed backward as arrow after arrow bit into Shank's back. Shank flung Alden's sword end over end at Lea. Somehow, she dropped to the ground fast enough to avoid the blade, but it still clipped off the end of her bow.

Ripping the blade from his chest was not the best tactic the Ragebourne could have used. Alden surmised doing so must have damaged Shank's second heart. The beast's odor was not nearly as pungent. And the new wound was beginning to cause the beast significant enough pain to force a retreat.

Shank whimpered loudly and dashed away, clutching the injury. Furious, Alden snatched Teth's axe and chased after Shank. His lungs burned. He coughed up blood into his mouth but forced himself to keep chasing, even as Shank easily gained ground. Realizing he could not catch the beast, he flung Teth's axe at him, but the projectile fell pitifully short.

Alden spat blood and wheezed with his hands on his knees. He found Teth's axe and returned to camp. Falcon knelt, leaning on his sword to catch his breath while he held his side. Alden guessed Shank broke some of his friend's ribs. The left side of Lea's face swelled up, fattening her lips and partially covering her eye, which had already begun to darken.

Olin half-carried Teth over to them. The large man's legs buckled with each step, but he was lucky to be alive, given the lacerations on the side of his ribs. Olin set Teth against a tree.

"I am exhausted, but Teth will survive," Olin huffed. "How did the rest of you fare?"

Falcon stood with a wince.

"I have been schooled enough to know how to quicken my own healing. I will recover with time."

Lea spoke with a slur and handed Alden his short

sword.

"We need to leave here, quickly."

Alden nodded and noticed the Divergent lying still on the ground, the dirt damp with her blood. He went to her and knelt down. She looked broken. The arrow stood, planted in her back, piercing the birthmark. Blood from her head and other wounds smeared her body, plastered her hair to her skin and stained his mother's amulet. He took the memento back, squeezing it tight before donning it.

Falcon wiped his blade clean and sheathed it.

"It was a noble thing she did for us."

Olin nodded, not taking his eyes from the Divergent.

"Sitara's forgiving heart be praised."

Alden placed his hand on her back to roll her onto her side. When he touched her, he swore he felt her heartbeat. He lowered his ear to her back, surprising those around him. It did still beat. He lifted his head to look at them, feeling relief so powerful he trembled.

"She's still alive," he said with a shaky voice.

Olin rushed to Alden and slid down to his knees. He placed his hand on her back.

"She is alive but is weakening. If only I weren't so fatigued, I could remove the arrow."

Alden glared at the priest.

"What does that mean?"

"I used much of my power saving Teth's life. Attempting to exert myself further, I could kill her."

"She will die anyway. Get this arrow out of her."

Olin looked at Falcon. The knight crossed his arms and looked to Alden.

"And what then?"

"What do you mean?"

"Look at her wounds. Even if we remove the arrow, those wounds will kill her or leave her vulnerable to Shank."

"Then we will tend to those wounds."

"We need to leave this forest. We don't have the time to wait for Olin to recover and we don't have enough supplies with us to even bandage her."

Alden gripped the arrow.

"Then we will take her with us. Heal the wound priest."

Alden, thankful Lea's arrows had field points for accuracy and not traditional broad heads, slid the arrow out of her back. The poison the assassin coated her arrows with would be another matter. He hoped it would be as ineffective on a Divergent as it had been on Shank.

As he pulled the arrow free, he heard Olin curse him under his breath. The priest lunged forward to cover the spurting wound, which began glowing softly with white light. Smoke, like breath on a winter night, rose from his hands. He shut his eyes, and his lips formed a prayer silently. Sweat ran down the sides of his face and the back of his bare head. Alden could only watch and hope. Falcon turned his back, understanding the risk Alden had forced Olin to take. The result could potentially be more gruesome than he cared to witness.

Olin pulled away with a gasp and nearly fell over unconscious, but he collected himself. The arrow wound looked very raw but was closed enough to stop the bleeding. Alden rolled the Divergent over and lifted her up in his arms.

Falcon stared at him hard.

"You can't take her. It is against the law."

"We have no choice. If we leave her, she will die, either from her own wounds or from Shank."

"I am aware of that, but the law isn't just to protect Divergents from exploitation. It's also meant to protect the citizenry from the Divergents. Can you imagine what would happen if you took her back and nursed her to health? A wild, uncalled Divergent would be loosed on the populace. There is no knowing how many she would kill. She could become a scourge worse than Shank."

"This one is not a manslayer, Falcon."

"How do you know?"

"I did not free her. She freed herself."

"What do you mean she freed herself?"

"She took the key from me. Somehow, she knew what it was and how to use it."

"But that does not mean she isn't a manslayer."

"She let me live and then assisted us against Shank."

"You only guess at her intentions. She had your sword, did she not? You returned to the camp without it. So, she must have taken it from you intending to go after Shank."

Alden raised the amulet up to show Falcon.

"No, she took this, too, and probably just followed me back to camp to find more."

Olin shot up to his feet, not so fatigued anymore.

"How dare you imply a Divergent could be a thief!"

"That's not what I was implying."

"It is what you were thinking."

"If you wish to follow my thoughts, priest, keep pace with them."

Lea carefully examined her broken bow, and then tossed it aside.

"Leave her, keep her, whatever. But I'll not stay a moment longer in this forest. And besides, knight, you make the same mistake you made with Shank. You only see them as rabbits or wolves."

Falcon regarded Lea with a raised eyebrow. Alden, for the first time, was glad she shared her opinion.

"She'll be my responsibility, Falcon. I'll see with all my resources she does not become a scourge. This, I swear to you."

"I do not like this. I fear your recent experiences and your father's death have impaired your judgment, but I will stand by your decision, as I always have."

"Thank you, Falcon."

"Do not thank me. By allowing you to take this path,

I've done you no favor."

Falcon grabbed his bedroll from his pack and gave it to Alden.

"Wrap her in this to keep her warm. By the time we exit, I expect you to have devised the necessary plans for her care. As you and I both know, you will not be able to return to your home in the capital with her."

Alden knew this, as he wrapped the Divergent in the blanket.

"Olin, can Teth walk?"

"Not alone."

"Don't let me slow you down, sir."

"Falcon, would you?"

Falcon, wincing, swooped to Teth's aide and helped him stand.

"Lea, please lead us out."

"My pleasure," the assassin said with a groan.

Alden sunk Teth's axe into a nearby tree. He planned to use it as a marker if he ever came back to this forest. He followed behind the others with Olin warily trailing behind him. He was more nervous about the priest's proximity than the Divergent he was holding in his arms, which he found remarkable.

Recovery

The sun drifted behind the cliffs overlooking Orsa Village by the time Alden and his party cleared the woodlands. It would be a few hours more before Sitara's Silver Star reached its apex. Its light dimmed the stars around it and cast shadows across the ground. He could not imagine what the night would be like without it. While there were cloudy nights, even stormy ones, he always knew the star was there, waiting for the sky to clear.

He drew a sense of peace from this knowing, even though he did not consider himself devout to Sitara, especially compared to Falcon, who carried Teth on his shoulder. Teth lost consciousness moments before they reached the Divergent Forest's edge. Olin feared the tracker's internal injuries had been aggravated. Falcon said nothing as he slung the large man across his shoulder and marched. Alden knew not how Falcon possessed the stamina and strength for such an act, but he was grateful for it. Teth was a good man and deserved a better end than this one.

Alden adjusted his hold on the Divergent. She remained unconscious as her bleeding seeped through the bedroll to stain his tunic. He decided he would take her to the Fieldman Inn. Emma's uncle, Marcus Fieldman, owned it and could be convinced to help or at least keep quiet for the night.

Falcon agreed to this plan and would take the others to the local militia building. There, Teth's injuries could be seen to, and Olin could rest properly and be able to do more with his blessed enchantments than any former battlefield surgeon, like Alden, could hope to accomplish. Teth was also well-known in this village and would be readily helped.

Alden split off from the party without a word. Olin attempted to follow, but Falcon grabbed him, almost losing his hold on Teth.

"With the rest of us, priest. Trust Alden to do what he must with her."

"Expect me as soon as I am able, good merchant," Olin sighed.

"Of course, just see to Teth, Lea, and Falcon's injuries first," Alden replied, hoping the priest was too fatigue to notice what he was thinking at that moment.

"Are not the Divergent's injuries more serious?" Olin inquired, not ready to give up so easily.

Alden glanced down at her.

"Perhaps, but I will attend to them tonight with more conventional methods. If she recovers too quickly, well, consider that."

Olin pursed his lips and ran his hand over his scalp.

"There is wisdom in what you say, but if her condition worsens, send for me immediately."

"Of course. Now go. Teth can't afford further delay."

Falcon called for Olin to follow, and the priest did this time. Lea remained silent, perhaps exhausted, as she leaned heavily on her staff and let her quiver dangle from her elbow. As if waking from a light sleep, she shook her head and trudged after Falcon. Alden felt the weariness, too, which came from the tingling in his chest, he assumed. Had they stayed just a few hours longer in those woods, he feared what the result might have been.

Alden found the local inn. The inn had three levels to it: a basement for storage, a main floor where food and drink were prepared and served, and the top floor held the rooms. The innkeeper, Marcus, emptied a mop bucket out the back door. A lantern lit the doorway behind him, and he rubbed his lower back, as he squinted to see Alden. His shadow obscured Alden's face, so he leaned just slightly off to one side.

"Alden, that you?" Marcus asked.

"It is."

Marcus untied his apron and slapped it over his shoulder.

"I almost didn't recognize you with that rash on your face."

"It should clear up soon, I hope."

Marcus tugged on his curly blonde beard; an action Alden had come to identify as a nervous habit of the man. Alden knew Marcus only wished to know one thing, but he probably thought it impolite to ask.

"We didn't get Shank."

Marcus wiped his face and took in a breath that bulged out his plump belly.

"I see. Well, why don't you come inside? I can get a bath ready for you and a meal."

Alden stood his ground.

"I'm sorry, Marcus. I'll stop him. I swore to you I would."

"It's okay. You did right by trying what you did. Entering the forest like that took a kind of courage few men have. Why don't you come in, now, and we'll have a drink."

Alden took a step forward. Marcus squinted, again.

"What's that you're carrying there?"

Before Alden could say anything, the inn owner's face went pale.

"By Sitara, tell me it's not another-"

Alden rushed up, but stopped short, thinking the better of getting closer to the man to reassure him right now.

"No, it's not another. This one is different."

Marcus looked him over, puzzled and relieved.

"Different?"

"I'm about to ask you for something. If you don't want to give it to me, I will understand, because it is dangerous. Some would call it foolhardy."

"What are you thinking of asking me for?"

"Your help."

"Well, you always have my help. You know that."

Alden gently touched the bundled Divergent in his arms with his free hand.

"This is different."

"Stop going in circles, Alden, and just tell me what you got."

Alden peeled down the bedroll to reveal her head to Marcus and the innkeeper stumbled back, catching the doorway.

Alden put a finger to his nose.

"No one must know of this."

Marcus steadied himself and spoke with a whisper that was almost shouting.

"You brought a Divergent to this village!"

"I know. Believe me, I know. But please, I had no choice."

"She looks asleep now, but she could tear you apart the moment she wakes up. She could tear this village apart!"

"Marcus, please listen for just a moment."

Marcus crossed his hairy arms.

"We both may only have a moment if she wakes."

"She's not a killer, Marcus. Shank attacked us, took us all by surprise. She came to our aid. She's the only reason we survived, but Shank hurt her. I need your help, Marcus. I need to tend to her injuries, now!"

Alden lifted her just enough to show Marcus the blood staining his tunic.

"Marcus, please. I ask you to trust me."

Marcus turned his back and grumbled quietly.

"Take her upstairs to the room on the far right of the north hall. No one else is staying up there tonight. I'll get together some supplies and be up there shortly. And Alden …"

"Yes?"

"However much I trust you, the law is the law."

"It won't come to that."

"I pray it doesn't."

Marcus stepped inside and Alden followed. He took the few steps leading up to the kitchen. Marcus had been in the process of cleaning it before he showed up at his backdoor with a Divergent. A stewpot simmered on the stove. He figured it was Marcus' dinner. The innkeeper climbed down the ladder leading to the basement as Alden moved quickly through the tavern area. A frail old man smoking a pipe at the bar took no notice of him as he slipped by.

He heard blood dripping on the hardwood as he climbed the stairs. He glanced back and saw a trail of droplets following behind him. He moved up the stairs with more expediency and hoped Marcus would see to the mess before anyone could ask questions.

Upstairs, lantern light from the hall barely illuminated the room enough for Alden to see. A large table, with an unlit lantern hanging above it sat in the center of the room. A couple of cots lined the wall facing the front of the inn and a small fireplace, adequate for boiling water, had been built into the side wall. This unusual, extra fireplace made sense, when Alden noticed a large wood tub taking up the corner of the room near a trunk.

He laid the Divergent on the table and went out into the hallway to borrow the lantern. With some kindling and wood chips, he started a fire and lit the lantern above the table. The brown bedroll seeped with so much blood it looked black. He dashed out and hung the lantern back in the hall, just as Marcus came up the stairs, wiping the blood trail clean.

"This is not a good sign, Alden."

"I know. Bring what you can."

"That room's sometimes used by the village midwife for delivering babes. She keeps fresh supplies in the trunk."

Alden nodded and hurried back to the room. He lifted the trunk's lid and took a quick inventory. It was as well stocked with medical supplies as any barracks in the capital.

Rolls of thread, clean cloth, liquor, and a set of small sharp knives numbered among the items inside. Even some tools normally used for picking locks had been adapted by this clever midwife. For a moment, Alden wondered as to her real identity and purpose in this village.

He gathered what he thought he would need on the table as Marcus came into the room with two buckets of freshwater and shut the door. Alden began unrolling the Divergent from the bedroll. Parts of it stuck to her wounds with crusted blood. He moistened those parts with a wet cloth and managed to free her without causing new bleeding.

In the lantern light he saw her shins and calves were terribly gashed to the bone in a few places. Her hands were not much better. Since he had never seen a living creature with wounds as serious as these before, he didn't have any idea how to stitch them. If a man bore such wounds and a priest weren't readily available, a surgeon would likely remove the limbs. While the gashes were open, raw, and moist, they weren't bleeding. He moved on from them for now.

Her neck and forehead bore deep bruises, but he didn't think anything seemed broken. Her head worried him, though. Three large lumps rose out of her scalp, where abrasions had peeled her hair away. These were caused by Shank striking her against the ground. He continued his triage, turning her over.

Immediately, he found the bleeding. It came not from the lacerations on her back, across her shoulder blades, ribs, and buttocks, left by Shank's claws. No, it came from the arrow wound Olin had supposedly healed. It oozed bright red blood and Alden had to wonder if this wound remained open from some kind of poison with which Lea had coated her arrowheads.

He rinsed and scrubbed his hands in a basin provided by Marcus and then soaked the blood up from around the wound with a cloth. He examined it as best he could before more blood filled the hole again. He picked out the cause of the wound remaining open—a silver arrowhead in the form of a sharply acute triangle. He cursed himself for forcing Olin to heal the wound. Attempting to magically close a wound around a foreign object gave the appearance of the wound being healed, while worsening the internal injuries by forcing the object deeper into the body.

Lea must have been saving that arrow specifically for Shank, he thought.

"Are those instruments ready yet, Marcus?"

Marcus came to the table with another basin holding a small knife and a pair of slender forceps bathing in boiling water. Marcus lifted them out of the water with strings tied to each of their ends. Alden let them drip dry for a moment before taking them. They were still hot to the touch, but he disregarded the pain.

He worked with delicate precision, even when he couldn't see the arrowhead clearly. He fought two battles by removing it. If he caused too much pain, he feared he would wake her, which would obviously be a dangerous thing to do with a knife at her back. But if he didn't get the arrowhead out quickly enough it was possible even for a Divergent to bleed to death.

Marcus watched silently, continuing to assist when needed. And when he wasn't needed, he just stood, biting the knuckle of his left forefinger.

It only took a few moments for Alden to remove the arrowhead. He held it up to the light, feeling utterly relieved and troubled at the same time. This was no ordinary arrowhead. Its sharpness frightened him, making him wonder if it bore some kind of enchantment, as the point stuck into the table's surface with just the force of its own weight and stood straight up. Fired from a bow, its pointed triangular head could easily pierce a man's skull, come out the other side, and hit his friend in the heart. He rinsed it, wrapped it, and put it into his pack.

"Marcus, could you get me a drink?"

"You still have to stitch her up, don't you?"

He looked down at the hole and the small cuts he had been forced to make to remove the arrowhead. The bleeding seemed to stop the moment he pulled the arrowhead out. The best thing he could do for her now, in his judgment, would be to clean and bandage her. Let her remarkable constitution do the rest.

"No, the bleeding's stopped. I think it's best for me to leave the rest up to her."

"Are you sure?"

"Yes, General Strife lost his thumb during the campaign to push the Lessers off the Southern Peninsula and it grew back in two weeks' time."

"I've heard of that, but I find it hard to believe. Not even a priest's magic can return a limb."

"Believe me, Marcus. If you had seen the things I've witnessed this girl to be capable of, you wouldn't doubt the regeneration of Strife's thumb."

Marcus reached for the door handle.

"I'll get your drink and a bowl of stew for you. You look like you need a good meal. Just promise me one thing."

"Of course."

"Don't ever confuse that Divergent with a girl again. I don't want to see you killed."

Alden nodded and proceeded to clean and bandage the Divergent, not the girl. Marcus returned carrying a tray with a mug of frothy ale and bowl of hot stew. He set the tray on one of the cots.

"Do you need anything else?"

"I hate to ask, but could you prepare a bath for me and see to my clothes? I'll gladly pay you for the trouble."

"It's no problem, there's a tub in the next room over. I'll get it ready for you and get you a change of clothes. The ones you're wearing will need to be burned, I think."

Alden smiled.

"We rinsed as best we could with our water. If any of the dust remains and gives you trouble, I have more of the root in my pack."

"I might have some, later. Just thinking about you and that dust makes me itchy."

Marcus started to step out. Alden stopped him.

"One more thing, could you find some simple clothes for her?"

Marcus looked back at him, perhaps trying to discern whether he was still sane.

"I'll see what I can do."

"Thanks again, Marcus."

Alden finished cleaning and bandaging her by the time Marcus had the bath ready. Most of her body was wrapped in cloth, including her head. He brought her from the table to one of the cots and laid her down there. He pulled a blanket from the trunk, folded it in half, and covered her with it.

"Please try not to wake while I'm away."

With that he grabbed his tray and went to the other room, shutting the door behind him. He ate his stew and drank his ale while he soaked. All the while, he listened intently to the room over. Marcus left him some simple farm clothes. He dried off and dressed, anxious to return.

He wasn't completely surprised to find Falcon waiting for him in the room with the Divergent. He burped, eating and drinking too quickly it seemed.

"You found a decent meal," Falcon grinned.

While he bathed, Marcus had cleaned the room, brought in a couple of chairs and set them by the table. Falcon sat in one, his legs casually crossed with his sheathed sword leaning against his side. He, too, had gotten a change of clothes from his own noble wardrobe, Alden assumed by their silken, clean material, and a bath at the barracks.

Alden took a seat, taking much pleasure in being off his feet. The Divergent hadn't moved at all since he laid her on the cot. She was breathing steadily, though. Falcon produced a wine flask and a couple of fine crystal shot glasses, the kind one could only find in the capital.

He filled each without a word.

"I thought we should drink to our own survival."

Alden took a glass.

"How is Teth?"

"In pain but on the mend. When Olin wakes, he'll do what he can."

"And you?"

Falcon roughly patted his side.

"My training has begun to pay off."

"Impressive."

Alden downed his glass and wiped his lips dry on the back of his hand. Falcon picked his up and tilted it back and forth, watching the red liquid roll from one side to the other.

"How does she fare?"

Alden set his glass down and Falcon filled it, again.

"She could recover completely by morning or need several weeks. I don't know."

"If she recovers by morning?"

"I will do what I can to see she doesn't attack any of us. I did have enough faith in her civility to bring her to this village."

Falcon downed his glass.

"You're holding something back."

Alden downed his second glass.

"Do you really want to know?"

"In this matter, yes."

"What if she doesn't want to go back?"

Falcon uncrossed his legs and sat up straight.

"She wasn't called."

"You don't know that."

"The Order makes such determinations."

"I know, but, again, what would any of us do if she desired to stay, un-called or not?"

Falcon poured another glass.

"That question is rhetorical. If anything, the Order would convene and reach a decision on the matter."

Alden flipped his glass upside down and placed it on the table.

"I respect the Order's authority, the emperor's authority, I do. But in my recent travels in these lands south of the capital, I've begun to recognize … You and I both know Shank would have been stopped long ago if he assaulted anyone in the capital."

"I should not have to remind you, of all the people in the Empire, the Order and the emperor are doing all they can while being pressed on two fronts by the Blackland Nation and the Volitors."

"How long will difficult times excuse what's happening to the people in the Chain?"

Falcon leaned forward, lowering his voice.

"We are friends, if not brothers, Alden, but know I do not take criticism of the emperor lightly."

Alden grinned.

"You would probably strike me down for such a thing."

Falcon's expression remained serious, and his words carried weight.

"I would."

Alden nodded and the pair sat in silence watching the Divergent sleep. Falcon eventually rose and collected the wine and glasses.

"Let us see what tomorrow brings."

Alden stood and offered his hand. Falcon took it, hand to wrist, and shook just once. The knight, his friend, closed the door softly behind him.

The Divergent slept peacefully. He knelt by her side, staring at her and wishing he could see her fate, whether she would have a place in this world.

Waking Up

If Alden slept at all during the night, he didn't remember it. He felt as if he had stayed awake, sitting at the foot of the cot where the Divergent lay, plotting. Growing up, he experienced similar nights when the emperor's generals tasked him with devising a strategy or critiquing a proposed battle plan. Typically, he would have fundamentally changed his thinking of the problem by morning. He could not say the same for his thinking this morning.

He rubbed his eyes and yawned. His whole body ached, especially his neck, but he was grateful he didn't itch and his breaths came a little easier than the night before. Dry blood crusted his lips from his coughing during the night. Thirsty, he went for the pitcher Marcus brought up the night before. He filled a wooden cup and chugged it until water dribbled out of the corners of his mouth.

He peered over the edge of the cup as drank. The Divergent wobbled on her wounded legs, trying to stand, but fell to her knees. Alden inhaled in shock and choked on the water. He doubled over, coughing it up. His lungs were still affected by the red powder, he realized. A full breath was worth just a half of a breath and choking on water brought him to his knees and threatened to steal his consciousness.

The Divergent didn't make any move, but just watched the spectacle. He noted his sword was on the opposite side of the room on top of a trunk, the Divergent in between. Not that having his sword would matter if she did decide to attack.

On his knees, he wiped his mouth and tried to make himself figure out what to say or do, but his mind just wouldn't work. He was too tired and too overwhelmed by everything. He just stared, noting how many bandages he had wrapped around her. It was as if he had bundled her for the winter with her shins, hands, wrists, lower back, upper back, buttocks, shoulders, and head all wrapped. And remarkably, all the bandages save for those covering the arrow wound in her back and her shins still looked fresh. Those two would need to be changed before too long.

She spoke to him. Her voice, child-like and hoarse, sent a shiver down his spine and back up.

"Alden."

He nodded.

"Yes, I'm Alden."

She pointed at the pitcher; he looked over his shoulder.

"You're thirsty. You want some water."

"Water."

He snatched the pitcher and a cup from the table and brought them both to the ground in front of her. He poured the water, his hands trembling as he filled the cup.

She took it with both her hands and poured as much on her face as she actually drank. The cup empty, she wanted more.

"Alden. Water."

He filled it, again, and she guzzled it. She put the cup down and belched.

"You drank it too fast."

She cocked her head to one side, shook it side-to-side dismissively, and then pinched the bandages wrapped around her chest, trying to hold them out to him.

"Those are bandages. You were wounded. I tended to your injuries. Do you understand me?"

Her forehead wrinkled; he didn't think she did. He pointed at the bandages.

"Bandages."

Becoming frustrated, he thought, she tried to stand and fell back to her knees. He almost went to catch her but stopped short.

"You're hurt. You need rest and time to mend."

He pointed at the cot against the wall, trying to fill his

voice with as much genuine concern as he could. It wasn't difficult to do. His concern was there, but so was his fear.

She curled her fingers into a claw and raised her hand into the air with a growl. He scooted back, reflexively. She growled again and swung her hand down through the air.

"Shank."

It was his turn to cock his head in puzzlement.

"Shank? You want to know what happened to him?"

She didn't seem to understand. He made his fingers into a sword and imitated stabbing down through his collar bone. Believing she gleaned their names, somehow, he acted out the battle with gestures and names. She followed him, her attention fixed on him with unnerving intensity.

At the end of his re-enactment, she gestured to the arrow wound on her back. Alden understood.

He held his hand up and carefully moved to his pack. He pulled out the arrowhead and unrolled it for her to see. She studied it carefully but didn't reach out to touch it as he worried she might.

He heard her stomach growl and pointed at her belly.

"Hungry."

She slapped her stomach playfully and did something he did not expect. She smiled at him. He wrapped the arrowhead up and put it back in his pack. When he turned around, she was at his heels. The urge to leap away was certainly there, but he kept his self-control and bent over.

"I'll get you some food, if you will stay here."

He acted out his words as much as he could. Pretending to eat invisible food and pointed at her and the spot on the floor where she knelt. She either didn't understand or didn't care to do what he said. She crawled after him.

He stopped at the door and backtracked to the cot. He grabbed the blanket.

"If you're going to follow me down, you should at least cover up."

He tried to enfold her in the blanket. She didn't seem to

mind, grasping the blanket and holding it around her. But as he tried to adjust her hold on it, his hand grazed her hands. His touch made her flinch and visibly tense up. It was obvious to him she didn't like it.

The word left her mouth, a pathetic yelp.

"No."

He raised his hands up defensively and backed away a step.

"Sorry."

The event made him even more curious about this creature. She didn't like his touch. It could be just his touch or the touch of all men. And if someone touched her, she could possibly be provoked to violence. This was something he did not want and would have to guard against until he understood it better.

He went back to the door to see if she would follow, and she did. Marcus hadn't rented any rooms last night and would likely keep his inn clear until the Divergent was gone. Alden was sure of this. The tavern below would be empty, too, as the vast majority of its patrons were farmers and hunters and were out pursuing both professions this early.

When they got to the stairs, Alden could hear Marcus at work below. The innkeeper was checking his inventory, tallying how many more barrels of spirits he would need to order from the capital. Thinking Marcus deserved some warning, he called down to the innkeeper.

"Marcus, I'm coming down with my guest. Please try to be calm."

Marcus stopped whatever he was doing and made his way around the bar to look up the stairs. He bit his knuckle, taking in the sight of the blanket draped Divergent sitting on her haunches next to Alden, a lock of red hair hanging loose from under the bandages.

"Calm? It'll be hard enough to try to be alive."

Alden grinned, gradually feeling more at ease, but still

wary. He took a couple steps and looked down to see if the Divergent was able to follow. She maneuvered them well enough, reaching her hands out first and bringing her knees down one at a time behind her.

"Can you get us some breakfast, something simple to eat?"

Marcus shook his head to regain himself.

"I have some bread and some fruit. It's not the freshest, but it's good."

The innkeeper disappeared into the kitchen as Alden slowly navigated the stairs, watching the Divergent each step. Ahead of her, he took quick strides to the front door and barred it just in case any patron thought to make an early visit.

Marcus had lit the fireplace in the corner. It wasn't a big fire, but it would be enough to make tea. The Divergent must have found its warmth inviting. She crawled to it and curled up in a ball on the floor, watching Alden with one eye hidden behind the blanket.

Her head shot up when Marcus returned with company. The innkeeper carried a basket of bread loaves and yellow and green fruit. He walked behind Falcon, who led the way into the tavern, fully armed and armored. The would-be True Silver Knight showed no sign his injuries bothered him. And his rashes had completely faded already.

His hand went to his hilt, and he froze midstride when he caught sight of the Divergent. She laid her head back down and yawned, not seeing Falcon as a threat perhaps, Alden assumed.

Falcon looked at Alden in disbelief.

"What is this?"

"She knows our names. I think she was watching us."

"She knows our names?

"That's what I said."

Marcus set the basket down and tossed Alden a yellow fruit shaped like a multi-point star.

"It's new. We call it star fruit. Some hunters found trees of them growing wild further south. Said it'll help you keep your wits. And you need your wits right now."

Alden sniffed the fruit. It had a tart smell, and its skin was smooth like polished stone. He took a bite. Very chewy, very tart.

Falcon let his hand slip from his hilt and leaned against the bar. All the while he did not let the Divergent out of his sight.

"How do you know she knows our names?"

Alden grabbed another of the star fruits and broke off a chunk of bread.

"She spoke mine and Shank's."

Those names caught her attention, shaking her from her drowsiness by the fire. Alden brought the bread and fruit to her and set them in front of her.

"Food for you."

He took a bite of his star fruit.

She sniffed the air then grabbed the fruit and bread. Switching between hands, she gorged on the small offerings, making a mess, but Marcus wasn't going to say anything about it. All three men just watched her eat, amused as if they had just fed an exotic household pet. When she finished, she pointed at the basket.

"Alden. Food."

Falcon stood from the bar.

"She does speak, but how?"

Alden grabbed what looked like a pear and some more bread. He brought them to her. Before he gave them to her, he pointed at his face and said his name. Then he pointed at Falcon.

The Divergent mimicked him and pointed at the knight.

"Falcon. Knight."

Those words even surprised Alden, who thought he was becoming used to surprises this day. He at least had the presence of mind to give her the food.

Falcon's mouth fell open and stayed that way for a lengthy moment. He shut it and licked his lips.

"She mimics our tongue."

Marcus threw his hands up in the air and went into the kitchen.

Alden sat on a nearby table.

"Mimics? Perhaps. I think she's learning our tongue and is a very fast learner from what I've witnessed."

"This is not right. We must take her to the Order as soon as we are able."

"I don't disagree, but we can't take her now. She will need time to recover and prepare."

"Prepare?"

"Learn about our people and our language."

"You want to teach her?"

"I guess you can call it that."

"Yes, she has some intelligence, but she is still a Divergent. You could very easily do something to provoke her to violence."

"That's possible. There's no other way than to take that risk, however."

Alden crossed his arms, weighing the situation in his mind. The damned fruit did seem to be helping him. Its taste alone was making him more lucid.

"Once she is able to walk, I'll try to take her further north. Jerle and Agraven are supposed to meet me here in a day's time. I can take her to their estate."

"Jerle and Agraven are fire elemental users. Are you sure that's wise?"

"They're good with children."

"She's not a child, Alden. Do not forget that ever or she will kill you."

"I've been given that warning before."

The Divergent slept by the fire, her second helping of food mostly eaten and sitting in a puddle of crumbs and juice.

"She needs a name."

Falcon crossed his arms.

"She is not a pet."

"We can't keep referring to her as the Divergent."

"The Order will not approve of naming her. It's their responsibility. They named General Strife, remember."

"They haven't named a new Divergent since."

"Because all the other fools brought out of the forest through force or trickery were wild, killed dozens, and had to be destroyed."

"Chilali."

"The name of my pet bird?"

"Our pet bird. My mother got it for me, and I let you keep it."

"It's too soft a name for something so dangerous. I think you're deluding yourself."

"I'm still alive. Her name is Chilali."

Falcon raised his hands in defeat.

"Chilali it is then. But do you know what happened to our pet of the same name?"

"You left the cage open, and it flew away."

Falcon shook his head.

"That's what I told you to save your feelings, but the truth is one of the palace cats made a meal of it."

Alden bit into another star fruit, the taste becoming more unpleasant.

Strife's Journal: 221st Day, 4057, Northern Hills

I saw a snowbird today. I almost mistook it for a wisp of snow clinging to a tree branch. It swooped low, gliding north with a bit of moss in its blue beak.

My 2nd Lieutenant called it a, "chilali." Recognizing the peculiarity of the word (it was not Talarian in origin, I was certain), I asked him where he learned it. He said the same place he learned all his words—from his mother. I let the matter rest.

Another day passes. I'm behind our line, frustrated and recovering. My wounds will heal completely and quickly, as they always do. But the arch priests still say nothing can be done about my thumb—they cannot restore what is cut away. And what was cut away throbs and tingles as if it were still attached. And it feels as if the bone is always piercing the flesh sewn over the nub. But this sharp pain may be cause for hope.

I notice slight growth each day. It is not my imagination. I will begin marking the growth on a stick to prove my case to the arch priests.

The young Ragebourne responsible for causing the injury remains in chains. Barely more than a cub, I underestimated his prowess with a short blade. Fool was I.

I think not to kill him. Few of his people remain in the north. The Blackland Nation has seen to this. Utterly eliminating the Lessers is the goal of the Nation, but it is a goal that overreaches, even if it is at the command of Father Night. The next great war will concern this matter, assuming we can even force the Volitors out of our lands. They are the most fearsome foes we will face on the battlefield.

—General Strife Ashwake

Sore Legs

Chilali woke to soreness and sharp pains. Her breaths came with stabbing pains. When she curled her toes, they stung with a tingling numbness and her head throbbed with her heartbeat. Were she not so exhausted the day before, she would not have slept at all in front of the fire, which burned low, but pleasantly warm. Its heat and the blanket had helped soothe her pain. She wanted to stay curled up on the tavern floor, but in the end her urge to move overpowered any desire she had for comfort, as it always did.

The man she came to know as Alden slept, sitting in a chair with his head resting on a table. A string of drool clung to his beard. The eyes of the other man, the knight called Falcon, the strong one, were closed and his breaths came deep and slow. He wasn't asleep, though. She could tell. He was far too rigid and still. And his heartbeat was much too steady for someone who should be dreaming. Fortunately, he was unaware of her or else his heartbeat would have quickened like it had in the past.

Upstairs, Marcus snored. The sound annoyed her and felt rough, akin to shimmying up a tree trunk. She pulled her attention away from the racket and decided it seemed safe enough to do some exploring.

She pushed herself to her hands and knees and arched her back to stretch it. Tingling pain ran up and down her spine. She winced and tried to stand. Her legs, below her knees, still felt numb and wobbly, but they were much improved from the morning. With care, she held her balance and managed stealthy steps, leaving the blanket behind.

There were many new sounds, smells, and sights in this place beyond her forest, but not the sight, sound, or scent she was hoping to find. She drove herself to go further and further from the center of the forest, even if going further meant less and less food. She didn't know what lay beyond, but now that she was here it was underwhelming. And the fact she crossed the threshold and still not found what she was searching for left a hollowing feeling in her gut.

What next, she wondered, as she crept into the kitchen. A small window gave her a glimpse of the village outside. She didn't remember passing through it but heard its sounds and caught its smells from inside the inn. A row of structures, buildings similar to the tavern but smaller, lined the side of a road made of stones.

Beyond the back door in the kitchen, she sensed animals, large ones, were not far. She couldn't be sure without going outside, but she estimated there were five or six clustered together in a wood structure. They made strange but pleasant sounds as they chewed straw and tamped the ground. They were content, she thought.

A variety of food filled the kitchen, but her appetite hadn't completely returned. She still felt full after eating the star fruit and bread. She had never eaten either before and didn't dislike them. They just didn't taste as good as meat or provide her the same pleasure as feasting on a fresh kill.

Marcus barred the backdoor before going to sleep; it was a simple enough mechanism for her to open. Into the night she went. Cool dark clouds brewed above, diffusing Sitara's star and giving the landscape a monochromatic silver glow. Her eyes were more than able to see in the gentle illumination, but a man would have much more trouble.

She moved through the village at a third her usual pace. It was the most she could do with her legs burning as they did, but it was still faster than any man in a full sprint. Several structures spread out from the village's center well. Only a few were larger than the tavern and most were smaller. People, those like Alden, slept soundly everywhere she went, save for a pair of men patrolling the streets by torchlight. They were armed with silver maces and armored with leather and chain but were easy enough to avoid.

The largest building stood at the edge of the village, ringed by short pointy trees and tended gardens. It was much different than the others, distinct in its design with circular walls and a multi-domed roof. Its walls were made of meticulously stacked and polished stones carved into neat rectangles, where the other buildings in the village were made of a much rougher, gray or brown stone. At the pinnacle of its largest dome stood a multi-point, silver star that twinkled even in the dim night light.

Firelight lit the slits in the dome and the main arch windows overlooking the building's courtyard. It looked familiar to her somehow, but she didn't understand why. She didn't know of Sitara beyond the vague references Alden and Falcon made in front of her.

She leapt onto the building's roof, the bottom of its dome, and crawled to the slits. The smell of burning oil and the agreeable sensation of hot air lofted through the slits. She peered inside one, while rubbing each of her calves in turn.

Olin, the bald man, stared into a large burning brazier at the center of a circular room with his hands tucked inside the sleeves of his robe. Opposite of him stood the woman, Lea, dressed in a similar robe.

Even though Lea was the first woman Chilali had seen, she seemed disfigured to her, grotesque even. Her blonde-gray hair seemed mottled and the warts and moles covering her face were absurd in their growth, almost blocking her vision. Where such a perception of ugliness came from, Chilali wasn't sure, but it existed inside her somehow.

The priest, that's what the others called Olin, she remembered. He slipped his hand from his sleeve and held it over the fire. It didn't seem to cause him pain, as she caught the stinking scent of burning flesh. Blisters bubbled on his skin, but he kept it there until his hand started to blacken before finally withdrawing it.

He held his crisp, trembling hand up for Lea to see and a white hue emanated from it. The damage the flame caused reversed. The blackened skin regained its pallid color as the blisters shriveled and disappeared.

The priest spoke with a harder, stronger voice than Chilali remembered him having. His words would not be denied her ears or her mind. They beat their way inside. The experience was unpleasant.

"Through Sitara, any wound may be healed, but limbs cannot be regenerated and sickness cannot be defeated. This is unfortunate. The consequences are obvious. What we cut away cannot be replaced. What sickness infects us will overtake us. And a sickness that forces us to cut away pieces of ourselves, doubly defeats us."

"I do not understand your riddles, priest."

"I only ask a question. What does one do when Sitara cannot help?"

"Try something else?"

Olin smiled and tucked his hand back inside his sleeve.

"A disappointingly broad response, but no. One must rely on himself to find a cure. That is the answer."

"Is that what you believe you are doing?"

"I'm searching for a cure, yes."

"But you haven't said what the sickness is."

"No, I have not. Return to Baigen and give him my message."

"Is that all?"

Olin moved around the brazier and placed his hand against the side of Lea's face. His fingers found grooves between the growths on her cheek.

"I see you as you really are, beneath this."

"You see another layer, no doubt."

Olin moved his lips closer to hers, breathing his words into her mouth. Chilali could barely hear them.

"And each new layer disgusts me more than the last. Be gone from this holy temple. Take a horse from the stables."

Lea pulled away without a word, just a blank expression. She touched her cheek where his hand had been and walked out.

The conversation both confused Chilali and bored her. She yawned and scurried down the side of the dome. She caught sight and scent of Lea walking behind the temple toward the stables, where more of those large riding animals called horses were kept. Perched on the temple's eave, she watched Lea saddle one of the horses and ride out.

With the same degree of stealth that she left the tavern, she returned. She barred the door smoothly, without making a sound and focused her senses on the main room where the fire burned. Alden still slept and Falcon remained as still as the furniture in the room. And upstairs, Marcus' snoring had thankfully quieted somewhat.

She crawled in front of the fire and wrapped herself in the blanket. She only remembered comfort like this one time in her life in her most distant memories from deep within the forest. Her mother would hold her warm, safe, and soft.

But her mother left her, ran away faster than she could keep up, and never returned. Her legs hurt almost as badly now as they did then, when she ran until she collapsed. The terrible feelings the memory evoked choked her up and tears came to her eyes. This was how she fell asleep many nights since that day.

Born from Fire

Alden woke, feeling as groggy as the day before. He wondered if this nauseous, light-headedness would ever entirely fade away. He stood and roughly massaged his lower back. Sleeping in a chair was not the best of decisions.

He blinked his eyes a few times to clear them. Chilali ate a raw fish on the floor by the fire. Blood and ichors smeared her face and the uncooked, un-cleaned meat pulled out from the fish in strings. The spectacle made him that much more nauseous.

Falcon watched casually from the bar with his legs crossed. He seemed to be mentally taking notes, little things he would report to the Order when they returned to the capital. It struck Alden this whole scene may be his friend's doing, a way to prove Chilali wasn't called, because only a savage would eat an unprepared fish.

Alden grunted as he made his way to the bar and Falcon.

"What is this?"

"She's eating breakfast."

"That I can see, but why didn't you cook it?"

"She doesn't mind, so why should I go through the trouble?"

Chilali bit another chunk out of the fish's belly and looked up at Alden with her mouth full. Alden grinned, noticing her bandages were filthy.

"As disgusted as I am by watching this, I will admit the fish was a hearty catch. It's longer than my forearm."

Chilali swallowed and slapped the fish on the ground with a thud.

"I caught it."

Alden looked at Falcon, who offered no answers.

"You left the tavern on your own?"

She shrugged and took another bite.

Falcon shook his head and stood from his seat at the bar.

"How do you know our tongue?"

Chilali ignored the knight, not really caring to answer questions that had obvious answers. Of course she left the tavern on her own. She said she caught the fish. She did wake before them and found the brook. And the fish did try to swim away from her, but she fell on it too fast in the shallow water. It flapped in her arms much of the way back. But as far as how she knew how to speak their tongue, it was her tongue, too. She knew it the same way they did, she assumed.

Alden rested his hand on Falcon's shoulder.

"Chilali."

He said that word to her, but she didn't know why.

"That's the name I've decided to give you. Do you approve?"

She never had a name. And in that moment not having a name seemed odd to her. She thought of herself as herself, but she had never been around anyone else requiring some term for them to reference her, other than "Divergent." A name would be a good thing to have.

She nodded.

"Well, Chilali, when you're finished eating, I'd like to change your bandages and help you clean up. I even have some clothes for you."

Clothes would be something new to try, she thought. It wasn't just that she didn't have a need for them. It was also the fact there were none lying around in the forest or growing from its trees. She nodded, again.

Falcon shook his head as Alden's hand fell from his shoulder.

"Since she can speak, perhaps you should tell her not to eat any of us."

Alden sighed.

"Tell her yourself."

Chilali stood, holding the messy remains of her breakfast by its tail.

"I don't want to eat you. I'm not hungry."

She smiled with bloody teeth and was acutely aware she had not comforted the two men at all.

Alden ran his hand down his face.

"I should strive to keep you well fed then."

Falcon slapped Alden on the back and headed to the back door.

"I'm going to see how Teth is doing," the knight spouted with an unusually cruel chuckle. "Sitara be with you."

Chilali finished her meal and Alden went about getting her and the tavern cleaned up. Discussion, as it had been thus far, was limited. She could speak their tongue but didn't seem to care much for conversation. She removed her mud-soaked bandages in silence. He noted even the most grievous of her injuries were well on their way to being completely healed and figured there was no need to bandage them again.

Washing her and clothing her were much trickier. As with removing the bandages, he made the cautious assumption she did not like to be touched, so he directed her on how to do both on her own. She took to his direction well, if a bit sloppily. Her hair remained a tangled mess hanging down to the middle of her back, but at least she smelled better or more like a girl and less like a wild animal.

The dress he gave her was a tan pullover that hung down to her knees and tied at her waist with a black ribbon. She seemed ambivalent about wearing it but didn't resist. He gave her sandals next, which she was uncomfortable wearing, constantly wiggling and rubbing her toes together.

The whole situation caused new questions to form in Alden's mind. Whether she was called or uncalled, he felt she was just going along with what he was asking. She wasn't guided by a desire to become civilized and walk in the Empire amongst men. She had some other motive, but he didn't think it wise to inquire at the time. Observe, he decided.

They went down the stairs together. Falcon stood at the bottom in a clean loose shirt with his sword sheathed at his waist, waiting. He appeared to not know what to say when he saw Chilali come down the steps cleaned and attired. But the knight did find something to say, eventually.

"Her hair is a mess."

"So it is," Alden rolled his eyes.

Chilali stepped around Alden to go to the fire, which burned out a while ago. The wounds on her shins were bright red gashes.

"The fire went out."

Alden grabbed his short sword from the chair where he spent the night and began fastening it around his waist.

"Don't worry. Either Agraven or Jerle can relight it."

"Who are they?" she asked.

"Friends and fire elemental users. I hired them for a scouting mission, and they should be returning today," Alden said. "We're going to meet them now and I'd like you to come with us."

Alden went to the front door, but Falcon intercepted him.

"You're just going to walk outside with her?"

"Yes," Alden smiled.

"You can't. You'll cause a panic."

"She's already gone out on her own."

"Can't we at least disguise her? Mask what she is?"

Alden rubbed his chin.

"I suppose we could. Have you spoken to Olin since our return?"

"Yes, he visited Teth at the same time. He said the old tracker will make a full recovery in a few days."

"That's some good news, but do you think you could

bring Olin here?"

"Why?"

"He's a skilled enchanter, for better or worse. I'd like to commission him to craft an item to disguise Chilali."

"Such an enchantment would be extremely complicated. I don't know if he can do it. And what about Agraven and Jerle?"

Alden turned to face Chilali.

"I'm sorry, but I must go meet them. Would you mind waiting for Falcon to return here with Olin?"

She tilted her head slightly to one side and pursed her lips.

"You want to add a layer."

Alden gave a single nod, puzzled by her word choice.

"Ideally, I'd like you to appear like a daughter of the Empire with golden hair and deep azure eyes."

She turned away from Alden and crouched in front of the ashes in the fireplace.

"Will you still be afraid of me?"

Alden didn't answer right away. He glanced at Falcon first to see his reaction.

"It's not what you look like. It's that you're a Divergent-"

"What is a Divergent?" Chilali interjected, whipping around.

Falcon licked his lips.

"She doesn't know what she is."

"Of course she doesn't!" Alden snapped more harshly at his friend than he intended.

He took a few steps toward Chilali and knelt in front of her to be at the same height.

"There's a lot you do not know, and I promise to tell you all that I can in time. But you will have to be patient. Do you approve?"

She stepped toward him casually and grabbed a lock of his hair between her fingers. He didn't flinch, which surprised himself.

"I want to look like you," she said curtly, letting his hair go to return to staring at the ashes.

Alden stood and faced Falcon.

"Please see to it Olin carries out my request. Provide him with whatever he needs."

Alden marched out the front door. Falcon turned to go into the daylight but paused at the doorway. He glanced over his shoulder, catching the image of Chilali in the light of day. She stirred the ashes with her finger in her plain dress. But beneath it, her hair and eyes sparkled, and her skin glowed in the sunray cast from the doorway.

She was as beautiful as she was powerful, like a great predator cat with a fine coat and ivory teeth. Naming her after a snowbird was a mistake and felt more and more like a terrible omen.

"We are fools playing with fire as she stirs our ashes," he spoke to himself and left, shutting the door.

Chilali heard his words, ones not meant for her. She licked the ashes blackening the tip of her finger. Grainy and unpleasant, she spat them out and wiped her tongue on her dress. She had no taste for the warm ruin flames left behind.

Aphephobia

From the corner of his eye Agraven watched a bead of sweat roll down Jerle's neck to the top of her plump breasts, which were bound tightly in a leather vest. Her short blonde hair curled up at her jaw, teasing her lips when the seldom breeze blew. He delighted seeing her like this, filthy, roughed up, and riding on horseback through the wilds. It let him dwell in the safety of the past; a time when he and Jerle were partners fulfilling guild missions together.

But that was before they were married, before they had a daughter, and before they lost that daughter.

Jerle caught him looking and teased more out of habit than interest.

"We'll be in our own bed again, soon."

"It's much softer and warmer than the ground," Agraven winked.

Agraven, a man fit enough to have stood above his peers as a knight, swallowed the last of the water in his skin and tied it to his saddle. He was never afforded such an opportunity. Orphaned and a groundling, a commoner in the capital, he was lucky to just be alive and not imprisoned. He owed much of that good fortune to the other reason he could never become a knight. In the back of his mind, he could feel it, a little searing spot. A dream-like heat radiated from it, the portal to the Fire King's prison in the sky.

The temptation to focus on the portal and feel its power surge through him waned, as the outskirts of Orsa came into sight around the edge of a thicket.

"You think Alden will be waiting for us?"

Jerle adjusted the bandage wrapped around her left bicep. It covered a seeping puncture wound.

"I do hope he is still alive. This wound needs his expertise before it begins to fester."

"I'm told a talented priest cares for this village."

"I'd rather my arm rot off."

Before Agraven could respond, Jerle pointed in the distance. Alden rode toward them on a white mare with a silver bridal. Likely he took Falcon's horse, Agraven guessed. The merchant shaved his beard recently, but his face was still rough and pink from the rash. His hair hung loose, instead of being neatly combed and tied. And even though he exuded youthfulness, compared to Agraven, he appeared to be weary. His friend, one of the few men Agraven would prescribe such a label to, always tried to carry too many burdens.

Jerle wound her reins one time around her hand.

"I do not know how he does it, but he remains punctual no matter his business."

"I imagine those rashes frayed many a nerve in that forsaken wilderness."

"Not unlike our second honeymoon in the Southern Wilds. Serves him right."

Alden waved to them and kicked his horse into a trot. He reined his mount, stopping within conversation distance.

"Jerle, Agraven, I've much, much to tell you."

"As do we," Agraven drew a black rock from his belt pouch and tossed it to Alden.

Alden caught it in his palm and examined it. He looked back, uncertain.

"It's black ore," Jerle explained. "We found the mine."

"But the Blackland Nation or at least one of its smaller tribes controls it and has established a settlement at the base of the mountain," Agraven continued.

"That's impossible. The mountains are far too high and steep to be passable," Alden countered, squeezing the ore tightly in his hand.

"We know they didn't come from the North, which only leaves one possibility—they found a way through the mountains."

Alden clutched the rock in his hand and cursed silently between his teeth.

"It never ends. I must report this to the Empire as soon as possible, and I'll need you to come along to share your accounting in more detail."

"We thought as much. If the Blackland Nation establishes a firm military presence in the south, the Empire will be flanked and fighting on three fronts," Jerle sighed. "But at least you have some good news? You manage to kill that child-murdering bastard?"

Alden shook his head, but kept his smile, raising his hands up to explain.

"We failed for the moment, but something remarkable has come of our failure."

"We'd love to hear your tale, but we've been rationing supplies since our daring escape from enemy lands-"

Jerle interjected with a laugh.

"And we could sure use a drink and a meal. The best Marcus has to offer."

Alden chuckled sheepishly.

"As you wish. I'll see to your arm, too."

* * *

By the time Falcon returned with Olin, Chilali explored all the rooms, closets, and stores. She found nothing of consequence to her. The whole experience was boring, so much so, she intended to leave the tavern, but returned to her spot by the fireplace before Olin and Falcon got to the door, unaware of her exploration.

Falcon entered first, but Olin quickly stepped around him, concern clear on his face. His robes looked dingier and older than those she saw him wearing the night before and he carried himself in a different posture. Last night his form reflected strength, but now he conveyed timidity with slumped shoulders and hands kept up at his sides in defense.

"We've returned, uh, Chilali," the priest croaked.

She paraded herself out from the shadows cast across the fireplace.

"You can make me look like a ..." she paused considering her words. "Like a daughter of the Empire?"

Olin nodded, slack jawed.

"Yes, yes I can," he turned to Falcon. "She knows our tongue. And she wears our clothes. What a delight this is."

Falcon ignored Olin and set a small silver comb on the table between him and Chilali.

"Do you know what this is?"

She didn't, but a few diabolic applications immediately came to mind.

"It's my comb. You can use it to straighten and untangle your hair," he continued, backing away from the table.

She strode over and took the item. It had a pleasant weight in her hand and the cool, smooth metal felt good to hold. Olin, though he did not have hair, motioned for her to run it through hers. She tried and felt it catch on tangle after tangle. She pulled through each of them with a satisfying pop.

When she finished, she set the comb on the table, a ball of red hair wound in its tines.

Falcon took the comb back and handed it to Olin.

"Will this be enough?"

The priest bobbed his head in affirmation, mesmerized by Chilali. To him, she was otherworldly, divine in her appearance—a god child. Despite her inexperience, her combed hair hung with a wild grace in smooth drapes and swung across her back with the slightest turn of her head from one of her elbows to the other.

Falcon grabbed his shoulder and gave him a shake to free the priest from his trance.

"Is it enough, Olin?"

Olin grabbed the comb and examined the hair. For an ordinary enchantment it would serve, but for something as extraordinary as he had in mind, he would need another ingredient.

"This is plenty. I should have it ready by nightfall. Is that soon enough?"

"That should be fine, good priest. Our friends will likely want to rest before returning to the road."

"The fire elemental users you told me about?"

"Yes.

"A tragic story. I will pray they find peace in their lives," Olin bit his bottom lip and let it go with a strong exhale. "And your plan is to bring the Divergent to the capital?"

"What is the capital?" Chilali chirped, beginning to distaste others talking about her as if she wasn't standing right in front of them or didn't understand their words.

"The capital is the heart of the Empire," Falcon answered.

"It is where the emperor's palace touches the sky, the Order guides our hearts, and the Senate convenes to argue." Olin added.

She tried to picture what they were speaking about, but couldn't, which added to her growing frustration.

"What is the Empire?" she asked.

"You're standing in it," Falcon shrugged.

"The Empire is one of the two nations of man," Olin beamed. "It has stood for nearly three centuries and holds Sitara and her teachings above all else."

"Who is Sitara?" she sighed.

Olin pointed dramatically through the roof.

"She is a goddess, the silver star that lights the night for us. She blesses us with her power to heal and battle to defend ourselves from the Lessers."

Each explanation led to even more questions. She resigned herself to the fact the quickest way to learn would be to just remain silent and watch. Her confusion was clear on her face with the way it made her wrinkle her forehead.

Olin moved forward and knelt before her. This would be the best way, he thought to himself and braced for the worst.

"Those wounds on your shins can be healed with Sitara's power. Would you like me to show you?"

"Olin, that is not a good idea," Falcon cautioned.

"Please sit," Olin drew a chair from a nearby table. Chilali sat.

"I will go to the capital," she stated flatly.

Her eyes fell on Olin as the priest reached for her leg. Anxiety began to build inside her, bringing tension to muscles that were loose a moment ago and a panic to her breathing. She experienced this before when Alden touched her but didn't understand why. She wasn't afraid of these people. She could kill them, but other contact was different. It made her lose control of her desire to devour them.

It brought to her memories of the terrible metal trap that pinned her in the forest. She watched Shank feed on the meat scraps with their overpowering bitter smell and made the decision to attack him. He was an intruder in her territory, and she had seen him bring others into the forest and play with them before killing them. It was unpleasant to watch him frighten them and torture them, especially when his prey looked so much like her in form and size.

He must have caught her scent a moment before she leapt, because he would not have heard her. She was always as silent as a shadow. Nonetheless, he batted her in midair. She landed on her hands and feet in a skid and felt the smooth metal panel give beneath her. The click, she remembered the sound keenly, sharp and fast. It released the jaws, and she reacted on instinct, jumping as high and hard as she could. But she wasn't fast enough, and Shank fled.

The click, the release of the jaws, was how she would describe the irrational panic rioting inside her. Olin's touch made it click and she couldn't stop the jaws from closing on him. The loss of control disgusted her as much as it frightened her. Why had his touch done this to her, she screamed inside where no one could hear her helplessness.

Olin laid his hand on her shin, covering the wound with warmth and light and a bit of malice. He felt a violent shiver roll through Chilali's body and knew he had erred. Falcon made a dash toward him, he remembered that much. A bright flash of red pain crossed his vision and preceded the darkness that swallowed him. He lost all sense of himself after that.

Chilali crouched on a table, ready to pounce on anyone who came near her and rip them to pieces, as a thin line of blood ran down her shin. Her eyes flitted in Falcon's direction as the knight desperately dragged the senseless priest away. The left side of the priest's face swelled, worse than she remembered Lea's swelling, giving his smooth head a lopsided proportion. His nose gushed blood and his jaw hung loose, as if one side had become unhinged.

Calm came to her when she couldn't understand how she had caused so much damage. She only struck him flat with her hand, but the sound was so loud, like a crack of thunder; it still resonated in her bones.

She didn't know what to do or think. She didn't want this to happen. Alden burst through the front door with a man and a woman. He didn't even look at her. He went straight to Olin and Falcon and began calling for supplies and giving orders.

There was noise, lots of noise and shouting, but it was all a silent confusion to her. The man and woman kept fearful watch on her, as she slinked back to the cold fireplace, her bleeding stopped. Falcon carried Olin upstairs and Alden came to her, his shirt wet with the priest's blood. His anger was obvious, fearless, and caught her by surprise.

"Why did you strike Olin?" he growled.

She tried to find the words to explain, but they were jumbled inside her.

"What is it that you want from us? Do you want to walk amongst us or return to your forest? Which is it?"

"He touched me," she stammered.

Alden calmed at the words.

"You can't bear our touch?"

She shook her head.

"What you're saying doesn't make sense. You touched my hair earlier today," he pressed.

She withdrew from him and his words, tears filling her eyes. The woman, with a scent not as strong or as sweet as Lea's, grabbed Alden's shoulder.

"Let her be, Alden. I understand what she says. For a long time, I was the same."

Alden took a deep breath.

"I apologize for losing my temper with you Chilali. I suspected your condition but said nothing of it to the others."

He took a few steps away from her.

"Olin's jaw is broken. I need to set it."

Alden went upstairs, leaving Chilali with the woman and man. She assumed they were the fire element users Alden mentioned, but so many terrible things swirled inside her, embarrassment, fear, disappointment, and guilt that she didn't care. She never felt so many black thoughts at once before. If only she could waste away like the ashes in the fireplace to make it all stop. Or maybe, she should just return to the forest.

The woman sat in front of her, and the man stepped up warily behind her.

"Jerle, I do not think this is a good idea."

She waved her hand.

"She's no more a threat to anyone here than you or I."

"Exactly my point," Agraven huffed.

The woman, with her short hair and muddy boots, locked eyes with Chilali.

"Chilali is your name, right? I'm Jerle and this is my

husband Agraven," she pointed over her head.

"I know how you feel. You didn't mean to harm the priest. Had you truly intended to do so, I've no doubt you would have killed him."

Chilali's eyes dipped to the floor.

"I didn't mean to."

"I know. I found myself in similar situations more than once while growing up. I don't blame you. Neither will the others in time."

"You're a fire elemental user?"

Jerle smiled.

"Both Agraven and I are."

"Can you relight the fire?"

"Of course."

Jerle rose and dusted herself off. She grabbed some logs from the stock and set them in the fireplace in a neat bundle. She turned to Chilali.

"Now watch."

The young woman waved her hand slowly in front of Chilali, as a rose color glow became a bright orange flame enwrapping Jerle's hand. Chilali reached for the flame and Jerle withdrew her hand.

"Just because it does not burn me, does not mean it will not burn you," Jerle cautioned.

"How?"

"Because of the connection my mind has to the Fire King's Realm. His power floods into me. I'm not burned by the fire, because I become the essence of fire when I channel the King's power."

"It's a dangerous power," Agraven interrupted. "Not something to be used lightly."

Jerle shut her eyes.

"This is true. The more power I channel, the stronger the pull on my mind becomes. It is like a tide washing in and receding. If I channel too much or lose my resolve, my mind will be pulled into the Fire King's Realm and trapped there for eternity."

Agraven crossed his arms.

"And all that remains of you is a body. It is a living death and is a terrible fate for your friends and family to endure. And still, it is not the worst possible outcome."

"You are so depressing," Jerle whined and touched the logs in the fireplace. The dry wood popped and cracked, taking alight easily and tossing cinders up the chimney chute. Warmth washed over Chilali and the tension in her body melted away.

Enraptured by Jerle's power, Chilali let herself forget about striking Olin.

"What's the worst?"

Jerle pulled her hand from the fire and theatrically blew out the flames covering her hand with a slow puff.

"The worst outcome, Chilali, is if too much of the Fire King's power enters you as your mind is ripped away. If that happens, the power will take control. And at that point what you were becomes an elemental, a denizen of the Fire King with semi-infinite power, for a brief period of time."

"It is extraordinarily rare. Few elemental users are even capable of drawing on such power. And such a thing has only happened twice in the two kingdoms of man in our recorded history," Agraven added. "But hundreds were killed."

The tone of Jerle's voice shifted, taking on a kindly seriousness.

"So, we take care in using our powers, reserving them only for dire circumstances."

"Or to cheer someone up," Agraven grumbled.

* * *

Falcon held Olin's head still on the table in the upstairs room, the same where Alden removed the arrowhead from Chilali's back.

"How bad is it?" Falcon asked, as Alden bound Olin's mouth shut with leather strands.

"There's too much swelling to know for sure how clean the break was. I've done all that I can."

Alden pulled his bloody shirt off, balled it up, and tossed it aside. Then he scrubbed his hands clean in a bowl of water. Falcon handed him a towel and a fresh shirt of dark gray, rough material befitting a groundling, not Alden.

Alden dried his hands and slipped on the shirt.

"It's your turn."

"I've never been very good at this. If I make a mistake, I could disfigure him."

"You won't."

Falcon took a deep breath and shut his eyes. His hands began to glow with white light on either side of Olin's head, illuminating the blood in the priest's skin. Sweat started rolling down Falcon's forehead and along his fair features and square jaw. The concentration and the strain it caused were tremendous for the knight, evident by his grimacing. Alden began to doubt his friend's ability, but all he could do was dry his friend's brow and continue to watch.

Falcon continued for several more breaths, and the effects on Olin were evident, but not outwardly dramatic. The main concern was to knit the bone and reduce the swelling around the priest's eye to prevent blindness. Falcon reached his limit and slumped into a nearby chair, completing both tasks.

Alden handed Falcon a cup of water.

"When he wakes, he should be able to finish the job?"

"Yes, it shouldn't be hard for him to heal himself."

"I meant the other job."

Falcon drank his water before replying.

"She's uncalled. It's obvious. Taking her to the capital would be a waste of time and endanger more people, including you."

"What happened to Olin was an accident. It wasn't her

intent to strike the priest."

"You think she has some sort of strange phobia?"

"Something of the sort, something that is part of her nature."

Falcon stood and pointed at the priest.

"What if someone else makes the same mistake as Olin?"

"I believe in time she can overcome it. I've touched her twice and not evoked a violent reaction."

"We should either return her to the forest or find a way to-"

"No," Olin mumbled and grabbed his sore face.

Alden went to the priest's side.

"Try not to talk. Falcon did the best he could to mend the bone, but it may still be weak."

Olin sat up, despite Alden trying to get him to lie back down. He placed his bloody hand on his swollen face, and it flared with blinding white light. Alden and Falcon both looked away from the piercing glare and still had spots in their eyes.

Olin slid off the table and stood with a groan, the terrible injury gone. His face was as it had been, except for dry blood and spittle. He felt the line of his jawbone with his thumb before untying the leather strands.

"It seems you did a fair job of setting the bone," the priest smirked. "And an even better job of properly mending it. Good work."

Falcon came to Olin's side.

"Are you all right, good priest?"

He nodded and looked at both men.

"She must be taken to the capital. Understand this and bear no malice toward her. My judgment was lacking. I sought to take some of her blood during the healing process to aid in the enchantment."

The priest waved his bloody hands.

"I got more than I wished, it seems, and paid the price

for it. No doubt my touch was especially irritating for her. I should have heeded Falcon's advice. Though a Divergent, she is just a child. Even Strife would have had trouble controlling his instincts had he come to us at such a young age."

"While I do not know much of the art, using a Divergent's blood for an enchantment seems dangerous," Falcon said, handing Olin a clean rag.

Olin wiped his hands on the rag and folded it to preserve the blood.

"That is true, but so much power surges through that one I feared an ordinary enchantment would be too weak to mask her true nature."

"You should have consulted me first," Alden fumed.

"My apologies, good merchant," Olin consoled and pulled Falcon's comb, still tangled with Chilali's hair, from inside his robe.

"I'll have the enchantment ready by morning. Just lend me this room for the night."

Alden nodded and stormed out of the room with Falcon.

The pair walked down the hall to the top of the stairs before stopping to talk.

Alden crossed his arms.

"He is much too powerful to be a priest in the Chain."

"I'm suspicious, too."

"The Order must have dispatched someone higher up to monitor our incursion into the forest. An arch priest perhaps?"

"Or perhaps he has always been stationed in this village to monitor incursions into the forest. I would have to see more to say for certain, but I would not cross him. You were wise not to strike him."

"So, you're beginning to develop that talent as well?"

Falcon shrugged.

"I'm not sure. I just noticed it now and only briefly. Perhaps it is related to my healing of the priest."

Alden moved to the top step. Falcon didn't. Alden noticed his friend was trembling. The knight wasn't telling him the entire truth and that worried Alden a great deal.

"I overexerted myself. I need to rest. I've never been good at healing others."

Alden patted his friend on the shoulder with a smile. "Sure, go rest."

Downstairs, Jerle, Agraven, and Chilali ate fruit as a stew pot simmered over the fire. Jerle enjoyed the Divergent's company but was perhaps making the same mistake Alden kept making. She was not a child of man. Agraven seemed more resistant to her charms, but Alden could tell even the hardened man was beginning to bend. Did Chilali resemble every lost child, Alden wondered.

Chilali left the table and went to Alden. Her haste surprised him, and his unease was unfortunately evident. She saw it in him and stopped well short. He didn't mean to keep signaling his own fear to her, but it was an instinct he doubted he would ever completely learn to control. And perhaps it was something she had to understand and accept if she were to walk among them.

"Olin," she stated as much as she asked.

He sighed and walked past her.

"He is as good as he was and will require isolation tonight to finish the enchantment."

"So, he is as talented as the rumors I've heard," Agraven commented, his voice laden with Alden's same suspicions, before chomping into a bread loaf.

Jerle marched to Alden and poked the middle of his chest harshly with her finger.

"You had dealings with Baigen."

The poke nudged Alden back a step and he raised his hands defensively.

"Where else was I to find a reliable mercenary?"

"Baigen does not hire out mercenaries. He hires out murderers. I can't believe you would do such a thing."

"The two of you were unavailable."

"You didn't even think of asking us. I wouldn't be surprised to learn you dispatched us, knowing you would go on this mission without us."

Alden rubbed the back of his head, caught, but not ready to surrender.

"Convincing the Order to allow passage into the Divergent Forest was hard enough without my trying to bring a pair of elemental users along, fire especially. And could I have really trusted any of Baigen's people with your task?"

"Lea wouldn't still be around, would she?" Agraven interjected, his voice dripping with black malice. Alden knew his friends had history with the Silver Talon Guild, even some with Lea, but Agraven's tone surprised Alden. Fortunately, he was able to hide his surprise this time with genuine indifference. There were other matters to be dealt with first.

He shook his head and carefully moved around Chilali to take a seat at Agraven's table.

"Can we save this discussion for another time, please?"

Agraven gave a curt nod and took another bite of his bread. Jerle sat next to Alden. Chilali kept standing, near the bottom of the staircase, uncertain.

"Come sit with us, Chilali," Alden said with feigned resignation. It was probably best not to tell her what the priest had done. Letting her feel guilty for the incident would be best for everyone.

She did as he said, pulling up a chair across from him and sliding it a safe distance from Agraven.

"I know I've not bathed, yet, but ..." Agraven joked, but earned no laughs, just a scowl from Jerle.

Alden took the wine bottle from in front of Agraven and poured a cup. He didn't drink it though. He just swirled it in his cup, feeling its weight. Then he began.

"Tomorrow we will begin traveling to the capital,

Chilali. We will stop at Jerle and Agraven's estate along the way. But ultimately, I will bring you to the Order. They will determine whether you have been called from your forest by Sitara or if you are wild, uncalled."

"And then what will happen?" Chilali asked, catching the strong odor coming from Alden's drink. The burning it caused made her wrinkle her nose.

"If you are called, you will go on to serve and protect the Empire. You will be trained in the arts of war and given a rank in the military. And if you are uncalled, I am not certain. They may try to return you to the forest or ..."

"They would try to kill me?"

Agraven and Jerle looked at each other across the table. Alden shook his head.

"I don't know. In the distant past, other Divergents were taken from the forest. They were uncalled and slew many before they were stopped."

"Why must she be uncalled and wild? Why can't she be uncalled and civilized?" Jerle asked.

"It is the way of things. A Divergent is wild and predatory, unless Sitara grants her the light of civility and reason. I was given the chance to read many of the Order's scriptures and records, and of what little is known of Divergents this is one of the few truths handed down by the Goddess. Perhaps you are an anomaly, Chilali, as Strife was. I cannot say. And we cannot operate under any sort of assumption that you are called, uncalled, or something else. We must see what the Order determines and work from there. Do you understand?"

Neither alternative appealed to her. If they decided she were uncalled she would not want to return to the forest. And if they tried to kill her, she would fight back. As far as training her for war and making her serve the Empire, she wasn't ready to commit to that. She didn't serve anyone and would never serve anyone. The idea of bending her will to another's infuriated her. She would die first, but she buried her feelings as deep as she could to hide it from them.

"I will go with you to the capital," she finally said. "But which do you want me to be, Alden?"

The question stunned Alden. As much as he thought things out ahead of time, he wasn't certain what to tell her. He hoped she was called, but also that he could retain control of her. That was his plan from the beginning, he told himself. He could use her to go after Shank and even the Blackland Nation's new mine, but what would he do after that? The Empire would not simply allow him to retain her indefinitely. She would inevitably end up in service to the Empire's military, fighting against the Volitors more than likely.

If she were uncalled, however, he knew he would likely face criminal charges for removing a Divergent, despite his best intentions. It was a risk he assumed the moment he was given permission to enter the damnable forest.

Perhaps the third option, as ridiculous as it seemed, would be best. Chilali could be an anomaly. Uncalled, but civilized, the Order would find difficulty in justifying returning her to the forest or executing her. As an anomaly, she would retain her freedom, ironically. Neither Sitara nor an animal's instincts would govern her actions.

"Whatever you are," Alden answered aloud.

Strife's Journal: 289th Day, 4056, Silver Sun Capital

The spirits of all continue to remain elevated after our first decisive victory. The battle to retake the city lasted days. The emperor and the other generals believe the best course of action is to mend wounds and restore defenses until warriors from the Blackland Nation can arrive in enough force to present a threat to the Volitors in the north.

I do not disagree.

I went for a walk alone today. Dogs and cats run feral through the city streets. The rats are wary. Many buildings crumble or smolder. I could smell the dead inside.

I came across a dying child. She suffered from the sickness bred on the nails of Talarian males. She shivered though the day was warm, and her body was stiff, paralyzed. She couldn't cry out, though I could see the intent in her eyes.

My presence frightened her, even after I chased away the dog that thought to make a meal of her bare feet. Had she been healthy, she would have run. So have many others. My people are the most fearsome and ferocious creatures walking this world; we kill all things. In more peaceful times, my presence in these city streets would have caused as much panic as a rabid bear.

To my dismay, even the men under my command (despite our success!) flinch at my approach. While I do not crave companionship or camaraderie, I do witness it taking place around me. Divergents are not beyond envy. Sometimes I find myself wishing that I could look like my men and move amongst them without stirring such apprehension, but I dare not ask the arch priests for such an enchantment. They look at such suggestions with much dismay.

I held the girl in one arm, and I showed her my elemental power—fire, bright and orange. I shaped the flame in my hand to resemble a man and made it walk, gesture, and dance like a buffoon with a fine ribbon of smoke trailing from his head. This made her smile as much as her condition would allow.

Then I made her into ash. She didn't suffer; her crumbling remains continued to hold that smile.

Perhaps if I smiled more often, I would not frighten those around me so much.

—Divergent Strife Ashwake

The Ribbon

Chilali woke once again in front of a dying flame. Embers smoldered, releasing a barely visible gray ribbon of smoke. She uncurled and stretched on the floor before standing. All her pain and soreness were gone. The wounds on her shins had been reduced to light pink marks with flaky bits of dry skin.

All still seemed to be asleep. The only sounds she could hear were steady breathing, the horses outside, and birds just beginning to wake. She bounded up the stairs soundlessly and with inhuman ease.

She crept along the hallway as it turned and stopped in front of Agraven and Jerle's room. Even though the door was closed, she could feel the room inside. The couple slept, one behind the other, back to front, Agraven holding onto Jerle. They slept as if they were enduring, not resting, but Chilali did not understand why.

She found Alden's room across from Olin's and next to Falcon's. The priest didn't sleep like the others, but maintained the same strange state in which she witnessed Falcon. And the knight, he slept deeply, hardly stirring, and had since early the night before. Alden, however, began to stir.

Not knowing any better, she opened his door and slipped inside. He sat at the edge of his bed naked with his blanket pulled over his lap. His chest and back bore a few scars from burns, cuts and scrapes. His frame, as a whole, was lean and tone, more so than she expected, but still small compared to Falcon.

Alden looked up at her groggily.

"It's polite to knock before entering someone's room."

She didn't respond to the comment.

"Tell me about Jerle and Agraven."

Alden pointed to his pants, which were draped on the back of a chair.

"Bring those to me first."

She did as he asked, noticing they were both cautious during the exchange not to touch. The situation pained her slightly.

She stepped back and he pointed at the door.

"Face that way a moment."

"Why?"

"Given your heritage, you have no shame, but do not think I wish to share mine with you."

"I don't understand."

"Modesty. I don't want you to see me naked."

She shrugged and faced the door, listening to him dress behind her back.

Bare to his waist now, Alden filled a bowl with water. He splashed himself a few times then dried his hands and face.

"Jerle and Agraven joined the Silver Talon Guild as children. They were talented fire users and often worked together. Both being fire users, they had little to fear from accidently harming the other."

Alden sat in the room's sole chair and began putting on his boots.

"In time, they fell in love."

"Love?"

"You'll figure it out yourself one day if you're fortunate," Alden said, but knew his words would only be true if she was able to overcome her inability to touch another.

"Soon, they wanted to marry and leave the guild. Baigen, the guild's leader, didn't like the prospect of losing two of his best mercenaries, but blessed their leaving or seemed to, anyway."

"Lea came from Baigen's guild?"

"She did. The Silver Talon Guild is the only guild recognized in the capital by the Senate. And it affords the nobles with military power beyond their standing armies outside the capital."

Alden grabbed his sword and drew it from its sheath to examine the blade.

"Agraven and Jerle left the guild and married. Not long after, Jerle gave birth to a daughter, Saveria. I had never seen those two so happy, so content in their own lives, despite their violent childhoods."

"Why would Saveria make them so happy?"

Alden scratched the back of his head.

"I wouldn't expect you to know. You probably don't even remember your own mother. Just know it would be best if you didn't mention Saveria to Agraven or Jerle."

"Why?"

"Because, Saveria, barely a toddler, was killed during a trip Agraven and Jerle took to the capital. An arrow shot from an impossible distance pierced her skull, as she walked hand in hand between them. You are no stranger to pain, Chilali, but even you have not known the magnitude of suffering that comes with losing a child. Pray you never do."

"They think Baigen did it."

Falcon sheathed his blade.

"There's no uncertainty. He ordered someone, probably Lea, to do it and likely planned it the moment he agreed to let them leave the guild. It is how Baigen thinks."

"They tried to kill him."

"They tried but were stopped by the emperor for reasons I do not know."

Alden put on his shirt and buttoned it.

"Don't repeat what I've told you, Chilali. This conversation must stay between us. Understand?"

She nodded and Alden stepped around her to the door.

"Let's go prepare for our trip. I want to leave before noon."

He tried to open the door, but she held it shut.

"What is it?"

"I remember my mother."

"You do? We've always been taught, as Strife wrote, 'Divergent mothers birth their ruby-haired, emerald-eyed daughters nameless and leave them as soon as they are able to walk.'"

"I tried to chase her, but she was too fast."

Alden squatted, realizing this was a delicate situation. It was the first time Chilali ever talked about herself and her time in the forest. He wasn't sure if she felt the same way an ordinary child would about being abandoned. By all of Strife's accounts, Divergents were solitary creatures.

"I'm sorry," was all he could say.

"Did Strife write why Divergent mothers leave their daughters?"

Alden licked his lips and shook his head.

"Not directly. It is assumed they leave their daughters to make them strong. And well, we know Divergents do not get along well with one another."

"We don't?"

"At the urging of the Order, Strife returned to the forest to try to recruit more Divergents. By the time the ordeal was over, the general slew three Divergents in self-defense or, perhaps, due to outright dislike. It was a catastrophe."

Alden stood and Chilali released her hold on the door.

"Come, let's see to breakfast, cooked, preferably."

Chilali imitated her own toothy grin from the morning before, but this time no ichors stained her teeth.

* * *

Chilali listened quietly as Jerle and Agraven shared their experiences in the Southern Wilds while eating spicy, cured meat and rolls. She ate the same food they ate, not caring for the hard, dry rolls, but savoring the mix of peppers in the meat. Alden often interrupted them to draw out more details on the land, the foliage, and the Wild

Briam. These creatures were also one of the Lesser races, like the Shank and the Ragebourne, but no description of them was given over breakfast.

Olin came down just as they began to clean the table. The priest walked as if sore from head to toe and avoided eye contact with Chilali, which everyone else seemed to do. But rather than being fearful of provoking her, it felt more like the priest just wanted to avoid her. It almost soured her relatively good mood, which had been brought on from healed wounds, tasty food, and the knowledge she gained from Alden.

The priest held an indigo-colored ribbon out to Alden.

"It was taxing, but I finished, good merchant."

Alden took the ribbon and held it between his hands.

"This is fine material."

"It was a gift from someone I helped many years ago. Now it is my gift to you and Chilali."

"How is the enchantment activated?"

"Because I used her blood, it will only work for Chilali. Merely tie her hair with it."

He used her blood, Chilali thought. She went to Alden, more curious than ever about the ribbon that would change her into a daughter of the Empire. Alden handed it to her. Its smooth texture was a pleasure to touch, but she wasn't quite sure how to tie hair. That's when Jerle came over.

The young woman advised her as best she could without touching her. The result was a simple ponytail with a lanky bow, which fit her wildly long hair. Even though she tied the ribbon in her hair, it seemed as if nothing happened.

Olin nervously scratched his bald head.

"The first time may take a moment. Enchantments of this nature must draw their power from a source. So, I believe that is what is happening now."

"From what source does this enchantment draw its power?" Alden scrutinized.

"Chilali's own physical stamina, but do not be alarmed. Divergents are untiring and the strain should be as minimal as if you were to hang a small bag of pebbles around your neck."

Chilali felt the ribbon's enchantment wash over her like a cold wind. It brought goose bumps to her skin and her vision tinted blue as if she dove deep beneath a clear lake. The experience continued for longer than she liked, a few short moments, but enough for her to reach back to remove the ribbon. Before she could free the bow, her vision returned to normal, the unnatural wind died, and warmth returned to her flesh.

Olin rubbed the stubble growing unevenly out of his chin and Alden just stared. Jerle took a step back, her hand covering her mouth. Falcon and Agraven both pretended to be unimpressed.

"Excellent work, Olin," Alden said, as he paced a circle around Chilali. "The enchantment is extremely convincing."

Chilali grabbed her hair to see. What was a deep red had become bright yellow, like a polished gold coin reflecting sunlight. She found it hard to believe and for a moment was afraid her hair would never be its original color again.

Olin's eyes narrowed and Chilali caught a glimpse of the priest's other self. Power and charisma returned to his sickly figure and his pallid skin took on a glow. But it was only a glimpse. The priest she mangled the day before remained and none of the others seemed to notice the brief transformation, which, for the first time, struck Chilali as unusual.

"This is odd," Olin commented weakly.

"Odd?" Alden asked.

"Falcon, do you see it, or I should say do you not see it?"

Falcon squinted at Chilali from the breakfast table.

"That is strange, good priest. But how would such a

thing be possible?"

"How would what be possible?" Alden insisted.

"All enchantments born of Sitara's power exude her power. Those like myself and Falcon, who are blessed with her power, are sensitive to such enchantments. We can see their power as it were a physical aura, a hue of light," Olin explained. "But we see no such power now, despite the strength of this enchantment."

"Could it be because Chilali is a Divergent?" Jerle put forth.

"Perhaps, but I cannot say. Nevertheless, the enchantment appears to be working. It should be safe to take Chilali to the capital without causing a panic," Olin said, while taking a seat next to Falcon.

"Are my eyes like yours now, too?" Chilali asked.

"Yes, you look just like a little girl from the capital," Jerle beamed.

"One that's been playing in the dirt all day," Agraven had to add.

Alden meant to answer Chilali's question, but he found himself too busy looking at all the new possibilities this ribbon afforded him. There must be some advantage to hiding the enchantment and Chilali's disguise from the Order. In fact, he began to weave an entirely new plan, a way to maintain some degree of control over Chilali's future.

But he also realized seeing her for what she truly was would be even more difficult now. Where once stood a fearsome slayer of men now stood a child of the Empire. Her skin was a shade or two darker than most, but her hair and eye color were undistinguishable from anyone else in the Empire. Yet somehow, her wild nature couldn't be completely masked by the enchantment. The ferocity in her eyes, like the eyes of a palace cat watching birds clean themselves in a courtyard fountain, remained. And the ease in which she carried herself, completely impassive, as if their world bored her, could not be masked. Or maybe their world, for the moment, failed to move with enough speed, failed to be propelled with enough chaos to capture her interest.

"Falcon, you still look quite tired. Do you think you'll be able to ride today?" Alden asked, interrupting his own thoughts upon noticing his friend's fatigue.

Falcon returned a nod to Alden.

"I look more tired than I feel."

"Do you think you could deliver a letter to my sister ahead of our arrival to the capital?"

"Considering you plan to stop at the estate, I don't think it would be a problem. But what could be so important that you would need to communicate it to your sister ahead of your arrival?"

"Nothing more than giving her a polite opportunity to prepare for so many guests."

"I'll go when you're ready."

"Thank you."

Falcon patted Olin on the back once, as he got up, and then went out the back.

Chilali went to the front door, but Alden called to her.

"Where are you going?"

"I'm going to walk around outside. I look like a daughter of the Empire now."

Jerle stood, eager to volunteer.

"I'll go with her."

Agraven grabbed his wife's wrist.

"Are you sure?"

"Absolutely. We'll just go for a walk, while the rest of you prepare the horses."

Alden didn't like the idea, but he didn't want to have a confrontation.

"Don't be too long. We'll be leaving shortly."

Jerle waved as she pushed open the front door and led Chilali out.

Strife's Journal: 395th Day, 4058, South Capital Road

An overcast sky let the morning fog linger for many hours into the afternoon. Not being able to see so clearly ahead is not something I am used to.

The campaign in the south is over. A short parade and party await us in the capital before I travel north again to contend with the Volitor remnants. Rumors indicate the Volitors have a champion unlike any other, a frightening beast of remarkable strength and size. I will deal with it when the time comes.

Sveta has begun to talk to me more now that I've shown an interest in her. This has caused more than a few whispers to spread amongst my ranks—whispers that I overhear.

Today while riding, she asked the origin of my name, which is admittedly unusual. I told her I was given it by the Magus; Divergents are birthed nameless. And she asked why the Magus would give me such a name. It was tradition, I told her, for Divergents to be given descriptors that act as names, going as far back as the last three Divergents Sitara called from the forest.

And then she asked me if I was not more than the description. Of course, I am more than a creature of war and fire, I told her.

She suggested I take my own name. I agreed. I will take my own name when this war is done; though, I do like my current name. Ren is a proponent of it as well.

—General Strife Ashwake

Just a Walk

Jerle followed Chilali, enjoying the breeze on her lips and the sunlight on her face. She knew Chilali was not Saveria, but she could pretend for a while. It was a false happiness, but it was better than none at all and a small respite from the pain she felt so acutely. The memories of that terrible day never left her, never even dulled. She could still feel Saveria's tender little hand spasm and go limp, followed by the forceful squeezing of her own hand to catch her child's dead weight.

It hurt again, so she focused on the burning spot in her mind where the gateway to the Fire King's realm existed. It stung to go there, to focus on it, but in the process, she gained control, again, as well as a distraction.

The main cobblestone street running through the center of the village was empty. Most people here were farmers, hunters, or fishermen and were already busy with their chosen profession. It was quiet, simple, and maybe even charming. Jerle could only guess how Chilali saw it, as the disguised Divergent meandered to the edge of the village to a place where the woodlands met an expanse of rolling plains.

Barefoot, Chilali followed a dirt road going uphill toward the bulk of the village's farming community. Wildflowers and flower-like weeds grew on either side of the road, lining it with pastels and briars. The Divergent stopped at the top of the hill, staring out across the farmland, endless rows of colorful crops and the occasional orchard.

Jerle caught up and stood beside her.

"It's pretty, isn't it?"

Chilali was locked onto something in the distance Jerle couldn't see. She pointed.

"What is that?"

Jerle squinted, but it was just too far, too small.

"I can't see what you're pointing at. It's too far for me."

Chilali took off in a dash, with the speed of a frightened horse. Jerle gasped and tried to follow, running full sprint, but less than half Chilali's speed. Even though she was a well-trained, well-exercised warrior, she could only run at full sprint for so long. Her lungs burning for air, she slowed and watched Chilali almost disappear in the distance.

Seeing the Divergent stop was enough to provoke her into a light jog. It was just too early in the morning for this, and she could taste her breakfast trying to come up. Her right calve was cramping, too. Not pleasant, she thought, and pushed forward.

Chilali was watching from the top of another hill overlooking an orchard when Jerle caught up to her.

"What is it," Jerle barely managed to ask between breaths.

Chilali pointed again, and this time Jerle could see what got the Divergent's attention. A Talarian servant girl rushed through the orchard screaming and ducking the nut-heavy branches. Though younger than most, she looked like every other Talarian. Her skin was smooth and ivory, like well-cleaned teeth, and she was slightly shorter and more slender than a daughter of the Empire would be at her age. Her hair hung in a long, dark teal drape with slightly thicker and more polished-looking strands than found on a man's head.

A Talarian's eyes and nails always unnerved Jerle, while many men in the Empire found them attractive. Their irises were silver and sparkled even in the dimmest light like a many-faceted gemstone. And their fingernails would grow to more of a point than a man's nails and were a reflective black.

Jerle caught sight of a one-armed man chasing this particular Talarian, awkwardly waving a leather strap over his head and shouting threats. More than once, both he and the Talarian slipped on the ample supply of the magenta-colored, eyeball-sized nuts covering the ground. And the

Talarian was having enough trouble holding her long skirt up to run.

"That's a Talarian servant, a young one. It seems this one has done something to upset her master," Jerle explained, getting her wind back.

"What is a Talarian?"

"One of the four Lesser races. Because their males pose such danger for men, only females are allowed to be kept as servants. They're mainly used for housekeeping chores and *recreation*."

"They must do as they're told, or they are killed?"

"More or less. But such is the price for beginning a war of annihilation and losing it."

"Alden told Shank that. I don't like it."

She didn't like it, Jerle thought. How should she respond to that? The enslavement of the Lessers, while a cruel fate, was still better than the alternative offered by the Blackland Nation. And it was the only way to be certain they would never threaten the kingdoms of man, again.

"You live in a much more peaceful era, Chilali. It is far easier to judge our actions ill, now, than it would have been two hundred years ago."

The one-armed man finally caught up to the Talarian and the inevitable beating ensued. Forward and backward, he swung his arm, slapping whatever part of her body he could with the strap and tearing her beige colored dress to get at her skin and humiliate her further. Such beatings were never pleasant to watch, but they were necessary at times, Jerle told herself.

The fire elemental user's eyes widened when the man tossed aside the strap and rolled the Talarian girl onto her stomach. The girl stopped her struggle halfway through the beating, but Jerle imagined she could hear her whimpering.

"Chilali, stay here," Jerle commanded more forcefully than she should have and ran toward the spectacle. Chilali followed behind, matching Jerle's frantic, but exhausted pace with little effort. Jerle didn't know if she could make it in time to stop what was about to happen. And she didn't bother to wonder whether or not she should even try.

She reached the orchard and maneuvered her way across the nuts without falling. She skidded to a stop by the one-armed man and the Talarian girl and held onto a tree with one hand to keep her knees from buckling. The one-armed man had his knee in the small of the Talarian girl's back and had gotten his belt unbuckled with his sole hand.

"Don't do this," Jerle cried out.

Startled, the man got off the Talarian, but didn't bother to fasten his belt, instead grabbing for the strap he discarded. Whoever removed his arm had done a good job of it, leaving no stump at all at the shoulder. Spittle clung to his beard and his face was red with fury. The Talarian girl crawled to the nearest tree, whimpering and holding her torn dress around her.

"This is not your business," the man spat, regaining his senses. "Leave my land."

"I've no problem with your beating her, sir, but this one is too young for anything more."

"That's my decision to make, not yours, woman," the man fumed and grabbed his strap from the ground.

Jerle stepped away from the tree and noticed Chilali standing behind her at a distance.

"If you don't leave right now, I'll beat you as badly as I beat her," the man pointed at the cringing Talarian, the welts already turning into deep blue bruises.

"Don't think to threaten me," Jerle returned hotly.

"I'm within the law. That Talarian's my property. I'll treat her how I wish. And if you don't leave my farm right now, I'll beat you in front of your daughter."

The words stung Jerle and tipped her psychologically off-balance. She couldn't focus on the burning place in her mind, and she wasn't ready for the man to lunge at her. She reacted sloppily, stepping back blindly. Her heel found a nut and she came down in a heap, rolling her ankle. The one-armed man closed on her in that instant. She braced herself for the first blow, catching the strap on her forearm. It bit like fire and struck as heavy and as hard as a club. Her whole arm went numb, and she couldn't help but to grab it in agony. He would land the second blow wherever he chose, and she wouldn't be able to stop him.

Just a few steps away, she made eye contact with the trembling Talarian. The empathy she felt in that moment for the girl made her sick with guilt. She was ready to take her beating, too. It was the price she would pay for her callousness.

Chilali barreled into the one-armed man's chest with the speed of an arrow and smashed him against a tree. Nuts fell in a great shower as the force rattled the branches. Jerle had to cover her head to shield herself from them. When she looked up, Chilali stood above the man. A line of blood rolled out the corner of his mouth as he sat against the tree. His eyes were open and still. He was clearly dead, evidenced by the fact his chest had been crushed, leaving a disturbing concavity beneath his simple brown shirt. The leather strap slipped from his still fingers.

Chilali leered at Jerle.

"I killed him," the pleasure in her words unsettled Jerle in a way she didn't think possible.

The pretty little daughter of the Empire in front of her was really a monster. She could see it for the first time but couldn't grasp it. As much as she tried to force it into her own mind, she couldn't make it settle inside. She held onto her swelling forearm and went to the Talarian.

There was no more time to think about things. She had to act. Despite the unusual circumstances, this scenario could be interpreted as murder. The evidence had to either be removed or altered to impugn someone else. She had always excelled at this while working for the guild.

"You're coming with us," Jerle told the Talarian girl

flatly.

The Talarian was frozen with fear and didn't even respond. She kept staring at Chilali.

"Chilali, drag him out to here," Jerle pointed at a spot on the ground two steps away.

Chilali responded not by dragging, but by tossing the man to the spot, emotionlessly slinging him by his sole arm. He crumbled like a sack of mismatched bones and more blood flooded out of him from beneath his darkening shirt.

"Now take the Talarian without hurting her and go back to the road."

The Talarian screamed and balled up as Chilali approached her.

"I'm a daughter of the Empire. I won't hurt you," Chilali told the Talarian, expecting she would actually believe the words.

"Go with her, damn you!" Jerle shouted at the Talarian.

Her words shocked the Talarian into obedience. The Talarian followed Chilali immediately and without question. She didn't even look back.

Jerle put her hand on the tree where Chilali crushed the farmer. She slid it to the base of the trunk and carefully lined it up with the farmer. The Fire King's power rolled into her and poured out of her hand into the tree. She used a technique she vowed not to use on another living creature ever again. It was the same technique that led her to such success as an assassin when she worked for Baigen. She mentally wound the Fire King's power like yarn into a ball, building it and thickening it inside the tree. A slight orange flame licking Jerle's fingers served as the only indication of her mental efforts.

She removed her hand and ran as far and as fast as she could. This was far too much running, even for her, she lamented. Behind her, she heard the dull pop, followed by a loud crack. Branches snapped as the tree folded over the exploded hole in the base of its trunk. The tree, not particularly tall, but high enough to be convincing, fell on top of the farmer's corpse, making even more of a mess.

It was the first thing that came to mind, she sighed. She caught up to Chilali and the Talarian. Alden and Agraven, especially, were not going to be happy with her and this turn of events. She was such a fool for rushing to the servant's aide to prevent the rape. Trying to spare this servant girl from that terrible fate would not change what happened to her so many years ago before she discovered her powers and joined the guild. And for a Talarian servant, such a thing was practically inevitable anyway.

It was just supposed to be a walk, she told herself and kept telling herself the whole way back to the tavern.

Past Mistakes

"That was Emma's father," Alden sighed and squeezed the bridge of his nose. "And Marcus' brother-in-law. I was the one who amputated his arm a season ago."

Jerle kept staring at the floor. This was not what she intended, but it still became such a catastrophe. Chilali didn't seem to be affected by the situation at all. While it wasn't outwardly obvious, Jerle had a horrible sense the Divergent felt some relief at being able to crush Emma's father by explosively ramming her little shoulder into the middle of his rib cage. The attack happened so fast, Jerle couldn't even recall what it sounded like when the man's torso burst.

Alden looked up at Olin and Agraven.

"No one can know of this. Are we in agreement?"

Agraven, holding onto Jerle's shoulders from behind, raised her bruised forearm.

"If I had been there, his body would still be burning right now."

Olin crossed his legs, sitting on a stool at the bar.

"I find this situation as troubling as it is interesting."

"What is your answer, priest?" Alden challenged, losing patience.

"I'll not discuss the matter with those in the village, but I must inform the Order of the incident."

"Then do not expect us to follow you to the capital," Agraven said, as he stepped in front of Jerle.

Alden patted Agraven on the shoulder.

"That is fine, Agraven, but only if you come with me to report on the Blackland mine. They can bring no charges against you."

Agraven nodded.

Alden stood in front of Chilali.

"In the future, use more discretion."

"I didn't know men were so fragile," Chilali replied,

chillingly. "Do you have any Talarian servants?"

Alden crossed his arms.

"Of course, they help run my house in the capital."

"Do you beat them?"

"Not personally. I leave their care and direction to men I've hired. But why are you asking?"

"If I were a Talarian, I would kill you."

Chilali stared at Alden with a piercing focus in her gaze. The others in the room tensed.

"Then it's a good thing you're not a Talarian," Alden remarked, hoping to break the tension in the room. He turned his back to her and moved to the kitchen and the rear exit.

He stopped.

"What happened to Oliven was unfortunate for us and his family, but I'll not lose sleep over it. Though he fought in the north against the Blackland Nation for nearly a decade, you are potentially much more important to the Empire, Chilali. Judge us as you will but know if you were a Talarian in the Blackland Nation, you would have been killed long ago."

"What are you going to do about the Talarian?" Olin asked, his eyes narrowing.

"I cleaned her wounds and bandaged her. She should be able to come with us. If Jerle and Agraven do not want to take her, I will," Alden turned and answered.

"I've no problem with adding her to our stock," Agraven stated.

"Good, then bring her down. I've settled my debts with Marcus. We'll be leaving shortly."

* * *

Chilali's legs were barely long enough to reach the stirrups and she found herself wondering how the horse she rode would taste. Neither she nor the caramel-colored beast enjoyed the arrangement. It was so fearful of her at first Olin had to force it to calm down and accept her with his powers. But the beast was not the only one that was fearful. As she rode, she felt the same anxiety that caused her to attack Olin, albeit not nearly as strongly. She wore riding pants, tucked into her boots, and a sleeveless buttoned shirt. The new outfit, more fitting for a boy, Jerle complained, worked to reduce contact and distracted her with new discomfort.

Her attention also kept wandering, because she didn't guide the beast so much as she just sat on top of it. Alden held onto the reins for her, riding slightly ahead on a white mare with a silver bridle. She couldn't focus her mind on any one thing in particular. Her world was one of annoyances and boredom, a combination she feared would lead her to lose control.

Jerle rode with the Talarian girl sitting in front. It was another awkward, but necessary paring. There were only so many horses to go around. Combined, the pair weighed as much as either Agraven or Alden and perhaps a little more than Olin. The Talarian had not said a word and kept her eyes forward as much as she could. Bruises streaked her face, arms, and legs. Their rich purple color marring her ivory skin went well with the gray dress and black shawl she wore, making her look that much prettier, Chilali thought. Still, the Talarian had been silent and afraid since the moment Jerle brought her down from the locked second floor room. Chilali was tiring of passively waiting to learn more about Talarians.

Agraven, the largest man in the party with Falcon's absence, lumbered behind Chilali on his thick, black steed. Like Jerle, Agraven was lightly armored with leather strapping and silver studding. He carried a sword at his belt, an unstrung bow on his back, and a knife on his thigh. He kicked his mount into a slightly faster pace to move up next to Jerle and the Talarian. He kept watch on the whole party and the surroundings, as if he expected something terrible would happen at any moment. Chilali wouldn't be so bored if that were actually the case. Her senses stretched well beyond the boundaries of his, but she didn't think to tell him to relax. Such a thing as cooperation on that kind of level wasn't part of her nature, yet.

Olin steered his mount, another caramel-colored stallion, next to Chilali. He held his staff, a slender silver rod with a multi-point star at the top of it, at an angle across his saddle in the same hand as the reins.

"There is not much to see on this road for quite a while more," the priest said, adjusting his grip on his staff.

That did seem to be the case, Chilali yawned. Once they cleared Orsa village and its fringe settlements, there had been nothing but rolling plains, crops of rocks, and the occasional thicket. The sky was depressingly overcast, and the air was stagnant. Chilali had to endure the stink of the beasts, the Talarian girl's fear, and Olin the entire ride. Olin's scent was so peculiar to her. While he smelled like any of the other men she had encountered, his odor had a pungent edge to it, a subtle foulness, but she couldn't tell what the cause was. This was also the fifth or sixth time the priest had tried to engage her in conversation. And like this time, the preceding attempts were failures.

Chilali's eyes shifted to the Talarian, who turned away quickly; trying to hide the fact she had just turned to see the priest.

"What do they call you?" Chilali asked the Talarian.

Alden slowed his mount to come between the Talarian and Chilali.

"It's not important."

Chilali leaned forward to peer around Alden.

"They decided to call me Chilali."

The Talarian's bottom lip trembled.

"She is too frightened to talk right now," Jerle dissuaded.

Chilali took the hint, but still found a way to give into her growing boredom.

"Jerle, how do you get an elemental power?"

"You must be born with one. But even those born with one, may not recognize it for what it is immediately. Some discover it when they are children and others not until much later in life."

"How would I know if I have one?"

"It is almost certain you do not have one," Olin interjected. "Divergents are Sitara's chosen people, and she counts the Elemental Kings as her enemies."

"Strife was a fire element user," Agraven argued.

"Yes, but Strife was an exception to many rules," Olin countered. "And in the end, it was his elemental power and not his enemies that brought about his end."

"Regardless, Chilali, one typically does not discover an elemental power until they have an absolute and desperate need for it," Alden said, answering Chilali's original question and hopefully averting an argument.

"How many Elemental Kings are there?" Chilali continued.

"More than is known," Olin quickly answered. "The Order recognizes, from the most common to least, fire, air, metal, light, and ice."

"Ice is just a myth put forth by the Blackland Nation" Agraven added.

"It is true there have only been three ice users in recorded history, but it is real. And a large number of tribes in the Blackland Nation do worship the Ice Queen," Alden said. "The real mystery is why there is no water element."

"The Water King died," the Talarian girl peeped.

"That is what a worshipper of the Elemental Kings would say," Olin agreed, snidely.

"It is a reasonable explanation that the Embracing Night deceived the Fire King into betraying the Water King," Jerle said, soothing the Talarian girl.

"An explanation that asserts Sitara fraternized with the Elemental Kings," Olin snapped.

Tiring of the ribbon in her hair, Chilali pulled it loose, and her façade dropped in front of the Talarian girl and the others. The sudden reemergence of her actual appearance surprised all of them. And again, while she didn't consciously acknowledge it, their reactions hurt her.

"A Divergent," the Talarian girl stammered and almost fell out of the saddle, but Jerle grabbed her.

"She won't hurt you or any of us," Jerle tried to calm her.

Chilali yawned and hopped off her horse, relieving both rider and mount. She walked alongside, holding the ribbon in her hand.

"You shouldn't be afraid of me. I wouldn't beat you," Chilali said matter-of-factly.

"What are you doing?" Alden asked Chilali.

"I'm tired of riding," she answered and moved ahead of the group. "This feels a lot better."

"Only for a bit, then you must use the ribbon again. I do not want to alarm any travelers that may be coming toward us."

Alden chewed his lip as he watched Chilali walk ahead of him. Her new clothing helped his mind make better sense of her true nature, even with the ribbon untied. As young and as small as she was, she carried herself like a warrior, lean and powerful. He could see the toned muscles in her arms and the ease of her stride. It was a beauty very different from her mask as a daughter of the Empire.

The Plantation

Agraven hadn't seen his home in months. It was just as he remembered, if not a bit more welcoming. The last two days he spent traveling from Orsa taxed his patience and fatigued him. He just didn't feel safe around the Divergent, and his wife riding with a Talarian didn't make the situation any easier for him. Along the way, Jerle got the girl to open up a little more, but he knew creating such a bond was a waste of effort. His wife would forget this servant in time, he believed.

Many men found Talarian women attractive. Agraven was not ashamed to admit their allure either, but he had no fondness for the Lessers. With the exception of the Fifth and the Volitors, he had no wish for their demise. He merely believed the Empire would be better off without them, the Talarians, Briam, and Ragebourne. It would create new opportunities for work for the groundlings. And maybe if he had been able to find an honest living, he would not have joined the Silver Talons. Maybe, his and Jerle's past could have been much less bloody if not for the Lessers.

Chilali barely took any notice of Agraven, who rode beside her in quiet thought. She was too busy absorbing all that she could of the plantation. This was the place where Jerle and Agraven lived, and she could hardly believe it. It teemed with life.

The Briam were unlike anything she had seen. Most were equal to her in height if not a bit taller, but they were just as wide. They had large almond shaped brown eyes and long trunks that hung just past their knees. Their skin color ranged from light gray to tan to pink with blue spots and their pointy little ears, which poked vertically out of the tops of their heads, could twist from side to side, facing together or apart.

Their scent, which was vestigial at best, given the

distance between her and the Briam working in the fields, was earthy, like the inside of a tree. And the way their trunks flopped over their mouths gave her the impression they were always smiling as they went about the fields picking vegetables, fruit, and fibers from the plants and carting them away in man-sized baskets. Most curious, however, was how they would walk together in chains. A Briam would grasp the tail of the one in front, usually the bigger one, with its trunk and they would link together like this in groups as short as two or longer than thirty.

Hundreds of Briam tended the fields and a handful of Talarian servant women moved among them, bringing them food and water. A few men on horseback oversaw the whole process and would occasionally bark out orders. Given their numbers, Chilali wondered for a moment why the Briam and Talarians didn't attack the men.

The answer was, they didn't think like her. She was different than them, all of them. The ribbon holding her hair in a ponytail was a tangible reminder of this. Her clothing and the fact she now rode a horse on her own were reminders, as well. Alden said it would look peculiar for a girl her age to ride a horse alone, but she grew weary of being led.

Jerle pointed across the fields to her estate. Chilali noticed the structure a long time ago. It appeared to have three floors, multiple rooms, and a front and rear entrance. Its walls were made of stone and wood, and its roof was tiled with some kind of flat red tablets. A stone wall as tall as a man encircled the structure, several gardens, and a pond. And the four breaks in the wall were marked with stone archways and cobbled walkways. It was easily the largest man-made structure she had seen so far, but it still failed to impress her.

"Look, there is your new home. It should be quite a pleasant change from where you were," Jerle said to the Talarian.

The girl's silver eyes had been opened wide since they reached the edge of the plantation. She turned her head to look up at Jerle.

"How many other Talarians are there in your house?"

"Many. It's hard for me to say exactly. We have a lot of land and a large estate. We accept many guests who need a place to stay for the night on their way between the Chain and the capital. So, we retain as many Talarians as we can reasonably sustain."

"That is a bit reckless," Olin said, trotting up beside Jerle on his horse.

"Treat them fairly with reasonable expectations and you won't have any problems," Agraven defended.

"And what do you consider to be reasonable?" Olin grinned.

"Treat them as you would a groundling," Agraven replied with a shrug.

"Groundling?" Chilali asked. "Is that another of the Lessers?"

"No, the groundlings are the common people of the Empire. They are mostly craftsmen, refining raw materials. They do not serve as militia men, knights, or as members of the Order and they are not of nobility, meaning they have no blood relation to the emperor," Alden was quick to answer.

"Are you a noble, Alden?" Chilali asked right back.

"Yes, my uncle is the emperor. I'm sixth in line for the throne, not that I desire it."

"Sir Eos will likely succeed Emperor Adelphos," Agraven added.

"My cousin, as young, impulsive, and ambitious as he is, has the makings of strong leader."

"The line of succession alone does not determine who is allowed to sit on the Silver Throne," Olin explained. "Sitara must accept him."

"Sir Eos is a True Silver Knight," Agraven half

complained, half stated.

"So he is," Olin conceded.

Despite the conversation and all the activity happening around her in the fields, Chilali didn't fail to notice the rider approaching them. A young man dressed much as she was, galloped toward them with a sword on his back and a wry smile beneath his short, boxed beard.

Agraven caught sight of the rider and galloped off to meet him.

"Raife," he bellowed out with a volume that surprised Chilali.

She could make out most of their conversation, as she and the rest of her party rode up to meet them. It was casual and inconsequential for her.

"Raife is Agraven's younger brother," Jerle told Chilali with a smile. "He must have been sent home from the northern border."

Raife swung his leg over his horse and stepped down. He patted his mount on the shoulder and greeted everyone with a slight bow.

"It's good to see you again, sister. And Alden, you look well. Falcon said he was worried the rashes you sustained in the forest would never leave you."

"It is good to see you home, Raife," Alden returned with a polite chuckle.

"And let me guess, the good priest here must be Olin, but I'm afraid I do not know of this charming young lady."

Raife swept a deep bow in front of Chilali and reached for her hand. She pulled her mount away, leaving Raife chagrin.

"Chilali's a bit shy," Jerle explained.

"I see. Chilali is a graceful name. While I would have to see it written to be certain, I would guess you are named for the most beautiful of the cold weather birds?"

"She is," Alden confirmed, as Chilali turned to look at him for the same indication as Raife.

He named her after a bird. That seemed strange to her, which was made even stranger by the fact she didn't even care about her name when he first gave her one. She was nothing like a bird. She couldn't fly. She wasn't fragile and she didn't sing. She slumped slightly in her saddle.

"Why don't we go inside now and clean up?" Jerle offered, as she dismounted and ran her hand through her horse's mane. It nuzzled her hand in return.

Chilali climbed off her mount, too, and Raife came to assist her. Fortunately, Alden moved in before him.

"She has to learn how to do it herself," Alden explained to Raife.

"Is she yours?" Raife asked and Chilali waited for Alden's response.

"Yes, she's my daughter."

"With a groundling woman?"

"I was too young a man."

"And her mother?"

"Passed."

"I see. Well, I wish you luck. She looks like a fine child, despite being of common birth."

"Truly, there is nothing common about her," Alden grinned, leading Raife behind Jerle, Agraven, and Olin.

Chilali rolled her eyes. He was hiding her now. The purpose of the ribbon went beyond disguising her so as not to frighten people. As much information as her instincts and intelligence allowed her to infer, Alden continued to surprise her.

Raife took notice of the Talarian.

"You purchased another one, Jerle?"

"This one was a gift," she replied with a toss of her hair.

"It appears she's seen better times."

Agraven came up behind Raife and put him in a playful headlock.

"Enough questions, tell me of the campaign to the north. And why are you back so soon?"

Chilali watched Raife struggle with his bulkier older brother. It sparked something inside her, a need for play, which was a pleasure she had forgotten after being alone for so long. Of course, if she got rough like that, she would likely kill them. Coming to this world, she traded one frustration for many new ones.

"Let me go, brother. The campaign goes well. A truce has been declared with the Blackland Nation."

Alden gasped.

"A truce?"

"Aye, it's been a hundred years, but we have some peace now."

Alden rubbed the stubble on his chin with his thumb. If what Raife said was true, something was very wrong. It's possible a catastrophe could have befallen the Blackland Nation, bringing a halt to their aggression. An inter-tribal war was more likely. Or maybe it had something to do with their breaching of the southern mountains.

"The situation is not as it appears," Agraven said and released his struggling younger brother.

"What makes you say that?" Raife returned.

"It must be a ploy to reposition their forces to the south."

Agraven nodded.

"We must leave for the capital as soon as possible."

Jerle draped one arm around the Talarian.

"Tomorrow morning then, but for now, let us go enjoy warm baths and hot meals."

She held the Talarian girl at arm's length.

"Now, tell me what your name is girl."

"Astra of Light," the girl meekly replied.

Jerle placed her hand on Astra's back and guided her toward the house.

"Welcome to my home, Astra."

Chilali saw Raife flinch and Agraven bite his bottom lip. Alden seemed lost in his thoughts. Olin shook his head.

Talarian servants rushed up to them to take the horses. They all looked like Astra, but with variations in the color of their hair and size. They all had long drapes, but the colors ranged from dark teal to a deep indigo. Some were a little thicker than others and some were taller. The difference between their scents was subtle and made it difficult to distinguish between them that way alone. But at the same time, the scent was familiar. Chilali wasn't sure why, as she followed the others inside.

Strife's Journal: 255th Day, 4057, North Master's Enclave

The daytime melt turns the ground to muck, and the nighttime freeze hardens it again. This is not a pleasant place to camp.

I stand in view of the North Master's Enclave. It is a mostly subterranean structure hollowed into a mountain. Steam clouds bubble out of its peak and I catch the slightest hint of sulfur in the wind.

I am told it is a place of warriors solely dedicated to improving themselves through rigorous combat training and something referred to as the Black Descent. While all peoples are invited to join the North Masters, provided they can pass the initiation, Divergents, Volitors, and the Fifth (not that they have need to join) are prohibited.

The Volitors are the only people the North Masters consider to be an enemy. The Fifth are the Fifth, supernatural and superior. And Divergents inherently lack the willpower to endure the training.

I thought to prove this assumption incorrect, but I am not permitted inside for another reason. It is a neutral place in this war. Only diplomats and scholars may enter.

Still, I hear whispers of another Divergent among the North Masters. If we are forced to camp here much longer while waiting for reinforcements from the Blackland Nation to arrive, my curiosity will get the better of me. I admit I salivate just a bit at the thought of testing the skill of the legendary Grandmaster Chael, the man who walks this world without equal in combat.

—General Strife Ashwake

Insomnia

For Chilali, it was much the same as it was back at the tavern. They ate and talked and retired shortly after sunset. Jerle provided her with a room, which she had to herself. The bed was softer than anything she had known and the blankets warm. But Chilali didn't want comfort. She paced in her room from corner to corner and eventually found her way through the balcony doors. Dressed in just a chemise, she stood on the stone railing at the edge of the balcony, letting the cool night breeze kiss her skin and her ruby hair blow free.

The sky remained overcast, but Sitara's Star was bright enough to light up a patch of clouds. In the distance across several plots, the Briam herd, as they were called, slept in their simple little conical tents in a bunch. And the Talarians slumbered in much more cramped quarters below the mansion in the stores with Astra. Everyone grew tired so much faster than she did. They were all now dormant and inactive, leaving her alone. She longed to run out into the night and dash through the crops, sinking her toes and fingers deep into the dew-damp soil for traction, but she had agreed not to run out on her own.

She heard a balcony door on the third-floor creak open and slipped back against the wall to hide. Alden stepped into the night, bare to his waist and candlelight aglow on his back. He raised a bottle to his lips and before he brought it back down, Chilali stood on the railing of his balcony. Too wound up in thought to react in fear, he set the bottle down and kept staring into the darkness.

"We'll be in the capital by tomorrow night."

She hopped off the railing and leaned against it next to him with both her elbows flat and her chin resting on her hands.

"You realize, you do not say much?"

"Your kind says too much."

"My kind is your kind. Sitara made you different, not the chaos of this world."

"Why aren't you sleeping like the others?"

"I'm having one of those nights," Alden sighed and took another sip from his bottle. "This Empire is all that there is for man. The Blackland Nation is one of our kingdoms, but it is savage, tribal, and worships Shyamon equally with Sitara. If our Empire falls, Chilali, the age of man will end."

Chilali let his words settle and watched him take another sip. As before, the scent from the drink was stringent, but inviting.

"I want to drink," she pointed.

Alden looked at the wine bottle, the crude, thick glass wrapped in twine and wax.

"Let's call it an experiment."

He slid the bottle to her across the broad stone handrail.

"Just take a sip."

She took it and tasted the red liquid. It wasn't sweet or sour or like anything she had tasted before. It was just strong with a fruit quality to it. It burned a little in her mouth, going down her throat and in her nostrils, but was pleasant in its own way. She slid the bottle back to Alden.

"You told Raife I was your daughter."

"I can't tell everyone you're a Divergent if I want to take you into the capital safely."

"What do you mean?"

"I'm taking you to the Order, because I have too much to lose if I do not. Others are not in the same position and would do anything they can to acquire you for political and military power."

"Power?"

"You don't grasp your own value, Chilali. When you are grown, you will be matchless in the Empire, the strongest of our warriors. You could become the greatest hero since Strife. Anyone fortunate enough to walk beside you during your ascent will reap untold benefits."

"If I am called."

Alden pointed at her.

"If you are."

She looked down at her toes.

"But I do not want to serve the Empire. I do not want to serve anyone."

Alden laughed and wiped his lips on the back of his hand. He passed the bottle back to Chilali.

"Of course you don't. You have no stake in our wars, our survival."

Chilali gulped a mouthful and handed it back to Alden. She hopped onto the railing, sitting with her back to the fall.

Alden took a couple deep gulps and looked across the dimly lit fields.

"What do you want, Chilali? If you're not called, why stay here? Why not just go back?"

"I want to see."

"See what? What is there for you to see in the kingdom of men?"

"Everything I haven't seen."

Alden stared at her hard, feeling the alcohol beginning to take effect. He would sleep soon, he hoped. He tired long ago of solving puzzles through to the morning.

"You don't really know why you're here," he observed.

Chilali didn't respond, didn't react at all. She tilted her head slightly, hearing something he couldn't.

"What do you hear that I cannot?"

A tear ran down her right cheek and dripped off her chin. He could only watch. She didn't whimper. Her breathing didn't change. She was just as impassive as he had seen her before, but still she cried.

"I hear Jerle and Agraven."

Alden felt a knot tighten in his throat.

"Jerle's crying. Agraven's telling her it will be all right." she continued.

"Saveria," he added.

She nodded slowly in affirmation.

"They loved her very, very much," he said, thinking it was the only thing he could say.

Her chin quivered and she spoke with a choked voice.

"Why didn't my mother love me like that?"

Alden wanted to reach over and sweep her up in his arms, as he would if she was his own daughter, but he couldn't. She would tear him to pieces. He could only comfort her with words, which seemed impossible.

"You're a Divergent, Chilali. It is how your people are. Take comfort in knowing whether you are called or not you have this chance to form new relationships. You don't have to be alone for the remainder of your days if you fight to preserve this Empire."

She wiped her cheek dry and rose to her feet on the railing.

"I want to go to sleep now."

"Good night, Chilali."

She leapt down to her balcony, a feat beyond any ordinary man. And even a well-trained one would only have attempted the leap as a last resort. She cleared the gap and took the fall with ease, on her way to bed. It astounded Alden, but so did her apparent vulnerability. She genuinely missed her mother and hadn't learned to cope with the loss. It was highly unlikely she would ever find her mother again and even if she did the meeting would likely result in a brawl.

He went back inside with his bottle and closed the balcony doors. The truce was a prelude to war. The Blackland Nation would come from the south, bypassing the majority of the Empire's defenses, but the trek must be difficult. It must necessitate the creation of an outpost in the south to maintain supply lines. The settlement Jerle and Agraven scouted was much more than a mine, he was certain of it now. Whatever happened with Chilali, he had to convince his uncle to attack the settlement and seal the breach in the border.

He sat at the foot of his bed. How much more would he need to drink before he could sleep, he mused. With his thumb he traced the mouth of the bottle. No man alive could say he drank with a Divergent. The thought brought a slight smile to his lips. He set the bottle on the night stand next to his bed and fell onto the soft furs.

Dreams of a grown Chilali riding at the front of a shimmering silver army, charging across endless plains, came to him. In those dreams, he found peace. The Empire would prevail, always.

The Road to the Capital

Dirt paths turned into cobblestone roads as they rode closer to the capital. Vast farmlands shrunk to smaller ones with more and more housing, mainly cottages and cabins built amongst trees. Briam and Talarians were even more prevalent, walking up and down the roads carting goods or tending to the fields. The groundlings they passed were busy with their livelihoods. Some hammered red-hot metal and others stitched fabric.

To Alden's unease, whether they were Talarian, Briam, or groundling, they took notice of Chilali and the rest of the party. Alden kept near her, holding onto her reins to keep up appearances. She dressed in the same riding gear Jerle said was better fit for a boy, and he was dressed to fit his class. His cream-colored button shirt and black overcoat were of finely woven materials with intricate silver stitched patterns. And his amulet hung on his chest with its jewel exposed for all to see.

Agraven and Olin drew just as much attention, riding behind. Agraven, though well-dressed, was also well-armed. He carried a heavy sword across his back and a knife on his thigh. He had also donned a hauberk of light-colored leather and silver chain. Olin, dressed as he always was in his white robes and carrying his silver staff, was still a priest of the Order. More than once groundlings came up to him asking for miracles, healing, counsel, and blessings.

As the population density grew the further they went, so did the size of the capital city on the horizon. Chilali watched it expanding in proportion with increasing amazement as they drew closer. Built on top of a steep plateau, it looked like its own mountain. Buildings, taller and larger than any she had seen, rose above the city's wall. Water flowed out of the city through gateways, draining in slender waterfalls that collected in pools all along the base of the plateau, where comparably smaller towns and markets were.

The most significant aspect of the capital and the thing that most boggled Chilali's mind, was the palace. It towered out of the center of the plateau, rising to the clouds like a silver needle. Smaller white towers with ivy drapes, which still dwarfed the surrounding structures, ringed this central sky tower, adding balconies, walls, and archways.

As much as she thought of herself, Chilali felt small facing this city, this Empire. It looked to be so much greater than she. The experience was humbling, but it inevitably led her to one question: what power could threaten this? Trying to imagine such a foe made her tremble with excitement and fear, a combination she was beginning to miss, last experiencing it when she attacked Shank.

"You're looking at the heart of the Empire," Alden told her, a trace of awe in his voice. "This is what I wish to protect and grow."

"You live up there?"

He nodded with a smile.

"I live within the third ring. You see, there's actually more up there than you can see. Beyond the first wall, there are two more even higher and thicker. And a lake stands at the base of the castle."

He pointed at the plateaus rock wall, which had numerous sloping paths and staircases carved into it.

"It's also not obvious from outside, but the capital goes significantly below ground. The pens where the Talarian males are kept, the castle's dungeon, the True Silver Knights training hall, the archives, and, well, other secrets, plumb great depths into the plateau."

She pointed at the top of the silver spire.

"The emperor is up there?"

Alden chuckled.

"My uncle usually keeps much closer to the ground in the main castle. The highest he will go is to his Silver Throne, which is halfway up the spire. Past that, the air becomes too thin."

Chilali leaned over to Alden.

"I'm the only Divergent amongst all the people in the capital?"

Alden regarded her for a moment. He almost gave the quick and easy answer. Of course, she was the only Divergent, but he didn't really know that. With shining blonde hair and blue eyes, he would not recognize her as a Divergent if he didn't know better. As talented as Olin seemed to be or pretended not to be, there had to be other enchanters capable of devising similar enchantments as the one on the ribbon in Chilali's hair. This prompted him to consider the slim possibility there could be other Divergents hidden in the capital. But he couldn't tell her that. He only had speculation.

"Yes, that does seem to be the case."

"Are there any other Divergents in the Empire?"

Alden assumed she was still holding onto the hope she would be reunited with her mother one day. But he didn't think she was ready to hear the truth. Her mother was more than likely deep within the Divergent Forest, wild and violent. She would be far better off never reuniting with her than facing the monster her mother likely was. Called or not, Chilali was not the indiscriminate killer other Divergents have been.

"There are rumors, just rumors, of another Divergent far to the North."

Despite his attempt to qualify the statement, he read clearly into Chilali's thought process. Given the chance, she would try to go north and find this Divergent. He couldn't have that happen.

"But the rumors are probably just exaggerated descriptions of the North Masters."

"North Masters?"

"They are an enclave of warriors that spend their lives training in combat. Their enclave is on the border between the Empire and the Blackland Nation and is considered a neutral territory. I don't know much more beyond that."

Agraven rode up next to Alden.

"Up ahead. Knights."

Chilali noticed them a while ago but didn't know they held some importance. Ten men on foot, dressed in silver chain mail and carrying maces and shields, blockaded the road ahead. One man in more elaborate silver armor made of plating and chain with hefty, spiked pauldrons sat proudly on top a horse behind the knights. He wore an open-faced helm and had a sword sheathed at his waist. She didn't even gauge him or the other men to be a threat.

"They're probably here to escort us," Olin added with a yawn.

Alden's eyes narrowed as he spoke to Agraven.

"They are not wearing the seal of the city's guard and we're still beyond the capital."

"That's what I thought," Agraven agreed.

Olin nudged his horse into a faster trot to ride up to Alden and Agraven.

"You believe these men belong to a noble's army and are here to take Chilali."

Alden didn't take his eyes off the men.

"Aye, priest."

"They're pretending not to see us," Agraven observed.

"So, there are more nearby, if not directly behind us, possibly dressed in plain clothes," Alden continued. "A fight seems unavoidable."

"I do not believe reason will resolve this situation," Olin sighed. "So be it. I will not let them have Chilali."

Alden took a quick count of those knights he could see and those groundling men around them he suspected of being enemies. They were outnumbered seven to one, excluding Chilali. He would prefer she did not fight, as it would cause too much of a disturbance. Without Chilali's help, the situation would force Olin to reveal more of his true abilities. He would take advantage of the opportunity to learn more about the priest, even if it meant risking his life.

Alden turned to Chilali.

"You understand what's happening?"

She nodded.

"If you can help it, try not to become involved. I don't want you to draw unnecessary attention."

She yawned in response.

"What is your plan then?" Agraven asked. "We're drawing closer to them."

"No plan. We're just going to ride straight to them. If we can, we'll just charge through. If not, yours and Olin's skills should be enough."

"I won't hold back, Alden. I'm going to return to Jerle," Agraven grimly stated.

Two by two, Alden and Agraven rode in front of Olin and Chilali. The knights waiting to meet them came to attention as their commander apparent, the man on the horse, raised his gauntleted hand to halt them. His thick eyebrows grayed at their ends, and he spoke with a whistle at the ends of his words.

"Alden Amos?"

"And you are?" Alden returned.

"Knight Captain Uriah. You and your party will come with me."

"Under Duke Medwin's authority?"

"It's not your concern. Come with us. I do not want there to be bloodshed."

"Then I suggest you let us pass."

Uriah looked them over, determining what kind of trouble this little band could cause. A crossbow was already trained on the priest. The armored warrior was known to be Agraven, a fire element user. Two bolts were aimed at him. He and the rest of his men should have little trouble taking Alden and his daughter. Still, he hadn't located the Divergent. If she were still around, the situation could become deadly. Assuming, there was actually a Divergent and it wasn't just a rumor.

"I think not. This is your last chance to come peacefully."

Agraven looked around and growled.

"They've got crossbowmen trained on us."

"So, you understand your situation then?" Uriah asked, his men holding their maces and shields ready.

The crowd around them began to thin as those passing by took notice, revealing Uriah's men. Three crossbowmen were stationed on the rooftops of nearby dwellings, and six more foot soldiers brandished swords behind them. Alden suspected Olin would handle the bolts or disable the crossbowmen.

"I understand it," Alden answered and drew his short sword.

Agraven did the same and Alden noticed Olin's knuckles turn white as the priest gripped his staff.

Uriah raised his hand.

"Take them down," he commanded, dropping his arm.

No bolts flew at Alden and his party to Uriah's surprise.

"They're asleep, knight captain," Olin wheezed, still squeezing his staff tight.

Alden kicked his mount forward and slashed at the knight captain. His blade clanked off Uriah's armored shoulder but tipped the knight off balance in his saddle. Agraven dismounted and charged the ten armed men, swinging his sword. They quickly surrounded him, but it struck Chilali he planned for them to do that. A burst of hot air blasted outward from Agraven, scalding all the exposed flesh in the vicinity. The men surrounding him fell to the ground quickly, screaming and holding their blistered faces.

Alden continued to clash with Uriah, swinging his sword defensively, as their horses nervously circled each other. The knight captain managed to maneuver his horse to buy the second he needed to draw his sword. His longer blade and armor gave him a significant advantage over Alden in a mount-to-mount fight or so he hoped. Alden was able to swing his blade around much faster in the close fight and he fought with a frightening, if not unexpected, ferocity. The merchant landed multiple blows, but they all clanked harmlessly off his armor.

His ten plain-dressed men dealt with Agraven more cautiously, taking up the crossbows they stashed around the street behind barrels and inside shrubs. They took shots at him as the fire user zigzagged across the street, taking cover, and engaging them with his sword when he got close enough. But the priest began another silent chant and Uriah suspected the rest of his men would fall soon enough.

He needed to change tactics if he wanted to survive this encounter. And only one new course came to mind, though it was despicable. He struck Alden in the face with his gauntleted hand, a glancing blow at best, and it opened him up to a piercing strike. Alden's sword dipped under the armor plating covering the right side of his ribcage and cut into the links. Still, his armor took the brunt, and he didn't even sustain a cut, just a hole and eventually a bruise. And in the exchange, he was able to push the merchant off balance in his saddle. The maneuver gave him the reprieve he needed to kick his horse around and make a break for the girl.

He rode past her, ripping her from her saddle with one arm. He halted his mount and spun it around to face Alden. He held his sword at the girl's throat and he could feel the panic in her. It disheartened him, but he reminded himself it was necessary. He had orders to carry out.

He looked across at Alden and the merchant looked petrified. His eyes were wide with shock. The priest and Agraven froze in mid-battle, as well, as if they were expecting something terrible to happen.

"Drop your weapons and surrender," he demanded. "Or I'll harm the child."

"Hurry, release her now. You must!" Alden shouted back.

Before he could respond, he felt a horrible pain in his side, an immense pressure. It burned, stung, and took his wind from him. He had never felt anything like it before. His whole body tensed up in response and he could barely move or breathe. He looked down and felt his head swim. The girl he held had thrust her fingers through the hole in his armor plating and into his rib cage. Her expression was full of such malevolence. Her eyes contained so much rage. She wasn't Alden's daughter, he thought. She was the Divergent.

She snapped her hand with a twist of her wrist then withdrew it with a quick jerk that felt like it cracked his entire body in half. A feeling of wetness going down his waist immediately followed. He blacked out just after noting something peculiar. She held bits of his ribs, bloody with his meat, in her hand. The last thought he remembered having was the realization his life was ended.

Alden wiped his mouth in shock, as Uriah fell out of his saddle. He dismounted and ran to Chilali. The remaining five or so plain-dressed men fled, as Agraven and Olin joined Alden in front of the Divergent. She hopped out of Uriah's saddle, discarded the clump of flesh and bone, and then bent down to wipe her hands clean on the deceased knight captain's cape.

"Must you use such violence?" Agraven stammered.

She tilted her head to one side, regarding him.

"I didn't know it mattered how you killed something," she replied, walking past him. "So long as it dies."

She hefted herself back into her own saddle. Alden stared at the gore on the ground. He had seen so much worse, but this level of brutality was always shocking. He turned to Agraven and Olin.

"We should go."

Olin waved his hand at the ten men writhing on the

ground and screaming from the pain their burns caused them.

"Should I heal them first?"

Alden shook his head.

"No, they are the Duke's men. Let him see to their care.

Agraven turned Uriah onto his back. It appeared as if all the blood had drained out of him and onto the ground from the hole in his side.

"It seems indecent to leave his body here in the open like this."

Alden shrugged.

"It is the price one pays for trying to use a child as a hostage."

"But Chilali is not a child," Agraven returned.

"And now Uriah is well aware of that fact. Leave him."

Agraven stood and grabbed Alden's shoulder.

"How can you ignore what she did to him? It was bestial."

Alden glanced at Chilali then turned his attention back to Agraven.

"Yes, it was, but is that not the point? She is a Divergent. Called or not, it's how they fight."

Agraven wiped his face, having nothing more to add.

Alden walked back to his mount, not looking at Chilali. He took her reigns again without even a word as Olin and Agraven joined him. They continued towards the capital down now empty streets.

The amazement Chilali felt moments before about seeing the capital waned, replaced with bitter confusion and self-disgust. She had lost control again and quite quickly. Alden told her not to become involved, but she didn't think the man would reach out and grab her. Panic instantly boiled inside her and cost the man his life. Still, there was no reason for the others to ride beside her in sullen silence. She defeated one of their enemies and instead of being celebrated for it they were only more disconcerted by her.

Strife's Journal: 327th Day, 4056, Northern Hills

Endless sleet that refuses to turn to snow.

The emperor promoted me to the rank of General today and placed just over 1,000 men under my command and 1 woman, who will serve as a scout if she is able. Three of the 1,000 men will be my captains. Two are relatively young and one is older, approaching middle age. I believe his name is Ren.

My own combat prowess aside, I've proven over the course of multiple skirmishes that I am able to limit our casualties while inflicting heavy damage to the enemy. I lead from the frontline, and I sense the battle in a way none of the other generals can by watching from afar.

Expecting the promotion, the men offered to tattoo my banner, a burning black sword pointing at the ground, upon our arms. But it seems not even an artist's ink will mark my flesh for long. Within two days more I expect the tattoo to be completely gone.

—General Strife Ashwake

The Amos Manor

Passage through the south gate of the capital's first wall went smoothly. The guards recognized Alden and let him and his party enter with little more than an affirming nod. The roads became so much more crowded inside the city, though, unsettling Chilali.

The groundlings, as Alden described them, were the common men and women of the city. They moved about the streets freely, chatting with each other and bartering. Others tended to their crafts, hammering red-hot metal, spinning pottery, or carving wood. Talarian females carried goods or followed behind nobles, made recognizable by their well-tailored coats. It occurred to Chilali that none of the groundlings had Talarian servants.

The Briam were far fewer in number than she saw outside the wall. Those within the capital did the same kinds of tasks Chilali saw horses do. More often than not, they would pair up and pull carts, wagons, or carriages, shuttling both people and goods. The nobles seemed to be particularly fond of this method. Some even went without wheels and used a pair of poles and four Briam to carry them around the square.

The structures were all made of what appeared to be smooth stone, ranging in color from gray to white to a subtle rose shade. As much as she tried with her exceptionally keen eyes, she couldn't see any seams between the stones. Some of the buildings reached four or five stories with domed roves, while others were one-story flats. The more elaborate buildings were a mixture of woodwork and seamless stone. They also sported silver frame windows with colored glass that depicted a variety of strange images. Some she recognized, like burning white stars depicting Sitara, others escaped her, like one of a man cloaked in flames and brandishing a heavy sword.

Alden led her horse and the group deeper, and the

crowd thickened ahead of them, becoming a wall of people. Chilali wasn't sure what to do. The few times strangers bumped into her, she flinched. And being amongst so many was only adding to her agitation. Passing through this crowd, without losing control, seemed impossible. She looked at Alden, hoping he would understand without her having to verbally admit to her fear and growing shame.

Alden stopped the party, letting Agraven move up to his flank.

"It was silly of me to forget such a thing," Alden sighed.

"I would have thought the Order would have shut down the Vineyard by now," Agraven mused.

"The Senate is not to be underestimated."

Olin spoke up from behind the pair loudly enough to be heard over the crowd noise.

"Talarian brothels are foul."

Alden noticed the concerned expression on Chilali's face. It was almost pleading.

"Agraven, let's put Chilali between us and muscle our way through."

"Three horses wide?"

"We'll let Olin lead. Olin?"

Olin pinched the bridge of his nose and maneuvered his horse in front. Alden and Agraven made their own adjustments to guard Chilali.

"What would you have me do, exactly, good merchant?" Olin asked without looking back.

"Preach?"

Olin resolutely grabbed his staff and pushed his mount forward. He gave what Alden believed to be his best stock sermon. The Lessers were the enemies of man. Sitara found them to be unworthy of her light. Cavorting with them was a sin against the Goddess and being intimate with them was an abomination.

Alden heard it all before, passing similar preachers on

his own secret trips to the Vineyard. He was a partial stakeholder in the establishment, which was a bit of information only he, his partners, and his older sister knew. Why his tastes ran so afoul, he didn't know. And with all the light of truth, he didn't care, not anymore, not since his father's passing.

The activity on the brothel's sole balcony off its third floor drew Chilali's attention, even as Agraven made a half-hearted attempt to block her line of sight with his body. A pair of Talarians danced to the cheers and chants of the crowd. They wore little clothing and flexed their lithe bodies in seductive ways as they transitioned from graceful twirls to sinuous arm movements to overtly jiggling their hips. The performance intrigued Chilali. The fluidity of their movements and their beauty reminded her of watching water ripple in a brook. And it also restored the appetite she lost when she entered the city and took in its numerous odors.

Olin accomplished his task, clearing out the crowd ahead of them so they could pass. Chilali made it through untouched, thankfully, Alden thought. The Divergent, too, seemed relieved. Though he had thought to shield her the same, but for other reasons. In this district, tastes ran even more afoul than his own did. Appearing to be a pretty young girl, she would most definitely run the risk of an attempted kidnapping. Such things happened more often than those in power beyond the capital's second wall cared to believe.

Dusk was near when they finally made it to Amos Manor, the mansion Alden and his older sister called home. For Alden, moving through the crowded city blocks with Chilali had been tedious work. He found himself watching for and trying to predict anything or anyone that might cause them trouble. Olin got them past the Vineyard, but not without drawing a lot of attention.

His lower back ached, and his cheek still throbbed from

the blow he took from Uriah. Both made him even happier to finally be home once, again. It had been weeks, so many he forgot what his own bed even felt like.

They walked their mounts up the manor gate with Alden tending to Chilali's horse. She kept her distance, but also kept close. Alden's home dwarfed even Agraven and Jerle's. It was so much bigger, taller, and even more spread out. It had two wings connected by tiered rows of archways. The entire roof of the main building was its own fountain. Water sprayed out of the top of a statue of a giant, bare woman with a crown of silver stars that radiated white light. Much smaller statues of men, Lessers, and even beasts formed two lines leading uphill to the woman, their hands held up to her in praise. These smaller statues also formed troughs which fed a pair of waterfalls spilling from the roof into fish-filled pools.

A pair of armored men carrying spears opened the gate for Alden, as three Talarian servants rushed out to take their horses.

"That is quite the artifact you have upon your mansion's roof," Olin noted.

"It predates the Nameless War, a reminder we were all once one people."

"Indeed, a tragic reminder."

Alden shrugged and led them through the courtyard, across two stone bridges, and finally to the main door.

"Remind me to ask for more the next time you send us out on a job," Agraven half-joked.

Alden gave a slight grin in response.

Most of the home's multi-colored windows were dark. Those with light beyond them were mainly at the wings. The door opened the moment they reached the step. Alden cursed himself. Chilali immediately crouched, readying herself to attack as soon as she caught sight and scent of the Ragebourne inside.

Aimon was his name and he had served the Amos

family for the last twenty years. Alden grew up trusting and respecting his family's personal bodyguard. Aimon was a gift from Alden's aunt, Empress Saveria, just a few years before her death. After a failed attempt by one of nobles to raze the mansion, Saveria ordered Aimon to be deployed to their home. At the time, Alden's father wasn't sure how to use the Ragebourne, allowing him to become a personal assistant, babysitter, butler, and interior decorator for the family.

"Calm yourself, Chilali. This is Aimon. He is family, of sorts," Alden soothed, stepping in front of the Divergent.

Aimon, who was younger looking, better groomed, and far more fashionable than Shank, wore a long coat and slacks and sniffed the air. His eyes narrowed on Chilali, and he spoke with disdain in his mellifluous voice.

"Lady Roche wishes to meet her new *niece*."

"Of course, take us to her," Alden nodded and followed Aimon inside.

The curved nails on the Ragebourne's toes made clicking noises as they moved across the marble floor. Chilali reached out to touch a painting of a great battle between knights and dark-skinned men she had yet to see, as they passed down hallway after hallway littered with artwork and tapestries.

"Please, do not touch anything," Aimon sighed.

Chilali returned a growl to which Alden interceded.

"It is all right Aimon. Let her touch what she will."

"Of course, Master Alden."

Aimon led them to a pair of heavy wood double doors. He stood in front of them.

"My apologies, but Lady Roche wishes to see only Master Alden and his niece. I can escort your guests to suitable quarters and have meals prepared for them, Master Alden."

"Aimon will take care of you. Once I'm done visiting with Roche, Chilali and I will meet you in the dining room," Alden said, turning to Olin and Agraven.

Olin raised his hand up in deference.

"Thank you, but there is no need for your hospitality. I will go and report to the Order. An escort for you should be dispatched tomorrow."

"Of course, good evening then, Olin. Allow Aimon to escort you out."

"Do not worry, I remember the way."

Olin bowed slightly and headed back the way they came.

Agraven crossed his arms.

"Unlike him, I very much want your hospitality, especially if I will find myself reporting before the Order, the acting True Silver Knight Captain, and the emperor's generals tomorrow," Agraven said and patted Aimon on the shoulder. "Let's go."

Aimon led Agraven away with a grunt, his toenails clicking the whole way.

"He misses Jerle," Chilali observed.

"Aimon will keep him company."

"Aimon is like Shank."

"Not exactly. They both are Ragebourne, but Shank is a cowardly monster. Aimon is loyal and kind."

"Why?"

"I always hoped it was because he felt accepted by my family, but really, he just seeks to honor his people's vow."

"Vow?"

"Yes, at the end of the war, the Ragebourne vowed to serve our kingdom. And their people take vows very seriously. They do not break them."

"Shank did."

"Shank was and is an outcast among the Ragebourne. Let's go see my older sister now."

Alden opened the heavy double doors, which marked the entrance to his father's study. A chandelier made of glowing white crystal lit the room from above. Books and manuscripts lined the walls and filled rows of bookcases. Chilali had never seen or smelled anything like it before. She found it difficult to even describe the smell other than to call it pleasant. It was an odor of sweet wood and leather mixed with the sharp tinge of ink. It was everywhere in this room, acidic and soft, and her head swam in it.

Roche sat at a small tea table, writing on parchment in the middle of the two-story room. A petite woman, she wore an ankle-length, strapless dress made of a creamy indigo material and augmented with silver stitching. A white ribbon twined through her long blonde locks and silver necklace faceted with many sapphire gems hugged her neck. If she were Alden's older sister, she didn't appear that way to Chilali. She looked much younger than him and smelled of wildflowers and honey.

Roche sipped tea from a delicate crystal cup before acknowledging Alden and Chilali's presence.

"You've arrived unscathed, brother."

"I have, mostly" Alden said, pointing to his bruised cheek as he slipped into the chair on the other side of the table. Chilali stood, focused on Roche.

"And this would be my new niece," she said with a dismissive flick of her hand at Chilali. "How could you? With a groundling? Were not Talarians bad enough?"

Alden collected himself.

"I assure you, there's more to the story."

"There always is," she rolled her eyes and settled them on Chilali, finally. "Well, there's still time for her to grow up to be pretty, maybe."

Alden wiped the corners of his mouth, feeling his stubble distinctly.

"Chilali, would you take off your ribbon?"

Chilali shrugged and pulled on the bow, releasing the ribbon. Roche's reaction was instant. She took one look at Chilali's true self, murmured something about Divergents, and then fainted. Alden caught her head before she could knock her teacup over.

"Well, I didn't expect that," he said to Chilali as he tried to revive his sister. "I guess I should have told her the truth in my letter."

Chilali wound the ribbon around her fist and paced down a row of bookcases. Roche revived soon after and slapped Alden.

"Are you mad? Having a Ragebourne in the manor is bad enough. Must we add a Divergent, too?"

Alden sat back in his chair with a groan and rubbing his twice sore face.

"It was unavoidable."

"Unavoidable? You didn't have to involve yourself in groundling business in the Chain, chasing that monster in the sacred forest."

"It cannot be changed now, Roche."

"Obviously! They'll execute you for this. Not even our uncle will be able to save you."

"It won't come to that."

"I can't believe Falcon let you do this. He was supposed to look after you. Wait until I see him again."

Chilali came back and stared at Roche, who immediately fell silent.

"I'm hungry, Alden. Are we done meeting Roche, yet?"

Alden went to Chilali's side with a chuckle.

"Yes, I think Roche is done meeting you."

Chilali followed behind Alden, as he headed out of the study.

"She's not staying here overnight, is she?" Roche called out but got no answer.

The Vineyard

Just as before, Chilali found herself put inside a ridiculously large room with a ridiculously soft bed. Not fatigued and absolutely bored, she hopped out of her fourth story window and explored the mansion's grounds for a while. She thought about trying one of the fish swimming in the ponds but wasn't very hungry. Alden fed her quite well, ordering his Talarian servants to prepare several different kinds of dishes.

Alden also provided her with many new clothes. She found an outfit similar to her riding clothes and put it on before going out. She was becoming used to clothing and found wearing boots cushioned her step, even if they made more noise when she walked. She made sure to tie her ribbon in her hair and was somewhat able to mimic the way Roche braided her ribbon into her blonde locks. The mirror in her bedroom was invaluable for that particular task. It also allowed her to see herself as she never had before, head to toe.

The experience was different than she expected. Her physical form looked so much softer and smoother than she imagined herself to be. She was also cleaner than she had ever been in her life and her hair wasn't a mess of tangles and cerulean leaves. But she couldn't find the creature Alden and the others so pretended not to fear, no matter how hard she searched.

She leaped over the estate's wall with little effort, even though it stood a man-and-a-half-high with needlepoint spires. Most of the streets were quiet and empty, while the structures built along them were filled with activity and light. She even heard music for the first time. Its rhythm, which she felt keenly, seduced her. Its melody captivated her. It was a mix of fast-paced percussion and subtle but powerful strings. A woman's voice flew alongside the sounds the instruments produced, occasionally parting with them to fill in silent gaps with staccato.

The music came from the building Agraven had called the Vineyard. She hid behind a stack of barrels on a side street to watch. A new pairing of Talarians danced on the balcony. Light poured from the windows and doors and the crowd, a mix of groundlings and nobles, almost entirely men, continuously flowed in and out. The music roared inside, and she wanted to get closer. Those coming out tended to stumble around and speak with slurred tongues more often than those going into the brothel.

She leapt wall to wall in the side street, propelling herself up a level with each spring. It was a tricky maneuver even for her, given the distance between the walls, the need for silence, and the fact certain areas of the walls were slicker than others. She landed safely on top of the shorter building then jumped up to the top of the taller one. The domed rooftops were difficult to run across and her footing was loose at best, due to bird droppings and weathering. Still, she made her way around to the Vineyard's roof, unnoticed by those below.

As one of the more elaborate buildings, its roof had eaves, tiles for shingling, and top floor windows. Those below and just outside the building could not see her as she crawled across. The music was much softer from above than at the street level, until she got closer to one of the windows. The light behind the multi-colored glass window was dim, but warm. She ran her hand along the outside frame, finding a hinging mechanism and deducing there was a latch on the inside. To get inside, she would have to break the glass. So, she moved onto the next and the next.

Circling around to the back of the building, she found one that was actually open. No light came from this room. There was only darkness. Her sense of smell had been dulled upon crossing through the first wall, but she recognized the scents inside. It was a strong combination of Agraven, a Talarian, musk, and other scents she had so far failed to identify.

She peaked around the window's edge, precariously holding her balance on the steep tiles. On a bed, Agraven lay bare, cradling a Talarian female in his arms as she rested her head on his chest. He steadily caressed the Talarian's upper arm with his thumb. Both were sweaty and their hearts beat with a quicker than normal rhythm.

They had their eyes closed, as if they were trying to fall asleep, but with the only source of light coming from outside the room, Chilali didn't think she would be able to sneak past them. They would notice her shadow cross over them if she dropped inside. Aggravated she couldn't get closer to the music, she worked her way back to the stack of barrels on the side street.

Another idea came to mind, as she peered around the edge of the barrels. She looked like a daughter of the Empire and could just go through the crowd. It was something she wouldn't have considered even a few days ago, but she felt relief at the thought she was adjusting to their world in some small way.

She went towards the crowd, and no one noticed at first until she got closer. Then it was strange. Those who did notice her just tried to ignore her. She got the sense she wasn't supposed to be among them, but they didn't want to bother with confronting her. Still, it was good enough for her for now. She moved through the crowd quickly, but with care to not touch anyone. It was difficult to do, but these people gave her space. They were actually trying not to walk over her.

At the door, a man with puffy blond sideburns and a scar running from his right cheek, across his lips, and curving to end at his chin glared at her. As far as size went, he was bigger than even Falcon and much thicker. He stepped right in her path and put his rough, hairy hands on his wide hips.

"Pardon me, mi'lady, but we don't permit children in

this establishment."

She peered around the man into the brothel. She could make out a raised circular platform beneath a brilliant chandelier of crystal, like the one in Alden's mansion. Beneath it, a woman with hair so long it hung down to her sandal wrapped feet, sang with her hands crossed over her stomach. The singer was part of a group of five performers. A young man, bare to the waist, pounded heavy jars, covered by tightly strapped leather, with a pair of short, curved sticks. A Talarian, the oldest she had ever seen with wrinkled skin and black hair, plucked the strings of a harp she held. Another Talarian, a child given her size, strummed a lute. And behind them all, sat a plump man with a crown of blond hair and a mustache. He held a long flute across his lap and tapped his foot to the beat, waiting for something.

The man with the puffy sideburns sidestepped to block Chilali's view.

"Why don't you be getting home, mi'lady? I can have someone escort you if you wish it. This is not a place for children."

"I want to go inside to listen," she snapped at the man, annoyed.

A potential patron standing behind Chilali came to her side. He was a gaunt noble with gloved hands and a cane of polished bone, which he held with a hand fitted with heavy rings.

"She is with me, Jamar. Let us pass," the noble said with a bit of cheer mixed with consternation.

Chilali took a moment to regard the man. He was no one she recognized by sight or smell. His face was shaved like Alden's, and he wore a long, black felt coat.

"As you wish Duke Medwin," Jamar said, reluctantly stepping inside. "But with my deepest respect, I ask you to remember she is just a child."

Medwin made eye contact with Jamar for a moment,

causing the doorman to shrink back a bit, and then stepped inside. Chilali didn't follow, recognizing his name from earlier in the day. The man she killed was one his.

"Come now. There's no need to give into fear so close to your goal," Medwin said, waving her inside.

She entered the brothel and was momentarily overwhelmed. So many things were happening at one time, so many conversations and actions. The place reeked of alcohol and scented oil. Neither of which she found to be pleasant. She followed Medwin through the melee of people, ducking and dodging scantly clothed Talarian servers carrying platters of drinks to tables and stumbling patrons. Despite her better efforts, she did get bumped into a few times, but was in such confusion she hardly noticed.

Medwin took her up a short staircase to a balcony. From above the floor, she was able to make more sense of her surroundings. She realized she was drawing more than a few stares. Some did it openly and others pretended not to. Several men, dressed like Jamar in black coats with a silver grapevine stitched on the breast, stood around the room, occasionally moving in small groups to drag people out of the establishment.

From above, she realized the floor had a large pit, taking up a fourth of the floor space. It was a half-circle at the back wall, perhaps two men deep. Many patrons stood around its edge, leaning on the wood handrail. They were waiting for something to fill it.

The balcony section turned and widened, making it parallel with the back wall and providing a good view of the pit. The people in this balcony section were much less rowdy than those below. They sat around dimly lit tables, sipping wine from slender crystal glasses. Chilali believed they were all nobles by the way they were dressed.

Medwin pulled out a chair for her at a crescent-shaped table at the balcony's edge. Four other men were already sitting, and they turned to regard her. She felt fear and apprehension roll off them in one great wave with one simultaneous realization. They knew she was a Divergent, as did Medwin.

"Please, have a seat," Medwin offered.

She sat, making the men even more nervous.

"Allow me to introduce my guest for the evening, daughter of Alden Amos, Lady Chilali Amos," Medwin said with obvious sarcasm.

Medwin took the last remaining seat beside her on her right, as she took a quick evaluation of the other men at the table. She believed they were all related. Their noses were long and narrow, and their ears were tight and round. They all also appeared to be Alden's age or older. The man to her immediate left wore a jeweled patch over his right eye and his slender fingers drummed the table in nervous sequence. Past him sat a feminine looking man with cherry red lips. He had some sort of knife hidden up his shirt sleeve. To Medwin's right a man with a long, full beard crossed his arms, revealing the fact he was missing the small finger from each of his hands. And to his right was a man with some measure of strength. His shoulders were broad and his chin square. He was the largest at the table and carried a decorated short sword at his waist that bore the same three words as Falcon's did on its gold handle: victory, sacrifice, and law.

"The gentleman with the eye patch is my brother, Duke Erschwin. To his left is my cousin, Duke Danival. On my right sits my other cousin, Lord Knight Thomlin. And to his right, sits my brother, True Silver Knight Vice-Captain Kern," Medwin said, indicating each with his upturned palm.

Chilali shrugged, impassive, but committed their names to memory easily enough.

"With the exception of Kern, we are all members of the Senate with Duke Danival being Speaker. You also sit among the second, third, fourth, fifth, and eighth in line for

Emperor Adelphos's throne," Medwin continued.

"First, second, third, fourth, and seventh, with me being the first," Danival corrected.

"I tell you, Eos is not lost," Kern said, not really believing his own words, but trying.

"It's been two weeks since we recovered Sir Gilan's remains. He is gone," Thomlin added, grimly.

Medwin sat back in his chair and grabbed a glass of wine.

"Let it rest. It would be rude to continue and not pay more attention to my guest."

The music stopped and Chilali looked down to see the performers stepping off the stage and leaving their instruments behind.

"They stopped," she groaned.

"Of course, tonight's main event begins shortly," Medwin agreed, sipping his wine.

Kern sat forward, putting both his heavy forearms on the table.

"Enough, you are not as you appear, Lady Amos," Kern said flatly.

"I'm not Alden's daughter," Chilali said, beginning to become bored, again.

"So, you are as the rumors suggest?" Erschwin asked with a cracking voice.

"What rumors?" Chilali asked, looking elsewhere in the room for something of interest.

"The ones that say you are a Divergent," Danival put forth, thinking himself clever as he watched to gauge her reaction to his statement.

"I am a Divergent," she said and looked at Medwin. "Are they going to play again?"

Everyone at the table held their breath for a moment before Medwin spoke.

"After the fights, perhaps."

Kern stood and leaned over the table to look at her.

"You do not look like a Divergent, girl, and I sense no aura of enchantment on you," the vice-captain accused.

"Uriah thought the same thing," she returned, entertained once again. "I killed him, though."

Medwin stood and put his hand on Kern's shoulder, as the knight gritted his teeth and balled his hands into tight fists.

"Calm yourself. You would gain nothing."

Kern turned to Medwin.

"Uriah was a friend!" he shouted and left the table in a quiet rage.

Medwin sat back down, as Chilali watched Kern force his way down the balcony stairs, knocking over a Talarian server and spilling a platter of drinks.

"My apologies, Lady Amos. Kern is more warrior than nobility. He can't divorce himself from personal matters," Medwin explained.

"Did you come here with Alden, Lady Amos?" Erschwin dared to ask.

Chilali shook her head and her response made Medwin smile.

"You know, Lady Amos, we could be of great help to you," Medwin said.

"I don't need help," Chilali replied.

"Are you sure? We could get you anything you would ever want. We could get you an entire troupe of performers to play for you whenever you wanted."

"What would I have to do?"

"Nothing beyond what you do already. Serve the Empire. The only difference would be that you count me and the remaining men at this table as your allies."

"Okay, you're my allies. Make them play again."

"Not so quickly," Medwin chuckled. "Things like this take time and to be our ally, you must disavow our enemies."

"Who are your enemies?"

"Well, the Lessers-

"The Talarians, Ragebourne, and Briam."

"Not quite, they are already defeated. No, the Lessers, as in the Volitors and the Fifth. And the Blackland Nation. But most importantly, we count Alden as one of our enemies."

"Alden?"

"Yes, you see, he believes things about the Empire that aren't necessarily true, things that could harm the Empire. And you, like us, want to protect the Empire, right?"

"No, not necessarily," she returned, drawing a dismayed expression from the normally stoic duke.

"You don't?"

She shrugged and rose from the table.

"Where are you going?" Medwin asked, standing with her.

"Down."

Medwin didn't follow as she headed down the steps and made her way to the stage where instruments lay, silent. The patrons mostly abandoned the stage, going to the pit. The harp leaned against a small wood stool. Its silver frame looked seamless. She circled around to pick it up.

"Chilali? What are you doing here?" Alden called out, rushing to her.

She clumsily strummed the harp's strings, feeling their delicious tension. They were sharp on her fingertips.

"I came to hear the music, but they stopped playing."

Alden took the harp from her and set it on the stage. He looked around the room.

"We should leave. It's not safe for you to be here."

Before Chilali could respond, all the men in black coats began rushing to the door to be sent tumbling away, until they quit getting back up. Kern struck them aside, bursting through them and the entrance with a two-handed mace. Even to Chilali, who saw things on a scale different than men, the mace Kern swung about seemed absurd in its size.

Its smooth black metal head had a silver ribbing encircling it and would be equal in size to Chilali if she curled up into a ball. The sight of Kern and his mace caused the patrons to spread out to the walls, the safest place to watch the show.

"We need to leave," Alden shouted at her.

Rather than following him, she stood her ground, enamored with Kern's violent approach. This was great, she thought, licking her lips. Alden stopped at the foot of the staircase and called out again.

"Chilali, come!"

She met Kern head on, rushing and leaping at him when he got close enough. She paid dearly for her excitement. He batted her out of the air and into a table and her body cracked into two. It took a moment for her to feel the pain in her side. The mace connected solidly with her ribs, which throbbed terribly. Cries of outrage came from patrons who had yet to realize Chilali was not as she appeared.

Sucking wind, she got to her feet and barely avoided a hard downward strike that blasted the stone floor. She found herself scurrying around, avoiding similar blows that left pits behind. If she got caught between one such blow and the floor, it would be over for her, she realized with exhilaration. This was what she had been missing the last several days.

Paying too much attention to the mace, she didn't see Kern's boot coming. It hooked up under her torso and punted her up into the air in front of Kern. Caught in midair, she saw the mace arcing around and tried to catch it with her hands. But the blow's force and her awkward angle buckled her elbows on impact. She took most of it with her face, tumbling head over heels across the room and into the back wall with a slap.

She fell into the pit on her hands and knees. Her nose and lips bled and throbbed worse than her side. Her eyes watered, blurring her vision. She wiped the tears away and pushed herself up against the back wall. She needed its support for the moment. She was still seeing stars.

There were two doors in the pit. Both were shut. She looked up, expecting to see Kern coming, but instead she saw Alden's back. He held his arms out wide with his short sword in one hand.

"Stop this, Kern. You're a True Silver Knight," she heard Alden plead.

Alden sidestepped a blow that crushed the handrail, causing it to break and snap all along the edge of the pit. Alden's sword followed his evasion, going in for a quick strike, but the blade found the mace's shaft instead. With a grunt and pushing with both his arms, Kern forced the mace against Alden and his blade, lifting him off his feet and into the pit.

Alden landed on his back with one rapid bounce and a loud, "oof," in front of her. His sword clanged off the back wall and fell next to her. For one excruciating moment, she watched Alden just lay there, barely able to move. She rolled and grabbed his sword with both her hands, just as Kern jumped into the pit. The patrons above ran to the pit's edge to watch.

His weight and that of the mace made him bend his knees low to absorb the fall. She didn't hesitate. She wouldn't give him a second to recover. With a hop, one short for her, she got enough height to swipe at his head. He ducked, stumbling back, but the sword tip cut open his brow. Blood began to spill into his right eye. Good, she thought, as she landed and pushed forward again with an upward vertical arc.

Kern pushed his mace down with a hand at each end and blocked the blow, but the force behind it stung him. It also altered Chilali's momentum, whipping her into a front flip. She came down with another vertical strike, hard and fast. He blocked this too, continuing her mid-air juggle by pushing her back.

As strong and fast as she was, the difference in their

weight gave him an advantage, he thought. He could push her around the pit by just blocking her. And the fact she had no skill with a blade helped as well. He charged her as she landed, butting her with his mace and knocking her against the back wall.

She pushed off the wall and came at him like a missile. Her sword cut deeply into his hip with a satisfying degree of resistance, despite his attempt to dodge it. He used the momentum he gained from the failed dodge to continue into a spin on his good leg, knowing she would land and come right back at him.

His mace came around in a wicked backspin Chilali didn't expect. She got her sword up in time to try to block it, but the mace just rolled over the blade and slammed into her shoulder. Spinning wildly, she tasted the wall again. It was bitter, more so than the last time.

The exhilaration she felt was gone. Now, it had become fear. She hurt all over. Her arm, below her left shoulder was numb and she could barely move it. Her right eye swelled, obscuring her vision. And her chest throbbed so much she felt like she could barely breathe. Gold and silver coins began to rain down all around her, clattering. The patrons above tossed them with cheers and shouts, calling for more.

More? She didn't know if she wanted more. And to her relief, Kern was having trouble standing. The wound she gashed into his hip bled severely. He covered it with his hand but couldn't hold his mace up with just one arm. Instead, he leaned on it.

"This is not over, Divergent," he roared. "I'll see you dead for killing Uriah."

The hand covering his wound flared with white fire and spit sprayed from his clenched teeth. He released the wound, now healed, and stood once again. To Chilali's growing regret, he grabbed the mace with both hands and steadily raised it once again.

It didn't seem fair to her he could just heal whatever

wounds she caused. She looked at the blade she held. It was slightly bent. Kern moved toward her, and she did the only thing that came to mind. She flung the weapon at him with all her might. Kern had no chance to react. The handle, not the blade, pierced his stomach, stopping at the hilt. She sighed inwardly. Alden had to stop carrying a sword with a hilt; it was always getting in her way.

Kern grabbed the blade and fell forward on his knees, dropping his mace. He tugged it out with a pained cry. Even more of his blood stained the pit's floor and even more would.

Chilali let go of herself and the crowd above cheered her on. She fell upon Kern and beat him with her bare fists, putting him on his back and straddling his chest. He made a half-hearted, if unaware effort, to block her with his arms, but she was relentless. Let him try to heal these wounds, she thought spitefully. She didn't stop until someone grabbed her by her hair and jerked her off.

She whirled on whoever pulled her away, enraged. Alden stood there, holding his side with one hand held up defensively.

"You must stop," he pleaded.

She took a step toward him, ready to hit him anyway, but regained herself. She could hear many more men coming, men in armor.

"We need to go," she told Alden, who looked at her disbelieving she would tell him such a thing. "What's behind these doors?"

"A way out," Alden said, understanding.

She tried to pick up Kern's mace but had difficulty getting the right leverage to lift something that weighed twice as much as she did. Instead, she dragged it to the nearest gate, making a loud grating sound. She swung it at the gate, rotating around it more than it rotated around her. It almost even slipped from her bloody hands, but in the end, it struck its intended target. The metal-bound wood door exploded. Behind it were a torch-lit corridor and a naked man wearing a mask covering just his eyes. He wisely ran the opposite direction.

Before they fled down the corridor, Chilali looked up to see Duke Medwin standing at the edge of the pit, waving goodbye with his heavily ringed hand.

* * *

Chilali was grateful the blood in her nose dried so thick it stopped it up. She could taste the acrid odors in the air all around her, as she and Alden sloshed through ankle-deep water full of things even she found unpleasant. Alden led her out the end of the tunnel, into the open night air, where she felt she could really breathe again.

They stood on the side of a canal that dropped off sharply as it headed for the city's first wall. Alden took a seat on the wall's foundation, which was an arm's length wider than the wall itself. She looked around. They were open to the night, but were surrounded by stone, like they had exited into a large vault. Alden called it a retention cell and pointed out a stone staircase at the far end from them that went up to street level.

She sat next to Alden and scooted to lean her back against the wall. Her body throbbed and she wished it would stop. At least it was quiet and dark here. It felt private and far away from the city, even though it was part of it. She almost let herself doze off, but Alden's voice stirred her.

"You just battled one of the Empire's strongest, most-revered warriors in the middle of a brothel," he said with an exasperated laugh, followed by a cough.

"Duke Medwin said his name was Kern," she acknowledged.

"You talked to Medwin?"

"He helped me get inside and brought me to the balcony

to meet Kern, Erschwin, Danival, and Thomlin."

Alden took a moment to think things over before speaking, again. Chilali watched him the whole time to gauge his reaction. He didn't reveal much.

"While I consider them adversaries, I admit they are necessary for the survival of the Empire. They help to balance out the Arch Magus and the Order."

"They promised to give me anything I wanted if I made you my enemy."

"Why didn't you?"

"They said I would have to serve the Empire."

"I see. Why would you be concerned for the survival of the Empire? You've been attacked twice by those who are a part of it."

Tiring of the stuffy sensation in her nose, she began scraping out the dry blood with her fingers.

"That's not very lady-like," Alden remarked.

"How else does a lady get the blood out?"

"I concede the point."

"Will Agraven be all right?"

"Agraven? You saw him there?"

"He was on the highest floor with a Talarian."

Alden rubbed the back of his neck.

"It would be best if you do not tell Jerle of this."

"Why would I tell Jerle what I saw?"

Chilali stopped her picking and flicking, satisfied with the airflow through her nose for the moment.

"I supposed you wouldn't understand, so I will drop the issue," Alden said. "But I would ask you to do something else for me."

"What?"

"The next time I ask you to run, please listen."

"Why?"

Alden gazed at her, his eyes full of genuine concern. Discomfort and warmth came to her, and she didn't know how to react.

"I don't want to see you killed," Alden spoke with a resigned tone. "And Kern would have done just that. You were fortunate tonight."

"I beat him. You stopped me."

"Kern is a True Silver Knight. Perhaps out of some desire to lessen his sin against Sitara for attacking one of her chosen, he did not use his powers actively."

"He's even stronger?"

"You must understand. Yes, you are a Divergent and could break an ordinary man like myself into pieces with little effort. But there are men like Kern, who are not so ordinary. And though you are a Divergent, you are not fully grown; the power of these men can surpass your own. In time you will become much, much stronger, but for now you should use more discretion."

"I'm going to grow to be stronger," she spoke to herself as much as him. The statement was something that never really occurred to her. And there was good reason it didn't, Alden surmised. Without a parent to compare herself to, she had no idea what she would mature to be.

Her sense of smell began to come back. She sniffed the air to make sure of what she thought.

"You have the strong scent of a Talarian on you," she said, curious. "Like Agraven."

Alden looked away, scratching the back of his head.

"I do."

"Why?"

"Because I made love to one."

"Made love?"

"It is something you will figure out on your own when the time comes," he said, knowing this was not the time to tell her it would likely never come, given her phobia.

"It is the same thing as what Olin said was unforgivable."

"Not the act itself, just my choice of partner. The Order believes men should not lie with Talarians, but their fairness has always had a certain allure for men. They are much gentler in their manner. And anyway, brothels like the Vineyard are a significant part of the economy in the Empire. A lot of resources go into the trade and rental of Talarians, as well as the breeding."

Chilali didn't really grasp everything he said but continued to listen.

"There is also the problem no one seems to want to face. Our Empire has three sons for every daughter. While it bolsters our military, it causes certain tensions to rise. And these tensions need to be released to maintain order, which requires an outlet."

He stopped himself, realizing he was probably talking of things well beyond Chilali's understanding. He stood and dusted off his pants. His feet were miserably soggy inside his boots.

"'The Love of Water,' by the way," he said.

Her brow wrinkled.

"It was the name of the song the minstrels were playing. It's an old Talarian hymn that has been adopted and revived by local musicians. The lyrics are in ancient Talarian and tell the tale of Sitara's romance with the Water King."

She got up slowly, hurting.

"Will they play again?"

"If we survive tomorrow, I'll have them give a private performance at my mansion just for you."

"Duke Medwin said he would do the same thing."

"Medwin doesn't own a third of the Vineyard," Alden said with a grin. "Let's go home. We both need baths before tomorrow, unless we want the Order to think we're both uncalled."

They left together and returned to the mansion without further incident. Chilali found her room much more inviting and was happy to find it so boring for the remainder of the night. She was also never so thankful she had a soft bed in which to lie. Her entire torso was well-bruised by the time she crawled under blankets and dreamed again of her mother leaving her.

Strife's Journal: 2nd Day, 4058, Silver Sun Capital

I see my breath. Frost covers the tops of tents and houses. Because of my element, I only feel enough of the cold to be able to notice it.

Many still feel the effects of the Starlight Festival. It is intended to be a celebration for the end of the 400-day calendar year, but the festival often acts as an excuse to correct the calendar. This year, the festival continued for three un-dated days to adjust the calendar. I am told scholars from the Order conferred with shamans from the Blackland Nation and even a scholar from the Talarian Empire at the North Masters' Enclave to come to the conclusion all peoples needed to throw a three-day party before the new year could begin.

A young noblewoman sought to court me at the festival (the emperor ordered me to attend the Noble's ball). I felt more surprised than flattered. She was beautiful, but I would not call her attractive. Or, I should say I was not attracted to her any more than I would be a Talarian or a Briam or a horse or the fish I had for dinner. Nevertheless, I was curious.

Though I am a Divergent, I know little of my people. Long has the belief been passed down that we are supposed to be an entirely female race. Clearly, I am an exception, but I do not know why. I've heard some suggest my existence finally explains how Divergents "continue through the ages."

My instinct suggests this is not the case, though I cannot say why.

I danced with the young woman. I set aside thoughts of what she might taste like. At the end of the night, I kissed her on the balcony and smelled the blood rush to her cheeks when she blushed.

Ren, one of my captains, suggested I pursue the

relationship further, but I decided to spare the woman any further heartache.

Perhaps when we finally begin the campaign in the south, I will take a day to return to the forest and seek out a female Divergent. I wonder what my reaction will be. I wonder what hers will be. I believe I can say with certainty the meeting will not involve soft music, wine, and dancing.

—General Strife Ashwake

Minnie

Giggling from just beyond the door to her room woke Chilali. She twitched at first to its sound, slowly regaining her awareness. She had burrowed under the thick blankets more than she had slept beneath them and had to dig her way out once again. The morning light was glaring through her colored balcony windows. She wiped the sand from the corners of her eyes. It had been a rough night, filled with frantic dreams of a never-ending, but always futile chase through the forest. Her mother was still gone. She would never catch up to her.

Much of her body bore splotchy plum-colored bruises, but she knew they would fade by the end of the day. After quickly knotting her ribbon in her hair, she went to her door, trying to feel who was behind the yellow varnished wood. Two people, she thought, and they were small, her size. The door creaked open as she peered through the crack into the hallway with its display of art and artifacts.

A boy, dressed in breeches and a shirt, walked on his hands, balancing with bent knees. Even upside down, Chilali could tell he was a little taller than her. His hair was dirty blonde and swung loose and wild down to the floor. His arms trembled under the strain of his own weight, but the cheers of a smaller girl further down the hall kept him going for the moment.

The girl clapped and laughed, egging the boy on to reach her. Her hair was so blonde and fair it looked like it was made of the sunlight coming through the hall's open windows. A dress, as soft and airy as Chilali's own chemise, blew in the gentle morning breeze from the open windows, making it seem like the girl was just hovering in the air, a white wisp of smoke and sunshine.

She had seen children before and watched Shank eat a couple of them. During her short travel to the capital, she witnessed them playing in the fields and streets or doing simple chores. She sensed some while in Orsa but did not think to interact with them. To her, they were just smaller, weaker adults. They posed neither threat nor interest. But she discovered she did not like to see them in pain, as she had when she watched Shank feast. They resembled her in form too much and she could not help but to empathize with them.

Chilali stepped into the hall, just as the boy lost his balance and flopped over onto his back. He wasn't hurt and got up quickly to look at Chilali, alarmed. The girl became silent, too, making Chilali wonder if they knew what she was.

"We're sorry, my lady. We did not mean to disturb you," the boy spoke, startled.

"We really are. We'll go play somewhere else," the girl apologized.

They both waited for a response; Chilali just shook her head with a yawn.

"Stay."

The boy didn't seem sure and looked at the girl. She smiled and wiggled her bare toes, with their filthy undersides.

"Thank you, my lady," the boy said with a playful bow.

"Who are you?" Chilali asked.

The boy scratched the back of his head.

"I'm Seth and that's my little sister, Marle," the boy answered, shyly. "Our mother is Lady Roche's assistant."

"Mother?"

"Yes, my lady, we're just groundlings, but Lady Roche lets us live here."

"I'm called Chilali," she offered, not sure what else to say.

"You're the master's daughter," he said.

She shrugged in response.

"Do you want to come with us?"

Marle grabbed Seth's shirttail.

"It's okay, Marle," the boy told her. "I can tell she's nice."

No one had ever called her "nice" before.

"Where?" she asked.

"We're going to the stables," the boy replied.

"To ride a horse?"

"No," the boy broke out laughing. "There is a Talarian girl there. We're going to go play with her."

Marle smiled and nodded in agreement.

"Okay," Chilali shrugged again, not really sure what the boy meant.

"We'll wait for you to get dressed," the boy said, blushing a bit. "It'll be fun."

Chilali dressed and washed, as she had been taught. Together, she and the two children navigated the lengthy hallways. Marle skipped, humming an awkward tune along the way. Chilali tried to follow it, but it lacked any kind of pattern.

Seth kept his hands in his pockets and strolled casually. Chilali could see the tension and nervousness in his movements and the way his eyes flitted to her and away. He said little though.

Seth led them out of the back of the mansion and through a garden full of flowers and purple plants suspended on poles with long leafy vines hanging to the ground. Marle was still barefoot, and it was beginning to make Chilali envious. Though, she did enjoy the extra traction her boots gave her. A pair of Talarian servants moved by them but didn't make eye contact. They bowed slightly at Chilali and moved clear of her approach. Seth sneered at them as they passed.

Unlike the other stables Chilali had seen, Alden's was made of stone and wood. It was long, narrow, and consisted of two aboveground levels. Grates with shutters let light and air through the roof and two heavy, banded wood doors with metal wheels built into each corner were swung open wide. Twelve horses filled the stable, six on either side and each in its own stall. The beasts were busy eating their breakfast of leafy greens and grains mixed together in troughs at each stall gate. Their ears all wiggled and they each seemed to take a moment to look up as the three of them entered the stables.

Marle went to one with a white nose. It bent its head down to lick her hand with its thick tongue. Marle laughed and withdrew it.

"Don't get so close, Marle," Seth said as he searched the stable, peering into the shadows within the stable.

Chilali pointed up the wood frame staircase leading to the second level.

"The Talarian is up there," she said.

"Then let's go," Seth replied with a smile and a wave of his hand. Marle skipped after him, wiping her hand dry on her increasingly dirty dress. Chilali followed, letting herself become an observer. This didn't amuse her in any way, but it did give her an opportunity to learn more about children.

The second floor was filled with tools, saddles, grain, and all the other things one would think to find in a stable. But the goods made a maze of sorts of the second level. Seth stood on his toes, trying to peer over and around the supplies. Chilali, her sense of smell still gradually adjusting to the capital, managed to pick out the Talarian's scent.

"Over there," she said, directing Seth with her eyes.

The boy kind of understood and went in the general direction. It helped that the Talarian girl let a whimper escape. Seth found her hiding behind a pile of grain sacks. He grabbed her by the wrist and tore her from her hiding place with a triumphant roar. Marle clapped and hopped.

The Talarian was a little taller than Marle, but more lithe. She whipped around like a long, wet blade of grass when Seth shook her. She screamed shrilly and tried to resist but did both for only just a moment. Seth threw her to the ground. Straws of old hay tangled in her short (for a

Talarian) indigo drape. The button fastening her dress at the back of her collar snapped off, exposing the top of her porcelain back and the edge of a charcoal bruise.

Seth circled her like a hungry dog.

"Her name's Minna of Wind. But we call her Minnie. She can make noises, but she doesn't talk," the boy explained, stopping in front of Chilali, who crossed her arms.

"Why not?"

"I don't know. She won't say."

Marle dashed away and came back carrying a muzzle with glee. She handed the leather strapping to Seth, who immediately fell on Minnie, just as the Talarian tried to scramble away. He pinned her face down and showed the device to Chilali.

"They use these on hunting dogs to keep them from biting the game, but Marle and I pretend it's a bridle," Seth casually explained as he wrestled the strapping over Minnie's face. One strap went under her chin and another across the bridge of her nose. Minnie whimpered and groaned sharply when Seth pulled the pair of buckles tight across the back of her head. One long strap, attached to each two smaller straps that connect to the mouth straps, hung loose. Seth took it, wound it around his fist, and stood, pulling the Talarian to her hands and knees and arching her neck.

"I'm too big to ride, but Marle can," Seth said as Marle scampered over.

Marle straddled Minnie's back and grabbed two fists of hair.

"Give her a good ride," Seth ordered Minnie with a pleasant tone Chilali found to be unsettling.

Minnie crawled around the floor in whichever direction Marle tugged her hair. The little blonde-hair girl bounced up and down on Minnie's back to get her to crawl faster.

"Whinny," the little girl ordered.

Minnie let out a sound that was close, but not close enough for Marle.

"Do it better!" Marle demanded.

Minnie tried again with the same result. Marle pulled her hair.

"She's not doing it right," Marle exclaimed to Seth.

It was at that point Minnie collapsed, unable to bear Marle's weight any longer. Marle took a tumble and skinned her elbow on the floorboards. She got up crying and ran to Seth, who looked at the wound.

"You'll be fine," Seth said, examining the wound, "It's just a scrape."

Marle nodded with teary eyes and looked back at Minnie, furiously.

"She was a bad horsey," Marle condemned.

Seth agreed and leered at Chilali.

"This is the fun part."

The boy grabbed a riding whip from a nearby post and set on Minnie, who again tried to crawl away. He grabbed the leather strap and twisted it around his hand. He pulled her up to the post and tied the strap on a high hook. Minnie stood on her toes trying to reach up and unbuckle the strap from her head.

"She's not strong enough to unbuckle it. Don't worry," Seth explained with the kind of certainty that only comes with experience in such matters.

He popped Minnie once across the stomach. It was a short strike, meant to scare more than cause pain. Minne still covered her midsection, desperate not to get hit in the same place twice.

"You want to try, Marle?" Seth asked.

The little girl was eager to run over and take the whip, and even more so to begin swinging it at Minnie with a determined look upon her face. Minnie groaned and moaned but couldn't open her mouth. She just twisted with each pop, trying her best to spread the blows around her skin. And fortunately for her, Marle lacked strength and accuracy. Seth did not, however.

"Marle, go downstairs. I'll come down when I'm done," the boy said, taking the whip from her.

"Why?" she whined.

"Go," he demanded, tapping her on the butt. Marle zipped down the stairs.

"That's not how you discipline a servant," Seth sighed and patted the end of the whip on his palm. "I bet you know how."

Chilali watched Minnie continue to dig at the buckles on the back of her head with her fingers.

"My father used to own a couple. He showed me how. You have to do more than just hit them. You have to humiliate them," Seth explained.

The boy grabbed the bottom of Minnie's dress and tried to pull it up, but she grabbed his hand. He swatted her arms until she stopped fighting him. He pulled the trim up over her head, obscuring her vision, and caught it on the same hook that held the muzzle. Minnie half stood and half hung bare from her shoulders down and unable to lower her arms. Like Astra, dark purple bruises, some of which oozed slightly, blotted her white skin.

Seth bent the whip and let it go with a snap. It caught Minnie right in the belly, leaving a red mark and causing her to try to curl up or bring her arms down. Seth did it again and she turned, twisting up her dress and the strap, lifting her slightly more off the ground.

"Watch this," Seth said to Chilali before rearing back and creasing Minnie across her bottom with a whistling pop. The blow immediately left a red line and stirred up Minnie more than ever. She shook and let out muted cries of pain.

Seth snickered.

"It's not like you didn't know it was coming," he told her before grabbing one of the sore cheeks and giving it a tight squeeze.

He flipped the whip around in his hand and offered the handle to Chilali.

"Care to try my lady?" he asked with a bright smile.

Chilali took the riding crop and swung it in the air, feeling its bend. She knew right away even she would flinch if she felt its bite.

"Why do this?" she asked the boy, flexing the whip between her hands and bowing it dramatically with her strength.

"It's fun. Try it. You'll see."

"But she can't hit you back."

"Of course not. Why would I want her to hit me back?"

"Because it would be fun."

"It's not fun to get whipped. My father made sure I knew that."

"Then why whip Minnie?"

"Why not? She's just a Lesser. They're the property of all the citizens of the Empire."

"Because of the war?"

The boy dismissed her with a wave of his head and grabbed the middle of the whip to try to take it back.

"I bet you've never whipped a servant before. I'll show you," he offered, but she didn't let go.

"I've done more than whipping, Seth," she said coldly.

"Show me," he said, ardently, and let the whip go.

She dropped the whip with a grin and reached back for the ribbon binding her hair. She pulled it loose, and the color drained from Seth's face as quickly as it drained from her hair. The boy fell over and scooted across the floor until a stack of feed stopped him.

"You're a-"

She slapped him with just her fingers, smearing his words and bursting his lips. He grabbed them, bawling.

"You're just like Shank, a monster. Touch Minnie again and I will eat you and your sister," she hissed with hot breath into his ear. The boy scurried to his feet and down the stairs. He caught Marle along the way and dragged her out screaming.

Chilali tied the ribbon back in her hair then went to help Minnie. She got her dress down by tearing the trim. The muzzle was soaked with tears and saliva. Minnie trembled before Chilali and stared at her with uncertain eyes.

"I'm Chilali," she said. "I'll get you down."

Seth was taller than her and she couldn't reach the hook and the strap. She did the next best thing by using brute force to break it. Her weight returned, Minnie stumbled, but caught the post. She held onto it for a long while, just breathing. Then she frantically went to work trying to get the muzzle off. She looked at Chilali with pleading eyes.

"Do it yourself," she replied and waited.

Minnie fought with the straps and cried and fought some more. With much effort, she got her black nails under the leather and pulled it loose from the first buckle a bit at a time. Undoing one was enough for her to peel it off her head with a gasp.

She collapsed and cried over the muzzle before throwing it across the floor.

"Get up. I'll take you to my room. You can stay there."

Minnie looked at her confused.

"I'm Lady Amos," Chilali explained, chagrined she would call herself that.

Minnie's eyes widened in surprise, and she stood quickly, trying to brush the wrinkles and dirt out of her dress with her hands and then smearing dirt across her face while trying to dry her tears. She then bowed her head slightly, looking at Chilali's feet.

"Do you have a mother," Chilali asked.

The girl shook her head.

"I didn't think so," Chilali said. "Come with me. I can show you how to brush your hair."

Minnie looked up with a quiver of a smile at the corners

of her lips.

In His Wisdom

Chilali watched Minnie brush her hair with an intensity that unsettled the Talarian girl. As a Divergent, she could feel this tension, but didn't want to look away. The brush passed so smoothly through the girl's hair, whereas it always caught on tangles and knots when she brought it through her own. She was envious in a way.

She let the girl wash in the adjacent lavatory and found her a clean dress, which was a little short, reaching down to the middle of the girl's thighs. Minnie was still grateful to be out of the ratty pullover she had worn for too long. And while Chilali didn't mind being dirty, she began to appreciate being clean as everyone else did. Minnie was no different and seemed sincerely happy to not smell like horse dung and hay, the latter of which irritated Chilali's nose.

A knock at the door broke the Divergent's vigil. She whipped around to see Alden enter with Olin close behind. The priest immediately moved in front, his mouth agape for a moment. He wore shorter robes of a finer material and leaned slightly on a more slender silver-star staff, giving his gaunt form a more vital appearance. He smelled better than she remembered, a hint of incense clinging to him sharp and minty.

"What is this, Alden? Why is there a Talarian child in her room?" the priest accused more than asked.

Alden stepped forward, glancing at the girl and then looking at Chilali.

"Why have you brought Minnie here?"

Chilali stood from her crouch at the foot of the bed, nearly matching Alden's height. Minnie stopped brushing and clasped the silver instrument tightly in her lap. The stable servant dared not look up, not now.

"I don't want her to stay in the stables anymore." Chilali answered honestly, but not hinting at what motivated her. It was a habit that grated on Alden's patience.

"Chilali, you must understand. She cannot remain in the manor."

"Why can't she?"

"For reasons of appearance."

"She's pretty."

"That's not what I mean. It is improper for nobles in the capital, such as us, to keep Talarian children in our homes. They can be housed in an exterior dwelling, but not inside the home."

Chilali stepped off the bed and went to her boots on the floor.

"I'm not a noble. I want her to stay in my room."

"Why? Do you feel sorry she lives in the stable and you have this room to just yourself?"

Chilali sat on the floor and wrestled with her left boot.

"Marle and Seth treat her like Shank. If she stays here, they won't bother her."

"What do you mean they treat her like Shank?" Alden asked and looked at Minnie. "Have those two been hurting you, child?"

"She can't talk," Chilali snapped at Alden more sharply than she intended.

Alden went to Minnie and tried to pull her dress off her shoulder to find the bruises he suspected were there. The girl cringed and Chilali was there in an instant, wearing just one boot and clasping Alden's wrist.

"Don't touch her," she said with intense restraint evident in her voice and released his wrist. Alden backed away from the girl, rubbing what would likely be a bruise come the next day.

"I'm sorry. She can stay in your room for the time being. I'll let Roche and the house servants know, as well."

Olin held his arms out wide.

"Enough, there are more important matters to which we must attend. Are there not?"

Alden nodded.

"Right, the moment of our judgment approaches. Are you ready, Chilali?"

She walked across the bed and grabbed her other boot. She pushed her foot inside it and buckled it tight.

"I am."

Olin frowned.

"I suppose you are, though I had hoped Alden would have dressed you more appropriately."

Chilali sniffed her riding outfit. It seemed fine to her.

"It is an accomplishment she is even wearing clothes," Alden replied with a sigh. Chilali blushed at the remark. She hated blushing.

"I'm ready," she fumed and left.

Olin looked to Alden for a response, but the merchant just shrugged in reply.

A white carriage trimmed with silver waited outside the estate for them. Knights in polished armor held positions in front and behind the carriage on mounts. Alden and Chilali both recognized Kern at the front and paused. They couldn't see his face, which was hidden behind by his helm, but they both recognized the menacing mace strapped awkwardly to his back. No other man in the Empire could wield such a weapon.

"The Order spent the better part of the night repairing his face," Olin yawned. "Do not worry, he was reprimanded for his actions last night and will bother you no more."

Kern turned his head, his faceplate revealing only his cold blue eyes, which locked on Chilali.

"Perhaps we should get into the carriage," Alden said, sucking in a breath.

"Where's Agraven?" Chilali asked, stopping.

"You were the last to see him, but do not worry. He'll make his presence known when it comes time to share his information with my uncle and the generals."

A knight opened the carriage door and Alden climbed

inside. The interior was roomier than he thought it would be and the seats, at the front and back, were padded. Curtains over the faceted windows blocked out most of the daylight, creating a calming dimness. Chilali followed and the knight shut the door behind her. She took the seat across from Alden, already feeling caged and cramped by being in such an enclosed structure so close to the man. The carriage started rolling with a slight jolt. Chilali fidgeted, digging one of her nails into the wood frame around the window.

"This trip will not take long," Alden said, trying to offer some relief and hopefully defuse the situation.

Chilali regarded the man, who was better dressed than she had ever seen him before with a slick overcoat, a leather vest, jeweled cufflinks, and silver rings. An ornamental short sword hung at his waist in an embroidered scabbard. He tried to hide his concern behind a congenial smile.

"I can't see what's outside," she said.

"It's more like people can't see what's inside," he replied. "You can remove the ribbon, if you want."

She shook her head and crossed her legs. Crossing her legs was a bit of learned habit she gleaned from watching Roche, Jerle, Talarians, and other women she came across. They would bring one knee on top of the other, whereas men like Alden would at most bring an ankle on top of a knee. The action surprised Alden, but he said nothing of it. It was only one more indicator she was called. A wild creature would not pick up such things.

Still, he was prepared for the worst. He gave Roche instructions on what to do if he found himself imprisoned or executed. He did not believe that would happen and refused to dwell on those scenarios. After all, he saved a Divergent who turned out to have some degree of civility. She had to be called, he told himself.

There was also the matter of the new Blackland Nation mine in the south. Agraven remained behind for the moment but would join him after the Order made its determination. The knowledge of this mine alone would be enough to barter for his own life and freedom, he hoped.

They traveled for a while, feeling the incline and decline of the capital streets and the jarring potholes. They were stopped at the gate to the second wall. Alden knew this, because he could hear Kern and Olin speaking to the guards. Beyond this wall lay the Order, government buildings, the university, the True Silver Knight barracks, and the majority of the most powerful noble families. He, himself, had not breached this wall since his father's passing and felt an urge to open the door a crack and peak outside, but it was an urge he fought.

Chilali lay across the bench, twirling one loose end of the ribbon around her finger. She sat up as the carriage eased to a stop.

"We're at the Order," she yawned.

"How do you know for sure? You've never been there."

"I've been listening to them talk," she replied.

"Really? What have they been saying?"

The carriage door opened before Chilali could respond. Olin stood outside.

"This way, please," the priest extended his hand toward a pristine building. Rows of arches layered on top of rows of stark columns with ribbons of silver flowing through them created the base of the gigantic white dome and the massive, multi-point silver star on its surface. Towers rose from each of the points at the dome's edge and each was topped with sharp white flames.

Chilali and Alden stood before this structure, as the carriage pulled away with the knights and Olin and Kern took to either side of them. The air was much fresher beyond the second wall than the first, Chilali noted, but she did detect a foul odor emanating from the direction of a walled-in area of the Order's courtyard.

"Chilali, hold in reverence this sacred structure, built with and protected by the Goddess' light, the Hieron," Olin spoke with mild reverie.

Chilali pointed to the walled-in area.

"What is over there?" she asked.

"It is the place where Talarian breeding is done," Kern grumbled. "This way."

The heavy knight led them through the Hieron's main doors. A foyer lit with crystals and attended to by priests, who looked similar to Olin but with hair, opened before them. The interior was the antithesis of Alden's home, utterly sparse. What furniture it did have was simple and used primarily for mediation or reading.

The foyer met the main hall, which branched into several other halls along its length. Chilali figured the other halls must ring around the middle of the building, which seemed to be where they were headed. Kern forced open a pair of massive black doors with a grunt.

Inside, the Order waited, Chilali knew. She could feel their collective body heat and an odor of incense similar to what she smelled on Olin. It like was having her head in a bucket of flowers; it suffocated her.

Several crystal chandeliers hung from points of another multi-point star on the domed ceiling, which was smaller and lower than the one seen from outside. Rows of tiered seating circled the walls and were filled with men and women, dressed in white robes and numbering more than Chilali could count. They were all worshippers of Sitara and for the first time, Chilali got a sense of the weight their divinely powered minds placed on her. It felt like she was totally exposed and vulnerable, as if she was standing beneath a giant rock that could fall at any moment and crush her. It was a sensation she did not enjoy.

Olin and Kern had them stand in the middle of the room. A short staircase led out of the ceiling to a platform supported by sloping pillars. Two men were on this platform. One sat in a throne that looked like it was formed of poured silver and the other stood wearing a glowing robe wound with a single silver chain that connected to the chin of a mirror-like silver mask.

Beneath the two men, among the pillars supporting the platform from the ground, at least ten more knights stood a silent guard. Even in the shadows of the pillars, Chilali could size them up in one way or another. They shared a scent similar to Kern's and held strength in their forms. From what little she could see, they each had a unique weapon and set of armor. One woman stood among them, too, made evident by the outline of her body, but she was the furthest away.

Chilali focused on the nearest figure, which peaked from just around the pillar, his face darkened by shadow. "Falcon," Chilali said silently to herself. His shield was strapped to his back and the corner of it poked out above his shoulder. She could even make out the gold color of his sword hilt. His height and hair were the same as she remembered, as well.

They must all be True Silver Knights, she thought with some alarm. Kern was tough enough and Alden claimed the knight was actually stronger than when she faced him. If they attacked her, if it came down to a fight, she feared she would be overmatched. Escape would be the best option.

"Uncle," Alden gasped, interrupting her train of thought. "Why has he come?"

"Uncle," Chilali managed to process the word despite her bewilderment. The man on the throne was Emperor Adelphos. His hair hung in long graying locks and his face was etched with strength and weariness. He kept his beard well-groomed and wore a silver breastplate crested with a black bird. An argent diadem, formed of stars, crowned his head.

Kern and Olin knelt and kept their heads low. Alden did too, coming to his senses. Chilali continued to stand, causing whispers to roll through the circular room. It felt like the air itself moved with those whispers.

Adelphos raised his hand, his wrinkled, calloused fingers encumbered with rings. The voices quieted. He licked his lips once and sat forward in his throne.

"What is your name, child?"

His voice carried through the room with surprising force. It intimidated Chilali, somewhat.

"Chilali," she replied.

"Won't you kneel before me to show respect?"

"Kneeling doesn't show respect," she returned.

"It is merely custom," he grinned. "But I see you know little of such things, though you know much of our language. Tell me, how did you learn our tongue?"

"My mother."

Alden glanced at her out of the corner of his eye, not wanting to move at all until asked to do so. It puzzled him why she would change her answer to this question now, but it made sense. Someone must have taught her. Language was not something even a Divergent could spontaneously pick up. But the answer only revealed more mystery. Her mother had to have learned it to teach it.

"And how did your mother learn to speak?" Adelphos followed Alden's logic.

"I do not know," Chilali replied.

"I see. Do you understand why you've been brought here today?"

Chilali nodded once and paced slightly in a circle like a caged beast. The air felt as thick as water. The rock hanging above her only grew heavier.

"You want to know if I am called or un-called."

"Exactly," Adelphos replied. "Would you mind undoing whatever enchantment disguises your true appearance? I would see you as you are."

She reached back and pulled her bow free. The gasps she had grown accustomed to hearing echoed through the chamber. Adelphos leaned forward even more.

"So, you are a Divergent. That is quite the clever

enchantment, too. Had those here, myself included, not known better, we would have mistaken you for my nephew's bastard daughter."

A rumbling chuckle filled the air, followed by another call to silence from Adelphos. The levity reduced the air's weight for a moment and Chilali was glad for it.

"And are you ready to be tested?" Adelphos asked.

She shrugged.

"Good priest Olin, would you please take the ribbon from her?"

Olin stepped up to Chilali and held his hand out to her. She reluctantly let it slide away from her. He held it tightly in his fist and smiled at her politely.

The emperor stood and loosed a dagger from his belt.

"Kern, take your place beside the good priest."

The emperor flicked the blade with its jeweled scabbard to Chilali, who snatched it out of the air. Olin and Kern moved aside, expecting something.

"The man who stands next to me is the Arch Magus, the most powerful and revered leader of the Order. He will observe the test and look deep into your mind to find Sitara's light," Adelphos explained.

Chilali unsheathed the blade and looked it over. The black edge was ultra-fine; she could shave bone with it, she surmised.

"Alden, please rise," Adelphos asked his nephew with menace tinging his voice.

Alden stood and flashed Chilali a quick smile before facing his uncle.

"Your actions have caused quite the disruption at all levels of the Empire. First, your crime of removing a Divergent from the forest, then the possibility of redemption by the Divergent being called—a serendipitous act for certain—and the accounts of violence and murder in Orsa and even in the capital, itself, reported to me. Now I hear word of a breach of the southern ranges and the establishment of a Blackland Nation mining operation. Information you received by hiring mercenaries, against my decree, to scout to the southern peninsula."

"My apologies, my emperor, I only strive to do what I believe to be best for the Empire."

"And that is your failing," Adelphos pounded his fist into the platform's railing. "You've no real faith in me, the Order, Sitara, our generals, our knights, no one but yourself to protect the Empire. You are talented, yes, but you are audacious, arrogant, and sometimes, misguided."

"I have faith in the Empire, my emperor," Alden returned.

Adelphos sat back on his throne.

"We shall see." Adelphos pointed at Chilali. "Divergent, your test is a simple one. I order you to bury the dagger in Alden's heart."

Alden turned to Chilali. She grasped the dagger in her hand, her eyes narrow and her visage fierce. She moved toward Alden, who knew running would do no good. He had not planned on this and could only guess what Chilali was thinking or what the real intention behind the test was.

He waged one gamble after another. There was nothing he could do to predict Chilali's actions now. He didn't understand the bond they had formed or her interest in him. But he believed they did have some connection on some level.

He dropped to his knees and began to unbutton his vest and shirt. The buttons would not come out of the holes fast enough. His fingers faltered with nervousness. He ripped open his garments, baring his chest and his mother's amulet to Chilali. If she were to stab him, he would give his life freely to her. He would not let himself be her prey.

And he began to understand this was not just a test of her civility, but of his own loyalty to the Empire. His uncle imposed this cruel test to take measure of his commitment to the Silver Throne and the Empire it served. It would be proof purchased with his life.

The act would also determine Chilali's status. If she followed his uncle's orders, despite her own feelings and instincts, she would be called, a true servant of the Empire. Any doubt as to his motives for removing her from the forest and taking her to the capital would be dispelled with his blood. She would ride at the front of the silver army he dreamed of so many times since finding her.

When the blade slipped into his heart, he would die a hero. Something he dearly wished in that moment both his mother and father were still alive to see. The emptiness their deaths carved into him embittered even this moment. Memories of the pain detached him from it. His arms slumped to his sides and his chest. Let it end and let it be a release.

Chilali placed her hand over his heart, where the amulet hung. The azure stone was cool, smooth to the touch, and also absolutely rigid. But beneath it and around it where the tips of her fingers touched, she could feel the muscles contract and the blood squeeze through the tissue. Its pace was wild beneath her hand, which felt so warm and small on Alden's skin. He would feel the pain soon, sharp and searing. His throat tightened with emotion and tears began to pool in his eyes. He didn't want to die a coward, but he could not hold back his own tears. He still wanted to live.

He raised his chin and met her eyes. She wasn't even looking at him; her eyes were set on Adelphos. He felt a little insulted and then amused his ego was such it could be bruised so easily. Then he was just relieved, as she dropped the black blade flat on the ground and faced Adelphos squarely.

"I don't want to kill him."

The room quieted so much Alden could only hear his own breathing. Adelphos leaned over the railing.

"I am your emperor, Divergent. Sitara demands you do as I say. Kill him, now."

Chilali belly laughed at the emperor, astounding all.

"Do I amuse you?" Adelphos tried to ask, but his mighty voice was drowned out by Chilali's laughter.

She stopped abruptly.

"Even if I was called, I wouldn't serve you," she spat.

Her words pricked Adelphos, causing his face to twist up a moment in anger, but the emperor of decades calmed. He nodded slowly and stepped back from the rail. He took a couple of breaths and adjusted his belt. The Arch Magus whispered something to Adelphos not even Chilali could hear.

Adelphos wiped the corners of his lips with one hand. Chilali noticed Kern was holding his mace in both hands, one at the bottom and the other near the head. The tension in the room was rising and she could feel the mental force of the crowd focusing more tightly on her, pressing down on her. The rock would soon fall, and she just wanted to get from beneath it.

"The test has concluded," Adelphos declared. "The Divergent is un-called, wild, a danger to all of us."

Chilali whipped around to face Kern, expecting him to attack immediately. The ones hidden among the pillars would come later. But Olin held the True Silver Knight vice-captain back with just his arm.

Alden stood, his legs a bit shaky, but he found his footing.

"Uncle, I beseech you. She is an anomaly, uncalled, but civil," Alden said.

Adelphos returned a look that saw only desperation in his nephew.

"I have faith in her, Uncle, as I do in you and the Empire, but I ask you to have faith in me."

Adelphos waived Kern to stand down. The knight begrudgingly relaxed.

"Have faith in you? What is there to have faith in?"

"I suggest a deal, an agreement between us."

"Ever the trader, I see."

"I reported the Blackland Nation has established a settlement in the south. Let me use Chilali and my own resources and some of your knights and we will seize it."

"I can spare no knights for a potentially foolish errand. You've no proof this settlement was not founded by an outcast tribe of the Nation."

"No, I do not, but there is only one way to be certain. I do not need your knights. Just Chilali and a choice of mercenaries should be enough."

"And what would you ask for in trade? Your life and freedom? Granting Chilali's patronage to you? Allowing you to continue running your little operations in the south of my Empire?"

"I ask nothing more than your permission to conduct the raid. Beyond that, I will yield to your wisdom."

Adelphos put his hands on the railing and leaned heavily on it. He stared down at the floor a moment, but not enough to cause his diadem to slide, never that far.

"You've shown me courage I did not think you possessed. And as selfless and honorable as your offer appears, this situation is not entirely about you. No, Chilali is more important. So, this is my offer, Divergent."

Chilali crossed her arms with a scowl to listen.

"Alden will be my prisoner and you will have thirty days, beginning with today, to destroy everything of the Nation in that settlement. If you fail, I will personally carry out the order you failed to follow. Succeed and I will give you his life."

Chilali zipped to Alden's side, facing Kern and readying herself to brawl. Even though his face was hidden, Chilali could tell the vice-captain was smiling, albeit painfully.

"No, there will be no violence here, Divergent. You will not fight, because I have already taken your companion, Agraven, into custody. I offer you the same deal for his life as I offer you for my nephew's."

"She can't do it by herself, uncle. She's still a child!" Alden pleaded. "Let me help her, I beseech you."

Adelphos smugly crossed his arms.

"No, you will offer her no assistance. We shall see, nephew, what value she truly places on your lives and those who live in the Empire, as well as her own capability" the emperor held his hand out and pointed to the southwest. "But know this Chilali. If you return to the forest and remain there, I will spare both of their lives without condition. If you choose that path, Arch Priest Olin will see to your return."

Chilali's shoulders slumped, and she glared at Olin, who stared at her, his eyes hard and judging. She turned to Alden, who looked down at her even more uncertain than when Adelphos ordered her to slay him. She grabbed his fore and middle fingers with her hand and squeezed them gently, before letting them go, before losing control.

"Whatever you wish, I will understand," Alden said and removed his amulet. He held it out to her, and she took it.

"I want you to have this," he said. "My mother told me it was enchanted with her love for me and would always protect me no matter where I went. I want you to have that, a mother's love, wherever you choose to go or whatever you choose to do."

Chilali straightened her posture and held her head defiantly. She grasped the amulet, letting the silver chain dangle.

"I'll never go back to the forest," she roared, turned, and marched out, shoving aside Olin on the way.

Alden tried to go after her, but Kern's gauntleted hand planted firmly on his chest stopped him cold. The Order burst into clamor and not even Adelphos could silence them, again. From the floor, Olin locked gazes with the emperor, bringing a terrible sense of unease to the man wearing the heaviest of crowns.

Adelphos had never been a fool and knew much of the Empire, especially its secrets. Olin was a secret he had not learned, assuredly as the masked man next to him was not the true Arch Magus. That would have to wait for another day.

Now came the task of monitoring the girl's actions. She had to be prevented from causing harm to the Empire and its citizens. As much as it disgusted him, Baigen would be the best option to find such a skilled spy and assassin. If the girl fell in battle, that would be one thing. If she were captured, someone would have to finish the job. He would not tolerate another Divergent falling into the Blackland Nation's ranks.

But as he glanced at Alden and noticed his nephew had not stopped looking in the direction the Divergent left, the most worrisome thing occurred to him. The girl could be successful. And if she were, what would he do? All called Divergents had to bend their wills to the demands of he who sits on the Silver Throne. It was the word of the Sitara, the price they paid for the light of her civility. But the girl resisted it. Two centuries ago, General Ashwake could be controlled; this one could not be. That was dangerous. Heroes who paid no allegiance to rulers threatened civilization itself. Kern was one option and Baigen another. And Adelphos knew he had countless more, if necessary, including one he overlooked until the young knight stepped into open sight, a mirror shield strapped to his back and a gold-hilted sword sheathed at his waist.

All Manner of Help

Chilali fled the Hieron, angry, confused, and adamant she wouldn't cry. She was stronger than them, she told herself. She could destroy this settlement. But the reality was she didn't even know where it was or how many warriors from the Blackland Nation were there. Only Agraven, Jerle, and Alden knew, meaning only Jerle could take her there. But if Jerle learned all Chilali had to do was return to the forest and both she and Agraven would be saved, she wouldn't help.

The odor from the breeding pens drafted to Chilali and she stopped, reminded of the filthy nature of man. She could just go back to the forest. If she was as strong as she believed, she could cope with that loneliness and force herself to accept she would never see her mother again. But she didn't even know why she thought her mother left the forest. She had no reason to think this other than the direction she chased her led away from the forest's depths and the fact her mother spoke this people's tongue and many others. The rest was instinct and feeling.

She donned the amulet in her hand and knotted the chain behind her neck. It was not the most eloquent method, but it kept the jewel above her navel. She tucked it inside her shirt, as Alden had always done. She felt connected to the merchant in some way. He was not the strongest of men, not even when she found him in forest. Perhaps, it was his kindness, his empathy. Or maybe it was the constant turmoil she could sense inside of him. He was a man always standing on the edge. He loved this empire, while despising it. And yet, he hoped she would serve it. From all she had seen, this last bastion of civilization for man would be just that.

But she would protect those she had come to know. These people were her first and only friends and the first intelligent creatures she came across and not been forced to kill. She craved that companionship. She craved it dearly. It was a weakness she dared to admit to, though, and began walking to where she believed the gate would be.

Exposed as a Divergent and meandering in this district of power, she drew attention. Knights, those on watch, priests, who had followed her out of the Hieron, and even nobles, who were going about their affairs, saw her and followed at a distance, curious and afraid.

She had barely made it down the first street from the Hieron and they were all around her. It infuriated her they wouldn't leave her alone.

"Where's the gate," she demanded of them, but no one responded.

"I'll take you to it," a familiar voice finally answered.

Falcon strode toward her, dripping with charisma and strength. His armor was a suit of half-plate and chain. It sparkled like water in the sunlight. His mirror-shield framed his back, and he rested his hand on the golden pommel of his sword. His figure was V-shaped, slender, but powerful. He took his steps lightly in line between his shoulders. He wore his hair tied back and his face was smooth. A medium-length dark blue cape waved behind him in the wind like the tide.

"Falcon," she said, stunned by his appearance.

The True Silver Knight knelt before her and bowed his head.

"As you are a member of the Amos family, I am sworn to protect you. If you would have me at your side?"

She shook her head, tossing her ruby locks.

"I'm not Alden's daughter."

"Really, Alden and Roche can provide papers that say otherwise. I, myself, filed them. And no laws bar such an adoption. Of Lessers, perhaps, but not Divergents."

Adoption? The world spun around her for a moment. Alden said nothing of this. All the time she thought it had been one of his ploys, a diversion. But the merchant took the extra step, and she didn't even get a say in the matter.

"But the emperor said he wouldn't spare any of his knights," she continued to challenge simply for the fact she was contrary by nature.

Falcon raised his head and stood. He was so much taller than her, so much more eminent. Would she ever grow to be so imposing herself, she wondered.

"That is true, but there are vows True Silver Knights take that must be honored. We cannot go back on our word. The emperor, once a True Silver Knight himself, understands this. He may well have suspected I would aid you and said nothing to stop me. Neither did the vice-captain. So, will you have me or should I return to my duties?"

She couldn't say, "Yes," fast enough.

"Come, we should stop by your estate before leaving the capital."

She marched beside the knight, Alden's friend. Together, they were a spectacle for all to behold, all the way back to Alden's estate. Rumors of her arrival and tales of her brawl with Kern in the Vineyard had apparently spread to all in the city. Those they passed called out in astonishment, "The Divergent has come!"

It occurred to Chilali they expected much of her. She was to be like General Strife, a savior to them. The thought humbled her but was ultimately conflicting. She didn't even believe they were worth saving and could not imagine what it was she could save them from. Falcon merely nodded, waved, and saluted, when appropriate. His presence alone seemed to be enough to validate her as their potential messiah and not a monster. And he seemed to enjoy the attention.

Aimon greeted them at the front door and took them to meet Roche in the study. Roche was writing on parchment surrounded by stacks of books at a small desk when they entered with Aimon close behind. She looked up at Falcon then returned to her work.

"So, my brother has exhausted our uncle's patience?" she inquired, trying to appear disinterested.

"So, it seems. The Order and your uncle determined Chilali is uncalled."

Roche glared at Chilali then studied Falcon's face, confused.

"How can that be? She's house broken," Roche stated with no intent at humor.

Falcon shrugged.

"It's not important at this point, Roche. What matters is the fact the emperor has struck a deal with Chilali. If she destroys the Blackland Nation mine in the south, he will spare Alden's life."

Roche shot to her feet.

"What? He truly means to execute my brother?"

"Yes, he does," Chilali answered with a hint of apology in her voice. Roche either didn't care or didn't notice.

"This is your fault, Divergent. Why couldn't you just stay in your forest? You were a bother to no one but trespassers there."

Falcon looked away, not wanting to give anything else away, but Roche knew the knight too well.

"There is more, isn't there?" Roche pursued.

Falcon removed his helm and held it under his arm.

"Yes, there is. If Chilali returns to the forest, the emperor will spare all their lives."

"Wait, what do you mean, 'all?'"

"Your uncle has Agraven, too," Chilali answered, her disgust with Adelphos and herself evident in her tone.

Roche walked around the table and stopped right in front of Chilali.

"Then the answer is a simple one. Go back to your damn forest," the young woman's tongue stabbed.

The words hurt Chilali for a moment, knocking her back a step. But she already made her decision.

"No, I'm never going back," she returned, meekly, too meekly.

"Why not, damn you?!" Roche demanded.

Chilali let loose, revealing part of what had been driving her this entire time. It was not something she cared to share, not even with Alden.

"I don't want to be alone, again! I want to find my mother! I won't go back!" she screamed, her voice cracking with genuine pain, enough so the outburst moved Roche.

The young noble pulled her dress up a bit to squat and be at eye level with Chilali.

"I lost my mother at a young age, too. That, I can understand. But I ask you, is this the best choice? Will you risk all that you've come to care about for yourself? And if you do, does that mean you really care about anyone other than yourself? If that is the case, then you are still alone."

Falcon placed his gauntleted hand lightly on Roche's shoulder. She blushed at the touch.

"Selfishness can be found in all things, but it is not such a sin if her chances for success are reasonable. And if she succeeds, the Empire will benefit greatly. We will have forced back an incursion and secured a black metal mine. It is a gamble, true, but you and I both know it is one Alden would take."

She stood and held the knight's hand on her shoulder. The armor was warm to the touch.

"And how do you know your chances are reasonable?"

Falcon held his arm out to Chilali.

"Well for one, we have a Divergent," he patted himself on the chest. "And the Empire's newest and most promising True Silver Knight. Add to that the fact we should be able to convince Jerle and Teth and we have the makings of a strong party."

"You could be up against hundreds of warriors and servants of the Embracing Night."

Falcon reached out with his other hand and clasped

Roche's.

"If that is the case, all in the Empire will need to know."
She pulled her hand away.

"What will you need?"

Falcon smiled at her and turned to Chilali.

"We will need all manner of help, but we should begin
with outfitting our champion here," Falcon gestured to
Chilali and continued. "Jerle will know for certain, but I
believe it takes more than a week to reach the mine from
Orsa. So, the turnaround time on this expedition will be
tight. Word will have to make it to the Empire before the
thirty-day deadline expires with Alden and Agraven's life.
We must be ready to leave within three days with as many
mercenaries as we can hire. I'll see to equipping Chilali."

Roche stepped past Falcon to speak to Aimon.

"Please, assist Falcon and Chilali with whatever they
need. I must begin making purchase orders for the goods
and will have to find the list of supplies Agraven and Jerle
originally put together to use for reference, as well as
petitioning the mercenary guilds," she spun around to face
Chilali. "When you do go, you will take that Talarian girl,
Minnie, with you. Your actions have made the other
Talarians suspicious of her, and that boy, despite being
scared to death, will likely plot some sort of revenge, I
suspect. A clever one he is."

Falcon raised an eyebrow, Chilali answered before he
could say anything.

"Okay, she will come with me."

"Are you-" Falcon tried to ask.

"Yes," Chilali interjected.

"So be it. Our next stop will be the smith." Falcon said,
letting the subject rest for the moment.

Dealings and Preparations

Minnie wouldn't leave the corner of the room. She curled herself into a ball and tried to cut herself off from the outside world. Chilali offered her food and drink and assured her, as best as she could, that she meant the girl no harm. But words wouldn't reach her; her mind had become as muted as her voice. So, Chilali left her alone.

She agreed to meet Falcon at the smith, which was a brick home a few blocks west from the estate. A large family lived there, three generations worth. Collectively, the grandfather, father, and son were some of the most talented and varied craftsmen in the Empire, servicing nobles and even the Order and the emperor on occasion. Only with Alden's reputation and past dealings was Falcon able to acquire their services and only at significant cost.

The son, who everyone called, "Hands," took her measurements. It was unpleasant, but he was extraordinarily quick with his measuring ribbon. At most, she felt a light pressure from his fingertips when he pinched the ribbon to hold his mark. Other than that, he took Falcon's advice not to touch her.

The thought of wearing armor didn't appeal to her. Adapting to clothes was difficult enough. The last thing she wanted was something else to encumber her, especially unwieldy metal plates or chain. Falcon assured her he had something else in mind.

As far as a weapon, she told the knight she wanted a sword like Alden's, but without a crosspiece. He dismissed her request, again, saying he had something else in mind, but also warning Divergents were not allowed to carry weapons within the capital. It was an ordinance that went back to Strife's time and there was no more explanation beyond that.

Dusk settled on the city with a dark purple haze. Pinpoints of firelight began to burn inside the windows of the buildings all around her, as she walked the streets. Without Falcon beside her, those in the streets kept their distance and their silence when she passed them. If they were coming from the opposite way and couldn't take a side street or turn around, they would stay as far to the other side of the cobblestone as they could manage.

The music that once drew her to the Vineyard echoed off the stone buildings. She was near the brothel and wondered if she had time to visit it again. It was a couple of blocks north or toward the second wall. She found her way to it along narrow alleys that were far darker than the actual streets, which were open to the firelight coming from the buildings. She hid behind the same barrels she hid behind when she first came to this place. A crowd was already gathering outside and a Talarian dancer wowed the onlookers with swinging balls of fire she twirled around herself. Chilali watched the fiery display for a moment, mesmerized by the way the light would streak across her vision.

She heard someone coming down the street, moving toward the brothel, and she dipped behind the barrels for more cover. It was a man, one she recognized immediately.

"Good evening to you, Divergent," Duke Medwin said, resting his weight on his heavy cane.

Chilali stepped out from behind the barrels. Medwin covered his mouth a moment with his ringed fingers but maintained his composure despite seeing her true self for the first time.

"Tell me, why are you out tonight?"

"I'm on my way to meet Falcon to get a new set of armor, but I heard the music and wanted to listen to it, again."

The Duke narrowed just his left eye.

"So, you've chosen to confront the Blackland Nation in the south rather than return to the forest?"

She nodded.

"Kern was most certain you would return to the forest, and he was most dismayed when his newest knight asked permission to join you."

"I didn't know Falcon asked permission. I thought it was his duty to come with me."

"Perhaps, child, but know that man would do anything to help Alden, even betray you."

That was something she hadn't considered. It was within Falcon's interests to return her to the forest, but the knight seemed trustworthy enough and she never sensed any duplicity from him. He lived like he fought, straightforward. But then again, he hadn't been completely honest with her.

"He won't betray me," she replied and turned to leave down the alleyway.

"Wait Divergent. Before you go, I have something to offer you."

She stopped but didn't turn around.

"I won't hurt Alden," she stated.

"You've already done a fine enough job of that," Medwin replied with a hard stare. "But no, I have something else in mind."

"What?"

The duke straightened his back and tossed up his cane to catch and hold it in its middle.

"I can offer you a Rageborne to assist in your assault."

She turned to examine the man. Everything she saw in him made her believe he was serious.

"A Ragebourne like Shank or like Aimon?"

"One in between. Far more civil than Shank and far more a warrior than that runt Aimon."

Aimon was a runt. That gave her pause. While he was more slender than Shank the two were nearly the same size. The thought there might be a bigger, tougher Ragebourne excited her, but she buried that excitement.

"You want something in return?"

"Of course, I want some, not all, of the mining rights, when you are successful. I'll even lend you ten of my knights from my very home, in addition to Beriszl."

She bit her bottom lip, trying to think it over, but realizing she didn't know anything about mining rights. Her goal wasn't to stay at the mine. It was to just kill everything there and report back. But Medwin seemed to have something else in mind.

"I will tell Falcon."

Medwin shrugged.

"I thought this was your task, not his."

The Duke had a point. Falcon was assisting her and a Ragebourne would be a strong ally. Alden, likely, wouldn't care about sharing the mining rights anyway, if it meant saving his life.

"It is my task. I accept your offer."

Medwin bowed with a smile beneath his beard.

"That is good news. I'll send Beriszl and ten of my knights to your estate at dawn. I take it you intend to set out in the morning, as well?"

"Yes," she answered, feeling like she had just stumbled into a trap, again. Her calves even tensed a moment as she briefly relived the painful memory of being bit by the steel jaws.

"Now, if you'll excuse me, there are men I must meet inside the Vineyard. Good evening."

With that, Medwin slipped into the crowd. It occurred to her in that moment there was more to this man than she was aware. As influential and powerful as he was supposed to be in the Empire, he moved about the streets alone, fearlessly. The other nobles she had seen always had a personal guard with them. If she ever got to speak to Alden again, she would ask him about the Duke.

She headed to her original destination and found the two-story brick building easily enough. Smoke still pumped from the rows of stacks poking out its inclined roof. And the sound of metal striking hot metal rang painfully in her ears over and over. She tried to ignore it, but it was still annoying.

Falcon let her inside. He was out of his armor and had been lounging around in common clothes, loose pants, and an open, long-sleeved shirt. The boy, Hands, stitched leather with a thick needle and a pair of pliers. His father, Gavin, worked the metal in the stuffy shop. Sweat pooled on his thick brow until he would lean his head forward enough to drain it, usually onto the red-hot metal he was working, causing a sizzle.

Falcon filled a pair of mugs from a spout jutting out of the side of a barrel. When he finished filling them, he plugged it with cork and handed her one of the mugs, which was about to foam over onto the floor.

"This is not normally given to children, but it helps pass the time."

Gavin grunted at the statement. The pair didn't seem to mind her presence, they were so focused on her work, which was good. She was weary of being the center of attention. She grasped the mug with both her hands and buried her face in the foam, sucking it up till she got to the bitter liquid.

"Slow down," Falcon chided and took a seat on a stool near Hands in the one room floor. The family lived on the second floor and stored supplies in the basement, which also happened to be connected to a series of tunnels. They did their work on the ground floor, where customers could come in and watch.

She wiped the sticky suds from her face on her shirt.

"I made a deal with Duke Medwin," she told the knight, who almost spat out a mouthful of mead upon hearing her words.

"Medwin? Why? What deal?"

"He's going to let us bring his Ragebourne, Beriszl, and ten of his knights on my raid."

Gavin stopped hammering and turned to regard the Divergent for a moment. Chilali was relieved the ringing stopped.

"And what does he want?" Falcon asked.

"He said he wants some of the mining rights."

"Mining rights?"

"Yes, but not all of them, he said."

"We're not going to secure the mine. We're going to force the Nation out of it. What is he thinking?"

"I don't know, but a Ragebourne will be good to have with us, right?"

Gavin doused the metal plate he was hammering with water, releasing a puff of steam.

"In this case, I do not know. Beriszl is considered by many to be the strongest of the Ragebourne. If Medwin's intentions aren't pure, we could find ourselves battling Beriszl and ten knights."

Chilali sipped her mead, letting Falcon's words settle.

Gavin doused the plate again with water and held it up to the firelight from the forge with a pair of long black tongs. He had worked the metal into the shape of a child-sized breastplate. Chilali recognized it was part of her armor, which she still had doubts about.

"Beriszl may be a beast in battle, but he is an honorable one. While he will do whatever his master asks, he refuses to knowingly engage in deception. If he's been ordered to turn on you at the opportune moment, he'll tell you first," the smith said before passing the breastplate off to Hands, who grabbed it with his pliers and set it on a nearby cold anvil before going back to his stitching.

Hands pricked his finger with the needle and sucked on it. His name came from the fact his hands were like a woman's, slender, graceful, and soft. None of which were characteristics that made one a good metal worker. But when it came to sewing, etching, and sculpting, few could match his talent or control.

"Perhaps you're right, Gavin, but I'll have a better idea once I've traveled with them for a time. If I think we should part ways, we can do so when we meet up with Jerle or when we make it to Orsa."

Gavin grabbed an odd-looking sword from the rear wall. It was short, wide, and thick, like a flat, upside-down club. The smith used both of his hands to carry it over to her, meaning its weight was significant for a man, at least. He handed it to her hilt first.

"This is yours, but you can't carry it within the city. I've no desire to be jailed for breaking the law."

She set her mug on the ground and grabbed the handle with one hand. She was more than strong enough to hold it aloft, but it probably weighed a third of what she did. While it tipped her off-balance, it wasn't nearly as bad as Kern's mace. It probably weighed a fifth of that monstrous weapon.

"It's meant to be wielded with both of your hands," Gavin explained.

That was good to know. It was easier to keep her balance with both hands on it. She could swing it probably more than twice as fast as she could with one hand. The weapon had a stubby crosspiece that was actually part of the blade. In fact, the whole weapon was one solid chunk of dull-silver metal. The boy, Hands, appeared to have woven the leather grip on the handle, though.

She held the blade out straight to get a better sense of it. It was probably as long as one of her legs, maybe a little shorter than the swords Alden carried. A thumb's width of the metal tracing the blade was highly polished from the sharpening. While it came to a fine edge, it widened quickly, making it have more in common with Teth's axe than the flatness of Falcon's sword.

"It's a heavy, sturdy weapon. Swing it and kill. It should be just right for a Divergent with little to no weapon training," Gavin continued. "But it's bulky and a standard sheath won't do you any good, so we're attaching a set of clasps into your armor to secure it."

She wasn't paying much attention to him at that point, as she swung the weapon and felt the resistance of the air and listened to the dull whiff it made. There was much power behind this blade when she wielded it. She figured she could chop Shank in half with one good strike or if she struck him flat with it, she could crack his skull.

Gavin held his hand out, wanting the weapon.

"Give it back young one. Hands still has to make it look pretty for you."

She nodded and hefted it up to him. He set it aside and stretched his back.

"Hands and I will be working through the night, Sir Falcon. We'll have your equipment delivered before dawn, so there's no sense in you hanging around here all night."

Falcon sipped his mug.

"Oh, there is much sense friend," the knight toasted the smith. "But you're right. It will be best if we're both completely rested for tomorrow's journey."

Falcon set his mug on the stool where he was sitting and grabbed his sword from the wall. It blended in quite well with the other masterpiece works on display; Chilali hadn't even noticed it until now. She followed Falcon into the night.

They walked side-by-side back to the estate. Falcon seemed to be elsewhere, though. The calm she normally sensed from him was absent. A quiet storm rumbled inside him. Perhaps it was the ale, she wondered.

The knight stopped outside the gate and regarded Chilali. He lifted his chin slightly then let it drop, his eyes focused on the bulge of Alden's medallion beneath her shirt.

"Alden was never one to part with that. Why did he give it to you?"

She pulled it out of her shirt to look at it. She hadn't

taken it from around her neck since putting it on and had become entirely used to it. Alden's words and the smooth, solid stone gave her a sense of security she had never experienced before but appreciated. Even in the world of man, she felt just a little less alone. And her abandonment by her mother became easier to not think about in quiet times.

"He wanted me to have a mother's love," she answered. "It will protect me, he said."

Falcon's shoulders dropped so slightly; only she, a Divergent, would have even noticed.

"A jewel, no matter how precious, cannot replace such a thing," Falcon said. "That has been my experience. It is best to not think about such things, because it will only bring pain. Focus on the path ahead and find new joy. This is what Sitara teaches."

She tucked the jewel into her shirt and said nothing. If only it were so easy to just disregard the past, she would have already done it, perhaps. But without the pain she felt she would never have been driven so far to the edge of the forest. She would not be walking in this great city of man next to one of its supreme warriors. In fact, she wondered if one should seek out new pain on the path ahead, as well as new joy.

Disguises, Expectations, and Beriszl

Morning came; Chilali had barely slept. Minnie stirred in the corner. Chilali had tossed her a blanket to keep warm and the girl clung to it, even as she slept. The Talarian took her time becoming aware of her surroundings. Chilali expected her to begin her routine again, curling up in the corner and shivering in fear. If only she still had the ribbon, then Minnie wouldn't be a problem.

She dressed herself in a fresh outfit, new riding gear provided to her by Roche. The material was softer, smoother, and fit better. She brushed her hair out next, having learned that brushing regularly meant less tangles. Her reflection gave her pause. She stared at her ruby locks. She recalled seeing herself with gold hair and wished she could go back to make things easier. She didn't want to drag Minnie out of the room kicking and screaming. Last night, Roche, again, made it clear to her the girl was to go with her.

Minnie's image in the corner of the mirror drew her emerald eyes. The girl sat up against the wall and watched her quietly. Perhaps her fear was gone, Chilali wondered. She looked over her shoulder at the girl and watched the Talarian tense under her gaze. Still afraid, Chilali thought and kept brushing, all the while wondering if she could find Olin and retrieve the ribbon.

The first few times the enchantment wrapped her in its new colors, she didn't notice anything, no sensation at all. The longer she went with it, the more she began to notice something. It sent a tingling through her whole body, beneath the skin. The tingling would swell inside of her until the enchantment took hold and then it would seem to die. The power was really still alive inside her, though changed. It became something more like a fleeting thought that never seemed to leave her mind entirely. It was like a dream she kept trying to remember but couldn't. Even now as she tried to regain the memory of its feeling her fingertips began to tingle. She looked at them, touching each one to her thumb in rapid succession. The tingling spread down her hands into her arms, up her shoulders, and through her torso, making her quiver. For a moment she was alarmed, not understanding what was happening, until she saw herself in the mirror. Her colors were changing. The ruby-red drained from her hair and the emerald of her eyes was overtaken with sapphire. She was one of them again and turned to face Minnie in exasperation.

The Talarian stood and took a step toward her, as she focused on the enchantment flowing through her blood. Yes, it was in her blood. She could feel it massing in her heart and bursting outward. She soon realized she may not be able to turn it off now and that sapped much of her excitement. There was no ribbon to remove. What was she to do?

Guessing her meditation on the moment of transition spurred this sudden change, she tried to go the other way. She concentrated on what it felt like for the enchantment to leave her. That fleeting thought would leave her mind and the tingling would rise up once again as it ebbed out of her. She walked herself through the memory of the process, trying to remember each sensation in detail. She knew it worked when Minnie took a quick step back.

She checked herself in the mirror and was herself, again.

"See? I can make myself look like them," she said to the girl, who didn't seem to know what to make of the situation. Multiple possibilities came to Chilali's mind. The first of which was to keep her discovery secret. Only she and Minnie knew of it and Minnie couldn't tell anyone.

"We'll be leaving soon, Minnie. You should get ready."

The girl showed no indication she even understood her words.

"Roche said you can't stay here anymore. So, you have

to come with me."

Minnie's brow wrinkled. Sounds of protest left her throat, but they were only sounds.

Chilali crossed her arms.

"You don't have to stay with me. When we get to Jerle's, you can stay there. She has a lot of Talarians."

Minnie made a mewing sound and looked down at the ground, her palms coming up to her eyes to try to seal the tears inside her head.

Chilali moved toward her, but she moved away.

"Why are you crying?" she asked.

The girl shook her head and clutched her throat. She tried desperately to speak, but only strained sounds came out.

"I don't understand," Chilali shrugged. "But you still have to leave with me. Go get ready."

The girl skulked to the lavatory just as a knock came at the door. Olin entered, dressed in short robes similar to the ones she last saw him wearing. She wondered if he ever wore anything other than robes. At least he didn't have a staff with him. He greeted her with a thin smile; she returned a frown.

"Why are you here?"

"I wanted to tell you I'm glad you chose to fight and not return to the forest, even if you do not have Sitara's light," the priest said, while pacing through the bedroom to peak into the lavatory where Minnie dressed, her back bruised. "And I'm coming with you."

She hadn't asked for his help. She liked him less than Medwin, even if her reasons weren't obvious to herself. While he was condescending and a member of the Order, there was something more to him, something that made her uneasy. Like those on the street, he revered her, but at the same time she disgusted him. That conflict in his behavior toward her disturbed her. She had experienced nothing like it before and hadn't learned how to respond to it.

"I didn't ask you to come with us," she returned.

"Falcon did. He thought you may be in need of a priest, and I was returning to Orsa anyway."

"Falcon asked you to come?"

"It was a wise decision on his part. He fears, as do I, a servant of the Embracing Night may be present at the mine. If so, you will need my help."

She shrugged and sat down on the floor to put her boots on. It was a childish act, but given her size, it was the best method. Olin seemed amused by it.

"Falcon told me of your dealings with Duke Medwin. Are you sure you require his assistance?"

"We get to take a Ragebourne with us."

"And may I ask, why that matters? You are a Divergent and are greater than any Lesser, even at your age."

She stood up and wiggled her toes inside her boots. The leather was new and a little stiff, but it didn't pinch her toes. She wasn't sure why it mattered so much to the priest that she had a Ragebourne to help. Beriszl was a Lesser, but he could tear apart men as easily as she.

Really, she wanted to learn more about them. Shank had shown her much, the differences in their relative abilities. Besides Kern, he was the only creature to ever challenge her strength. In a way, she felt it was a way to test her limits.

"He's strong," she finally replied with a shrug, as Minnie came out the lavatory, dressed in the same pullover dress she had been wearing.

Olin regarded the Lesser and licked his lips.

"And what of this Lesser? Is it true you intend to take her along?"

"She can't stay here anymore. Roche said so," she answered, watching the girl creep towards her without taking her silver irises from the priest. She feared Olin more than she feared a Divergent. That surprised Chilali.

"I do not approve of taking so many Lessers with us,

but at least the girl seems to be warming to you without the ribbon. It was confiscated from me, if you were curious. Neither the Order, nor the emperor, felt it wise to allow a Divergent, especially an uncalled one, to walk amongst us disguised."

"Where's Falcon?" she asked, not caring about an explanation of their reasoning.

"He should be at the stables, preparing your mount. He's found you a young stallion, one a fair bit smaller than your previous mount. He already had me enchant it for you. In fact, he dispatched me to take you and the Talarian to the front of the estate to leave."

"Then let's go," she said and moved past him, Minnie following closely behind. Olin caught up to them with a sigh.

Roche was waiting at the open front door, her hands on her hips and worry on her face.

"I do not like the looks of this, Divergent. I trust Falcon's judgment in many things, but yours I find severely lacking in this particular instance."

Rows of mounted knights and lightly armored mercenaries waited outside the front gate in two columns. There were many more men than Medwin promised, but they didn't all seem to be from him. The seals they wore differed. She could pick out their designs, some of fierce birds and others of flowers, from inside the manor.

"I didn't do this," she replied, confused, and swept out the door with Minnie. Falcon came to her in haste with a Talarian servant and two horses. One of which was to be hers, she surmised, given its smaller size.

"We have a bit of a problem," the knight exclaimed.

The army, that's what it was, crowded the street outside the estate. There were hundreds of men with supplies on horses and wagons. All were standing impatiently and fidgeting. They would whisper things to each other from time to time, but nothing she could hear.

"What is this?" she asked.

"Roche hired a few more than one hundred, but apparently word spread you accepted help from Medwin. This was the result. Nearly every noble house with a standing army contributed men and supplies, hoping to have a share of the mining rights."

"So, we have more men."

Olin stepped forward and waved his hand at the army, which watched them from over the wall.

"The emperor will not be pleased by this."

"I know he will not," Falcon sighed. "But what are we to do? We cannot turn them away. That would certainly worsen the matter."

She scanned the crowd, looking for the Ragebourne. Where was he? The walkway sloped down to the gate, and she could see well over the wall, but there was no Ragebourne. She'd rather have Beriszl than all these men fighting at her side for the simple fact his strength could challenge hers.

"I don't see Beriszl," she said, drawing looks from Falcon, Olin, and Roche, who came out of the house.

"The Ragebourne is the least of our problems," Falcon explained. "I did not plan on these extra men; I prepared for the number Roche hired. Now, moving a force this size will take more time. Leading so many rival houses will also be a challenge. They all likely have their own agendas. Furthermore, there is no guarantee the mine will be the resource the nobles believe it is. Black metal has always been scarce on our side of the mountains."

Chilali mounted her horse. The saddle smelled fresh. And her mount hardly noticed when she climbed onto its back. Olin had placed it into a trance of some sort.

"You can figure it out on the way to Jerle's," she said, disappointed. Where was the Ragebourne Medwin promised?

She caught Aimon's scent and looked up within the

courtyard. The Ragebourne sauntered side-by-side with another Ragebourne, the one for which she had been waiting, from the direction opposite the stables. She didn't even think to question why the pair came from the gardens on that side of the mansion.

The other Ragebourne's scent came to her on the breeze soon after Aimon's. It was muskier, earthier. This one spent much more time outdoors compared to Aimon. He was also larger on the same scale of comparing Falcon to Olin. This one had much more muscle, in impressive coils and lumps. His shoulders were wider than she was tall and his canines were as long as her middle fingers and just as thick.

This was Beriszl. And as intimidating, even to her, as he was, something was amiss. Aimon's eyes were sharper and more focused. They peered into everything with intelligence. Beriszl's were lackadaisical. Though his form was well-muscled, his arms had an awkward length. He picked at his clawed toes with his clawed fingers as he took bobbing steps. Someone had also forced armor on the creature, but not armor tailored for him. It was the same armor knights wore, a combination of plate and chain. It looked as if he were squeezed into any piece he could possible fit. He even wore a helm with a waving, bright red plume. Just looking at him made her want to run screaming from putting on her own armor.

And the last thing she noticed before she hopped off her horse and dashed toward him was the relatively tiny silver-star mace hanging from his belt. It was meant to be wielded by a man with one hand and was no longer than her new sword. One of his hands was big enough to wrap around a third of the shaft. Certainly, he should have a weapon more like Kern's mace than that pitiful instrument.

The Ragebourne saw her coming toward them and stopped. Beriszl sniffed the air, flaring his nostrils. He let out a raspy laugh. Aimon sighed.

Chilali slowed to a halt several paces from him. Falcon

and the others she left watched her suspiciously, but in silence. They were confused as to her intentions, she knew. Aimon slipped off to the side to return to his duties inside the house, caring little for the spectacle.

"Divergent Chilali?" Beriszl asked with a voice uncharacteristically rough for a Ragebourne.

"I am. And you are Beriszl?"

He nodded and scratched the tops of his feet with his claws.

"Why are you wearing armor?"

He looked away from her and at the men waiting outside and then shrugged.

"Duke Medwin told me to help you take the settlement."

"Yes, we made a deal."

"There are a lot of people with you."

"I didn't know they were coming."

He regarded her a moment.

"You're really small. I thought you would be bigger."

She looked at herself and returned a grin.

"Alden said I will be."

"Good, when you're bigger you won't need my help."

"I won't," she agreed.

He pulled at his breastplate to let some air slip between his fur and the padding.

"We should go. It's getting hot."

"Okay," she said and turned to Falcon, genuinely content the Ragebourne had come.

"Let's go Falcon. Beriszl is here."

The knight waved in response, held Roche's hand for a moment, and took to his horse. Olin was there, too, but she didn't pay him any mind. She walked back to her young horse with the Ragebourne at her side. Her mount nuzzled his hand as she climbed into the saddle.

"You don't have a horse," she asked.

He let out a raspy chuckle.

"Horses should ride me."

She grinned at that and took measure of Beriszl again. His relaxed attitude didn't come from laziness or disinterest. She sensed it came from experience. There was something else to him as well. She didn't feel threatened by him at all, which seemed odd to her. In any case, she planned to learn as much as she could from him. Her ultimate goal was to hunt and kill Shank.

Minnie cried out with an inarticulate noise. Both Chilali and Beriszl took notice of her.

"Who is this?" the Ragebourne asked, adjusting his helm.

"Minnie. She's coming with me."

Beriszl looked around, making brief eye contact with Falcon, Olin, and Roche.

"She doesn't have a horse."

"Falcon," she looked at the knight, awaiting an answer.

"The girl hasn't been trained to ride. Put her on a horse and she'll just harm herself. If we must, we can put her in one of the wagons so she will be out of the way."

Minnie stared at Chilali with frightened eyes, but the Divergent was scoping out the handful of wagons the nobles provided. They were full of mercenaries and supplies. Given her experience, placing Minnie in one of them would not be a wise decision. But she couldn't let the girl ride with her; she would lose control.

"Can she ride with you Falcon?"

The knight shook his head.

"I'm sorry, but no. I need to be able to move about the column. The extra weight would be too much of a strain on my mount. But do not worry for her safety; I will place Olin with her in the wagon."

Minnie did not like that suggestion and pressed herself against Chilali's mount.

Beriszl groaned.

"If she must go, I will carry her," the Ragebourne

grinned at the Talarian, who returned a curious, uncertain expression. "But I would ask you give her a blanket, Divergent Chilali. She can shade us both on the road."

Falcon unfastened his cape and handed it to Beriszl.

"Take it. I respect sacrifice and it would just become dirty on the road.

The Ragebourne was hesitant to take it and bowed his head slightly in gratitude. He crouched in front of Minnie. The girl understood his intention but was hesitant. She climbed onto Beriszl's right shoulder, fitting with room to spare. The Ragebourne held her there by her hip with just one hand and stood back to his full, hunched-over height. The plume from his helm tickled Minnie's face, causing her to let out a strained giggle when the Ragebourne shifted his head. He handed the girl the cape and she held it open and above Beriszl's head.

"Now we can leave," the Ragebourne chuckled. "It is cooler already."

Strife's Journal: 261st Day, 4057, North Master's Enclave

The weather has improved, but more clouds gather to the north.

My head continues to ache and the vision in my left eye remains distorted.

Tales of Master Chael's prowess are not exaggerated. Not in any significant way. There was no joy to be had in fighting him. None at all. I wholly regret the disrespect I showed him. And I will make it one of my ambitions to never slight him again.

I will likely continue to be mocked for days to come by my men but seeing me so soundly defeated has put them more at ease around me, which is at least some benefit to be had from this humiliation.

—General Strife Ashwake

The March

Beriszl panted and adjusted Minnie's placement on his shoulder. He and the horses, perhaps more so, were tiring under the midday heat. And Minnie, too, had long since stopped holding Falcon's cap aloft for shade. She held it over her head and across her shoulders, covering Beriszl's back and about half of his helmeted head.

Chilali rode next to him and felt her mount proceeding wearily. The heat hadn't bothered her. She hadn't even broken a sweat, even though Beriszl left a trail of droplets behind him, and Minnie left a wet spot on his shoulder. The only other person not visibly affected by the heat was Olin, who pretended to wipe sweat from his bald crown, dabbing it with a fine white cloth.

A hot breeze blew across the farmlands around them and swirled up dust from the road. Falcon shielded his eyes from the gust and pushed his mount to catch up to Chilali, who rode ahead of the column.

"This weather is unseasonable," the knight stated. "Many of the men have stripped down to the waist."

"We haven't too much further to go," Olin spoke aloud from behind.

Falcon pulled out his water skin and doused his face and hair with it.

"That is true, but we may want to stop at that thicket up ahead and shelter in the shade for a short time," the knight pointed to a spec on the horizon.

Chilali glanced at it, making sense of the heat-distorted image. It didn't seem like it would be big enough to fit the five hundred or more men riding with them, their horses, the forty or so wagons, and Beriszl.

"How do you fare, Chilali?" Falcon asked.

"I'm fine. But we should stop soon to rest," she agreed.

Besides being bored and frustrated and having to ride this beast and not just run to Jerle's on foot, she was fine.

She checked Beriszl and Minnie, feeling a little guilty the Ragebourne carried the girl. Even she would find that tiring after a while, a really long while.

"Can I have some of your water?"

The knight handed her his skin.

"You haven't taken a drop, yet. I was beginning to wonder if you even needed to drink."

"I don't," she said and offered the skin to Beriszl. "Have some. We'll stop soon."

Beriszl clutched the skin and shot a spurt into his mouth before reaching it up to Minnie.

"Thank you, Chilali," the Ragebourne said.

Minnie imitated her mount or tried to and sprayed water all over her face. Falcon and Chilali smiled at that. But Olin was not amused. Minnie wiped her face with her hands and carelessly tossed the skin to Chilali, who caught it even more carelessly. Both actions caused concern for Falcon, who feared they'd drop the skin, and it would be trampled.

The Divergent handed it back to the knight, but he refused for the moment.

"You should have some, too."

"I'm not thirsty or hot."

She forced the skin back onto the knight.

"But you must be, unless you are taking ill?"

Olin pushed his mount in between theirs.

"Divergents do not become ill, but I do find it unusual you haven't even broken a sweat."

"Neither have you," she returned, becoming irritated because the priest had moved closer to her.

"Sitara protects me from the Fire King," the priest offered, his tone heavy with condescension. "Tell me of the command situation, Sir Falcon."

Falcon pulled a long indigo strand of hair from his skin and swallowed a squirt.

"To say one exists may not be truthful. Twenty noble houses contributed men to this expedition, a combination of knights and mercenaries. And each has its own appointed commander that claims he will only answer to the Divergent leading the expedition or me, acting as her second in command, of course."

"All is not what it appears," the priest sighed. "I've gleaned enough of their thoughts to know they all have their own agendas. If we succeed, good knight, we may be faced with a sudden spat of infighting within our own ranks."

"I suspected as much. Many of these men were sent along, not for mining rights, but because their rivals joined our crusade. The legend that is Chilali has grown much in people's minds."

"As does the possibility to exploit her," the priest lamented.

Chilali shrugged, finding the situation amusing, but not letting on that she did. She also puzzled over Olin's ability to perceive another's thoughts. She witnessed mention of it before, but never so directly. And she felt the power of the Order personally inside the Hieron, but she still wasn't ready to accept the priest could see her thoughts.

"Do they know that when we are successful, I can kill all of them?"

Falcon pursed his lips at the remark, pretending to think it over.

"It hasn't crossed their minds yet, but it will eventually."

"Such a tactic will not be necessary," the priest sighed. "Do try to rein in your uncalled nature, Chilali."

The admonishment drew a hoarse chuckle from Beriszl.

"Why do you laugh, Ragebourne?" the priest asked.

The Ragebourne cocked one red eye at Olin.

"Chilali was joking."

Yes, and it allowed her to learn much about her companions. Olin either wasn't using his ability to glean thoughts on her or he couldn't. Falcon misunderstood her intentions. And Beriszl knew her better than both.

"You can't read her," Beriszl wheezed, following Chilali's reasoning. She wished the Ragebourne kept the observation to himself.

"Perhaps not," Olin said, scratching the back of his head.

"We should still think about killing them," she said, changing the subject and filling it with the laughter of her companions and even a smile from Olin.

It was a warm moment, one of few she had shared with others since leaving the forest. And even on a hot road, she was grateful for it and sad at the same time. Alden and Agraven remained hostages and this arrangement with Falcon and others, she knew, would not last forever. This battle would have its end.

Shade

The thicket offered a welcome reprieve from the wrath of the imprisoned Fire King, which was both the blinding orb in the sky that brought daylight and the jealous lover of Sitara. From a distance, Chilali thought the cropping of trees and bushes along the road would be too small and too dense to cover so many, but Falcon ordered the wagons wheeled out to the perimeter. The knight assured her it would only be for a moment of rest and maybe a quick meal, but fatigue was evident even in Falcon. He stripped off the larger pieces of his armor as soon as he was able.

A small brook cut through the fields and bisected the thicket. The water flowed over smooth gray and magenta stones and was clean and clear enough for the horses to drink. Though, there were so many beasts they had to be brought to the water in ordered groups. Further upstream, others covered the mouths of their skins with cloth and refilled them.

She just sat on a tree branch about two men in height above the ground, waiting and watching. Minnie tried to climb up to her but was only able to make it to a branch beneath her with Beriszl's help. She wrapped Falcon's cape around her and leaned against the trunk, threatening to doze off. Below, the mighty Ragebourne lapped water out of his plumed helm, his pointy ears occasionally twitching.

Falcon passed below, looking for her perhaps.

"Above you," she called to him.

The knight looked up and used his hand to shade his eyes. Even beneath trees, sunrays found their way through to the ground.

"The commanders want to make camp for the night. While we are close to Jerle's, we are also halfway to Orsa."

"What are you saying?"

"There is no reason to rush these men to Orsa in a day, and they have no business with Jerle. So, they do not need to continue for the day. They can travel to Orsa tomorrow without losing much time."

"We have business with Jerle."

"Yes, we do, which is why I'm prepared to continue riding with you. We can make it to her estate by nightfall."

Beriszl dumped his helm out and forced it back on with a grimace.

"I will go with you," he burped.

Minnie climbed off the tree branch and onto Beriszl's shoulder. The Ragebourne paid her no mind, except to grab hold of her.

"Of course, Beriszl. Minnie must come along with us anyway," Falcon said with a nod and a smile.

Chilali hopped off the branch and landed in a stiff legged fashion. The fall made Falcon wince, but it really had no effect on the Divergent.

"I'm prepared to leave Olin in charge during our absence. The commanders agreed to this, at least until they reach Orsa," the knight said to the Divergent, as she passed by him.

A man standing as tall as Falcon, but nearly twice as thick with a braided beard stared at her from across the camp. Heavy leather bracers wrapped his arms, and his pectoral muscles twitched at Chilali's approach. Both his eyes were blue, but his left one was off-color, faded or clouded over. Sweat drained off his bald head as he rested his hand on the hilt of a dagger sheathed in his belt.

Chilali could feel his intent, his desire to challenge her. His stare burned her with it and that excited her. The urge to destroy him swelled inside her. Savagery, violence, the cupric taste of it in her mouth pushed her forward, despite knowing Falcon, Olin, and many others would protest her actions.

The camp quieted, feeling the tension rise in the air, and fanned out from the man. Those returning with horses stopped at the edge of the thicket. Falcon and Beriszl came to Chilali's side as soon as they realized what was about to happen.

"You want something little girl?" the man asked.

"No, she does not, Kergen. And neither do you," Falcon interjected, stepping out to the side to look at both of them.

"You know him," Chilali asked the knight with a sideways glance.

"He knows me well, girl. He stole my place among the True Silver Knights. Purchased it with his friendship with the merchant, he did. He didn't have to earn it like the rest of us," Kergen spat.

"Watch your words, Kergen," Falcon ordered and explained to Chilali, "He is one of the commanders and is of Duke Danival's house."

"Tch, you haven't seen a third of the battles I have boy. To think they put you and the girl in command disgusts me."

"Are you going to attack me, or do I have to attack you?" Chilali asked, disregarding Kergen's insult.

Kergen pulled the dagger from his belt and gripped it tight, causing the leather wrapping the handle to squeak slightly. Falcon drew his sword in reaction.

"No, I won't allow this. We are all of the Empire, and we go to face a mutual enemy."

Kergen turned on Falcon.

"What? Do you fear I'll expose this child for a weakling not even worthy to service General Strife, rather less pretend to carry his legacy?"

"I'll attack you, then," Chilali growled.

Falcon tried to catch her, but she dodged him and went straight at Kergen. Surprised by her speed and the suddenness of her attack, the muscled man was prepared to only swipe at her once with his blade. He gashed her forearm, but that was all he was able to do. She caught his arm as it swung down at her with her right hand, spun half a turn to get a foot between his feet, and then grabbed the inside of his thigh with her left hand. Those were the handholds she needed. She heaved him off the ground and whipped him around, flinging him into a tree. Kergen smacked into the trunk sideways and dropped onto the gnarled roots with a groan. The dagger fell from his hand, and he could do little more than lie there, hold his broken ribs, and cough.

Chilali scanned the onlookers, but they avoided eye contact. Blood ran down her left arm to the top of her hand. A couple of her fingers tingled with numbness, but she didn't mind. The bleeding was already beginning to stop.

Her expression stoic, she called out to them.

"I can throw the rest of you further than I can throw him."

She turned to Falcon.

"Let's go to Jerle's. I'm tired of waiting here."

Falcon nodded and took one more look at Kergen. It was true he and Kergen competed to gain entrance in the True Silver Knights. But while Kergen was physically superior and had more battle experience, neither served him well against Chilali. Kergen lacked the spiritual powers and cunning Falcon possessed. Those talents were the real strength of a True Silver Knight. And Falcon knew, as he followed Chilali to their horses, he would need command of all his skills to complete the mission the emperor gave him.

Olin tended to Kergen at the base of the tree, a thin smile on his lips.

Bad News

Minnie slapped her hands together with a smile and Beriszl chuckled. Even Falcon found it hard to suppress a smile. Looking back, he actually felt sorry he possessed more restraint than Chilali. He would have loved to do the same to Kergen.

Chilali flexed her fingers. Falcon noticed she had been doing that every few moments since being cut. He knew he should have had Olin take a look at the wound before they left, but Chilali wanted no more discussion. She rode ahead, quiet and intentionally putting distance between them.

Falcon rode beside her. He had something on his mind, and he felt now was the proper time to address it.

"Chilali."

"What is it?"

"It would be best if we do not tell Jerle about the other part of the emperor's bargain."

"What do you mean?"

"She shouldn't be told the emperor will spare both Alden and Agraven if you return to the forest."

"You and Roche know."

"Roche is a more logical woman. And while she cares for Alden, she holds the Empire higher in her heart. I cannot say the same for Jerle and Agraven. If we tell her, she can refuse to guide us to the settlement."

"But then she would lose Agraven."

"And you and I would lose Agraven and Alden. Consider it this way. This settlement needs to be destroyed to preserve the Empire. It is in everyone's best interest to win this battle. So, we should do whatever it takes to secure victory, even if it means withholding information from Jerle."

"I won't tell her then."

"Good, that will be best. Trust me."

Jerle's plantation came into sight as the Embracing

Night's black enmity began to engulf the Fire King. And still Sitara's light twinkled brightly, and Falcon was glad for it. He always held a sense of amazement in his heart that the little light in the sky was his goddess, looking down on him, protecting him, and loving him. He could always look up to see her and feel her. Her light was warm, and her power enwrapped his soul with serenity and security. In this life, he was never alone.

A pair of overseers on horseback led chains of Briam to their pointy tents, where spiced meat cooked over open fires. An extra reward before the harvest season ended, Falcon thought. Another overseer, weary from the day's work, saw them and stopped. The straw he chewed fell from his mouth. The shock of their appearance could not be helped, Falcon knew.

"We're friends of Jerle. Is she home?" the knight called out with a wave.

The sky turned a soft amber with ridges of periwinkle clouds flowing out from a crest of vivid navy on the horizon. Chilali cared not for the spectacle, as she picked out Jerle amongst a handful of Talarians tending a garden at the rear of the mansion.

Chilali pointed for the benefit of Falcon.

"She's over there."

Falcon nodded in affirmation, just as the overseer kicked his horse into a gallop and rode to Jerle. The fire wielder stood and dusted herself off upon the overseer's approach. She stared at them across an empty field and ran toward them, sensing something was wrong. And clearly something was, as Agraven was not among them.

Chilali climbed off her mount and walked the rest of the way. Her forearm throbbed, but she ignored the pain. The numbness in her fingers was steadily fading.

Jerle stopped well short of them, surprised by Chilali's appearance. There was no ribbon this time to offer a false sense of security. Her hands bunched up the dirty apron she wore, and her toes curled into the warm dirt of the road. A breeze blew through her hair, causing a few loose strands to wave across her face.

"Chilali? Falcon? Why have you come? Where are Agraven and Alden?"

Falcon climbed off his mount and stood by Chilali's side.

"The emperor holds Agraven and Alden," the knight said.

"Holds them? Why?"

"I am uncalled," Chilali stated flatly.

"I don't understand."

"The emperor was dismayed by Alden's recent actions and ordered Chilali to kill him. She refused, thankfully, I admit. But the result was the striking of a bargain. To save Alden and Agraven from execution, Chilali must go and clear the Blackland Nation settlement, the one you scouted."

"What? That can't be? How could he ask that of her? And how can he ransom Agraven like that?"

Falcon shook his head. She knew the answer, even if she didn't want to accept it. The emperor's word was law.

"Olin and I … It was our duty to report the truth of our experiences with Chilali. The emperor likely justifies holding Agraven for the crimes you committed in Orsa."

"He can't hold Agraven for my crimes!?"

"Agraven will be executed alongside Alden if we are not successful …"

Jerle felt like she suddenly stood on a teetering stack of crates. The whole world wobbled, and she thought she would be sick, as fear filled her gut. She kept her composure the only way she knew how, by becoming angry.

Falcon looked away and down at Chilali. Jerle's eyes narrowed on them both.

"There is something you aren't telling me," she

charged.

Chilali shut her eyes and lied.

"That is all."

Jerle stood stunned, her hand coming to her abdomen.

"We have an army and a Ragebourne and me," Chilali exclaimed. "I'll destroy them, and the emperor will let Alden and Agraven go."

She turned to Chilali, regarding the Divergent for a moment.

"You've never fought in such a battle before and have no concept of the danger. The warriors of the Blackland Nation are fierce and cunning. And, I assume, I will be the one to guide you to the settlement," Jerle spoke with breathless words, not wanting to single out Chilali for her misplaced wrath, but not being able to stop. Her life was much simpler before the Divergent was taken from the forest.

"I'll protect you," Falcon tried to soothe.

Beriszl brought Minnie forward, holding the girl's comparatively tiny hand.

Jerle's eyes drifted to the girl, and she already surmised the servant's story. This one, another one, was Chilali's doing.

"Who is she?"

"She is Minnie, a Talarian from Alden's home. Roche wouldn't let her stay there anymore, so I brought her to you," Chilali explained.

Jerle bit her bottom lip, but it wasn't enough to keep her thoughts to herself.

"No, she can't stay here."

"Is there some sort of problem?" Falcon asked, confused.

Jerle turned on Chilali.

"No, there is no problem. I only want Chilali to know what it is like to take someone you care about into battle, so she will learn something of vulnerability."

"You can't be serious?" Falcon questioned.

"I am," Jerle shouted. "She goes with us, or I will not go at all. Agraven would not blame me. After leaving the guild we vowed we would never serve as mercenaries for the Empire to fight in its wars."

"You're lying," Chilali said.

"Test me then," Jerle challenged.

Chilali looked at Minnie, who trembled with uncertainty.

"Minnie will come with us," Chilali resigned, realizing it would be in her interests to supplicate the fire element user. It was the same rationale Falcon imparted to her. They needed Jerle to find the settlement.

Falcon moved between them.

"Jerle, please, this is not necessary."

"It is, Falcon. It is. And you must ask yourself if you want my help or not. I assume the emperor only gave you so much time to complete this task."

"We've little less than thirty days."

Jerle's eyes widened at the number, betraying some of her own fear, Chilali realized. The time they were given to accomplish this task never concerned the Divergent before now. These people moved much more slowly than she. If Jerle seemed worried, then she should be concerned, as well.

"At least lend us another Talarian to look after the girl. We won't be able to spare Beriszl to always see to her wellbeing," Falcon said.

Jerle looked at Minnie and nodded. She was making it all up as she went along, trying to recover from saying something she didn't intend. She had no true desire to torment Chilali or the servant girl; she just needed a direction in which to vent her frustration.

"We'll take Astra with us. She knows how to ride, is capable with a bow, I discovered, and would be the most appropriate choice," she suggested, hoping this would possibly allow her to wash her hands of both Talarians in time.

Jerle took her apron off and slung it over her shoulder.

"Where is your army?" she asked Chilali.

"They're going to meet us tomorrow in Orsa. We've five hundred men, most from various noble houses and Olin at our side," Falcon answered.

"I see. Let's go inside then and have a meal."

Jerle walked past Chilali, glaring at the Divergent. Chilali anticipated the fire elemental user would be upset, but this felt different. It felt real, like it came from deep within Jerle. Would this animosity ever go away, Chilali found herself wondering as she followed Jerle and Falcon inside.

Beriszl placed his hand lightly on Minnie's head to reassure her and led her to the house. The old Ragebourne witnessed their divisiveness the entire trip, but experienced enough in his considerable lifetime to know these broken relationships would reconstitute themselves the moment they all engaged a mutual enemy.

His only hopes for the future were for Chilali's success, Minnie's safety, and his own death, the only honorable way to bring an end to a lifetime of slavery. This Divergent was more special than Strife, he had told himself the moment he saw her. Aimon sensed the same but was not ready to admit it. Despite their nature, Ragebourne enjoyed calm and stability and possessed a six-sense of sorts when it came to forecasting disruption. And Chilali, like Strife, made the tops of his feet itch, a sure signal she would bring chaos into this world. And this world needed such chaos if his people were to survive through the next generation.

He gave Minnie a toothy grin. The Talarian was just an innocent. But she was of the kind cursed with the terrible fate of becoming a motivation for someone else. Her life would end tragically; Beriszl believed this. It was the reason why he willingly carried her so far and would continue to do so. His second heart fluttered at the thought.

Strife's Journal: 252nd Day, 4056, Blackland Mountains

The mountains are quiet and still. Low hanging clouds bunch and swirl around the peaks.

The head of the Order of Sitara, the Magus, gave this journal to me. He told me to detail my thoughts and observations, explaining they would have value to future generations.

I find this difficult to believe. I was called by the Silver Goddess to save mankind from the Lessers, not to scribble idle notes. But perhaps these notes could offer some tactical value to others. This will be my first entry.

Right now, our best tactic seems to be hiding in these mountains. Men, survivors trickle in, but we've yet to amass a large enough force to even think of making an attempt to retake the capital. Each day we delay gives the Lessers, mainly the Talarians and Ragebourne, that much more time to restore defenses and build a supply base.

I think to go alone and perhaps conduct quick hit-and-run raids at night. I could target their provisions and reduce their stocks before winter. We must weaken them.

General Aiden thinks otherwise, however. He and the Magus tell me to be patient. They hold to the belief warriors from the Blackland Nation will push through the north and arrive to assist us. But even if this is the case, I do not think it wise to invite them into our land, even if they are brothers, even if they have had far more success than us at purging the Lessers from their lands.

The mountains are too quiet and still.

—Divergent Strife Ashwake

One More Night

Falcon adjusted the angle of his spreading knife so its tip would better align with his spoon. His silverware representation of the wall being constructed around the Blackland settlement drew Jerle's scrutiny. She sipped wine from her goblet before pointing to a pair of black berries placed just inside the imaginary joint shared between the spoon and knife. She rolled the berries further apart from each other with her fingertip.

"The towers were spaced more apart, but the wall was still being constructed. It was only half a man high in most places when we first scouted it."

Falcon rubbed his chin.

"If they have made any significant progress toward finishing this wall, we may be substantially delayed."

Jerle shook her head and popped one of the black berries into her mouth. She squished it slowly between her molars.

"We've also no real idea how many men the settlement has for defense."

Chilali smacked the juicy, but tough, spiced meat as she chewed. Light colored with dark skin and still attached to the bone, she savored every bite, while making a mess at the table. Jerle and Falcon frowned at the Divergent, which drew a chuckle from the silent Ragebourne sitting at end of the lengthy dinner table.

Falcon shook his head and focused on the matter at hand.

"We need more information."

"Water will also be a problem for us with so many men. The nearest supply Agraven and I were able to find was days away in the Southern Wilds, excluding the mountain peaks. The Fire King parches the whole area."

"You were not able to discern their water source?"

"No, so even if we chase them from the settlement, we

won't be able to hold it."

"The emperor didn't order us to hold the settlement."

Jerle glanced at Chilali.

"But Medwin was promised mining rights for his assistance. His men will not be pleased if we leave the mine."

"I anticipate the whole matter will be resolved with violence, even if there was a water source."

"That is likely true, but it still doesn't resolve our primary problem: how do we attack them?"

Beriszl coughed politely to get Jerle's and Falcon's attention.

"Do you have a suggestion, Ragebourne?" Jerle asked, incredulously.

Beriszl hoisted himself out of his seat, pressing with his massive hands against the table to rise, but without even leaving the slightest scratch on the finely varnished wood behind. He sauntered to the knight and the fire elemental user, while wiping the corners of his jowls clean with a cloth napkin. Fascinated, Chilali watched him take a seat next to Falcon. He made the knight look like a boy, sitting next to him at the table.

"We must not expose our numbers or assault the settlement, itself," the Ragebourne explained. "We would be best served with several quick attacks against their towers."

"The guards in the towers will see us and alert the others," Falcon sighed.

"Not at night," the Ragebourne returned.

"The night is a perilous time for men."

"So it is, but not for me and not for her," the Ragebourne motioned with his snout at Chilali. "Together, we can scale the towers, attack, and escape."

"To what end? In hopes of drawing out search parties to ambush?"

"Perhaps, but also to reduce their numbers and gain

information on the settlement without exposing our main force. More so, we should seek to wound and not kill those in the towers to tire their healers. And if these towers are as you describe, I can destroy them."

"And you think they will sit idle while you strike at them over and over? That they will not track you back to our camp, exposing our numbers and location?"

Beriszl let out a rasping chuckle.

"Chilali and I are too fast. At night we can come and go as we choose, and they will not be able to stay with us. If they try to track us, we can lead them away or attack their trackers."

"It is a sound suggestion, albeit one component of a larger plan."

"Thank you," the Ragebourne said with a slight nod of his head before getting up and leaving the dining room with its paintings of various locations in the capital. One of them, a colorful depiction of the fountain on top of Alden's manor caught his eye on the way out of the room. He mocked himself for feeling nostalgic. Even though he would own nothing but his memories in the remainder of his life, he still wished he could keep that painting as a reminder of the fountain, a symbol of a distant time.

Chilali tried to slink away from the table and drew Falcon's ire.

"Where do you think you are going? You've a battle to plan with us."

She cocked her head in reaction, half-sitting in the heavy wood chair, her face spattered with food. She grabbed her cloth napkin and wiped her face mostly clean before responding.

"I like what Beriszl said. He and I can attack their towers."

Falcon shook his head.

"We will need to do more than that, especially if the settlement holds significant numbers."

Chilali shrugged.

"We don't know how many men they have," the Divergent returned as a matter of fact.

Raife strutted into the room wearing a loose shirt revealing his chest and a black tattoo of a fiery bird over his left breast. He paused for a moment, struck by Chilali's presence and shook his shock away. He took the seat next to Falcon without a word, revealing his smaller frame by comparison to the knight. His scent was strong with that of a Talarian. Chilali had yet to learn how to distinguish between them reliably, however.

Jerle rolled her eyes at him.

"Good of you to join us."

The young man's wry grin faded.

"What is this I hear of my brother being executed?"

Jerle sighed.

"It's simple. The emperor will execute Alden and Agraven if we do not clear the Blackland Nation settlement in the south."

"If that is the case then count on my blade."

Falcon regarded the cocky young man. He heard stories of Raife's skill and talent during the day-to-day skirmishes that plagued the North, as well as tales of the young man's recklessness and inability to follow orders exactly as intended. He also showed no interest in pursuing knighthood, which relegated him to being a low militiaman, a position that did not reflect his ability. But Raife seemed fearless to Falcon, arrogantly so, which contrasted with Chilali, who was fearless because of her heritage. Falcon admired that and would not pass up such a skilled fighter or the chance to push Raife toward more noble pursuits.

"So, we will. I would have you guard Jerle at all times."

"His presence does not make me feel any safer," Jerle remarked, luring Raife's grin back out into the open.

"But will this not mean the end of the truce we've established with the Blackland Nation?"

Falcon expected this question. While he understood the truce was likely a ploy by the Blackland Nation to purchase time to secretly establish itself in the south, Alden's theory, the Empire sought to honor its agreements, always. The emperor was wise, and his plotting was to be commended. If a rogue army of noble soldiers led by an uncalled Divergent, an unknown True Silver Knight, and a local Sitaran priest were to attack the Blackland Nation, it would not technically constitute a breach of the truce agreement.

"No, it won't."

"Then I am relieved I won't be responsible for starting a new war," Raife laughed before filling a goblet with wine.

Chilali sighed.

"I'm going."

"And the battle plan?" Falcon was quick to ask.

"Kill them. I'm going to find Beriszl."

Falcon gave her a curt nod, one that failed to hide his frustration with her, and she left the table without any concern. Both he and Jerle had been sharp with her since reaching the mansion and sitting down to eat. A part of her definitely wanted to lash back at them, especially Jerle for making them take Minnie along, but she restrained herself. She needed them to save Alden. She didn't have to explain herself to them or ask their permission for anything. She hated the fact they even thought she should, which is why she lied, a skill she was steadily developing. No, she was not going to find Beriszl. She had to satisfy her curiosity.

The Briam ate and gathered in their tent city, and she would see them and how they lived. In the capital, they traveled in small groups, usually carrying goods or nobles up and down the streets. Here they behaved differently. She would know why. She also enjoyed being away from the capital and its populace. The air was so much fresher without them and their waste and would be even more so outside the mansion.

She slipped out the backdoor in the kitchen, passing a

group of five Talarians on the way. Her presence startled them and sent them away from their duties and whispering amongst themselves. They were unaware she could hear their words clearly, but she didn't understand them all. Together, they spoke in a mix of Talarian, she assumed, and the tongue of the Silver Sun Empire. Still, she was able to glean they were afraid of her and feared what she might do. This was obvious by just their reaction alone. The one thing that caught Chilali's attention and one of the few things she understood was the mention of Astra spending much time in Raife's bedroom.

From outside, where the only light came from the night sky and the candles in the mansion, Chilali picked out Raife's room on the third floor at the corner of the building. She caught a glimpse of Astra through the crack in the curtains. Even to her eyes it was more shadow than substance, but it was enough to spur her into leaping between the three balcony tiers. She needed the activity anyway.

Outside and low to the floor on her hands and feet, she peered into the slit of light where the curtains parted. Astra, her bruises healing and appearing to be little more than sooty smudges, cleaned herself in a wash tub. She wore a short robe and scrubbed a limb at a time with a wet washcloth. Chilali distinctly heard her sniffling and she believed she could taste the Talarian's tears in the air, even though a draft blew into the room. Despite the heat from earlier in the day, the night air was cool and crisp.

Not hearing anyone else on the floor, she slipped inside as quietly as only she could and stood before Astra a fair length of time before the Talarian even realized the Divergent was there. The washcloth splashed into the bucket as Astra's hands covered her own mouth.

This close to Astra, even with the scrubbing, she could smell Raife's scent on the Talarian's skin and the other aromas similar to what she captured the night she found

Agraven and a Talarian sleeping at the top of the Vineyard. Her reaction became one of disappointment and was evident in her body language by the way her shoulders slumped a bit and she looked down and away from the Talarian. Yet, she didn't understand her own reaction; she merely felt it, because Astra felt it.

Those soft, slender hands covering Astra's mouth curled into fists as if she were trying to force the cries back down her throat. Her tears flowed more freely then, and she collapsed to her knees in the tub.

Chilali went to her, forcing herself to smile. Astra was too distant to care about the Divergent's proximity, even as Chilali reached into the tub to take the washcloth. She squeezed the water from the rag with such force it seemed as if it went dry between her hands. With careful effort, she brushed Astra's tears away with the cloth.

Astra stared at the Divergent for a moment, daring to peer into the wild depths of those emerald eyes where murder always lurked in an attempt to find where this apparent sympathy sprang. Chilali returned the stare, catching her tiny reflections in the Talarian's sparkling silver irises and little else.

"Do you know why I cry?" Astra asked in less than a whisper.

Chilali sat on her heels.

"No."

"Then why do you wipe them away?"

"Because, you wouldn't."

The sound of soft-soled boots crossing the floor alerted Chilali to the fact she needed to leave. Before Astra could take another breath to even speak a word, the Divergent was gone into the night, the balcony door shutting with just enough momentum to close quietly. Raife entered the room wearing his characteristic grin. He slid the bolt closed and went to his Talarian. She was young, maybe too young, and was at least a head shorter than him, but he wanted that. It made him feel more powerful, more dominant over her. Her skin still wet, it glistened in the candlelight as she stood up in the tub in her damp robe. With one hand, he teased open the robe and with the other, he wound her hair around his fist.

Astra decided then she would endure another night with the young man and possibly many more, where moments before she hoped to discover a way to drown herself in the washtub. She learned something from the Divergent and was grateful for it, even more so when Raife's weight on her back felt like it would suffocate her.

* * *

The fields had thinned with the harvest. Chilali moved low and between the stalks and their emptied pods. Hot smoke drifted low like fog from the systematic burning of some of the used crops. But Chilali found the sharp aroma to be pleasant, like a mix of dusty, rich soil, grain, and soot. The soil itself radiated consoling warmth, still heated from the Fire King. Chilali grabbed handfuls of the dirt as she crawled, just to squeeze it between her fingers and feel its grit and moisture.

She hid herself well at the edge of the Briam camp, lying on her belly and peeping at them from beneath the stalks. Much of the earlier activity she witnessed was gone, but some milled about, going between the numerous conical tents. Smoke ribbons curled out of the tops of the tents, and she could pick out the tasty odor of the spiced meat. Her mouth watered with memories of dinner.

She wrenched herself around to look behind her, just barely hearing the sound of rustling stalks, but she couldn't smell anything. The wind blew away from her. But the black form standing shoulders above the stalks was unmistakable. Beriszl called out to her, revealing both of them to the Briam, who peered into the darkness with curiosity and alarm.

"Chilali, where are you?"

Chilali sighed and stood, not bothering to brush herself off. She moved to Beriszl, wondering what the Ragebourne wanted and hoping Falcon had not sent Beriszl to bring her back. She saw Beriszl squinting to see her, which surprised her. Even under the overcast night sky, she was able to see fairly well with just the firelights from the mansion and the Briam camp.

"Are you here? I cannot see you."

Once she got closer, she saw the Ragebourne's shoulders rise and fall with relief. Meanwhile, all the Briam had gone into their tents, afraid perhaps. She wasn't sure; she was too far away.

"Why are you crawling around in the fields?" the Ragebourne asked with genuine confusion.

"I wanted to watch the Briam."

He nodded with more motion than a man, which made the action appear exaggerated.

"They are the most simple of peoples. Left alone, they become feral, bigger, and stronger. Very dangerous."

She shrugged and moved past the Ragebourne, ducking empty pods along the way. Beriszl turned to go after her.

"Wait a moment, I would speak with you."

She stopped and looked at the Ragebourne, waiting.

"Do you think ill of Jerle?"

"Do I think ill of her?"

"Yes, are you angry with her over her decision to force Minnie to come along with us?"

Chilali halved a stalk with a slice of her hand.

"Yes."

"But you must realize now why she does it. Yes?"

Chilali hewed another stalk.

"She wants me to know what it is like to go into battle with someone I care about."

"But she lies, for your benefit, perhaps, and for

Minnie's and Astra's."

She tried to take down one more stalk, but Beriszl caught her hand, completely encasing it with his own. His swiftness shocked her, as did the strength of his grip. So surprised she was, it took a moment for her to feel the anxiety welling inside her again. She jerked her hand free.

She stared at the Ragebourne, furious with him for grabbing her, stopping her. But Beriszl remained calm.

"Destroy only the deserving, Chilali. This is good advice, I think."

She wound his words through her mind and took note of the fallen stalks. Beriszl squatted, bringing his head below the stalks and stretching out his arms to keep balanced on his toes. Now both were hidden among the fields, isolated in their own private, dark world.

"Jerle brings Minnie and Astra to protect them from Raife, as much as she can."

"Protect them?" she asked, her brow wrinkled.

"You smelled the Talarian's scent on the boy, did you not?"

She nodded in reply, unsure of where this was going.

"So, you understand then?"

Chilali returned a blank stare.

"I see. So you do not know of such things and what they mean. You are still an innocent."

"Innocent," she had never been called such a thing and, truthfully, she didn't completely understand the meaning of the word. In the past, when encountering words and phrases she didn't understand, she relied on her reading of the speaker's body language, scent, and the overall context to make sense of the word, as well as the comparative usage. But this was different. She needed to understand what the Ragebourne meant.

"What does 'innocent' mean?"

Beriszl nodded his head knowingly.

"One who knows not evil."

"And evil?"

Beriszl chuckled.

"If I were to tell you, you would no longer be an innocent."

"Tell me."

Beriszl waved his hand across her entire field of vision, dismissing her demand.

"You will know it in time. Just believe Jerle wishes to protect Astra and Minnie and bear no grudge against her."

She sighed.

"I will try."

"What do you want in this life?" the Ragebourne asked, leaning forward on his knuckles and bent arms.

She returned a blank stare. Beriszl scratched the tops of his feet.

"Do you intend to serve the Empire, become its champion, as Strife did?"

"No."

"Then what do you intend?"

"To save Alden."

"Beyond that."

"Kill Shank."

The answer surprised the wise Ragebourne. He made note of it.

"And beyond that?"

"Find my mother."

"Your mother? Do not Divergents mothers abandon their daughters?"

"She left me alone in the forest."

"So, you will return to the forest?"

"No, she's outside the forest."

"Why do you think that?"

Chilali shrugged.

"Why do you care for Talarians?"

Her brow wrinkled at the question.

"Care for them?"

"Aimon told me you protected Minnie from the boy. And I was told the story about how Astra came to live here."

"I didn't like how they were treated. It reminded me of what Shank would do in the forest."

"You watched Shank kill the children?"

"I didn't like it. He wouldn't just eat them. He kept scaring them and hurting them. I had never seen a Ragebourne or a girl before. I didn't understand. I thought they were strong like me. I didn't know until Alden came. He spoke like my mother spoke and I could understand him. I listened to him talk to the others about Saveria. I watched him have nightmares and become sick at the smell of the strange meat Olin put down. He wanted to stop Shank. I tried to help. That's how I got trapped."

She explained all of this as she squatted down and wrapped her arms around her knees. Balancing on her toes she hid her face between her kneecaps.

Beriszl, absentminded, scribbled in the soil with one of his claws. This Divergent did know evil. She had seen it, tasted it, and felt it, but she had not recognized it for what it is. Her purity was refreshing and rare. The old Ragebourne witnessed none like it before, which meant a time would soon come when she would gain such understanding. And when she did, her rage would consume the kingdoms of man. The Silver Throne was destined to become a pile of cinders, seated by a blackened skeleton. Beriszl could feel this on the tops of his feet; they itched so exquisitely.

"Your situation is difficult. I would not trust your allies," he finally advised.

She raised her head to regard the Ragebourne.

"But like the Talarians and the Briam, I am just a slave. I am bound by my oath to serve the Empire, up to the loss of my own life. Then, I will be free. So, I care not whether I am betrayed or a betrayer."

With that, Beriszl lumbered back to the mansion, a

serene sadness in his pace. Chilali tipped backwards and rolled onto her back. The Ragebourne's parting words were a mystery to her, but the soft soil felt great. It was good, or maybe even better than the bed awaiting her in the mansion. She stared into the cloudy sky, picking out Sitara's diffused light and noting the approximate location of her star. Drowsiness followed with the drift of the clouds above.

* * *

Falcon stoked the logs, making them crackle and pop inside the circular hearth. He looked over his shoulder to see Jerle staring at the renewed flames.

"How quickly the chill comes with the night."

The pair listened to Beriszl's entrance with the subtle sound of clicking nails on the stone floor, the heavy, but soft footfalls on the staircase, and the creaking of the floorboards overhead. Jerle sighed and wrapped herself tightly in a worn shawl. She knelt before the fire on the black fur rug, the centerpiece of this room. Falcon chose to stand and circle the fireplace with its open sides and bronze flume.

"Earlier today, when you suggested Minnie be forced to come along with us. What was your true intent?"

Jerle lifted her chin and locked her jaw to look at the knight.

"Dipping into my thoughts, are we?"

Falcon shrugged and poked at the logs again, adjusted them into an even neater pile.

"True Silver Knights are not often gifted with such abilities. Mine is amateurish at best, but it is enough to recognize deceit."

"Is it?" Jerle asked incredulously.

"I am right about your intentions with the Talarian girl, aren't I?"

"I meant; does it help you expose your own deceits?"

Falcon stopped his methodical pacing and poking of the fire.

"Sitara is the light that exposes all that is hidden, but her guardians must keep their secrets to protect her chosen. And they must follow the law, the word of the emperor, no matter the sacrifices they must make to achieve victory. So yes, I've deceived you slightly, but only to carry out my mission and with the best of intentions."

Jerle stood, anger flickering in her eyes with the firelight.

"And how have you deceived me?"

"A truth for a truth then?"

"So be it."

"The emperor has no intention of sparing Agraven and Alden's lives, even if Chilali is successful."

Jerle heard the words, but it took a moment for her to force herself to completely comprehend them and their ramifications, as unpleasant as they were.

"What are you saying? Was that not the bargain?"

"I made my own bargain with the emperor. The Blackland Nation will be purged from our lands, yes, but there is another part. Chilali must be put down.

"Kill her? How could you!"

"The emperor and I agree, Chilali is uncalled and a danger to the Empire, but there is more. She is a danger to Alden. She has become his obsession and must be stopped. And she is a danger to Agraven, you, and many others. She cares not for our laws or values. She heeds not the emperor's words. She is wild and savage and must be stopped before she causes more harm."

Jerle looked away.

"You speak the truth? This is the only way Agraven will be spared?"

Falcon returned a grim stare and a solemn nod.

"After the battle is won or when victory is imminent and we no longer need her, then we will carry out the deed.

But I fear I will not be able to do it alone, swiftly and mercifully. I will need your help."

Jerle bit her bottom lip and stood, holding the shawl tightly around her.

"I need to think about this, Falcon. I can't just … I mean …"

The knight returned a slight but knowing smile.

"You have time to prepare yourself, but I urge you to examine the child and her actions in these coming days. I'm certain this will make your decision easier. But as for my question, why do you wish the Talarians to come with us?"

She turned her back to him.

"I wished to keep Raife away from them, but now that he is coming along, I don't know how possible it will be to do so."

"He is a young man. When he finds a woman worthy, such activities should cease."

"I hope so," she said before leaving the room.

Falcon prodded the fire, continuing to make it grow, even as stray cinders bit at his hand.

The Asael

Jerle rode next to Falcon at the head of the group on a spotted mare. Equipped in her usual road gear and a short sword hanging from her waist, she seemed more like the woman Chilali knew. Beriszl lumbered alongside her, quiet and avoiding eye contact. The Ragebourne balanced Minnie on his shoulder as he sliced up fruit and passed the slices to the little Talarian and occasionally to himself.

Raife rode behind them, towing Astra and her black mare. The young man appeared to nap, wearing a wide-brimmed hat low on his eyes and slumping in his saddle. Chilali knew better. Like Beriszl, he feigned his lazy, careless attitude.

Far into the horizon where even Chilali had to squint to see, multiple plumes of smoke billowed into the sky. She couldn't smell anything on the wind, though. It was still quite far away.

Riding in the middle of the group on the crisp morning, they all seemed to have lost themselves in thought. Chilali's voice snapped them out of their daze.

"I see smoke ahead."

Jerle waved it off.

"That's not unusual. You're likely just seeing cooking fires."

Falcon used his hand as a visor, as if it would help his vision come close to matching a Divergent's.

"I cannot see anything."

Beriszl licked his snout and squinted.

"I do not see anything, either."

Chilali pointed, frustrated.

"There are six, maybe seven trails of smoke."

Falcon rubbed his chin.

"Remain calm. Even if it is smoke, it does not mean anything unusual. Jerle is right. It could be coming from cooking fires."

Chilali didn't like that answer. Something about the smoke bothered her. Watching it, she knew something was wrong. Perhaps her instincts were that much better than Beriszl's. But her growing alarm was not to be attributed to paranoia or anxiety. Something ahead was dangerous and waiting for her. She made her decision.

"I'm going ahead."

"Going ahead where?" Jerle asked, confused.

"To Orsa."

"You shouldn't go alone as you are. You will frighten people. And you don't even know if the smoke is coming from Orsa. If you become lost, we may not be able to find you in a reasonable amount of time," the knight cautioned.

She dismounted and began sprinting ahead many times faster than their casual trot.

"Watch my horse," she called back.

Raife lifted his head.

"Should we send the Ragebourne after her? A man on a horse won't be able to catch her."

Falcon glanced back at Beriszl. The Ragebourne scratched his nose.

"I do not think I could catch up to her. She's very fast."

Falcon wiped his face.

"Well, let us pick up our own pace. The sooner we reach Orsa or can see these fires, the better. She's probably just witnessing some farmer burning part of his field."

"She didn't bring a weapon," the Ragebourne rasped.

"Yes, I left her equipment with Olin, but I do not think we have anything to fear. If the situation was an emergency, Sitara would make me aware of it," Falcon mused. "The promise of battle must be making her anxious."

"She's been behaving oddly since this morning," Jerle observed. "Do we know where she was during the night?"

Falcon shook his head and they both looked back at Beriszl.

"I left her in the fields." the Ragebourne offered.

"She was probably chasing rabbits and field mice," Raife joked.

* * *

The smoke on the horizon and its source became clearer as Chilali dashed toward it. The trails of smoke grew taller, and she could see there were at least twice as many as she believed. Her small legs whipped her down the dirt road, leaving a cloud of dust in her wake. She hadn't run so fast in such a long time. The drag from the wind pulling at her and tearing at her hair roared in her ears. Her heart beat with ferocity at her fervid pace and her breathes came fast and deep, but there was no fatigue. She could run like this for a very long time. If only she could have run like this when she chased her mother and failed to catch her, she lamented, then refocused her attention.

While the road winded and she zipped up and down hills, she never lost sight of the smoke until the source of it came into view. Orsa burned. All the buildings, even the Fieldman Inn, burgeoned with flames. Beams cracked and fell. One house collapsed under its own burning weight, tilting to one side before falling into itself. The smoke, hot and sharp, burned Chilali's disbelieving nose and carried the fetid scent of burning flesh, which she keenly remembered from the night she spied on Olin and Lea.

She slowed to a stop at the village's outskirts and hid amongst the foliage, low and to the ground. She needed a moment to comprehend the sight. Never since leaving the forest did she believe anything she had witnessed in the realm of man could be so quickly and effectively destroyed. Orsa would be there forever, as would Alden and the Empire, she assumed without ever really thinking it through. Her understanding of her current predicament, her bargain with the emperor, and the consequences for failure crystallized in the midst of a cloud of hot smoke and ash.

Lost in the moment, she still noticed a man unlike any she had seen before, dragging a middle-aged woman along by the hair toward the temple, which remained intact. This man was leaner than those of the Empire and his muscles were much more toned. His head was shaven more cleanly and smoothly than Olin's and he had no beard. His skin was dark like leather and marked with splotches of grayish blue. The whites of his eyes were not white but were colored blue-black. He wore a light suit of tight-fitting armor made of charred wood splints that covered his upper torso, exposing his stomach, his waist, and his upper thighs. His wrists and shins were bound in the same armor and all the pieces were overlaid with black metal rings. He hefted a double spear on his shoulder. The tips were made of the same black metal and were long enough and thick enough to be short swords on their own. Its middle was made of the same unusual obsidian wood with knots along its length.

Chilali marveled how a man would fight with such a weapon, but not that he was a man. His scent, while different, still belonged to a man. She also didn't have to make much of a leap of logic to know this man came from the Blackland Nation. And so, he would be her prey if she were to save Alden and Agraven.

She focused her attention on the temple as the man disappeared behind the walls with the woman. She discovered there were many inside its walled-in courtyard. She could barely make out their murmurs over the roar and crackle of the fires around her. The tree line did not reach the temple and there was much open ground to cover in daylight without being spotted, but with preternatural speed, she dashed to the wall at the rear of the temple and leaped on top of it. She crouched and didn't notice anyone below her. The temple blocked her view of the courtyard. She jumped on top of the stables and carefully managed her way across its thatched roof, feeling for the frame beneath the tightly bound straw.

She landed on the ground and kept low on her hands and feet. Another quick bound took her to the edge of the temple's roof, where she circled around its many domes until she could see the courtyard. Below and unaware, five men from the Blackland Nation kept guard over a handful of survivors. Marcus Fieldman numbered among them. He was the only man, and he covered his gut with a bloody hand. The rest were women, mothers, daughters, and grandmothers. Some showed bruises, scrapes, and burns, but none were seriously injured as far as Chilali could discern or cared to. They were all terrified, Marcus, too. Chilali didn't like the smell of fear and they reeked of it. As a group they outnumbered their captors more than two to one but were too weak to do anything but yield to these five men of the Blackland Nation and their odd weapons.

She compared them. All were bald and shaven. Their armors resembled each other's but had different patterns of rings and covered different amounts of skin. She took note of the fact the patterns of the blue-gray splotches varied among them, not just in shape and size, but in how much of their bodies they blotted. The one who bore the most was the one Chilali first saw. The others looked to him for direction. And his eyes were the only ones that were not white.

He pointed at Marcus with one end of his spear and spoke angrily at the youngest of the five.

"Why does his still breathe, Abdiel?"

Their language was the same as the one the men of the Empire spoke, but their accents were sharper and harder.

Abdiel's eyes dropped to the ground. He would not look at his leader.

"He bleeds from his stomach, Asael. I meant not to disobey."

Asael's eyes widened. His hand slapped down on the back of Abdiel's neck, forcing him into a standing slouch and an equally painful grimace as Asael's fingers pinched hard.

"I told you to deliver the killing blow. So, you will kill him with your blow. He will not die any other way. Now go."

Asael shoved Abdiel forward. The younger, smaller warrior righted his posture and stood before Marcus. He raised his spear with both hands and twirled it slowly with an upturned chin. The innkeeper stared up at him with clenched teeth and rage in his eyes. Even wounded as he was, Marcus managed a fierce visage. He was a son of the Empire and would do no less than die proudly with courage. But he would not die today; Chilali would not allow it.

She slammed into Abdiel's side with snake-strike speed. Her sudden presence rocked all, even Marcus, with irrational fright. Screams, even from the warriors, filled the air before anyone took any other action. But that gave Chilali more than enough time to squeeze her fingers through Abdiel's throat and leave him gurgling blood.

Asael was the first to act. His blades came at Chilali one after the other in what seemed like an unending rhythm. He whirled his spear around his body with such speed Chilali was both impressed and worried. During the first few rotations she took a handful of nicks and at least one deep slice across the bridge of her nose, which stung terribly and made her eyes water. She covered it reflexively with one hand and her reaction almost cost her an even deeper cut to her torso, but she squirmed out of the way.

Quickly, she pulled back to get some distance from Asael to reengage him with a better understanding of his abilities. He seemed to be able to hit her no matter how quickly she moved. But Asael had no intention of letting her recover. The other three men fell on her swiftly, running to surround her at Asael's silent direction. They moved her where they wanted her to go with coordinated combinations of swipes and pokes. Their movements were sped with the fear of death and their eyes were so wide and white they burned into Chilali's vision as she danced to avoid more wounds.

She was aware of their tactic to corral her and was frustrated by the fact she couldn't grab the spears as they came at her. Her hands were more than fast enough, but the blades were as long as her arms. If they were only as half as short, she wouldn't have had a problem, but the reality was when she overextended herself to try to grab one, she would take another nick or poke. Already she was bleeding from multiple, painful spots, including her underarms, the backs of her knees and ankles, and her stomach. And these wounds were making her that much slower, which began to provoke memories of her fight with Kern and the desperation she felt.

She could lose. These weaker things called men could kill her. The thought made her sick and burned her ego, but she finally learned the lesson experience was trying to teach her. Men were dangerous and not to be underestimated. If she could not handle just five of them, how did she ever believe she would be able to attack an army and succeed?

During the scuffle, Orsa's survivors tried to escape the courtyard, but were cut off by three more Blackland warriors, who forced them back. These new combatants were not a welcome sight for Chilali and even less so for Marcus and the others. The warriors beat them to the ground. The middle-aged woman Chilali first saw lost her top front teeth on the tip of one of their boots. And another warrior crunched Marcus' nose with the palm of his hand.

Chilali cursed her foolishness even more, as she continued to contort her body and dig into the ground with her hands and feet to spring about and avoid blows that would otherwise cleave her. She couldn't afford to let any degree of her attention wander to Orsa's survivors, as Asael joined the original four and they managed to cleanly encircle her. Refocused and more cautious, she readied herself for the new challenge even though she was still uncertain how to face the last one.

"Abdiels, draw back. I wish a word with this beast."

The four men who had been whittling away at her fell back a step but kept their weapons ready. And she had learned "Abdiel" was not a name, but some type of rank.

The Asael raised his spear at her and motioned to both her bloody hands with a waving motion.

"You wet your hands with the blood of our youngest and the voice of my god shrieks at you with outrage. I would have you know this before I kill you and take your eyes as trophies."

She sneered at him.

The Asael made eye contact with the four encircling her.

"The killing blow is mine. Shyamon commands it."

With those words, they came at her again with less immediacy, but more intelligence to their attacks. The result, however, was not what the warriors expected. To win against her they needed more speed and less strategy. Less speed meant a wider opening for her and limited their ability to execute any kind of coordinated defense in time. They continued as they had, but this time she ducked, dived, rolled to her side, and boosted herself beneath a stab by digging her fingers and toes into the earth for traction. Before the other warriors could react, she was on top of one of the Abdiels, tearing out his throat with a quick swipe.

The death enraged the other Abdiels, who madly pressed their attack, but lost their encircling flank. The Asael's displeasure with the break in formation did not escape Chilali, who scooped up the fallen warrior's spear with her slick red hands. She had no idea how to wield the weapon but could feel right away that swinging it without holding it exactly in the middle would greatly imbalance her. Thinking it would be more manageable if she broke it into pieces, she tried snapping the shaft, but wasn't strong enough, to her surprise. It bowed slightly and no further.

The warriors came at her, but she ran away, not with enough speed to outpace them, but enough to stay out of range. With no warning to her pursuers, she planted a foot, tossed the spear out to choke up on just one end, and came around with the weapon with such force, the spear warped into a crescent shape. The warriors coming after her were ill prepared for the attack and suffered debilitating cuts, deep and across their hips. The spear's blade dipped into the soft organs causing blood and waste to ooze. The four men of the Blackland Nation fell to the ground, screaming and clutching their wounds.

Chilali's victory did not come without a defeat, however. Swinging one end of the spear as quickly and recklessly as she did caused the other end to rake across her chest, cutting and peeling up a layer of skin. The inadvertent wound flooded her body with a dizzy weakness, and she let the spear fly out of her hands and embed in the courtyard wall.

The Asael recognized the extent of the injury and came at the Divergent, leaping over the bodies of his wounded subordinates. He whipped his spear around with a backward rotation of his body and came up with a powerful arch. Chilali flinched but pushed herself far enough to one side to only catch the tip of the spear vertically across her left elbow.

The voice of Shyamon screamed inside the Asael's head how to slay the Divergent. And he was able to anticipate the evasion and program it into his next movement, which shortened his grip on the other end of his spear. He pulled it out of the spin and jutted it out with lethal precision. His aim was for the Divergent's heart and Chilali could not avoid it. Her feet shuffled beneath her, begging the ground for traction, but receiving none.

The spear tip found Alden's amulet before it found Chilali's flesh and rolled off the gemstone to a target higher than the Asael intended. The black metal found Chilali's clavicle and slipped beneath the bone. The difference in their height caused the blade to pierce downward through the top of Chilali's lung and out her back. Her eyes widened in shock from the pain and a sharp yelp escaped her. She tried to scream more when the Asael twisted the spear, but burped out a mouthful of blood. The black blade's undulating edge worked to widen the wound inside and out, but the stabbing also shortened the length of the blade, allowing Chilali to grab the shaft in frantic reaction.

Weak though she was, she ripped the spear from the Asael's hands, pulling hard with her hips, and tore the blade free of herself with a slight turn. Her scream was little more than a bloody gurgle and she felt like she could not breathe no matter how much she tried or wanted to do so. The Asael, speckled in her blood, howled for her to die and came at her swinging. The voice in his head roared for her blood so loudly, he could no longer hear his own thoughts. His fists found their marks on the sides of her face, but they bled more than drew blood. A man's bones were brittle compared to a Divergent's and the Asael felt like he was trying to beat a stone to death, but he kept up his attempt to pummel the stunned Chilali with mangled hands. Shyamon would permit no less.

Chilali regained enough sense to stop her staggering. She countered by striking the Asael's knees with his own spear, taking him off his feet. The blow was not fatal. The Asael was too close for the blade, but the shaft worked well enough. He tried to catch himself with his hands, as he fell, but she struck his outward elbow, cracking it and dropping the warrior onto his cheek. Her next blow came down and hard on the back of his neck, leaving it concaved and swollen and the Asael dead.

Chilali let the spear go and turned her attention to the three remaining Abdiels. Despite her wounds, she still stood alive and as a Divergent, a creature of legend. So, they ran, unknowing how little fight remained in her. She wanted to chase them, to tear out their throats as she had done to the other two, but she couldn't. It was too hard to breathe and her whole body tingled. Blood ran down her stomach and thighs and soaked the inside of her boots. But the blood from the wound across her nose was already drying and partially obstructing her vision with its thick crusting. And some trickled out of her nose and into her mouth. She found herself swallowing more of it than she cared to.

She slumped to her knees, coughing blood and spittle, and determined to breathe through it all. Her wounds be damned. No one would come to help her, not one of the survivors. They kept their distance for the same reason her attackers fled. This disheartened her on one level, but she was glad none of them came to her and touched her. Hurting as she was, she had no doubt any who made that mistake would be killed.

A few of the women did manage to come over to kick and spit on the Abdiels, who were still in the process of suffering and dying from the wounds across their hips. Watching them, feeling terrible pains that would not abide and just trying to breathe, time seemed to slow and move faster. Each second was a new agony, but her mind became so detached and unfocused she couldn't remember the second before.

A time did come where the roar of battle cries of hundreds of men echoed off the courtyard walls and inside Chilali's throbbing head. The nauseating scent of hundreds of men caused her to vomit out the blood collecting in her stomach, leaving a cupric, acidic taste behind and irritating her chest wounds further. Despite the smell, Chilali felt some relief when the knights and mercenaries rushed into the courtyard, swords, shields, and maces at the ready. Her handiwork was obvious to them and most seemed genuinely impressed. The rest stood in quiet fright. The moment, however, didn't last long. She saw Olin hurrying toward her, passing Orsa's survivors without a glance and carrying an expression of exasperated concern on his face. She wished he would just go away, the last thought she would have before losing consciousness.

Strife's Journal: 260th Day, 4057, North Master's Enclave

Lightning continues to streak the sky and a light rain persists. The thunder is strangely mute.

Reinforcements from the Blackland Nation arrived, another 5,000 men, led by an Avidan and a pair of Asael's. They were the first such warriors I ever met. I knew only of their reputation through stories repeated in awe by my men.

"Avidan" means, "blade of god," and Asael mean, "warrior created by god."

The combat skills of those who hold the rank of Asael rival and potentially exceed that of our own True Silver Knights. They are the divine warriors of Father Night, and he whispers to them how to move and attack to kill. Combined with the fluid and deadly combat style of the double spear, I understand why Lesser and man alike seek to avoid combat with them.

While the Asael are strong, the Avidan represent the greatest warriors in all of the Blackland Nation. They not only hear Father Night's whispers, but they command an element that Father Night can direct them to use.

Still, I do not fear these warriors. They present the same weaknesses I see in their lower ranks and in elemental users.

First, their double-spear style is more dance than fighting. It has a rhythm that can be timed and countered if one can recognize and memorize the pattern. Few men are capable of this, but such rapid memorization comes easy for me.

Second, the more elemental power one uses, the more they must focus or risk succumbing to the Living Death. I can only speculate having a god whisper inside one's mind would be distracting.

Third, these men are so bonded to their tribe and nation they do not know how to fight for only themselves or trust only in their own ability to achieve victory.

Fourth, they rely far too much on their black metal. When faced with a foreign opponent, like myself, who also happens to be armed with a black metal weapon (a heavy two-handed sword) and possessed of many times their strength, even an Avidan will find himself overmatched quite quickly.

As the commander of the Blackland Nation reinforcements, the Avidan had a responsibility to see to it his men arrived on schedule. I thought it necessary to remind him of this fact.

—General Strife Ashwake

Orsa in Ruins

Falcon and Jerle forced their way through the small crowd of mercenaries and knights that gathered around the wagon at the edge of Orsa. Olin climbed out of the wagon, easing out from between the leather drapes. He wiped his nose on the back of his hand to avoid smearing anymore blood on his face. Blood seeped one sleeve of his robes and stained the rest in random spots. He squeezed the wet sleeve, wringing out a short red stream before recognizing Falcon and Jerle.

"How is she?" Falcon asked, staring at the blood puddle at Olin's feet.

"She will clean up well enough I'm sure, unlike these robes."

Falcon stepped around Olin to look inside the wagon, but Olin grabbed his shoulder and stopped them.

"For Sitara's sake, let her rest."

"You weren't able to heal her, priest?" Jerle asked, trying to peek inside.

Olin stepped away from the wagon.

"No, I tried, but she would not accept Sitara's light, even while unconscious. The degree of stubbornness … It does not matter. I bandaged her wounds, and she still breathes. It is a victory, I think."

Olin massaged the back of his bald head, covering it with blood.

"There are others who still need my attention."

"Go then, good priest. Know I dispatched Beriszl to track down the escaping Abdiels. He'll likely return with their heads before sundown."

Olin nodded and walked away. Falcon looked at the men standing around them and the wagon.

"What is it? Do you not have work to do?"

A mercenary Falcon recognized as being in Duke Erschwin's employ spoke up.

"If not for her my elder sister would be dead. I would thank her."

The man was of medium build and probably medium skill with the mace hanging at his waist. But there was sincerity in the wide features of his face and his slightly crooked nose. A red tattoo of an upside-down flaming sword marked the side of his thick neck, a symbol representing General Ashwake.

Falcon dismissed the man's gratitude.

"Chilali fights for the Empire, not your thanks. If you are truly grateful, go ready yourself for the battle to come."

Another man, this one a knight, stepped in front of the other men. Falcon didn't know this man, but the black carnation embossed on the upper right corner of breastplate signified he belonged to Lord Knight Thomlin. The fact he still had the small fingers on each of his hands meant he was not high-ranking. Thomlin had his truly elite sever these fingers to prove their loyalty to him. Any who refused was considered a traitor.

"Sir, is it true she killed five, an Asael among them, unarmed?"

Falcon looked over his shoulder at Jerle. The fire elemental user shrugged.

"That is the truth priest Olin has given to me," Falcon answered. "And it seems she has paid for the attempt."

"She is a Divergent, sir. She will recover."

Falcon slapped the man on the shoulder.

"Of course she will," he called out to those around him. "Now, enough of this vigil, we must prepare and establish a perimeter for the night."

With that the men left with reluctance in their stride. Jerle stood next to Falcon and spoke in a hushed voice.

"This is our fault."

"We didn't know."

"She could have been killed. An Asael was here!"

"I've already dispatched a messenger to the capital."

Jerle looked back at the wagon.

"She defeated an Asael, alone. That is something I would have liked to witness."

"I know, just as I had wished to see her battle with the vice-captain."

"That is not what I meant."

"You worry we won't be able to keep our bargain."

"An Asael, Falcon? Does that not frighten you? One such warrior could stand against our best and the one she slew was not alone."

Falcon let a slight smile escape.

"Do not worry. My friendship with Alden has taught me to do nothing without a plan and contingencies. Now, where is Raife?"

Jerle pointed across the smoldering village where a set of tents stood.

"Should we not leave someone to watch over Chilali?"

"I intend to task the Talarians with it, which is why I wish to find Raife."

Jerle crossed her arms and sighed before leading the knight to the tents. Men knocked down the blackened frames of buildings that had not yet collapsed while others dragged charred bodies out from the ruins. She knew a little more than two hundred people occupied the village but was unsure of how many were slain. The piles of the dead, stacks of horrifically contorted bodies, continued to grow in size. It seemed more than likely the handful of women Chilali saved would be all that remained, and Falcon had sent them to the capital with an escort. Orsa would be no more. The attack was a tragedy and caused such a severe wound none of them felt the pain yet, Jerle understood, but the pain would come, slow and inevitable, and herald a renewed blood rage.

Marcus Fieldman burst from the nearest tent, shirtless and holding his bandaged gut. He went straight to Falcon, tears welling.

"It's good to see you."

The burly innkeeper hugged the knight as best as he could manage with his wound.

"I don't care what they say, but it was right of you to care for that Divergent and bring her here. She saved my life, lots of lives."

Falcon glanced at Jerle and nodded his head in agreement.

"Yes, she did. The rest of us could not have made it to Orsa in time," the knight explained to Marcus, as well as Jerle.

Marcus nodded and wiped his eyes.

"She'll be up soon, won't she?"

Falcon laughed half-heartedly.

"She's had worse. Don't worry."

Raife ran toward them from the road leading out to the orchards. He called out to Falcon and Jerle, as he slowed to a stop and stood panting with his hands on his knees.

"We've a problem. The outlying plantations fell victim, too. The Briam herds are gathering together out of fear and the Talarians are hiding in the fields."

Falcon didn't have to think. He got the attention of the two nearest men, mercenaries.

"Take as many as you need and go round up the Briam and the Talarians, as far as the lake, and bring them here unharmed."

They looked at each other and then at Falcon.

"That's an order," the knight returned impatiently. "We don't have time to waste."

They both nodded without saying a word and hurried off to gather more men.

Raife moved closer to Falcon, Jerle, and Marcus.

"What do you plan to do? They are too many gathered together."

"Too many to take back to the capital for auction," Marcus added.

Falcon bit his bottom lip as he stared off into the distance, his expression becoming grim. Jerle figured out what he was thinking and called him on it.

"We're not going to slaughter them for our own convenience."

Raife avoided eye contact, but Marcus cleared his throat before speaking.

"Poison," the innkeeper offered quietly.

"No," Jerle returned.

"We've no choice. The amount of men we would need to leave behind to guard them and even keep them in the fields working to feed themselves …" Marcus trailed off.

"There must be another way."

Falcon looked at Jerle.

"Can you think of one?"

Jerle turned away, disgusted with the situation. She spat an answer back without thinking.

"We can take them with us."

"We don't have the supplies," Falcon sighed.

"We have plenty of Briam. They can carry more than what we will need," she returned, undeterred and bent on proving her rushed suggestion was the right one.

"And how do you propose we fight a battle with so many Lessers at our backs?"

"They won't be a problem for us. Once they see we're battling the Blackland Nation they will know their lives are at stake."

Falcon shook his head.

"Give me time to think about it and get a better idea of how many Lessers we would have to take with us."

Jerle smiled at Falcon and turned to Raife. She lost her smile just as quickly.

"Where are Astra and Minnie?"

Raife pointed over his shoulder with his thumb at the wood line.

"I tied them to a tree. They're fine."

"You are so fortunate Chilali is wounded," Jerle huffed and marched to the woods.

Falcon spoke quietly to Marcus and Raife.

"Raife, help Marcus ready the poison."

Raife scratched the back of his head and took Marcus by the arm.

"Let's go do some herb collecting."

Raife practically dragged the stumbling innkeeper behind him, leaving Falcon alone amidst the activity of the camp. Many thoughts tried to pull his mind into many different directions. The complexity of the task before him felt overwhelming, but he believed it was all a test, one given to him by the Silver Goddess. He vowed not to disappoint her.

* * *

Chilali woke, shaking. Something terrible happened to her, a nightmare she couldn't remember. And its effects, a cold sensation of powerlessness and vulnerability, still lingered. Only bandages clothed her and were tied neatly and tightly in pretty knots. She sat up and felt a wave of fire roll down her chest. She pressed her hand against the wounds until the pain eased. A new outfit lay on the bench to her side with her amulet resting on top. She took it and dressed as quickly as she could manage.

Outside the wagon, her army worked, each man going about some particular task, occasionally stopping to chat in groups as they dragged burnt bodies to one of the many piles. Others tended to horses or readied food supplies. The buildings, the homes, and shops that once lined Orsa's main road were burned out mounds. The brick structure of the Fieldman Inn stood like a sooty skeleton and Chilali could see the fireplace where she spent time recovering from the injuries she sustained from her battles with Shank. And here she was, again, injured and waiting to mend.

Her nose stuffed with dry blood; she couldn't pick up any scent but was grateful for it. Nausea still pinched the back of her neck, and she wasn't ready to absorb the odor storm around her.

The clamor of Talarians and the trumpeting of Briam caught her attention. Across the village, men on horseback herded many Lessers, more than she had ever seen gathered in a single place. Even though the Briam and Talarians were brought together, they kept themselves segregated. Their body language, the Talarians' in particular, indicated how fearful they were of their current situation. They moved pensively with uncertain steps. Their eyes kept to their sandaled feet, occasionally glancing around to see where they were.

Chilali spotted Falcon and Raife coming out of a tent. She went to them, beginning to draw much attention to herself. Some men saluted her, bringing one arm across their chests. She wasn't sure how to respond other than to acknowledge the gesture with a nod.

Falcon noticed the growing commotion on the other side of the village. He looked and found Chilali, as he expected. He touched Raife on the shoulder and together they went toward the Divergent.

"What is this?" Chilali asked, watching the Lessers being corralled into nearby fields.

"The Blackland warriors slew the owners and left the Lessers to wander on their own, a deliberate attempt to seed chaos in our lands. And there are hundreds."

"What will happen to them?"

"Jerle wants to take them with us and use the Briam to carry supplies, but I think their presence will slow us down too much. The Talarians are fragile creatures and will have difficulty keeping pace."

Something in Falcon's tone betrayed the true intent of his words. For an instant, Chilali saw the charismatic knight as something else, something dangerous and not to be trusted. It made her feel cold inside and shiver, which drew puzzled expressions from Raife and Falcon.

"You cannot be cold, the air here is stifling," Raife remarked.

Chilali glared at the young man then stared at Falcon. It occurred to her what he might be planning, but she wasn't certain.

"You want to kill them," she spoke, prepared to gauge his reaction to her words.

Falcon already committed himself to his plan, the Divergent be damned.

"Not all of them. We need to reduce their numbers by half. The rest we can take with us. I've spoken to the other commanders, and they agreed to divvy up the remaining Lessers, which would facilitate any possible mining or settlement plans."

"But they don't know about the scarcity of water in the area," Raife whispered with a wink, which only earned him a cowing stare from Falcon.

Chilali girded herself.

"I won't let you, Falcon. You shouldn't harm the undeserving."

Falcon wasn't fazed.

"Lessers are always deserving, Chilali. They persist at our mercy. You should learn to accept this, especially if you want to save Alden and Agraven's lives. For if we try to take so many Lessers south we will waste more time than we have and draw more attention to our movements from the Blackland Nation than we want. It is either them or Alden, Divergent. Which do you hold higher?"

Chilali balled her fists, trembling, but relaxed and turned away without another word. Falcon felt himself twitch at the thought she might attack him right there. Why she didn't, he wasn't sure. Fear had no place in his mind and neither did uncertainty. But she stirred both inside him. He would kill these Lessers not to be cruel, but to save

Alden and the Empire. Not even Alden would fault him for it.

Dusk neared, promising a clear sky and a bright night. Chilali didn't take peace from the thought. She clenched her teeth so tight her gums bled. She wanted to beat Falcon, bounce his head off her fists, but she held back, held onto reason. She needed his help and hated admitting the fact. She knew she was in no condition to fight. The stab wound through her torso and the slice across her chest were slowing her down far too much and it was hard enough to just stand and walk when breaths came so shallow. But in the back of her mind, she noticed that he flinched.

Ahead of her and behind a fern, Jerle sat on a log in a small clearing with Astra and Minnie. A fire, fueled with burning nuts and moss, burned hotly and with much gray smoke. Its sweet scent enticed Chilali to get closer to it, which gave her presence away to the trio.

Chilali immediately got the impression Jerle didn't want to see her. And Minnie and Astra were as apprehensive as ever. She kept her distance, too frustrated with everything else to let it sting her. Her wounds were doing enough of that already.

Heavy footfalls and cracking branches caught Chilali's attention. She tried to sniff the wind but couldn't get any air. Making matters worse was the fact her nose was too sore to even be picked and was darkened with a deep purple bruise. She caught sight of the visitor before Jerle, and the others even heard him approaching from behind.

Beriszl closed in on their little camp with bloody armor. He carried his helmet under one arm and leaned on the occasional tree as he walked. Chilali could see his left leg had a cut just above his knee. The bleeding stopped long ago, though.

Chilali pointed behind Jerle.

"Beriszl is coming."

Jerle stood and scanned the forest until she finally

picked out the Ragebourne. Beriszl waved lazily in response.

"I hope he was successful in chasing down the remaining Abdiels," Jerle offered. "He looks wounded."

"He has a cut on his leg," Chilali confirmed.

The Ragebourne made it to their camp and sat at the base of a tree. He leaned his head against the trunk and straightened out his wounded leg with a grunt. Jerle pulled some clean cloth from her pack and went to him. She tied the cloth around the wound, drawing a grimace from the Ragebourne.

"Will it heal?"

Beriszl nodded and asked for water with a dry rasp. Minnie brought a skin to him from Jerle's pack.

"Did you get them?" Jerle asked as Beriszl swallowed a squirt.

"All three."

"Where are their heads?"

"Too messy to carry," the Ragebourne chuckled.

Chilali stood closer to get a better look at the Ragebourne. His red eyes fell on her and were full of fatigue.

"You killed an Asael."

She shrugged.

"That is no small feat, Chilali. An Asael is to the Embracing Night what a True Silver Knight is to Sitara."

Chilali puzzled over that a moment. The Asael didn't seem to be that tough. He pushed her as far as Kern, if not a little further, but he had help. Kern didn't.

Beriszl guessed what she was thinking and pointed at her chest wounds.

"He almost hit your heart, almost killed you."

She touched the amulet, feeling the tiny groove the spear etched into the gemstone.

"Kern was stronger."

Beriszl chuckled.

"Strength is not necessarily strength. The Embracing Night gives the Asael vision of all around him. That's why his eyes were colored strangely. He can see all your weaknesses. He knows how to attack you. The Embracing Night tells such things."

"And all their warriors have black metal weapons, Chilali. The metal is lighter and harder than the silver metal we use, and it can be sharpened to such a deadly edge it will leave notches in a defending silver weapon or even cleave through your bones," Jerle added. "Fortunately, it is very hard to smith. Only a skilled fire elemental user can really work the metal."

Beriszl gripped the tree to climb to his feet. He took another squirt of water and passed the skin to Minnie.

"I must report to Falcon."

"I'll go with you," Jerle said. "Chilali can watch the Talarians for the night."

Astra and Minnie looked at Chilali, both chilled by the prospect a Divergent was now their owner. Chilali was oblivious to their concern. She watched the fire elemental user and Ragebourne walk back into the village or what remained of it and then turned her attention to Astra and Minnie. She could tell them about Falcon's plan and have them tell the others. It was a pleasing thought, but it could prevent her from getting to Blackland Nation settlement in time. She wasn't certain it would be worth the risk and took a moment to pick the dry blood from her nose to think it over. The Talarians winced at the sight.

Chilali pulled most of it out, despite the tearing pain it caused, and sniffed the air once. She made up her mind.

"Astra," she said, but the older Talarian just looked at her.

"Falcon intends to kill half of the Talarians and Briam. He said we can't take all of you with us, because you will slow us down too much and make it harder for us to hide from the Blackland Nation."

Minnie went still and Astra's mouth went agape. Her brow wrinkled in horror and her hands went to cover her mouth.

"Can your people keep up?"

Astra stared at her a long moment before nodding.

"Can they move quietly?"

She nodded again.

Chilali grinned at her next thought.

"Will they listen to you?"

"I don't know …" the Talarian finally spoke.

"They know you?"

"Yes, but I am young. We-we listen to our older sisters. They may hear what I say, but I've been gone for many days and have been kept from them even now."

"And the Briam?"

Minnie nodded, imitating one of their trunks with her arm.

Astra agreed.

"The Briam trust us. We look after each other."

Chilali straightened her posture with a yawn and a grimace. Searing pain arched across her chest, but she still managed a smile.

"Let's go talk to your sisters."

Astra stood and held Minnie's hand. Chilali took the most direct path across the village to the Talarians. They sat in two separate fields, huddled together in small groups. Men surrounded them, sitting on stumps, rocks, fences, or whatever would get them off their feet. The Briam were being kept in another pair of fields further down the road to the orchards. Falcon observed Marcus, who stirred a large cauldron of simmering stew, at the edge of the easternmost Talarian field. Sweat dripped down the innkeeper's face, clueing Chilali into the man's anxiety. A subtle odor hid within the aroma of the cooking stew. It was an odor familiar to Chilali, one she hadn't really noticed until she had been away from it for a time. It was of the red chutes that left dust on her forest's floor. Marcus must have added some of this dust to the stew and she knew enough of what it did to non-Divergents to realize Falcon planned to poison the Talarians.

The knight sensed the Divergent's approach and moved to intercept her.

"You should be resting."

She returned a murderous glare, her whole posture becoming wild and tense, throwing the knight off balance.

"Astra says they can keep up with us and hide from the Blackland Nation."

Falcon looked at the two Talarians standing behind Chilali. They both stared at the ground. The knight nodded in understanding.

"They are just trying to save the others. They will say anything."

"So will you to save Alden," she returned.

"Isn't that what we're both trying to do?"

"I don't want you to kill them."

"Why do you care so much!? They're Lessers! You're a Divergent! Sitara made you to kill them!"

Falcon words came out more harshly and loudly than he intended. He never lost his composure, but she drove him to do so.

Marcus stopped stirring the stew. The ladle trembled in his hand.

"Keep stirring, Marcus," the knight commanded. "This one has no answer for her motives, just irrational sympathy."

Chilali scooped up a rock from the ground with a motion so swift Falcon was barely able to follow it. The little piece of granite had a good weight to it and fit nicely in her hand. She could just about curl her fingers around the flat stone.

"I have a reason, Falcon. I'm stronger than you and I said so," she growled, less than a moment before side-arming the stone squarely at the stew pot. The concussion knocked the pot off the fire and onto the ground with a dull clang, causing Marcus to yelp and dance away from the scalding, poisonous stew, ladle still in hand.

"It's the same reason your people use," she finished.

Falcon reacted, absolutely infuriated by the temerity of Chilali's actions, by drawing his sword.

"You little-"

Falcon tried to take a swipe at Chilali, but she stepped back and out of the way with ease. Astra and Minnie fell to the ground, holding each other and hoping they would escape the knight's wrath. Falcon took another measured slash and Chilali, again, dodged it. He wasn't serious yet, Chilali knew. She wondered if he was just being cautious or if he was just that afraid of her. The worst was to come, she expected, but needed to make a stand, despite her injuries. More importantly, she wanted to make a stand.

Fortunately, Beriszl and Jerle came running, shouting at them to stop. Olin and Raife approached from another direction, echoing the same thing. Falcon, his face red, his breaths hard and heavy, forced himself to sheath his weapon. He pointed at her.

"If we fail, you will be the one to blame, Divergent, not I!" he roared and stomped off in the opposite direction, inconsolable for the moment. Even the others were shocked by the radical shift in the knight's demeanor. Chilali could only grin. She beat him and it felt good. Being in control in general in such an overt way was a new delight. She wondered why she hadn't exerted herself earlier and blamed her reliance on Falcon as the cause.

Her stand against Falcon effected a change inside of her and her way of thinking. It gave her a new insight into Alden and why she was so drawn to him in the forest. He was a leader of men and now she had a better understanding of what that meant.

"All of the Talarians are coming with us. Feed them

good food," Chilali barked to all those within earshot. The men manning the field were dumbstruck by her confrontation with Falcon and the knight's withdrawal, but her orders did not go unnoticed.

"Chilali-" Jerle tried to interject, but the Divergent glowered at Jerle, shutting the woman up in midsentence and gave her next direction to the priest.

"Olin, heal Beriszl's injury."

The priest drew back in revulsion.

"I cannot heal a Lesser."

Beriszl seemed sheepish about the prospect as well.

"I will be fine on my own in time."

"We won't have time. Heal him, Olin," she returned with an inarguable tone.

Olin gawked, but silently agreed with a lick of his lips. He took the Ragebourne by the wrist and led the uncertain beast away.

Raife moved to help Astra stand, but she didn't take his hand. Miffed, he grabbed the Talarian's wrist and pulled her to her feet, while leaving Minnie on the ground. The action, while happening in the background, did not go unnoticed by Chilali.

"Let Astra go and never touch her again," she dictated.

Raife returned a confused expression, as did Jerle.

"You cannot," the young man protested.

"Astra and Minnie are mine," she returned and took a step toward him. He backed away, one step wiser than before.

"As you wish," he stammered and backed away.

Jerle watched Raife slink away, stunned by the sudden change in Chilali's attitude, but she was also relieved. The Divergent saved dozens of Talarians and hundreds of Briam. Whether that would prove the correct decision or not on the battlefield was another matter. She also saved Astra and potentially Minnie from Raife. The fire elemental user began to wonder if she misjudged the Divergent, if she was too hard on her. A child and a stranger in this land, Chilali did not deserve to be a scapegoat for all of her frustrations. And most importantly, Falcon could have misjudged her, as well. Chilali did not act like a wild, dangerous beast. A beast would not pity a Lesser or risk its life to fend off enemies of unknown strength, unarmed, to save women and children.

Jerle's contemplation grinded to a stop; Lea entered the village with Teth leaning heavily on one of her shoulders. The disgusting growths covering the woman's face were just as Jerle remembered and she carried a bow on her other shoulder. The tails of many arrows bobbed side to side behind her head as the pair walked. A crude splint kept Teth's leg straight and a deep gash on the side of his face exposed the inside of his mouth. Others went to their aid, but Jerle couldn't move. She wasn't sure whether she should strike out that moment and burn the archer where she stood or take the time to think things through and confront her about Saveria's murder.

Chilali passed right in front of the pair, stopping for a moment, recognizing them. Their eyes fell on her, and their expressions bore both alarm and curiosity. The Divergent flashed a slight smile.

"You fought Shank," she said.

"Aye," Teth grunted.

"And you shot me with an arrow," she turned to Lea.

"I'm not apologizing," Lea returned. "You got in the way."

Chilali smirked at the comment and noticed Lea's scent. She had caught it before when the woman was at the temple with Olin, but she didn't recognize it for what it was. She cocked an eyebrow at Lea but said nothing of the woman being a Talarian in disguise.

"My face isn't getting any prettier, girl," Lea huffed, as she handed Teth off to some of the men who came to help. "You should stop staring."

The archer's eyes flitted to Minnie and Astra.

"Why do you have a couple Talarians following you around this carcass?"

Chilali disregarded the question and turned to Astra.

"Go tell the others."

Astra looked at Chilali confused, not by the meaning of Chilali's words, but by the autonomy the command gave her. Chilali waved her away.

"Tell them they must keep up and must be quiet."

Astra nodded and left with Minnie, drawing a befuddled look from the old archer. Jerle came up behind Chilali, her arms crossed, and her hip pushed out to one side. She strummed her fingers across her bicep with one hand.

"Lea," she said, her tone venomous. Chilali stepped aside a bit to better see the exchange.

"And a good day to you, sizzle crotch, but I don't see Agraven anywhere. Perhaps he's enjoying himself in a brothel?"

Jerle took an angry step forward and Lea took a frightened step back, one hand taking her bow from her shoulder and the other drawing and notching an arrow. Her actions were well practiced and very fluid and left Chilali wondering how quickly the woman would be able to draw her arrow back and release it.

Jerle bit her bottom lip. This was not the right time to do this. There were other enemies out there. And she wasn't even armed. Lea only needed the distance she already had to draw the arrow and fire it. She needed to escape from this situation, so she turned her head and looked at Chilali.

"You're supposed to stop us from fighting each other."

Chilali shrugged at her and continued on her way, leaving Lea and Jerle to each other. Jerle sighed and Lea relaxed her firing stance a little.

"This isn't over, yet, assassin," Jerle vowed and left.

Chilali intended to go back to the little fire in the woods and spend the night there. Tomorrow, they would march

again, and she needed rest more than ever. She hadn't ached
so much since being trapped by Shank in the forest.

But the night did not come without interruption. Several
men, soldiers in her army, visited her modest camp to give
thanks to her for saving the remaining Orsa villagers.
Others came to get a good look at the Divergent who
defeated an Asael. A few offered blankets and food from
their supplies or desired to share a drink of mead or wine
with her. She accepted it all until her belly bulged and her
head felt light enough to float from her shoulders. The
fellowship she received was a warrior's fellowship. As
feared and even respected as she was, conversation was
minimal, to the point, and exactly how she preferred to
speak.

By the middle of night, all quieted down, save for the
creatures in the woodlands and the crackles of campfires.
Astra and Minnie came to sleep near the fire, wrapped in
riding blankets, with Astra holding Minnie with the girl's
head just beneath her chin. Chilali sat and watched them
sleep with full bellies and some degree of peace. The site
comforted her and reinforced her belief she did the right
thing by forcing Falcon from his plan to poison the
Talarians, as the doubts, the fear of failure, did come in
those quiet hours before she fell asleep.

Peace Offering

Falcon found Chilali's little camp in the woodlands just off the edge of the village. A light fog clung to the ground and dew collected on fern leaves. Chilali appeared to sleep sitting up with her head resting on her knees and her back to a log. Across from her the Talarians held each other beneath riding blankets, well protected from the morning's chill.

The knight approached cautiously. It was not his intention to surprise the Divergent. He saw one of her emerald eyes open and leer at him without her raising her head. He held out the heavy, bulky leather pack he carried on his shoulder and spoke softly.

"A peace offering."

She stood, her stiff joints popping as she straightened and stretched. He handed her the pack, which was large enough to fit her inside of it, and she unfastened the ties. Her armor and sword were inside, but they were not quite what she expected. The armor had taken on a blackened polish and was not sparkling silver. The sword was finished much the same way, except for a finger's width at the edge, which was bright silver, almost like white light. And it appeared Hands etched the words, "Victory," "Sacrifice," and "Law," along the center length of both sides of the blade with austere calligraphy.

She looked up at the knight, genuinely appreciative, but wary. He motioned with his head for her to follow and she did. He brought her to the rear of the temple in front of the empty stables. He grabbed a wood beam and rested part of his weight on it before speaking.

"I must apologize. I spent the night meditating and realized Sitara would not have wanted the Lessers to be exterminated to aid our victory. It is not her way."

She didn't say anything in response and drew her sword from the pack to feel its weight again. Her chest aching, the blade felt heavier than she remembered, but it moved much more smoothly through the air than before. Falcon watched her wave it about, amused.

He pointed at the pack the Divergent left on the ground.

"You've seven pieces of armor, a hauberk, a fauld with tassets, a pair of bracers and greaves, and a helm. Gavin reduced the pieces, so they will provide only the most basic protection and will keep you from feeling restrained."

She flipped the sword around in her hand and forced its tip into the ground to make it stand on its own. The action dismayed Falcon, but he said nothing, as she dug through the pack, removing the armor pieces. He instructed Gavin to make the armor fasten on as simply as possible, so Chilali could do it herself. Gavin seemed to have succeeded, as the Divergent donned and strapped on each piece without much difficulty.

The armor consisted of plated segments over chain. The plates covered only the most vital areas, like the heart. The hauberk formed the only solid piece of the suit, a strong frame built around the shoulders and shoulder blades and running down the sternum. The back of which had the mounted clasps for Chilali's sword, which could be sheathed in the clasps at an angle across her back. The fauld, with its frayed chain skirt and short segmented tassets, covered her hips and much of her upper legs. The greaves strapped over her boots and climbed just above her knees. The bracers clasped on and covered from her wrists to just past the point of her elbows. Though the suit was simple in its design and bore little to no ornamentation, Gavin did a good job, the knight told himself.

The helm still lay on the ground and Chilali showed no interest in wearing it. He pointed to it.

"You're forgetting a piece."

She examined herself in the armor, moving her arms and twisting at her waist to see if the armor would impede her at all.

"I'm not wearing that."

Falcon grabbed the helm from the ground and looked at it. It was a simple open-faced helm, smooth all around and flared at its base. It would protect one's jaw line and the sides, top, and rear of one's head.

"A helm is the most important piece of armor one can wear," he argued.

She shrugged.

"It will get in the way."

"No, it won't."

She pulled her sword from the ground and shook the dirt from its tip. She reached overhead with it and searched to find the clasp. It would take some practice before she would get a sense of where it was exactly on her back. But the blade eventually slid in smoothly and its weight and a slight notch at its base kept it secure. Chill felt the weapon's weight shift slightly in her hand as the notch locked onto the edge of the clasp. To draw it, she would have to lift the blade slightly to free the notch, she figured.

Falcon stood there, holding the helm out to her. She just shook her head and walked away. The knight bit his bottom lip. His task just became more difficult because she refused to wear the helmet. And it was clear there would be no way to convince her otherwise.

Strife's Journal: 355th Day, 4058, Burning Sea

Humidity saturates everything and the constant steam from the Burning Sea drives my men to thirst.

The Talarians launched a desperate counterattack with the last of their remaining elemental user corps.

By Sitara, I'm still shaking. Damn them. Damn myself. I was reckless. I pushed myself too far. The Magus warned me of the power of the Time King's amulet. But it is more curse than power. Burns mark my body and I nearly lost my mind to the Fire King's prison. I pulled so much power I thought I would burn up inside. The Talarians who stood against me were no more before I was even aware of the fire I unleashed upon them. Their skeletons still stand!

Then the pull came, rising inside of me like a wretch of the deep. I felt it dragging me into the inferno. I felt myself slipping away from my own body even as I clawed and bit to stay. It was akin to being ripped in two or maybe, being peeled apart.

I still tremble.

The living death is a terrible fate. More than terrible. Indescribable. This war has seen many elemental users succumb to it. I look upon them all with much sympathy now. At least no elementals have been spawned. All living creatures should be thankful for this.

If I ever succumb to the living death ...

In that horrible moment when I almost lost myself forever, I felt the other mind, the hateful, spiteful, madly enraged mind of the Fire King.

By Sitara, let me never become an elemental. I fear some of him may have remained inside of me like a slow burning ember.

Morning will come soon, and I dread the sunrise, the Fire King's rise. I know his malice and I care not to look upon it. He knows my cowardice and insecurities and will mock me until Father Nights pushes him aside again.

—General Strife Ashwake

The Edge of the Abyss

Chilali found herself adjusting to the armor. It was lighter than she thought it would be and didn't seem to constrict her in any significant way. She had also been wearing it since dawn and hadn't felt any discomfort, even though it was well past midday.

She looked over her shoulder at the train of wagons, mercenaries and knights on horseback, Talarians, and Briam. Astra rode on top of her own mount with Minnie at the front of the Talarian line. The Talarians trudged, fatigued, but with an understanding their lives were at stake. Beriszl walked with them, too, and would occasionally carry one that needed a rest. But Chilali knew doing such a thing would eventually tire the Ragebourne, as well, even if his leg was completely healed.

At the rear of their line marched the Briam in a tail to trunk train, four wide and hundreds long. Together, they carried large sacks full of food, water, and other supplies. Falcon and Raife worried the extra food supplies would become rotten before they would be able to find more. Jerle seemed to think the Briam could persist on the nuts they collected from the orchards.

Chilali wished she could fall back from the front of the line and join Beriszl and the Lessers. They seemed more inviting than her current road companions. Falcon said nothing more to her since giving her the armor and sword. Jerle did all that she could to keep some distance between them. And neither Raife nor Olin was eager to be around her, because of the night before.

Only Teth would acknowledge her from time to time, mostly out of curiosity. But their exchanges were short. Other than that, he would bicker with Lea and occasionally ask Jerle about the area. Jerle explained they were still on the easiest part of the trip and were traveling across plains and hills with random thickets, but this would change to a dense, black forest with tall slender trees. In this forest, Wild Briam roamed. She and Agraven encountered them more than once and each time they had to fight for their lives.

Even though her understanding of the world outside the forest had matured and her situation was both serious and dire, she found herself hoping they would run across some of the Wild Briam. She was desperate to kill something with her new sword.

Jerle motioned towards the horizon, the black line rising to meet them. Chilali could make out the edge of a dark forest with rows of black trees with dark green leaves.

"Agraven and I believe this part of the forest was the thinnest and easiest to cross. It will take a few days to pass through, and when we do, we should come to parched plains littered with rocks at the base of the southern Blackland Mountain range. We will need all the water and food we can find in the forest. It will be a two- or three-day march across those plains just to reach the settlement," Jerle explained.

"As long as there are no Divergents hiding in this forest, I do not care," Lea hissed. Teth gave her a look like she was mad and immediately apologized on her behalf.

"She didn't mean it mi'lady."

Teth's use of "mi'lady" irked Chilali, even though she tried to hide this fact. He had been using it to address her since the start of the morning, though, and it was beginning to grate on her. Jerle and Falcon were well aware of this fact and shared a knowing grin.

"She's not going to eat you woodsman," Raife chuckled. "Try to relax."

Teth agreed with an inaudible mumble and scratched the bandage tied to the side of his face.

"Do not pick at your wound," Olin chastised. "I will finish healing it tonight if you do not make it worse."

Teth's shoulders sunk a bit.

"After we save Alden, I'm going to hunt Shank. Do you want to come with me, Teth?" Chilali asked while rubbing her eyes.

The old tracker didn't know how to take the question. He wiped the sides of his bearded lips and looked at Falcon and Olin for some guidance. They didn't know what to say either.

"One thing at a time, Chilali," Jerle said with a slight stutter and a sideways glance at Falcon.

The knight's shoulders bobbed once with a deep breath.

"It would be prudent to see what plans Alden has, first, and you will need approval from the Order to enter the, well, to bring others into the forest."

Chilali turned her head to Olin. The priest pinched the bridge of his nose.

"I would need to speak to the Order to obtain approval, but even with a Divergent at our side, convincing them could be difficult."

"I'm not going, so don't even ask," Lea chimed.

"No one was asking-" Teth tried to insult, but Falcon cut him off with a raised hand.

"We need not worry about this now, Chilali. Fall back and speak to Astra. Explain to her the Talarians and Briam must pull together tightly and not get separated when we enter the forest, else Wild Briam may run off with stragglers," the knight advised.

Chilali was not going to argue. He gave her the excuse she needed to leave the front of the line. She slipped off her horse without losing a step and handed the reins to Teth as the tracker passed her.

She received a few salutes and affirming nods as the men moved past her. Beriszl, Minnie, and Astra caught up to her and she matched their pace. The Talarians following behind Astra and being flanked by lines of mounted men, shrunk back a step from Chilali, practically backing the whole line up a step and frustrating the men overseeing them, who urged them forward with shouts.

Beriszl set a Talarian woman down and she darted behind him to get some distance between herself and Chilali.

"Her condition has improved," Beriszl chuckled and flicked the pommel of Chilali's sword with a claw, causing a "tink" sound. "You have a weapon now."

"And armor," she added. "Falcon had a smith in the capital make it for me."

"Falcon did? Not Alden?"

"Yes, Falcon."

Beriszl licked his chops and took his helmet off. He held it out to Chilali.

"You're missing a piece."

She withdrew from the helm with the same disgust an ordinary girl her age would withdraw from a snail. Beriszl laughed, again, with a rolling rasp. Minnie joined in the fun by clapping. Chilali turned her attention to her pair of Talarians.

"Astra, Falcon said the Talarians and the Briam need to stay as close together as they can when we're in the forest, so no one gets separated and taken by Wild Briam."

Astra looked over her shoulder at the Talarians walking directly behind her in their long, pale dresses and sandals. The tallest one gave Astra an affirming look and whispered to each of her sisters the instructions. They in turn passed the information down the line, Chilali assumed. But they spoke in Talarian, so while Chilali could hear it, she couldn't understand what they were saying.

Beriszl leaned in close to Chilali to whisper in her ear. She flinched in response and pulled away a bit.

"Prepare yourself. We will most certainly be attacked in this forest."

Chilali peered ahead but couldn't see much of the forest as the line curved slightly, blocking her vision.

"We can go and kill whatever will attack us."

"We should," the Ragebourne showed a toothy grin.

He picked up his pace, patting Minnie once on the head as he passed. Chilali followed, matching one of his strides with three or four of her own. They caught up to Falcon and the front of the line quickly.

"What is it?" the knight questioned.

"Beriszl thinks we will be attacked in the forest, so we're going to go kill whatever will attack us," Chilali answered.

"You want to take the point position, then, Beriszl," Falcon asked.

"With Chilali, yes."

Falcon looked to Jerle for confirmation.

"It's a straight shot through the forest," she said.

Falcon waved them forward.

"Do not lose sight of us," he told them, whether or not they heard, as they sprinted toward the dark forest was another matter. The two were locked in a friendly race, both pushing as hard as they could. Beriszl, not as fast of foot, stayed ahead with his much longer stride, the better traction the claws on his toes provided and the occasional boost from his long arms. Chilali ran hard with an even pace but didn't seem to tire. Both stopped at the edge of the black forest, excited by the unknown and what adversaries may lie in wait for them.

Inside the forest, the trees were the most distinguishing feature, exceptionally tall, thin, and jet. Their wiry branches exploded above in massive domes of deep-viridian leaves, the size and shape of fingers. Their collective canopy nearly blocked out all of the Fire King's light, while vegetation sparsely covered the floor, where a persistent fog swirled up to Chilali's waist. Lichen-covered rocks and boulders jutted from the soft looking ground, occasionally in crops, and water trickled down nearby rises and hills, flowing into one-stride-wide streams.

But there was more and Beriszl watched Chilali to see if

she would notice. The forest, while emanating the strong odor of vegetative decay, hid another odor, a sour one. Chilali looked at Beriszl, seeking an answer even though she hadn't asked the question.

"There are many hot springs here. That is what you smell," the Ragebourne answered, as he scanned the forest.

The forest, with its slender trees, was disorienting for Beriszl and even more so for Chilali. Both could see exceptionally far and well in low light, but the forest created an illusion of depth. It gave the impression the pair were seeing further than they actually were, but in truth their vision was ultimately blocked by successive trees and shadows.

Chilali moved forward and Beriszl cautiously followed. After moving deeper into the forest for a few moments, Beriszl stopped and looked back the way they came. He could barely discern where they had entered. Chilali kept going.

"Chilali, we should wait for the others," Beriszl examined the path they had taken, noting the distances between trees. "It will be difficult for them to move wagons through here."

Chilali paused and looked over her shoulder. Beriszl was right. The trees, as well as at least one moss-draped boulder, pinched the natural path they took. But moving the wagons through wasn't her main concern. This forest was too still and silent, save for the sound of gurgling water. She neither heard nor smelled smaller creatures. And her eyes detected no motion in the shadows around her or above her. Unnerved by the fact she couldn't find another single living creature, she followed Beriszl's lead back to the forest's edge.

Falcon and the others were perplexed as to what to do about the wagons once they reached the forest. Chilali, bored by then, shimmied up one of the trees. Finding nothing of interest, she leapt between trees and slid down.

By then, the knight and the other commanders resigned themselves to the fact they would need to strip the wagons of supplies and bundle them onto their horses. Everyone would be walking from this point forward, but it would take time to shuffle the supplies and unlatch the horses from the wagons.

"I feared this would be the case," Jerle muttered while inadvertently leaning on the tree onto which Chilali clung. "If we had more time and men, we could cut a path."

Teth arched his lower back, jammed his thumbs into it with a soft grunt.

"The way I'm feeling now, I can't say I'd like to be one of those extra men."

Jerle playfully backhanded the old tracker's exposed gut.

"You could use the work, I think."

He released his stretch with a grin, as Chilali inverted herself on the tree trunk and hopped off to land in front of Jerle, startling the fire elemental user.

"Chilali!"

The Divergent checked to see if her sword came loose after the maneuver, before responding to Jerle. It remained securely in place.

"Want to go take a walk in the forest?" Chilali asked, strands of ruby hair crisscrossing in front of her eyes.

Jerle pursed her lips and saw Falcon and some of the commanders bickering with one another. She also noticed the Lessers remained out in the direct sunlight, sitting to the sides of the trodden path.

"We need to bring the Lessers closer to the forest's edge, first."

Chilali shouted Astra's name and the young Talarian came running with Minnie trailing behind her.

"They took your horse already," Jerle observed.

Astra gave a slight nod.

"Bring the Talarians and the Briam into the shade,"

Chilali said.

Minnie shook her head and Astra looked at the ground.

"The overseers want to keep us from the forest," Astra explained.

"Do they really think you will try to run into this forest?" Jerle asked, the ridiculousness of the rationale reflected in the tone of her voice.

By then, Falcon headed toward them with Olin at his heels.

"They have more supplies than they can burden their horses with. They want to make the Briam carry the excess."

Jerle tossed her hair.

"Then we are quite fortunate someone knocked over Marcus' stew pot last night."

Falcon scowled.

"It is not that simple. The Briam are already burdened with the supplies we scavenged from Orsa and its orchards."

"What are you getting at?" Jerle pushed.

"The excess supplies they want to take with us do not just include weapons, armor, food, water, or the usual supplies. They've brought mining tools."

"And they don't want to leave their tools behind, because they're expecting to reap untold amounts of black metal from the mine. But what do they want you to leave behind?"

"The extra food the Briam carry for their own feeding," Olin stated coldly.

A pause followed as they looked to each other for solutions.

"No," Chilali interjected. "They can leave the tools with the wagons and get them later. They need more manpower to cut a trail, anyway."

Jerle's shoulders rose and fell with a shrug.

"She has a point. Even if they can mine, they won't be

able to bring large amounts of ore back without a wagon trail."

"There is hope Sitara's light may find you yet, Chilali," Olin praised. "I'll go inform the commanders of our decision and the rationale behind it."

"Bring the Talarians and Briam into the shade," Chilali added, halting Olin in mid-stride.

The priest checked with Falcon first, who waved him on.

"We've another problem," the knight spoke with a sullen tone. "There are rumblings amongst the men about putting the Talarians to use."

Minnie slid ever so slightly behind Astra, who didn't shy away from the discussion. Jerle ran her hand through her hair and scratched the back of her head.

"Are they serious? We're at the edge of this abyssal wilderness, possibly under imminent attack by the Blackland Nation or Wild Briam or worse."

Falcon returned a look that made Jerle think she should have known better than to ask the question.

"I do not think we can deny them this vice, Jerle. Other than this, the Talarians are good for little more than tending gardens or performing household chores. Military code does not forbid it, either, as we aren't an official standing army of the Empire," the knight explained.

"I don't understand," Chilali said, looking up at the taller knight and fire elemental user.

Jerle blinked and gave Falcon a knowing, sad look. She turned to Chilali.

"It's trivial, Chilali. They want the Talarians to clean their clothes, while there is fresh water nearby in the forest. Let us go take that walk and scout ahead of the others tonight. We'll take Beriszl, Astra, and Minnie with us."

"That sounds like a wise plan. I would know what lies ahead of us. Turn back to us in the morning, Chilali," Falcon advised.

The Divergent didn't miss the nonverbal cues or the fact Astra and Minnie stood remarkably still as if every muscle in their bodies had turned to wood. But the enticement that came from wanting to explore the forest helped to turn her away from her better judgment or else she would have pressed the issue.

Jerle waved Beriszl over from helping Marcus with moving satchels of dry goods. She suspected the Ragebourne was close enough to have heard the discussion and she was right. He came over with her horse, which was loaded with supplies, and handed her the reins. He then scooped Minnie up into his arms and held her face to his breast to hide her sudden tears from Chilali.

"Plenty of supplies have been moved to your horse, Jerle," the Ragebourne spoke more loudly than usual, as if he were forcing the words out of his throat.

Chilali couldn't smell Minnie's tears, masked as they were by Beriszl's own scent, but she knew something was amiss. And yet, the unknown that was the forest kept her distracted, excited, and unwitting. She went into the forest with Beriszl, Astra, Minnie, and Jerle, leaving the Talarians to do the laundry for her army.

The Southern Wilds

"There's nothing," Chilali spoke to the forest with disappointment and a bit of worry, as she spun between every other stride to try to find something in the forest beyond trees, fog, and water.

Jerle rubbed her arms for heat, walking leisurely behind with Astra.

"Much of what lives in this forest lives beneath the ground in caverns and tunnels and surfaces at night," Jerle explained, a shiver in her voice. "And the trees bear no fruit this time of year, so there are no birds."

Beriszl lumbered behind with Minnie in one arm and holding the reins of the horse with the other. He let the reins slip for a moment and reached for a blanket from the saddle to hand it to Jerle. She waved it off.

"I'm fine. It is just the cool damp air here. I'm unaccustomed to it," she said, rubbing herself more roughly and then stopping.

Beriszl draped the blanket over the groggy Minnie and pulled the meandering horse back to him without a glance.

"It is hard to tell how soon nightfall will come," Beriszl grunted.

"It will be in moments," Astra offered meekly.

"My feet are inclined to agree with you," Jerle sighed and pointed to a rock-littered clearing ahead. "That would be a good place to camp."

Beriszl shook his head.

"We should stay away from the rocks. Something may live beneath them."

Chilali's ears perked up at Beriszl's words.

"Then we should camp by the rocks."

Jerle sighed and stopped where she stood.

"Right here will do then. It's flat and as open as we're going to get and there aren't any rocks."

Beriszl scratched his chin and the tuft of hair sprouting

from beneath it.

"Yes, this is good. We will need wood and a fire."

Astra went to work, gathering fallen branches off the ground. Jerle found enough fist-sized stones to make a ring of sufficient size. By just snapping some moss between her fingers, she had the fire growing and puffing white smoke as Astra methodically added branches, building a conical structure. Beriszl wrapped Minnie in the blanket and laid her near the fire. She slept soundly, exhausted from her travels.

Jerle looked around, tired and irritated. The Divergent meandered off without a word. She turned to the Ragebourne for answers, as he tied Jerle's horse to a sapling and hung a feedbag on it.

"Where did Chilali go?"

Beriszl tossed his snout off in an aimless direction.

"She goes to the spring, I think. There is one nearby."

"A spring?"

"Yes, but its odor is not as strong as the others. It must be cooler."

Jerle rubbed her hands together with a smile.

"My feet could use a good soaking," she said and took Astra's wrist. The young Talarian let out a little yelp.

"You deserve a chance to relax, too," Jerle told the Talarian, who stopped her passive protest. "Beriszl, would you mind the camp while we're gone?"

"Do not get lost. Chilali and I have difficulty scenting in this forest," the old Ragebourne advised with a groan as he plopped against the base of a tree, rattling its branches. "And do not go unarmed, not even Astra."

Jerle went to the horse and pulled an unstrung bow and quiver from beneath a stack of blankets. She passed them off to Astra and checked the strapping on her own short sword. Beriszl gave them a tired wave as Jerle led Astra away at a bouncy pace.

* * *

Lichen covered rocks at a cliff base ringed a steaming pool that glowed with a soft indigo light. Scalding water trickled down the steep rock face into the pool and the night sky pierced the forest canvas above, shedding some of Sitara's light into the bleak forest and scattering silver glimmers across the water's chaotic surface.

Chilali adjusted to the sulfur odor the pool exuded, mostly by mouth breathing. Even then, the taste it left in the air made her wrinkle her nose just a bit. She stroked her fingertips lightly across its surface to gauge the temperature. The others she ran across burned her fingers, but this pool was much milder. Her whole hand swam in its thick water, as she lay down next to it on the lichen padding. She heard Jerle and Astra coming toward her, sat up, and shook her hand dry.

"How hot is it?" Jerle asked when she and Astra came upon the pool.

"Hot," Chilali answered, noticing Astra had a bow slung over her shoulder and a full quiver dangling from the crook of her lithe elbow.

Jerle sat on the rock ledge and knelt by the water's edge. She held her hand over it to feel the heat and steam.

"It doesn't feel too bad," she remarked.

"What are you doing?" Chilali was quick to question when Jerle started to wrestle her boots off. Astra paced slightly and nervously, holding the quiver on her shoulder so it wouldn't slide back down her arm.

"I'm going to take a bath," she deadpanned.

The thought made Chilali poke her tongue out in revulsion.

"In there?!"

"Oh yes," Jerle answered with a tone full of more determination than Chilali had ever witnessed in the woman. "These springs are the one redeeming thing about this entire journey."

Jerle got her boots off and rolled her riding pants up to below her knees. She dropped her feet in the pool, not shy about splashing and wetting Chilali's hair. The Divergent reflexively shook it dry.

"It smells," she protested, pulling back from the pool.

Jerle began stripping her armor off a piece at a time and setting them neatly aside. She kept her sword next to her, always.

"The smell is a small price to pay," Jerle scoffed and waved Astra over.

The Talarian came, looking at Jerle, uncertain.

"Don't look at me like that," Jerle laughed. "Come soak."

Astra touched the bowstring cutting across her chest.

"Don't worry. Nothing is going to sneak up on us while we have a Divergent to protect us."

Astra submitted, setting her bow and quiver on the ground. She unfastened and removed her sandals before hiking her gown up to above her knees. She sat timidly next to Jerle and eased her feet in one at a time with a muted gasp. Beneath the water, she flexed her toes, letting out a quiet sigh and a soft moan.

Jerle finished with her armor and began on her clothes next. She tore her vest and blouse off, followed by a bit of wiggling to slide out of her riding pants while sitting. She had to stand to remove her undergarments. A warrior woman, mercenary, and assassin, her body bore its scars. She was accustomed to bearing them to Agraven, but with Astra and Chilali, she felt a tinge of shame. A thick, hard ridge of off-colored flesh crossed a hand span on the side of her hip. A thumb-sized, V-shaped bump bubbled up on her left hamstring, just above the back of her knee. And a thumb-sized splotch beneath her left arm on her rib cage mirrored itself on her back.

The sight caused Chilali and Astra to blush. Jerle broke

into a fit of nervous laughter at their reaction.

"Why are the two of you being so modest? You blush at neither bird nor beast, so why blush at me?"

Jerle slid into the water, releasing a relaxed moan and rubbing her shoulders with a crisscrossing of her arms.

"It's not as deep as it appears," she said, bouncing on her toes with a wry grin, the tops of her breasts just above the water's surface. "Even you can reach the bottom, Astra."

Astra returned a hopeless look. She stood and worked her gown over her head. The slave, too, had her scars, pink lines streaking her porcelain back, left by her one-armed master's strap. She slipped into the water with a yelp as it rushed up to her chin. She knew not how to swim and struggled to stand barely tall enough on her tip toes.

"It's not that deep by me," Jerle soothed and pulled the Talarian toward her.

Astra stood taller in the water.

"The bottom is slimy," she said, as Jerle straightened the Talarian's teal hair, which sank in the water.

"You get used to it," the fire elemental user returned and looked at Chilali, who came back to the water's edge.

"What about you, Divergent? Will you brave these merciless waters, too?" she taunted.

Chilali suddenly readied herself to spring into the oblong pool. Jerle raised her hands.

"Take off your armor first, unless you intend to drown," she chastised.

Chilali forgot she was even wearing it and began unclasping the pieces and letting them fall where they may. Her clothes came next just as haphazardly. She set her sword across Jerle's on the ledge and stood before them bare in a mixture of indigo and silver glare.

Jerle and Astra couldn't help but to stare. Her small form held so much power. Her muscles were so lean and well-defined they looked like tree roots beneath her perfect skin. Despite all her wounds, her body did not seem to remember the horrors it had endured. It forgot the bite of Alden's trap and the crushing force of Kern's mace, and it would eventually forgive the Asael's spear. Envy and awe came to Jerle and Astra.

"She has no scars," Astra observed absent-mindedly.

Chilali pointed to the wounds across her chest, which had become light pink marks, in protest.

"That's not a scar, Chilali," Jerle corrected. "It'll be gone by tomorrow night."

She spun around, showing her back, and pointed to a black mark on the small.

"That's a birthmark-" Jerle began to say but stopped herself. She swished closer to Chilali to get a better look at the odd mark. In the low light, making it out was difficult and Jerle found it hard to believe what she saw.

"It's a black star," she said, to herself, puzzling over it.

Chilali turned back around.

"It's what?"

Jerle blinked.

"I've no idea. We should have Olin look at it when we meet up with them again."

Chilali swung her hand across her form dismissively.

"No, I don't want him to look at me. Not ever."

The sudden surge of emotion surprised even herself. Chilali didn't know where it came from, but just hearing his name filled her with a sharp coldness that made her insides feel like they were shriveling.

"Okay, forget it," Jerle came back, shocked by the Divergent's reaction. "Alden would know more anyway."

Chilali stepped off the ledge and fell into the pool. She broke the bubbly surface with a small splash and shot back up just as quickly. She treaded the water, easily, even though she moved her arms twice as hard as an ordinary person would have a need to do. Divergents were just that much denser, Jerle thought, while puzzling over the black multi-point star.

Chilali coughed and gagged, fighting to get the smelly water out of her throat and nose.

"Aside from the odor, how does it feel," Jerle asked coyly.

She hovered with just her eyes above the water and her hair spread out across its surface. That was answer enough for Jerle. Astra slowly put distance between herself and the Divergent.

Jerle grabbed the Talarian by the shoulders and pulled her close, making the girl gasp.

"She won't hurt you so long as you don't touch her. So, stop being so skittish."

The Talarian's skin was hot and smoother than her own. Jerle could begin to understand the appeal men felt for these poor creatures. She pressed her thumbs in Astra's shoulder muscles, massaging them. Astra fidgeted for a moment but began to melt beneath Jerle's hands.

"Don't doze off. Pay attention so you can do the same for me. I don't have Agraven here this time."

Chilali surfaced enough to speak as Astra moaned into the water, causing her hair to drape over the sides of her face.

"What are you doing?"

"I'm massaging Astra's shoulders. It helps to loosen up the muscles and relax them," Jerle explained, kneading the girl's back.

"I wish I could do that," Chilali said, her sigh turning into bubbles.

Jerle paused in her work on Astra for a moment and regained her senses. It was too dangerous a thing to try to touch Chilali. She nearly killed Olin and he only tried to heal her. But the thought of not being able to know such contact frightened her and made her pity the flawless child for a time.

Jerle finished and let Astra go. The Talarian slipped

away as loose as rope and turned around, a slight smile on her lips.

"Your turn," Jerle said and turned her back.

The Talarian mimicked what she felt as best as she could and Jerle enjoyed it, but her hands weren't half as strong as Agraven's. They were much smoother, though, and warmer, but not half as strong.

Chilali bobbed to the surface.

"You both look like my mother."

Jerle examined the Divergent out of the corner of her eye. Those emerald eyes watched her from just above the water's surface, while her arms and legs kicked and pushed furiously beneath.

"What do you mean?"

Chilali lifted her chin above the water.

"You have those on your chest," she pointed with her eyes and continued with an in-water back flip.

Jerle laughed and waited for her to surface, again. She grabbed her breasts and gave them a hearty heft.

"You'll have your own set one day, too, sore back included," she offered.

"I will?" the Divergent pressed.

Jerle's mind raced back to Falcon and their bargain with the emperor. Her heart cracked a little, but she nodded with a thin smile on her lips and sorrow in her eyes. At the same moment, a tingle shot down her spine all the way to her toes. The Talarian's hot lips pressed against her back, once, twice, slowly and deliberately going lower.

Jerle twisted around quickly, not sure how to react. The water swished with her like a storm, frightening Astra back. The Talarian's lips trembled. She had displeased her master, despite her best efforts. She stood paralyzed, until Jerle engulfed her in a hug.

She whispered into the slave's ear.

"Never like that. Not with me. You never," she whispered into the slave's ear, as her tears dripped down the Talarian's back, cooler than the water in which they bathed.

Chilali watched but didn't surface. For the first time, she felt naked below the water.

Strife's Journal: 385th Day, 4058, Ivory (Bone) Cliffs

Clear with a warm breeze blowing in from the southeast. I stand on the edge of the chalky cliffs with the emerald ocean fatally below me.

The campaign in the south is complete. The Talarian Empire stands no more.

We've taken Talarian survivors by the thousands, mostly women and children. We will take them to the capital to be slaves. It is a cruel fate, one that will likely persist until this war is no longer remembered.

But it is a better fate than those in the Blackland Nation chose for them. We surrendered half of the Talarians to them—to rape and slaughter.

Father Night has become Shyamon, the Embracing Night. Politics begin their shift. Our priests decry the ancient name of Father Night.

I see this new schism forming between the two nations of man. I saw it well in advance. But I did not wish for it to happen so quickly.

I've grown tired of war. I want to stop. Though, runners bring word of new Volitor movement in the north.

Ren, my friend, his hair beginning to gray, told me he intends to return to the capital when the war is done and take a wife. He wants a family.

I admit to wanting the same. I still regret my return to the forest. It is clear to me I cannot be with a female of my race. But there is one under my command, a scout, no, my best scout. I've run across her on the many nights I have gone out on my own scouting missions.

She is the first child of man I have found attractive, and her name is Sveta.

I deserve to have some comfort in this life. But it will not be given to me. This is something I must take for myself if I truly desire it.

I do not want to be alone.

—*General Strife Ashwake*

Motivating Factor

The cold damp air brought relief to Jerle, as she picked her way past low ferns and fallen branches, fanning herself with one hand while lighting her way with the other. Her flame ravenously licked the spaces between her fingers and winded around them until escaping at the tips. Her armor and her vest lay across her shoulder and her sword belt loosely wrapped around the side of her exposed stomach and part of her hip.

The three of them, she, Astra, and Chilali hadn't gone far, and she made certain to mentally mark her path, but the campfire did not burn in the black distance.

"Chilali," she spoke, expecting some kind of response.

The Divergent seemed distracted and had been since they left the hot spring. She climbed out early and dried herself in the night air before donning all her clothes and armor. All the time her emerald eyes remained watchful of their surroundings; so much so Jerle wondered if she were avoiding Astra and her.

The Talarian kept silent, as she always did, but stayed close to Jerle. The incident in the pool caused a bond to form between them. Jerle was glad for it, in a way, but hated it. She knew such a thing would only cause her more suffering. Astra was attractive by any standard and would only become more so, especially with her budding sense of independence. Astra was gaining the one thing daughters of the Empire had over her slave race, a sense of self, free will of a sort, with some degree of self-determination. But the women of the Empire could at the very least tell a man, "No." Astra's refusal, if it ever came to that, would end at knifepoint.

Jerle showed the girl a smile and got a slight one in return, as she continued to scan the forest, not seeing much beyond trees and shadow.

"There," Chilali said suddenly and with uncharacteristic

alarm.

She darted into the darkness ahead of them so quickly Jerle was barely able to follow her by the firelight reflecting off her ruby hair. And she risked leaving Astra behind, who made as much haste as she could in a wet gown and sandals, carrying both bow and quiver.

Chilali stopped and remained still. Her mind refused to accept what she saw and begged to be able to scent the scene to verify it. But the pool and its soothing waters temporarily stripped her of the sense. It was like being made deaf by a constant loud sound and her nose wouldn't stop ringing. But her eyes still saw the truth in the pitch.

Beriszl lay on his side, thick blood draining from a wound in his torso and out of his mouth and nose. The head of his mace was jammed into a tree trunk and its handle poked out into the air. Bits of bone and meat clung to it and matted Beriszl's fur. The branches used for the fire were scattered all around her, some glowing with dull orange specks and others just smoking. Bodies, the remains of several Blackland warriors lay about in gory pools around her. The horse, too, had been slain.

Chilali swallowed hard, her throat clenching.

Jerle brought firelight to nightmare. All the emotion in her face fell away and she shoved Astra back to try to shield her from the spectacle. The Talarian fell onto her hands and knees, wailing.

Jerle dropped what she was carrying and loosed her short sword from its sheath, revealing its partially serrated blade.

"Where, Chilali?"

The Divergent tried as hard as she could. But the forest remained quiet, still, and dark.

"Where?" Jerle demanded.

Chilali glared at the fire elemental user and returned to her spying.

Beriszl twitched and Chilali felt her heart flutter. She

was on top of him, rolling him onto his back before Jerle could get a word out.

"His heart beats," Chilali confirmed. "But it's slow."

Jerle dropped her sword and examined the chest wound. She covered her mouth in horror and shook with nervousness.

"Sitara, no," she stammered and slapped her hand over the wound. "His second heart has been pierced. He's in agony."

"Help him!" Chilali screamed at her so loud, she felt the force of the Divergent's voice in her teeth.

Jerle shook her head.

"I don't know if even Olin could help. It's his second heart. It burst and now it's poisoning him, paralyzing him."

"Make it stop!" the Divergent child screamed again.

"There's nothing I can do!" she shouted back, hysterical.

She placed her hand on the side of the Ragebourne's head to look into his cold red eyes. Beriszl's mind slipped away with each new heartbeat. His tongue hung limp and his nose was hot. He blinked once slowly and Jerle knew what she had to do.

"Okay, okay, I'll do it," the fire elemental user said and began to cry. She scooped her sword from the ground and straddled the Ragebourne. She tried to swipe at Beriszl's throat, but Chilali caught her wrist, furious. Her grip was like having a booted man step on her and made her hand go instantly numb. Her sword slipped free. Chilali shoved her almost immediately afterward. The force sent her rolling through the air and well clear of Beriszl, breaking her concentration and extinguishing her flame.

Mostly unharmed, Jerle scrambled to her feet to face Chilali in the dark.

"He wants us to do this. It's like there is a slow-moving fire burning inside his body. He's suffering horribly Chilali. We have to-"

Chilali refused, wildly shaking her head.

"No, we have to save him."

"This is the only thing we can do," Jerle pleaded.

A blinding white light erupted behind Chilali. She stood like an eclipse before Jerle, who quickly covered her eyes and looked away. The bright red and green spots still lingering on her eyelids, she opened them, rubbed them, and tried to see again. She reignited her flame and saw Astra weeping on Beriszl's chest as the Ragebourne's heavy hand stroked her back.

Jerle stood at Chilali's side. The Divergent was as lost as she.

"Astra," was the first thing to come to Jerle's mind and out of her mouth.

The Talarian looked at her, her lips forming words of apology that would not leave her throat.

Beriszl sat up slowly, the wound in his chest bloody and raw. He covered it quickly and panted hard.

"Do not kill her," the Ragebourne begged. "Please."

Jerle fit the pieces together and it felt like the world fell away beneath her.

"Astra, you've Sitara's light."

Chilali cocked her head to one side, as Jerle stepped forward. Beriszl twisted the Talarian to the ground to shield her with his body.

"Please, no," he gurgled.

"I, the law, this is," Jerle mumbled.

"Jerle won't kill you," Chilali said.

Jerle regarded the Divergent.

"Whole families have been put to death for hiding such Lessers. Whole families, by the Order," Jerle said to the Divergent, expecting her to understand, when she didn't understand herself.

"I said, 'No,'" Chilali growled, drawing the heavy sword from her back. Jerle blinked.

"I don't want to Chilali. I don't, but Beriszl. He knows.

We can't."

"No," the Divergent's green eyes narrowed with sinister intent.

"Agraven is not in danger," Beriszl coughed in resignation. "Take this truth I give you for Astra's life. Know what it costs me to betray my oath. Please."

"What do you mean?" Jerle snapped.

"He is not the emperor's prisoner. He works for the emperor," Beriszl explained, the words sour in his mouth.

Jerle shook her head.

"Agraven, we do not work for the Empire, ever."

Beriszl shook his head with a hard grimace.

"It is true. I know not why. But spare her, so we can leave."

"Where's Minnie?" Chilali barked at the Ragebourne.

The Ragebourne rolled off Astra. The Talarian's gown showed deep dark blood stains.

"An Avidan took her. We must flee. He stalks us. Our only hope is to make it to the others."

Jerle gasped and scooped up her sword. The flames licking her fingers erupted with new brightness, expanding her field of vision.

"What is an Avidan doing here?"

"I do not know," the Ragebourne said, trying to stand with Astra's help. "But he is out there, his spear sharp as death, and he had others with him."

Chilali sniffed once and flitted to one side with preternatural speed. A phantom fell upon her, its many arms swaying with inertia and spear slashing with snake-strike speed. Jerle caught a glimpse of the figure, before he punted Chilali beyond her firelight and pursued. He sneered at her with a cobalt face, inked like an ancient tome with eyes like dry blood. His teeth glistened like moist blackberries, and he wore a many-tailed cloak of fine black chain, like a fan of blades. This was an Avidan and not seen in the Empire's lands since the Nameless War.

They were all dead, Jerle knew. Maybe with enough time to mature and train with a weapon, Chilali could stand against such a monster with Beriszl's and her assistance. But with the Ragebourne wounded and Chilali fighting like a wild beast, there was nothing to be done.

An Asael was just a man, but a master of his weapon and blessed by Shyamon with an unnatural sense. It was as if the Embracing Night himself whispered to him how to best attack to kill and guided his movements in doing so. The most skilled of the Asael could give his body completely over to the Night God, become his instrument and gain unnatural quickness, coordination, and foresight. But an Avidan was an Asael who also controlled an element.

She pushed her fear aside, knowing she had no choice but to fight as hard as she could and pray to Sitara she would get lucky. She rushed after Chilali and the Avidan, her sword in one hand and her arm wrapped in flames.

She didn't need to run far, Chilali battled the inevitable, swinging her sword around as if it were a club and accomplishing little more than churning the night air. She looked like an angry dog hopping around, snapping, and snarling. The Avidan would strike her dead at any moment. He danced around her, his steps measured, firm, and balanced. He knew where he needed to be at all times as he slung his spear around his body, one end following after the other in a constant hum.

Jerle joined the battle, tossing her sword to her burning arm and engaging the enemy from behind. This was no surprise attack. None could hope to surprise such a warrior, but Jerle hoped Chilali would be able to take advantage of the momentary distraction a searing blade would provide.

The black spear drummed her blade before she could even bring it down, twice to deflect it wide, twice more to keep it wide, and one more time to slice through the hot orange metal. This warrior possessed such skill his attacks against her also fended off Chilali, parrying the Divergent's wild swings and sending her off-balance with her own tremendous momentum. And when the last slice cut Jerle's sword in half, the Divergent felt the bite of the black spear across her back.

If there was any doubt about their chances for survival, for the duration of the entire flurry, the Avidan hadn't even looked back at fire elemental user. Jerle never felt so ineffective before. And then the end came as a whirlwind. It spontaneously surrounded her, pushing her to the ground it blew so fiercely, and extinguished her mystical fire like it was a candle. The wind whistled by her so quickly she couldn't take in a breath and dirt blew into her eyes, nose, and ears with the larger particles scraping her skin. Her ears popped and her chest tightened, like someone heavy was standing on it. The Avidan commanded the power of the Wind King, she realized, and wished she could just see Agraven one more time.

Chilali covered her eyes for a moment to shield them from the dirt and leaves blowing up in the whirlwind. The Avidan took advantage of this and sliced open the back of one of the Divergent's sword hands, as she spun away. But, Chilali did not drop her blade, even though it felt like the top of her hand was being pressed against a boiling pot.

This felt like the same battle she had with the Asael. He was able to completely maneuver her and trap her with his attacks, his unceasing attacks. The sword she carried was as much use as an ineffective shield. She could never get close enough with her comparatively short reach and his carefully measured attacks. If she ever got within the arc of his blades this fight would be over, she believed and seethed, after taking a painful slice across her forehead. He had meant to open her throat with the attack, but she pulled herself down and away in time. Despite his skill, she was still much stronger and faster.

Jerle suffered inside the whirlwind, clawing at the

ground to get free of it, Chilali saw, as she maneuvered to a nearby tree, hoping to gain some cover. Blood ran down her face and into one eye. She tried to wipe it away with her free hand, but the burning grit remained, and she took another cut across the side of her stomach for the effort. She was becoming tired of bleeding all the time. And except for the slash against her back, her armor failed to block anything. The Avidan could pick his way around the metal pieces whenever he wanted to, it seemed.

She rushed the tree she intended to use for protection. She ran up its trunk, three steps, before shooting off it above the Avidan's reach, hoping to land a safe distance behind him by Jerle. But her momentum suddenly shifted. The sense of the fall became the feeling of acceleration in a new direction. A blast of wind slapped her, pressing on every inch of her body and not letting go. She sailed backward, toward the Avidan, and could see out of the corner of her eye he waited to deliver the killing thrust to her heart. Squirming in the air, she tried to wrench herself around to face his attack, but there wasn't enough time.

Beriszl joined the fight, charging the Avidan as if he were trying to run the man over. The Avidan adjusted his tactics. He reset his stance to intercept Beriszl with a thrust, while mentally pushing Chilali over and past him with one more gust.

The Ragebourne dipped quickly to the side to avoid the thrust aimed at the wound on his chest. His gory mace swung out hard with a powerful backhand at the Avidan, but didn't connect, as the warrior spun out of the way, his spear matching his movements. The first blade ripped open the thick muscles, just above the Ragebourne's kneecap, causing Beriszl to drop to a knee and intercept the second blade. His mace blocked the strike solidly, but the Avidan sprung off the deflection and came around on Beriszl's weak side.

The Ragebourne raised his arm up to defend the blow,

hoping it would be just thick enough to not be dismembered. He would never find out, though, as Chilali rushed back in the fray, shortening the Avidan's attack by forcing him to back off to avoid the Divergent's rush.

The Avidan feigned a lethal counterattack, prompting Chilali to try to defend her heart, again, and went low. Chilali hopped the attack, which would have hewn her from her own feet, and rolled forward into the whirlwind with Jerle.

The force the wind exerted was impressive, more so than she anticipated, but it was not nearly strong enough to pin her to the ground. She could feel it trying to suck away her very breath, a frightening sensation even for her. She snatched Jerle's heel and dove out of the whirlwind, jerking the fire elemental user behind her.

The Avidan was not amused and hammered the Divergent from behind with another wind blast, launching her away, while turning his attention to ending the Ragebourne, again. Chilali landed in a roll and prepared to sprint back. The Ragebourne hobbled away from the Avidan, mounting a marginal defense with his mace. His only goal seemed to be to avoid a lethal thrust to his heart, head, or neck. It was clear to her the old Ragebourne was trying to hang on for her to rescue him.

But something made her pause, an ill feeling, as if a cold metal rod had been run up her spine. She glanced above and to her right. Minnie hung upside down on a tree. Rope wrapped her from shins to shoulders and bound her to the tree. The tension in the cording broke the girl's skin in places. Her eyes bulged and a slight bit of blood pooled around them. Her tongue barely stuck out of the side of her mouth, and it dribbled more blood down her face. The tips of her pretty indigo hair swayed in the night breeze, gently sweeping the leaves on the forest floor. That was the only motion Chilali saw from the girl, and she felt something crack inside her and a new emotion leak out—hatred, utter and pure.

All her efforts to control herself and her instincts to walk among these people left her. They weren't forced away by the emotional trauma she suffered at seeing Minnie dead. She sent them away, cursed them away. She let herself go, let the trap inside her spring and bite on the whole damn world.

The Avidan finished slicing up the muscles in Beriszl's arms enough to prevent the Ragebourne from protecting his heart any longer. He spat in the Lesser's face and thrust his spear at the bloody wound, absolutely intent on reopening it. But he stopped himself, feeling a dangerous shift. The manic whisper in his head from his god, his second self, screamed. He never experienced such a thing before, nothing he would call fright from the whisper of his god. He didn't understand the danger. He turned to face the Divergent child and found the beast he had been anticipating to face. This was not surprising, but why did he feel such alarm?

Chilali rushed the Avidan, drowning in her overwhelming instinct for violence. She saw him turn away from Beriszl, calm and unaware of exactly what he was now facing. She felt the wind gather in front of her and dodged to the side to avoid a powerful blast. The Avidan thought the attack unavoidable, but Chilali was faster than before. The result was he set himself late to receive the Divergent. He avoided her initial lunge, but she came right back at him.

He fell into a defensive barrage and carefully stepped to maneuver himself away from her. But he couldn't keep her out of his circle. She forced her way closer and closer to him. His spear dipped into her skin in multiple places and sparked off her armor. It clanged off her sword, cutting shavings from the blade. But he could not force her back.

He drew upon the place in the back of his mind, a constant, low howl he always heard, but not with his ears. It

was where the power from the Wind King's prison drafted
into him. He began to inhale it, more so than he had when
he forced the fire elemental user to the ground and stole her
breath. Gorging on so much of the power was dangerous
and risked a fate worse than dying. Draining the power
created a vacuum, one that would suck, pull, and tear one's
mind into the Wind King's prison. And not even the
Embracing Night could pull his mind from such a place if it
passed into the cursed realm. It was an eternal death, the
worst of suffering. But taking the risk was the only thing he
could do to force the Divergent back.

A shrieking howl erupted. The air around Chilali
exploded with sudden velocity. Above her it collected and
spun, tightening and drawing itself into a white ring.
Seemingly solid and altering the direction of the wind as it
changed course, the ring darted at her. She didn't need to
think at all to know she needed to avoid it, as it cut between
her and the trembling Avidan, who halted his spear assault.

The ring hovered between them, parallel to the ground.
The gusts spinning off it blew the blood from Chilali's
armor and wounds, spattering it all over the forest and her
comrades. Her hair flapped like a torn sail threatening to
tear from the mast. Tree branches cracked and fell around
them.

The Avidan spoke, but his words were lost to the
torrent. Chilali could read his lips, though. He promised to
take her eyes as trophies, just as the Asael had. The ring
came for her at that moment with speed greater than she
was capable of on foot. She dug her hands and feet hard
into the ground to push away as fast as she could to try to
dodge it. It clipped the bracer on her left arm and ripped it
off, bending the clasps open and lacerating the skin to
which they held.

Chilali watched the armor piece spin away and embed
high into the trunk of a tree. The ring was already swooping
for her a second time. She didn't care though, because there

was now an open path between her and the Avidan. She went at him, but his movements were slower and his strikes more desperate. Sweat ran down his face and his breaths were fast. The ring came for her from behind, but not with nearly as much speed. The warrior had difficulty managing the ring and his own defense at the same time. She avoided it by moving around the Avidan, forcing him to constantly and quickly adjust his stance, attack pattern, and the careful manipulation of the ring that would rend him even more easily than it would her, she believed.

She steadily broke his defense down, pounding him with frightfully strong sword swings and forcing herself closer and closer. He found it harder and harder to block her attacks blade-to-blade and caught more and more on the shaft of his spear. This is what Chilali wanted. She slipped past a swoop from the ring, hopped a swipe from the spear, and came around with a two-handed slash. Her sword cleaved through the spear shaft, blowing the extraordinarily dense wood into splinters and sending cracks through its entire length.

The ring rocketed into the sky and dissipated at that instant. She drew her blade back, ready to cut the Avidan into chunks, but he was unmoving. His blood-colored eyes were still and staring into a distant place. By the time she thought to lower her blade, that something was wrong, he collapsed. He lay on the ground alive, but lifeless. His heart beat, his lungs breathed, but he said nothing, heard nothing, and thought nothing.

Chilali took a moment to collect herself, to regain control, to see that her allies were still moving, and to check her own injuries. She was hurt and her strength was diminishing with each breath, but she would recover. Jerle began to climb to her feet and Astra came out of hiding to help Beriszl stand.

She took a deep breath and remembered Minnie was still tied to a tree, no longer alive. She dropped her sword, felt her rage build to an uncontrollable level again, and fell upon the Avidan's living body. Her allies watched stoically as she ripped him apart and ate the meat from his ribs and thighs.

Never had a meal been so satisfying, while tasting so bitter.

None Could Console Her

Falcon approached with his sword drawn and his shield raised. He took his steps with great care, not wanting to agitate the Divergent. She lay curled up at the base of a tree, listless but awake. Crusted blood, bits of raw sinew, and dry ichors caked her. She fed well the night before it seemed. The remains of her meal, three-quarters of a man by weight Falcon estimated, lay scattered about. The smell was as terrible as he suspected.

Her pupils slid to point at him, but her body remained as still as death. Falcon paused and some of the men he ordered to circle the Divergent, while keeping their distance, flinched. He raised his hand to calm them. Their nerves were already well-frayed from the night before, because of the ambush. A frantic battle broke out, tent-to-tent, wagon-to-wagon. Forces intermixed chaotically. Many died or lost limbs to survive. Falcon, himself, suffered a laceration to his arm that he spent much of the morning mending. Olin slept for the moment under guard after having gone through to the morning conservatively healing all that he could.

Falcon cursed his luck twice, for the attack and for this incident with Chilali. Jerle explained what happened as best as she was willing. Being forced into a fight with an Avidan was a terror he hoped he would never have to face in his lifetime. It was by Sitara's will alone the Avidan fell victim to his own element. Otherwise, not Beriszl, Astra, Jerle, or even Chilali would have survived. Losing Minnie, though saddening in a way, was a blessing.

He spoke to the Divergent with a gentle voice.

"Chilali, can you hear me?"

She blinked, gradually recovering from her bloody stupor.

"We need you to come back to us," the knight continued.

She blinked again and lifted her head from her folded arms.

"We've readied a pyre for Minnie at Jerle's request. I thought you would want to come see it alight."

The fallen Talarian girl's name stirred awareness in Chilali. The haze in her eyes lifted and she sat up against the tree.

"Chilali?" the knight asked, seeking some verbal interaction.

She looked herself over and at the Avidan's remains. Flies buzzed all around her, landing on the rotting meat to lay their eggs. Their sound, while noticeable to the men encircling her, made her ears throb. The fetid meat turned her stomach and rekindled the red nightmare of the night before. The taste of it painted her tongue and throat, slimy, but dry. Powerful shame welled in the pit of her stomach, and she hung her head to savor its torment.

"Chilali," the knight repeated.

She pushed against the tree and slid up its trunk to stand. Stiff and aching, as usual, she thought. Her hair hung in uneven clumps where it crusted together. The sword she cast away pointed at her on the ground. She finally responded to the knight.

"I'm going to bathe," she spoke with a weak voice and walked out of the circle of men. Falcon didn't follow and motioned for his men to let her pass, not that they would have engaged her anyway. He took her sword from the ground and looked the blade over. The Avidan notched it well, but the blade's unusual thickness kept it from being sheered outright like Jerle's weapon. It still seemed usable, but would need a little work, first.

* * *

Beriszl held Astra close to his side and buried his snout in the side of her hair. She held his head and looked on at the pyre, at Minnie. Falcon's tattered, dirty cape covered her little body, which they placed on a stack of stones and branches. Jerle stood at the foot of it, lost in her thoughts. The fire elemental user's eyes hadn't left the corpse since it was set on the pyre.

Minnie was the last that would be burned this day, and the spectacle drew a small crowd of mourners. Rumors already spread of the violent battle between Chilali and the Avidan. Some claimed she held her own, single-handedly. Others said she would not have survived without the Ragebourne's help. But none questioned her victory. Falcon thought to quell the rumors, but the men needed something to occupy their minds as they tended to the dead and prepared to continue the march.

He allowed the surviving Talarians to attend. Their night had been twice as harsh. The ambush occurred shortly after they were dragged into the forest one at a time by different men seeking comfort. The irony was the ones in the forest were the ones that survived with the fewest injuries. The ones in the camp were the first target for the Blackland warriors. Most were killed and those that were maimed died by the dawn. And so they bore their own wounds this morning, inside and out, and Falcon could pity them this one thing.

Teth stood by Lea. The pair had not bickered once this day. Falcon was glad he took the old tracker along. He fought as bravely and as powerful as any man, saving lives and ending many more. Lea, the assassin, earned her title. The Blackland warriors made a poor judgment of their numbers and attacked with only a couple hundred warriors. Outnumbered at least two to one, the battle eventually shifted against them, and many tried to flee. Because of Lea, none escaped. She spent her entire quiver. There was satisfaction to be had from that, but the woman seemed silently distraught over the night's events and Minnie. But when were women not made distraught in some way when faced with death and war, Falcon mused. Life givers had no strength in their hearts for it. Men were the life takers.

Raife, the hero of the battle who took command of the men engaged in the forest, wasn't present. Falcon could not blame him. The young man lost part of his left arm, from just above the elbow down. Not even Sitara's light could restore a limb, but it did help to ease his pain and stop the blood loss. His sickly face was blank this morning. Though it was his non-dominant arm, continuing his career as a warrior seemed unlikely. Falcon tried to console him, speaking of things beyond the battle and of the future, but he knew the young man's life was over. Raife would never recover from that wound.

Chilali emerged from the depths of the forest. Waiting for her was a wise decision. He took note of the fact her armor, her missing bracer included, was scrubbed clean, as were her clothes, which were still damp. Her hair hung heavy, too. But all the cleaning and bathing would not repair the scars in the plating, the torn chain, or the wounds mottling her body. Time and effort would be required to repair both armor and body.

He intercepted the Divergent, stopping her approach to the pyre. All watched, but none spoke. He handed her back her sword. She took it and sheathed the weapon without looking up at him.

"We've been waiting for you," the knight whispered.

She walked around him and went to the body, which was at eye level for her. She stood by Minnie's covered head and reached her hand out to touch it. But she drew it back at the last moment. Her eyes locked on Jerle.

The fire elemental user nodded once with a sad smile and set her hand on the branches. Fire sprouted like flowers all around Minnie's body. They sprouted and bloomed until the Talarian became a stinking field of them. Chilali was glad for the fact the hot spring dulled her sense of smell this time. She stood close, feeling the heat and the smoke, as the fire crackled and hissed. The comfort it brought felt painfully false.

Falcon came to her side, and she barely noticed his approach.

"Remember her with your blade," he whispered and almost touched her on the shoulder. He stopped his hand, and she returned a smile as sad as Jerle's.

"I only hurt like this when my mother left. I didn't want to hurt like this, again. It doesn't go away," she spoke, her voice cracking, before walking off into the forest.

It will, Falcon thought grimly.

Blood-Soaked Boots

Jerle climbed to the top of the low ridge where Falcon and Raife stood. She kicked up dust clouds as she walked over the dry ground. Her boots crunched across it like it was a shallow layer of fresh snow. The camp lay behind her on the horizon. Cooking fires trailed smoke and black specks moved about in the growing twilight. Her brother-in-law hid his wound behind his cloak as she drew near. She loathed to tell this part of her misadventure to Agraven when they were reunited, knowing it would devastate him.

Falcon peered across the landscape. Arid land, littered with boulders and crags, lay before him as far as he could see. And beyond that, the jagged, needle points of the Blackland Mountains bit into the clouds, drawing white blood. The entire range was like this, Falcon thought, impenetrable. No man could hope to pass over them. In the distant past, some tried and were taken by the cold, the thin air, or the unstable surface.

And yet somehow, the Blackland Nation found a way through. A cave system perhaps, Falcon wondered. However they did it, they opened a new front in the war. A slight pang of guilt made the knight's mouth twitch. Alden was right.

"We're half a day from the settlement and three from the forest," Jerle explained. "Our water supply continues to dwindle."

"The men are aware of the situation," Falcon huffed.

The knight turned on his heel and headed back to the camp, his new crimson-colored cape billowing in the warm night wind. Raife, his face thin and his eyes angry, followed.

"Have Chilali and Beriszl returned?" Jerle asked, not sure she wanted to know the answer.

"No, but both seek more blood than the rest of us it seems," he waved without breaking his stride. "Regardless, we will march soon and attack with the dawn."

Jerle looked out and rubbed her arms, feeling a slight chill, despite the lingering heat from the day rising from the ground. She waited for the two men to reach the camp before she returned herself. Her tent stood at the edge of all the others, at her request. Besides Lea, she was the only other woman and wanted some privacy. She also wanted some space.

She felt safer alone on the ridge than she did in the camp. The atmosphere changed. A powerful, cold rage had built in all their hearts over the last several days it took to march to within striking distance of their destination. Fist fights and brawls broke out at what seemed like every hour. The Talarians that survived struggled against the advances of some of the men, who were becoming increasingly rough. They often had to be forced to fulfill their role, while some surrendered so fully they held no more interest for the men.

Of course, Falcon would not have permitted it all had Chilali actually been among them at the time. It might have been the pragmatic thing to do, but Jerle found it cowardly. Their Divergent leader left with Beriszl night after night the last several days, raiding and attacking the Blackland settlement. This was part of the original plan, but it was difficult to judge what kind of effect the Divergent and the Ragebourne were having. They brought back only their words and a fresh set of wounds each night.

The situation irritated Falcon, not because it interfered with his plans, but because the men began to watch for Chilali's return. They came to respect and rely on the Divergent and awaited tales of her small victories each morning. Falcon felt slighted by this. Chilali's successes seemed to delegitimize him in their eyes and reduce his status. Despite his claims otherwise, this did not sit well with the knight and left him in a contemptuous, brooding mood.

Jerle just wanted it all to be over. She just wanted to be home with Agraven to smell him again and touch his face. More than that, she wanted to be safe. Hiding her illness the last few days was difficult. The vomiting seemed to happen after eating certain meals and the nausea often was strongest in the morning. She refused to believe it, believe she could be carrying another child. Building up so much hope and having it stripped away when nothing happened or did not happen as planned, had already scarred her over and over.

Maybe that was why she hid her suspicion from Falcon. She feared the knight would bar her from battle. Letting a woman participate in general was prohibited. Only the absolutely most skilled, like Lea, elemental users, like herself, or priestesses were allowed to stand in the ranks of men. Letting a pregnant one fight would be an affront to the honor of the men fighting with her and Sitara.

But she would see this through. And by doing so, she wouldn't be giving into false hope. If she fought then she truly didn't believe she was with child and wouldn't be hurt again as a result. She couldn't stand to lose another pregnancy. But the vomiting dehydrated her, and water was scarce. She already drank some of Astra's ration, as meager as it was, to get by.

Astra turned the carcass of a small animal Jerle didn't recognize with a makeshift spit of sticks and twine over their meager fire. It smelled good enough to eat and the Talarian seasoned it with some wild herbs she collected in the forest. It was enough for the two of them to share without filling their stomachs completely and that was fine with Jerle. They would march again soon and battle without a rest. She couldn't afford to be sick again.

"It smells good," Jerle commented, as she eased down next to the Talarian.

Astra smiled weakly and focused on the sizzling meat.

Jerle noticed Lea sitting alone in the distance. Her only

company was Teth, and he seemed to hate her. The urge to walk over and throttle the truth from the old hag plagued Jerle night after night. But she maintained her self-control. Now was not the time, she told herself, as she had so many times before. After the battle, she would learn the truth if she had to burn every scrap of flesh off that woman's old bones.

"Are Beriszl and Lady Chilali all right?" Astra asked under her breath.

Jerle put her arm around the girl, drawing a warm smile from her sad face.

"They've not failed to return, yet."

"And me," she whispered, not taking her eyes from her cooking.

Jerle glanced about and quickly kissed the top of her head when she saw no one was looking.

"Only Beriszl, Chilali, and I know. So, no one will know if you keep your promise."

The girl nodded, but Jerle knew she would never truly believe her words. Jerle wasn't certain she believed them, either. The risk was too great. If the Order ever learned of Astra's secret anyone found complicit in keeping it and their immediate family would be executed.

* * *

Beriszl picked his teeth with the point of the claws on his ring finger. Man meat was so very stringy in places, he lamented, while finally freeing the irritating bit from his gum line. That is why he hated to bite a man. He spat out the loosed food and stretched his arms and chest. The wound over his heart remained tender, but it hurt in a good way to tense those muscles. They finished early tonight, and he was glad to have a bit of rest. The continuous raiding wore on him.

Chilali washed the blood from her face. Her water skin

was still about half full. She seemed to need so little, Beriszl thought. He wished he had enough to rinse the stink and filth from his fur, but he barely had enough left to quench his thirst.

She sat on the ground and pulled her boots off to drain the blood from them. A dissatisfying thin stream dripped out.

"It was not a good night," Beriszl sighed.

Chilali flexed her bloody toes as she shook her boots dry.

"I squished some out during the last battle, I think."

She slid her red feet back into the boots and stood with a yawn.

She leaped on top of a finger-shaped rock formation poking out of the ground. In the distance too vast for the eyes of men to see, the Blackland settlement remained in chaos. The fire, the one Beriszl set to their food supplies, still burned. The wounded that could crawl, did so across the ground, begging for help. The others just passed away into unconsciousness and death. The few women and children in the settlement cried and pawed at the bodies of their loved ones. Chilali savored it, the pain she felt and the pain she inflicted.

Beyond the attrition and suffering, the pair accomplished their original mission, taking out the towers one by one. The Blackland Nation built the settlement near the base of the mountains and constructed basic fortifications. A low wall semi-circled the settlement and remained under construction. Five short towers traced the perimeter, but they were small and fragile things. They stood maybe two men in height and one more in diameter and were largely composed of stone blocks. A single ladder led up to the top and its floor of rough planks. On the first night, a pair of Blackland warriors would have stood guard in a tower. By the fifth night, five waited.

It didn't matter how many men they put outside the base

of the towers or in their tops or even how they were constructed. Chilali and Beriszl struck each one, sometimes feigning an attack to draw forces away from another. Beriszl would smash the stones with his mace and collapse them, while she took care of the warriors with their spears and arrows. The darkness of night was always their greatest ally.

"They will begin the assault at dawn," the Ragebourne rasped as he rewrapped a slender cord around the remains of the splintered shaft that had once been one head of a Blackland double spear. Chilali tore the black blade free from that particular spear and had done so many times to other spears since learning of their weakness in her battle with the Avidan. Beriszl now replaced his mace with it after warping the weapon beyond use in their most recent raid.

"Will we have enough?" she asked, stepping off the rock and landing on the ground.

"We will stand one-to-one with them, I think," the Ragebourne sighed.

"But we've killed and wounded so many," she argued.

"Nearly a hundred," he tied off the wrapping with a grunt. "More importantly, we killed their last Asael."

"The one who led the search party?"

"I believe so."

Chilali tried to press the metal poking out of her right bracer flat again. It would bend easily enough for her, but not far enough to stay that way. Her entire suit had such gouges, nicks, and tears in it. But it had saved her half as many wounds and, blackened with soot and coal, it helped to hide her in the night.

Beriszl, too, had seen better days. He taught her how to stitch wounds and so she had a couple of times for him. Silk stitches crisscrossed his right shoulder and back. He was not nearly as nimble as Chilali, especially in his old age and with his size.

Chilali pulled her sword from the ground and examined

it. Rust speckled the many notched blade, and she used it several times to loose stones from the towers. Had it not been so thick, forged like an ordinary sword, it would have broken three times by now, she figured, even though she knew nothing of swords.

"It is more club now than sword," Beriszl remarked with a belly laugh.

Chilali pointed to a deep notch.

"This is where I tried to break the blade of that one that tried to run away from that last tower."

"You shattered his wrist and that is enough," the Ragebourne continued his laughter and took a slurp from his own water skin. "But it is no matter, Falcon or Olin can repair it for you."

She scratched her head.

"How?"

Beriszl tapped the silver armor he wore with one of his claws.

"It is made of blessed silver and enchanted with Sitara's restorative powers. It can be mended by those with her light."

"Mended?"

"Healed like a wound."

Chilali pursed her lips at the thought and wiggled her sword into the dinged-up clasps on the back of her hauberk.

"Why haven't they fixed my armor?" Chilali waved her damaged bracer in front of him.

"Maybe they didn't have time to enchant it," Beriszl shrugged.

"We should get back to camp. I'm hungry."

"My pads are sore and my claws smooth," the Ragebourne whined.

"There's no food here," she returned.

He pointed back the way they came to where they ambushed the search party. Several men lay dead there.

"There's still food back there," he offered, his red eyes

narrowing on her.

She shook her head.

"I'm never going to eat that kind of meat again."

"It is very stringy."

She smiled and led him off into the overcast night. They did not have to travel far or long before coming across their army. Falcon walked his horse at the head of the line with Raife and Jerle following close behind. Chilali also noticed Astra stood at the head of the Talarians at the rear of the line with Lea and Teth. She carried the same short bow across her back as she did the night the Avidan attacked. Arming her caused animosity to breed among the men and the Talarians, Chilali heard Falcon mention to Jerle when they were still in the forest.

Their armor camouflaged and Sitara's star hidden by clouds, Chilali and Beriszl made their way to the front of the line without being seen or heard, staying just far enough outside the torch light. Their sudden appearance from the night ahead startled even Falcon, who skipped a step in his gait to reach for his sword.

"You were supposed to return sooner," the knight chastised.

The pair fell into stride beside everyone else.

"A search party led by an Asael tracked us. We had to fight again," the Ragebourne explained unapologetically.

"An Asael?" Jerle gasped.

"The last," Chilali answered coldly.

Falcon's eyes, too, narrowed at the casual nature by which they made the claim. He wasn't sure he could believe them. Their recounting always seemed embellished. The ease by which they would rush a tower from the night, battle those on guard, damage the tower's base, and retreat with speed the Blackland warriors could not hope to match, did not seem plausible to the knight. Beriszl may be a veteran and Chilali a Divergent, but the pair simply weren't good enough to do what they claimed.

Chilali drew her sword, flipped it end over end, and caught it at the tip. She reached the handle out to Falcon.

"Beriszl said you can mend it."

Falcon took the blade and looked it over, aghast at the damage.

"What have you been doing with it?!"

"Smashing towers and breaking spears," she offered.

The knight passed the sword to Olin, who trod wearily and seemed distanced from everything going on around him. The priest took the blade with a sigh. His eyes and the purple rings around them barely flitted over the blade.

"This will take much work. Every nick in it I repair is worth ten more in flesh tomorrow."

The priest passed it back to Falcon.

"There you have it, Chilali," the knight said with a shrug and gave the sword back to her. "Flesh is more important."

She forced it back into the clasps on her back.

"I'm hungry."

"I'll help you find something," Jerle said, adjusting her sword belt. The longer, heavier weapon it now held caused it to slide too much to one side. It was a weapon taken from one of the men who fell in battle, which was considered bad luck. She didn't care, as one would have far worse luck entering a battle without a weapon. She was also wearing a heavier than normal suit of leather and chain, meant for a small man, and it slowed her down noticeably. She hated this last stretch of the march.

She fell back into the line with the Divergent. Men saluted or nodded at Chilali as they passed. Jerle found some rations, dried, salted meat, and nuts, in one of the rear wagons. Their supplies were starting to run dangerously low. The last five days they spent waiting for Beriszl and Chilali to clear the towers had exhausted much. She could only hope it had been worth it, as did Falcon, who she often saw praying on the same ridge she found him on with Raife earlier.

The Divergent snacked on the meat and the nuts, switching between them and crunching and tearing her way through the meager portions. It made Jerle wince, but she already warned Chilali to crack open the shells to get at the meat inside and not eat them whole. But the Divergent had been eating them that way for days and it didn't seem to matter to her. Where an ordinary person would have cracked their teeth or injured their jaw, Chilali found an extra food source. Jerle could not persuade the Divergent otherwise.

She and Chilali walked off to the side of the line, dragging behind it a bit. Jerle didn't care, she felt exhausted and sweat ran down her back and chest. She didn't even notice Astra and the Talarians catch up to them until Chilali fell into stride next to Astra.

The Talarians were ragged, drifting along like ghosts. Their pastel gowns were tattered and dirty. And some were torn. Shame, pain, and desperation brought dark coloring to their pale faces. Their eyes stared forward at the never-ending horizon while their feet shuffled and their breaths came short and often. The stronger, healthier ones carried the tired, wounded ones, but in truth, they were slowing the whole line down. The riders acting as overseers knew better than to try to make them pick up the pace, however. Anymore and they would all just collapse. They were bred to be housemaids, gardeners, and concubines, not soldiers.

In contrast to them was Astra. Her stride was strong, and her eyes were filled with many times the confidence they had in theirs collectively. Jerle just wasn't sure if it was admiration or animosity she saw in the faces of the trailing Talarians that looked upon the favored Astra, but she suspected the latter.

Chilali looked over her shoulder at the lagging Talarians and saw a growing divide forming between them and the rest of the line. The Briam began to back up into them, too.

"Astra, they need to walk faster," she said, naively.

Astra turned her head and flashed a concerned look at the row of Talarians walking immediately behind her. They acknowledged the request and tried to walk a little faster.

"They look so weak," the Divergent observed.

"Many of them have not slept soundly in recent nights," Astra returned with a sharp whisper.

Chilali cocked her head at the comment, confused. Astra stared back at her, confused by the Divergent's puzzled expression.

"They have not been able to sleep at night, because of the men," Astra expounded, politely.

Chilali looked ahead at her army and back at Astra. Jerle came over by that time and caught onto where the conversation was leading.

"Astra," she hushed the Talarian.

Astra shied away, but Chilali did not. She sniffed the air.

"I can smell the men on them," she charged. "And the other scent."

"Don't worry about it, Chilali," Jerle sighed, rubbing her forehead. "We've more important things to concern ourselves with."

But there was no mysterious forest to distract her this time.

"The men were lying with the Talarians," she put forth to gauge Jerle's reaction. And Jerle did react, flinching and blushing a bit with embarrassment.

"You don't even know what you're talking about. So, let it go," she tried to deflect and began walking a bit faster.

"I do," she spat back. "I've smelled it."

"Have you now?" Jerle rolled her eyes and picked her pace up a bit more.

"With Astra and Raife at your mansion."

Jerle bit her tongue and looked the Divergent over. Astra's eyes took to the path ahead of her and the Talarians were still lagging behind the rest of them, slowing the Briam behind them.

"What did you see?" Jerle stopped and turned, hoping she could dispel this conversation for the moment at least.

"I smelled Raife's scent all over Astra and Astra's on Raife and that other smell," she reiterated.

"Other smell?" Jerle raised an eyebrow.

"Yes, like at the Vineyard."

Jerle sucked in a sharp breath at the name of the infamous brothel, her face turning beat. She did not want to be having this conversation right now, especially in front of the men at the rear who began to slow their pace to stay in earshot and the other men acting as overseers, who were pretending not to be listening. She blinked and asked the most obvious question.

"What were you doing at the Vineyard in the first place?"

"I like the music," she answered without missing a beat. A likely excuse, Jerle caught herself thinking.

"What you smelled at the Vineyard is the same thing you smell right now on them," she waved her hand at the Talarians.

"What is it?"

"Something men do," she answered, desperately looking for a way out of this predicament.

"Then they should stop so the Talarians can rest," Chilali said, her brow furrowed.

Jerle smiled weakly and agreed by repeatedly nodding her head.

"Chilali has said the men are to let the Talarians rest the next night," she shouted.

The order drew a few moans, groans, and curses as it passed down the line, but none challenged it, not the Divergent's order. The fact many of them may not see the next night also weighed into their complacency.

And at the order, the Talarians regained a spark, a

night's reprieve. Their spirits rekindled for the moment, they pushed themselves even harder. Together they closed the gap between themselves and the line.

Jerle caught Lea staring at Chilali but dismissed it as nothing. Few people didn't stare at the Divergent. Together, they returned to the front of the line, Chilali's hunger sated for the moment and Jerle relieved to be able to pass off some of the responsibility of rearing her. Beriszl gave her a knowing grin.

* * *

Near the end, Chilali marched ahead of the line, everyone else following behind her, fatigued. The Fire King's light just began to tinge the clouds on the horizon, and it signaled the coming of bloodshed. The Divergent could feel the rise in tension from those around her, exciting her.

The settlement was within her sight a while before Falcon was able to see it. Smoke rose from the main building in the center where the food supplies were kept. Several outlying stone buildings circled this main structure, spreading out to a low wall and five rock piles. The knight knew them to be towers, but he never suspected Chilali and Beriszl would be able to collapse them so completely.

The wall remained unfinished and was open where it circled around the base of the mountain. It would not be able to deter a small force, rather less one that was a few hundred or more strong. He searched for two other strategic landmarks, the mine and a water source. He could determine neither.

"Where is the mine located?"

Jerle, never wanting to cast her eyes on the settlement again, indicated a cave entrance around a crevice at the mountain base, meaning it was hidden from direct line of sight. But Jerle did not know where they got their water.

The only rational explanations were they either brought it in from their own lands or they brought snow and ice down from the mountain peaks.

He raised his hand to stop the line and held it out to his side, level with his shoulder, signaling the line to swing out and face the settlement. He himself began unfastening what little remained of the surplus supplies on his horse and mounted. The animal whinnied, exhausted from the trip as well and not desiring to carry an armored rider.

As his line swung out and men armed themselves and mounted, the spectacle caught the full attention of the Blackland warriors. Those guarding the wall screamed and shouted. More spilled out of the multiple structures, some of which were simple tents. They rallied outside the settlement's wall, knowing it would offer them no protection. They had no mounts and numbered more than three hundred strong when they formed into columns.

"A servant leads them," Olin growled, showing the first sign he hadn't been completely drained over the last several days from healing the wounded.

Falcon looked down his line. He ordered Raife and the other wounded, who still chose to fight, to stay behind the line. This way, they could still thicken the appearance of the line without giving the enemy an idea of their true conditions.

Jerle fidgeted in her saddle and trembled with nervousness, as did many of the men still new to war.

"They have us with numbers," she said.

"They've no more elite warriors," Beriszl chuckled and lightly smacked the flat of his black spearhead against his small buckler.

Behind them, the overseers ordered the Briam and Talarians to sit. Any who moved would be killed. This was war and it was serious. The Lessers understood and clung to each other for support, each with their own.

Jerle kept Astra with her, letting her ride on Chilali's

horse. Using Lessers in battle was not unheard of in the Empire, Beriszl as evidence, but using a Talarian was highly unusual. Falcon didn't like it, but if it put one more distraction between the fire elemental user and the Blackland Nation, he was glad for it. He promised she would survive this fight and ordered her to not engage immediately and to linger behind with Raife and the wounded. Lea would also be near to pick off any and all that threatened them. And Teth volunteered to guard Lea, surprisingly.

Hot wind gusted up brown dust clouds between them and the enemy line. And rocks littered the battlefield. Footing would be a tricky thing for all, but offered a slight advantage to his men, who relied less on finesse and more on brute force.

A commotion erupted along the line. The men were pointing at something in the distance, something Falcon failed to notice. But Beriszl and Chilali knew what it was, sharing a laugh. What Falcon thought was ground littered with black rocks from the mountains, just behind the settlement, was something else entirely, the casualties the Ragebourne and Divergent inflicted.

It was custom for those of the Blackland Nation to expose a body fallen in battle to the night sky for seven days. What remained would be pushed into a shallow hole and covered. So many rotted in the open air that if the wind shifted, Falcon feared all his men would be made ill by the smell.

"By Sitara," he said aloud. "You killed so many."

And so, the chant of Chilali's name erupted. Hearing such a soft name bellowed over and over by warriors in such a way felt out of place to Falcon, but that seemed to be the problem with the Divergent in general. Still, had those men been alive the outcome of this battle would be grave for the Empire.

"The servant approaches," Olin hissed.

Chilali moved forward, as if she were going to run him down and slay him.

"Stop, he approaches to parley," Falcon bade her.

She heeded his words for the moment.

"It is your place to come with me to speak to him. But do not attack, unless he does so first," the knight explained and dismounted. "The rules of war must be obeyed always."

It was also customary among the nations of men to meet an opponent on equal footing. The Blackland Nation had few horses and kept them almost entirely in the north. As the Servant came on foot, so would he.

"Be cautious," Olin called out to the knight and Divergent. "I do not like the looks of this one."

Chilali stared at the man before her. Blue splotches covered his skin as it had all the others she had seen. And his head was just as bald and smooth. His eyes glinted with a dim green light, which felt unnatural to her. He wore a brown robe with a hood he had pulled back and he kept his hands open and out to his sides to show he hid nothing. He smelled like a bouquet of withered flowers, something she experienced once or twice in Alden's mansion.

"I've seen him before," she told the knight. "He heals the others."

"He is a Servant of Shyamon, one of the Embracing Night's priests. His powers are not to be trifled with."

"Why does their skin always look like that?"

"The blue-gray markings?"

"Yes, yours is not like that."

"They imbibe a ritual concoction to celebrate achievements. It marks their skin so."

Falcon shushed her before she could ask another question. They were within range enough to converse with the Servant.

"You've come to parley?" Falcon asked.

The Servant bowed slightly and spoke with a peculiar

voice. It was pleasant and calm but hid a sound like the distant buzzing of insect wings.

"I am Lysander, a Servant of the Embracing Night. I've come to ask you to allow us to withdraw."

"Let you run away?"

"Take the settlement and the mine. We've known enough bloodshed."

"You are not one to decide that, I think. You invaded our lands and attacked our people."

"We were not aware of the truce."

"We were aware."

"And yet, you came?"

Falcon waved his gauntleted hand at the line behind him.

"We do not carry the Empire's banner. We are an independent expedition force, comprised of knights and mercenaries from various noble houses."

The Servants strange eyes focused on Chilali.

"A Divergent stands by your side."

"She is uncalled and does not hear Sitara's voice," Falcon returned.

"That explains the vicious methods she employs."

"It does."

"What will you do then, True Silver Knight? Your Divergent and Ragebourne destroyed our food stores and we've lost half our warriors to this misunderstanding. The few women and children we brought with us hide in fear. If you do not allow us to withdraw, we will fight to the last man."

"You've no more warriors of the rank of Asael or higher or else they would be here."

"Perhaps, that is true, but your losses will be heavy regardless."

Falcon glanced at Chilali and tightened his fists. Maybe it was his mental abilities as a True Silver Knight beginning to develop, but he could feel the blind urge to kill growing inside Chilali. He knew what her answer would be. But he found himself wondering if he should accept the withdrawal. His mission would be accomplished, part of it anyway. The nobles would have their settlement and mine, even if they didn't have food or water within three days travel. But no glory would come with such a victory and no vengeance would be taken. His becoming the new True Silver Knight Captain above Kern would be a hollow thing.

No, this was his battle, his test from Sitara.

"I will return to my commanders, and you will know our decision," he finally answered, his heart pounding in his chest and head. "Come, Chilali."

She growled and followed him back to the line. Falcon mounted his horse as the others looked at him for some indication as to what was said. Chilali remained silent, but tense, utterly focused on Lysander across the field.

"Kill him as soon as you are able," Olin whispered to the Divergent and Ragebourne.

Beriszl returned a blank stare and lapped his snout once.

Falcon trotted out to the middle of the line and looked *his* army over. For an irregular force, they had done well enough. Their efforts deserved to be recognized by the emperor when he finally returned.

"The Servant made an offer," he bellowed, his voice like rolling thunder and his shield glowing like fire in the rising light of the morning. "Let them withdraw back to their lands or they will fight to the last man. I say, let them fight to the last coward."

The men roared at his words, and he felt exhilaration like none before. Sitara blessed him that moment, he felt. Her star never seemed so bright to him before. He drew his sword with its gold hilt and the three virtues etched on it and he pointed at the enemy.

"For Orsa!" he shouted and kicked his reluctant mount into a full gallop with his army following behind. Collectively, they glistened like water as they charged and surged with as much force.

They met the frightened front line of Blackland warriors, who desperately tried to defeat the charge by planting one end of their spears beneath a foot and holding the other up and out. While such a simple tactic caught inexperienced horsemen, the others were experienced enough to divert the protruding blades aside and position their mount to pass through the opening to trample the spear holder. And the tactic did little to fend against those on foot who followed almost immediately behind.

Before Falcon was aware, he fell into the melee, swinging and hacking, while fending against attacks with his shield. As the commander, he found himself quickly singled out by the enemy. Spears cut deep into his mount's flanks, dropping him and the animal to the ground. It kicked and whinnied with the fear and pain of death as he scrambled to his feet, trying to mount an intelligent defense, while looking for his men. But all around him he saw only the stained faces of angry Blackland warriors.

A spear stabbed through his thigh plate, and he collapsed on the shaft, screaming and trying to swipe at the wielder. Another found the gap in the plating covering his hip and knifed into the bone. He wailed and tasted blood in his mouth. So quickly the end came, he thought, and shut his eyes for the killing blow.

Instead, he felt an intense wave of heat that made him instantly and profusely sweat. His eyes blurred but he was still able to discern Jerle. Like the warrior empress, she cut a swath through the men, two hands swinging an orange-hot sword, and set the two stabbing him ablaze. They darted in random directions like moths set aflame until falling to the ground.

While the heat was a good deterrent to the advance of the other Abdiels, the Blackland warriors quickly closed their circle around them. They knew what their weapons would do to such a malleable blade if they landed a solid hit. Jerle knew this, too.

She screamed and heated the sword further. The hot air was unbearable to Falcon, and he felt he could not even breathe. Just as the blade turned white in her hands, she spun it over her head, using the centrifugal force to sling molten bits at the surrounding warriors. Falcon never heard men squeal in such agony quite like that before. The white-hot metal stuck to the fine black metal chains covering their splinted armors and seared right through, burning cavernous holes into their bodies.

Jerle held little more than a molten hilt and a few of the warriors avoided the spray. Arrows took them down in sequence. The fire elemental user turned, hoping to see Astra, and instead she found Lea. The old woman stood well clear of the battle but was able to rain death with such accuracy. She already had another arrow notched and another target, a warrior Teth wrestled on the ground, selected. The old tracker slammed his elbow into the Blackland warrior's face over and over, but the younger man got the better of him and rolled on top. Before he could run a dagger into the underside of Teth's jaw, Lea stole his life.

Her supply of arrows was finite, and she used half, already. She notched and sighted for a new target. At the edge of the line, a mass of Blackland warriors churned around Chilali and Beriszl. The sight gave her pause and she knew not what to do.

It appeared the Divergent learned to use the slower Ragebourne as a living shield. She maneuvered around him with such ease that he seemed oblivious to her tactic. He always moved forward to the next nearest target, and she killed whoever came at her or directly for him. When she needed cover, she retreated to his front to get his attention and expose the enemy to his wrath. His long arms, black blade, and shield crushed all that they collided with, and he swung with absolute abandon, completely unconcerned about inadvertently striking Chilali.

Beriszl unleashed a clearing strike with his blade, finding flesh once or twice. He was losing breath and becoming tired, but he feared calling upon the blood rage his second heart would bring. He did not know how healed it was or if it had been healed at all by Astra's taboo power. The splintered shaft he wrapped with cord and used as a handle for his blade was beginning to crack and collapse in his powerful grip. The rim of his small shield also became more warped as it struck and cracked skull after skull.

And still the enemy came. He and Chilali made a game of it, the never-ending slaughter. In his extensive lifetime, he knew warriors that kept track of their kills in a battle and made wagers. But they had developed something new and unique to them. It was a simple challenge; how bloody could they make Chilali's boots by the end of the night, or in this case, the battle? He knew they were doing well, hearing the squish of blood from the padding inside her boots with each of her frantic steps.

Beriszl understood their goal needed to be to slay the Servant and he worked his way toward the stoic man with the dimly glowing green eyes. Chilali flitted all around him, not quite aware of his intentions, but being effective, nonetheless. The Servant recognized the tactic and chose to flee. The Ragebourne made a mental note to watch for his return.

Chilali darted up from between his legs and beneath his horizontal swing. She caught a ducking warrior and slashed him across his face. She followed the maneuver by springing to Beriszl's right and cutting a defending spear in half, leaving that warrior open to Beriszl's sheering swipe. When the second warrior fell onto his back from the mortal gash across his chest, Chilali got a glimpse of the rest of the battlefield. The Talarians were in trouble.

The overseers formed their horses into a line and fought hard against a unit of Blackland warriors, maybe twenty in size. But as she observed, mounts offered little advantage to the riders in that kind of situation. The Blackland warriors slashed at the slender legs of the horses to terrible effect. Riders tumbled off their collapsing mounts, often suffering injuries or being pinned by the pain-crazed animals. And as the overseers dropped, the Talarians became more vulnerable, sitting on the ground, defenseless and too fearful to move.

Astra came to their aid, running to them and clumsily lobbing arrow after arrow into the air, hoping it would fall onto an enemy. Lea, too, drew a bead on them, and her arrows found their marks, piercing men through necks and torsos. But her quiver was three arrows from being empty and Teth lay on the ground, trying to stop the bleeding from a deep wound on his leg.

Chilali lingered too long in one place and one of the dozen of spears aimed at her caught her ear and sliced it into two flaps. She recoiled and rolled out of the way, while Beriszl punished the attacker with a jaw-breaking swing of his shield. She scurried on the ground, avoiding strikes, but didn't see a way to get to the Talarians. She tried to force a route, breaking from Beriszl, but almost found herself surrounded. Their screams barely rose above the rest of the cacophony around her, the men with their grunting and screaming, the clang and scrape of metal on metal, and the occasional wet squish, which mostly came from Beriszl's fighting.

The cries of the Briam roared, inhuman, low, bestial, and louder than anything else. Each made the noise for as long and as hard as it could and then stopping for a moment to do it over again. As some dropped out, others picked back up. Some went silent forever. There was sadness in the sound, simple and plain, and it struck Chilali inside, going past her pain and bloodlust. Her violent instincts withdrew for the moment, leaving her exposed but enlightened. As Alden explained to her, the Empire was all there was for man and the Lessers. This battle became larger for her than just Minnie, Agraven, and the merchant who took her from her forest. The lives of all the Lessers, others like Beriszl, Astra, and Minnie, were at stake all across the Empire.

"Beriszl," she shouted and the Ragebourne immediately understood.

He roared, baring his fangs, and bowled forward without regard for the danger. Spears found their way to him, clipping and gouging him as he rushed passed, but none had the angle to really stab and stop him. She went with his push and punished those she could, but the linear shift in their motion exposed them to arrows, as they left a clear path behind them.

In her recent battles, Chilali learned some, but not all of the Blackland warriors could twist a metal centerpiece on their spears and cause them to bow out with a tight string. The warriors with these spears carried short arrows inside flat pouches on their thighs. The tautness of the bow and the short draw of the arrows let them loose many of the bolts quickly and with great velocity.

Slender black projectiles whizzed at them in mass. Many missed, because the speed at which they ran was so fast it was difficult for the Blackland archers to measure, but a few found their mark. The diamond-shaped heads bit deep into their flesh. A pair of arrows poked out of Beriszl's back, stuck into his shoulder blade. The red feathers of another wagged back and forth after becoming stuck in Chilali's right buttock, making the muscles go numb with pain. She tore the arrow out, surprised by how deep it penetrated, and kept running.

Beriszl cleared the Blackland mass, which collected behind them in a pursuing surge. Chilali zipped around the Ragebourne, sprinting with a slight limp as the pain in her buttocks radiated up her lower back. A secondary melee engulfed the Lessers. The surviving overseers, supported by the wounded, battled fifty or more warriors, who seemed to pay more attention to the random running and screaming Talarians than the men with swords and maces.

Lea joined Astra in the melee, firing off desperate shots with their remaining arrows, while trying to stay covered behind a wall of three armored knights. Chilali flew into the fray just as Lea managed to steal a handful of arrows out of the quiver of a nearby ally and send half of them into Blackland warriors.

Chilali ripped open an exposed back with a crossing slash. She thought with her help they could turn this battle quickly and she could return to aide Beriszl, but the Divergent failed to consider one thing. A wave of warriors still pursued her. Her eyes went wide when she spun to take the leg from a warrior trying to run down and impale a Talarian in the back and became aware of the pursuit. Only a small segment continued to follow Beriszl, but the wounded Ragebourne was wise enough to find a mass of his allies and seek support.

She made a visual count of those warriors coming after her and put their number at less than forty. The Briam rushed around her, continuing their harrowing song. Falcon and Jerle were nowhere in sight. She had to face these warriors, or they might break off after the Lessers.

Raife came to her side, panting and bleeding.

"We have this," he shouted in her ear and rushed to aid a mercenary, who was favoring a broken leg and found himself at the mercy of a Blackland warrior intent on piercing his gut. Raife burst open the attacker's side with a backhand slash and booted him away.

Chilali shifted her attention back to her pursuers; they were near. She kicked hard into the ground, trying to build as much speed as quickly as she could. She pierced the head of the mass, breaking spears and severing limbs. Her sword was an uneven, jagged mess with more sharp points than a nettled tree. It no longer cut anything evenly but tore everything apart like a wild beast.

They circled her, but this time she was without Beriszl and began to take hits. They didn't allow her much space to maneuver, but she became much more used to their peculiar fighting style and weapon. She could grasp the rhythm of their attacks and that made them easier to evade and easier for her to time her own strikes. She whittled at their numbers and had no doubt she would succeed in besting the entire mass on her own, until her sword broke in two.

Left with a sharp, metal nub, she hurled it into the face of the nearest attacker, killing him, and scrambled to find another weapon, just anything but one of the spears. She took a hit to her chest, but her armor absorbed most of it. She managed to grab the foe that landed the blow and fling him into several others, pushing the pack.

She saw the glimmer of a mace in the sunlight and broke for it. They ran after her, swinging to try to slow her. She hopped over the blades and zigzagged to avoid any thrusts. She swooped up the mace from next to the fallen knight who wielded it and turned back. It was longer than her sword, but lighter. She liked how its center of mass felt concentrated on the spiky head. She tried it out by crashing it through a spear shaft and thrusting forward with two hands, as she had seen Kern do to her. With her strength, she cracked the warrior's sternum, forcing blood to flow from his mouth.

The melee continued and she kept moving, beginning to breathe a bit faster, but much less so than the men pursuing her. Their movements slowed and some trailed behind the others as she shifted the position of the pack. The mace worked better than she expected, smashing through spear shafts and making her attacks nearly indefensible. The Blackland warriors were left with two options: avoid the swing or parry with the motion of the strike to avoid broken wrists, hands, or spears.

Chilali felt invincible for a short moment in the eternity of battle, until a warrior got lucky and blocked one of her swings with his blade against her shaft, shearing the head free. Left with only a metal stick, she panicked and searched for another discarded weapon. But this time, she shifted the pack so far from the original field of battle no new weapons were in sight.

An arcing spear almost cut the back of her neck, but she ducked forward, losing part of her hair. She countered by slamming the rod into the knees of the warrior, cracking them both. Another warrior slashed her across the back, piercing her armor and slicing open the muscles. The wound stole her wind from her, and she nearly doubled over. The rod fell from her grip, but she caught herself on her hands and clawed her way forward and back to her feet.

Half as many were left as had begun this dance with her, but she was in trouble and knew it. Her only option was to run, and she tried, but, as always, they excelled at corralling her. She could try to keep evading them, but eventually one would land a blow that would drop her dead. She knew this and hoped Beriszl would rejoin her.

The blaring sound from the Briam faded and a roar of multiple voices rose over the tumult. Falcon led a regrouped charge of knights and mercenaries. They outnumbered the warriors attacking her two or more to one. They clashed with men ramming their shields into the Blackland warriors and taking them off their feet.

The True Silver Knight was the first to reach her. He tossed a heavy, two-handed sword to her flat and without spin. She snatched it from the air by the handle and wheeled around with it at the warriors behind her. She crumpled one who tried to block the blow with his spear and slew the one next to him, even cutting through his belt and loincloth, leaving the dead man exposed.

Chilali slew a handful more, losing two hand spans from the tip of her sword in the process. And then there were no more. She searched, listened, and looked all around. There were no more. The horrible sounds of war became the dull, quiet noises the wounded and the dying made.

A Blackland warrior bleeding from his stomach on the ground, raised his hand up to Falcon and the knight responded by thrusting his sword through the man's heart with one hand on the handle and the other on the pummel.

"No prisoners," he ordered, breathless and barely able to stand.

The Knight freed his weapon from the corpse. He had been wounded several times, judging by the dents and holes in his armor, Chilali observed. And he healed each one on the spot. His trademark mirror shield looked like a flag of silver ribbons frozen in the wind. Blood dripped from his armor. He freed his hand from one of his gauntlets with his teeth and wiped the sweat from his brow with it. The Divergent came to his side as he surveyed his losses.

Jerle survived without suffering any major wounds. Her dangerous tactic with the molten sword saved his life and he was grateful for the woman's participation in the battle, but she earned a new scar. An arrow pierced one of her arms. She tended to the Ragebourne, who lay on his back, unconscious from exhaustion and blood loss.

Across from them, Lea tied a splint on her own leg as Astra watched. The Talarian girl made a few kills without suffering anything more than fright. Teth was not as lucky. A pair of knights carried him away, knowing they would have to remove the arrows piercing his leg and shoulder. Raife worked with other men to regroup the Lessers and offer limited assistance to any superficial injuries they suffered. Maimed Talarians were worthless in the Empire, as were Briam who couldn't work. It was best to let them die.

Olin waited at the edge of the battlefield with Marcus as the wounded were brought to them. The priest made quick judgments as to who would live without his help, who would need his help, and who was going to die regardless.

He sorted them into three spots on the ground and went to work, rolling up the sleeves of his robe. An actual count would need to be made, but the knight suspected little more than half of his force remained. Disease and sickness would claim even more.

The Talarians looked to be a third or less than what they set out with from Orsa. And the Briam lost the most. Of the few thousand that were alive at the start of this battle, only several hundred still gathered in weeping packs. As hearty as they were, they were also fragile creatures that stressed to the point of death, easily, which was why so many of their bodies littered the battlefield without any wounds. Meekness only invites death, he thought with contempt.

Chilali plopped down on the ground. He looked at her, curious.

"Fatigued?"

She shook her head and started taking her boots off.

"What are you doing?"

"I'm seeing how well we did," she answered and poured a steady stream of blood from her boot and then the next. Falcon smiled grimly, just beginning to second guess himself and the day's losses.

"It shouldn't count if it's your blood," he said, tired and numb.

She returned a fierce look, as if he had falsely accused her of cheating.

"It's not."

Kergen, the man Chilali bested in the thicket on the road to Orsa, approached and shouted to Falcon.

"Spoils of war hiding in the settlement, sir."

Chilali twiddled her toes, not interested in the brute anymore. Falcon shouted back.

"What's that?"

"Blackland women, maybe ten or fifteen. They bled the children before we could."

Falcon wiped his face on the back of his hand and

hollered back, "Spoils of war."

Kergen grinned and sprinted toward the settlement.

The knight looked down at Chilali and her red feet.

"The sick and injured will need fresh water and you still seem able enough with your injuries," he pointed at the Blackland Mountains. "Can you climb to where ice forms and bring as much as you can back?"

She stared at the mountains and stood barefoot.

"I'll go."

"Take your boots with you. It will be cold. And try to find large, clean leather bags, like the kind we use for rations."

She stretched and headed off to perform her errand without complaint, a sense of relief budding inside of her, warm like sunlight and as refreshing as the breeze.

The Cost of Victory

"She heads into the mountains," Falcon stated, squatting in front of Jerle to bandage her arm. His face seemed dark when he spoke the words or maybe it was a trick of the early morning light and the shadow his growing beard seemed to cast.

Jerle adjusted her sitting position on the rock, feeling uncomfortable.

"This doesn't seem right," she spoke meekly, her eyes dropping from his face.

"We do this at the emperor's order," he returned sharply, pinching her wounded arm just hard enough to grab her attention. His breath was hot and sour, and his fierce blue eyes contained such weariness. Like she, he wanted this entire ordeal to be behind them. The only way he believed he could do that was to take the Divergent's life.

"But the emperor doesn't know what she has done. We owe her this victory."

"We owe her nothing," he seethed.

She tore her arm from his grip.

"You did not slay a single Asael, or the Avidan."

"Agraven," he said bluntly and stood. "If you want to save him, this is the only way."

She bit her lip and stood to face him. He was more than a head taller with a much larger frame, but she was not intimidated by his stature.

"Why should I even believe you?"

"Why wouldn't you?" he asked, his tone full of suspicion.

"You've lied to me before."

"I have and I will again to serve the emperor."

His words surprised her.

"What other lies have you told me, then?"

He rested his hand on his sword pummel. The action did

not go unnoticed by Jerle, who already began to hone in on the burning place inside her mind.

"The emperor gave Chilali an option to avoid all of this, an option she turned down."

"What are you talking about?"

"He offered to allow her to return to the forest and he would free Alden and Agraven. And we would have avoided this battle, all its hardships, and all its risks. The Imperial Army would have seen to it with much greater force and far fewer casualties."

Jerle stood stunned, her thoughts so jumbled she couldn't make sense of them. She didn't know whether to believe Falcon or why Chilali would not return to the forest if he were telling the truth.

"She chose this bloody path for us, Jerle. She risked your husband's life for her own childish, selfish reasons. And now you must decide whether you will help us bring an end to the misery and death she breeds as an uncalled."

Jerle turned halfway away.

"I'm not a murderer anymore."

He grabbed her shoulders and turned her to face him.

"This is not murder."

He waved his hand across the battlefield as men went about euthanizing the wounded horses with a blade.

"This is mercy," he finished with a sigh.

"What do you need me to do?" she asked with a sniffle.

"I have a plan so she won't suffer, and we will not be put in danger, but I need your talent to carry it out properly."

"Tell me what it is."

"You will know when it is time. It will be better that way. Trust me. Now, prepare yourself. We will leave as soon as Olin is finished."

The knight left her weeping and defeated. Her emotions were as mixed as the blood and dirt around her and the throbbing pain in her arm was more than she could bear at the moment. Lea entered her field of vision, hobbling along on a splinted, broken leg by using a ruined spear for a crutch. Jerle feared she would not be able to control herself, but something seemed pitiful about the old woman, lonely. She came straight toward Jerle, which puzzled the already confused fire elemental user even more.

Lea made a spot on the stone next to Jerle, pushing her off a bit. Her presence made Jerle tremble with rage, but she didn't seem to care. She kept her head forward and peered over the growths on her cheek with one eye at Jerle.

"Let's get this done. Ask me."

Jerle turned a bit and pushed the guttural words out of her throat.

"Did you kill Saveria?"

Lea leaned forward on her crutch a bit and stared at the ground.

"If I did, would you blame me? Would I be responsible for it? Or would you save your rage for the one who ordered it?"

"What does it matter if you were ordered or not? You still had a choice."

"Just as you have a choice now."

"What do you know of my choices?"

"I'm not here by accident, child. I was ordered to stop Sir Charisma and that vile priest from killing the Divergent. But now, I'm no longer able, physically at least."

"Then you know why I have to do it."

"Then hold fast to that rationale when I tell you I fired the arrow that ended your daughter's life. I try not to regret it. I took a life to protect the one I love, as you intend. But seeing the hatred in you, one who suffered the loss, I wonder if I should have let her die."

"Her?" Jerle said, her voice cracking.

"My daughter."

"You have a daughter, and you did this to me? How could-"

"I know your misery."

"Do you really?"

Jerle waited as Lea gathered her words.

"Sitting here next to you, my life is already yours to take. So, I will tell you this. I made a deal with Baigen to protect my daughter. She was to live safely and in comfort at a noble house. And to keep our secrets he made sure she would always be a quiet child through means I care not to consider," she explained, wiping her nose. "So, I was quite surprised to find her gone from the house and on this ill-fated march in your company."

"Who? I don't …" Jerle said, her eyes opening wide with realization.

Lea shook her head.

"You lit her pyre aflame."

Jerle felt her heart break for the woman who murdered her daughter. And with that, there was no more rage, just sorrow, sickening and unfading. It felt like someone plunged a hand into her chest and twisted everything inside.

"Never had I loathed the Silver Goddess so much before," Lea said, rising.

Jerle grabbed her arm, coming to her senses enough to ask the most important question.

"Who ordered it? Was it Baigen?"

"No, it was someone powerful in the Empire. That is all I know."

"And what will you do?"

"That depends on what you do," she answered coolly.

"Do you know if it is true that the emperor gave Chilali the option to return to the forest?"

"I don't."

The disguised Talarian started hobbling away and Jerle actually felt sympathy for her. She could barely begin to understand the loneliness and hopelessness the woman faced and the detachment she was forced to feign.

"Olin won't heal your leg, will he?"

Lea shrugged.

"Do not trouble yourself for me. I will continue to work my charms on the pig-faced tracker," she said with a cackle, returning to character.

Jerle stood with a slight smile and wiped her cheeks dry. She could see Olin washing after treating the last of the wounded. They would be heading for the mountains soon. She was running out of time to make up her mind. It seemed easy to hold Chilali responsible for all this death, as callously as she played with it. But Lea's revelations made it all fuzzy. She had to learn the truth and there was only one person she could trust for it, if he knew.

Beriszl lay among the wounded, wheezing. His chest rose and fell at an uneven pace and his numerous wounds were not bandaged. This was not due to the fact he was a Lesser, but because there was a shortage and his blood had already clotted. Jerle knelt at his side, watching him fade in and out of awareness. She brushed her hand through the short spiky fur on top of his head. He seemed to recognize her.

"I need to know something Beriszl. It's important, so you must tell me the truth."

He blinked slowly, looking at her.

"Did the emperor tell Chilali to return to the forest and he would spare Alden and Agraven?"

The Ragebourne raised one of his heavy hands. It wobbled with weakness. She held it.

"Yes," he spoke with a droning hiss and squeezed her hand as if he wanted to tell her more.

She stared at the Ragebourne.

"Why?"

"Find her mother," he managed to get out between coughs.

"Her mother?"

The Ragebourne passed out and could answer no more questions. Olin stood above her like a corpse. He leaned heavily on his silver staff.

"I hope what the Lesser told you will not keep you from doing what the emperor asks," the priest said, fatigue tainting his voice.

"It won't," she assured him, knowing he could read her thoughts. But she didn't care, because Beriszl words had not swayed her one way or another. She had to ask Chilali before she would end the Divergent's life.

"Falcon is waiting," the priest said, offering his hand to help her stand.

She stood on her own.

"Astra will come with us. I don't want to leave her unprotected here and her presence will help keep us from alarming Chilali."

"That is wise," he agreed, withdrawing his hand. "Meet us behind the settlement."

He grabbed her shoulder as he passed and stared hard into her eyes. She found Astra among her people, helping as much as she could. But the Lessers were not a priority, and supplies would not be wasted on them.

"We need to go," she told the Talarian, even though it was clear she wanted to stay and hold the hands of the dying.

"You do not want to stay here alone," she hinted.

The girl did as she was told. Jerle found a bow and a nearly empty quiver on the battlefield. She handed them to the Talarian and kept walking. They passed through the settlement, hearing the awful cries of the Blackland Nation women inside the stone structures.

"The spoils of war," she said to herself, shutting out the painful sounds and dragging Astra along.

Falcon, armed with a whole but worn shield, and Olin met them. Both men were silent and Jerle could feel Astra's fright. She was afraid, too.

"How will you find her?" she asked of them.

"Her armor bears enchantments," the priest answered

and began walking up the slope. "This way."

"As tired as we are, this will not be an easy trek. Focus on your footing and keep your weight forward, always," the knight offered and followed the priest. Jerle sighed and fell into pace behind them with Astra.

They climbed until Jerle could see the settlement, the battlefield, and the camp where the wounded were treated, and the dead were being stacked for the pyre. They climbed further, until the brown dirt gave way to more and more to black rock. They zigzagged to lessen the sharpness of the rising slope, but it just dragged the journey out longer.

Astra held onto her, barely able to keep up with the men who were blessed with divine stamina. They never slowed, even as Jerle's legs burned. Methodically, they continued their climb, pausing at times to let her and Astra catch up.

The wind blew with increasing strength as they climbed and the air cooled. Soon her breath left her mouth in puffs and looking back dizzied her with its height. The settlement and the battlefield were small things. And the forest trimmed the horizon at the edge of the rust-colored smear that was the arid plain at the mountain base.

They reached a level ledge and the Fire King burned brightly above them. She was cold, but still sweating. She forgot to take water and hoped her thirst would hold out long enough to survive the rest of the climb and the descent. The ledge wrapped around into a crevasse, formed by a gradual split between two of the peaks.

Olin pointed.

"Ahead, through there."

Falcon led them through the narrow passage. The knight had to turn sideways to squeeze through. They passed into a circular open area, like a scoop taken out of the mountain. It was a large area, big enough for fifty men to camp, and the middle featured a hole large enough to swallow a wagon. It appeared to Jerle water would drain into it, falling forever into the ground. Ahead of them was a long, snaking path with a sharp incline, leading to another plateau where snow collected. It was a smooth path, littered with little stone bits. This is where the water comes from when the snow melts, Jerle figured.

"She approaches," Olin said, staring up at the snowy plateau. "Falcon and I will handle this part, Jerle. When the time is right, we will ask you to assist."

Chilali's head appeared over the edge of the plateau, followed by the rest of her. She saw them and smiled. Her tiny arms dragged a pair of leather sacks as big as her and both were full of ice and snow. She hopped and skidded her way down the treacherous slope. But they were all used to seeing her perform such precarious actions.

She stopped at the bottom and held the bags up for them to see.

"I have plenty of ice."

Falcon approached casually and took the bags from her. He set them aside and knelt before her. She looked him over, curious and bothered by his silent calm.

"Thank you for all you have done for us and the Empire."

She shrugged.

"We need to hurry back and tell the emperor so he will let Alden and Agraven go."

"Don't worry. I intend to go myself as quickly as I can with Olin. Alden and Agraven will both be fine."

"I'm faster," she suggested.

"You are," he agreed. "But your armor is a mess. It should be repaired before you present yourself to the emperor."

"You can heal it like a wound?"

He smiled.

"Better than how we heal wounds. You see, with flesh, we cannot repair what is cut away or completely destroyed. We only speed that which would happen naturally. But with enchanted metal we can cause growth, so long as we can envision the form."

"Can you?" she asked, examining her armor and its multiple tears, gouges, and holes.

"I'll show you," he said and reached out to touch her breastplate. She flinched and stepped back.

"I only intend to touch your armor. You do not need to worry. And also, why don't you remove Alden's amulet? It could interfere with the enchantment."

"Why is that?"

"Because of its power. Did not Alden tell you it carries his mother's love? And there is no enchantment greater than that."

She took the amulet off and looked at the spinning blue jewel with the little nick in it. She dropped it in Falcon's shield hand and glanced at Jerle. The fire elemental user's scent was thick with the odors of stress and exhaustion.

Falcon touched her breastplate, surprising her. A soft, white light radiated from the metal, beneath the camouflage, and Falcon stepped back to watch. The holes began to knit themselves and she felt the armor bending and moving to regain its original form. The experience unsettled her, but she didn't feel threatened until she saw Jerle begin to cry.

She whipped around to look at Falcon, suspicious of the situation now. That's when the armor's re-growth became growth. The silver metal began to spread out from the individual pieces, thick and tight on her skin. She screamed and tore at it with her fingers, clawing up as much of her own skin as she did metal. But her efforts weren't enough. The armor grew over her arms and hands and began to harden. She used all her strength to try to move, to try to reach Falcon. But the armor continued to thicken, halting her movement mid-stride and making it very difficult to breathe or speak.

She heard Olin speak unintelligible sounds, his eyes radiating white light, as her heart beat in her ears and the pressure continued to build inside her head. Her whole body was covered in silver metal from her neck down with random strands wrapping her head but exposing enough of her face and ears to see and hear. Fear overwhelmed her. She squirmed and fought but couldn't move at all. She screamed and screamed inside her head to be let loose and to not do this to her. Each thought became more unbearable than the next.

"It worked, but the enchantment will lose its power soon. We must act quickly," the priest said, ending his incantation.

Falcon nodded and faced her.

"I'm sorry for this, but it is the only way the emperor would truly spare Alden and Agraven. If you chose to wear the helmet, this would have been easier for all of us."

Astra tried to run to Chilali and Olin blocked her path, his visage fierce with his glowing eyes. He backhanded the Talarian, knocking her down.

"Mind your place," he growled.

Falcon beckoned Jerle to him.

"Jerle, use your power to end this peacefully. I can't cut the metal with my sword without breaking the enchantment."

Jerle forced herself to stay calm and she stepped forward and looked into Chilali's eyes. She heard the Divergent's muffled, helpless screams.

"Hurry," Olin shouted.

She shook her head and focused on Chilali.

"Why did you not go back to your forest?"

The Divergent went silent. Tears welled in her eyes.

"Why damn you!?" she asked again.

Falcon grabbed her shoulders from behind.

"It does not matter. You must do it now or we will all be in danger. She defeated an Avidan, so you know what she is capable of. Do it for Agraven and Alden and the Empire."

He shoved her forward gently and she fell to her knees, with her hands on Chilali's chest. "Why?" she mouthed.

Chilali screamed and tried to say something over and over, but it was muted by the metal and her inability to move her jaw. But Jerle understood. It was the same reason Berisz1 gave, a child's reasoning, "mother."

Jerle's head fell.

"Your mother is gone, Chilali. She left you and you will never find her again, no matter how hard you look. Forgive me this and find peace."

Jerle raced to the burning place in her mind and felt its heat enwrap her, enthrall her. She drew on its power, siphoning it from the Fire King's realm with care and precision. Falcon intended for her to use the same trick she used to topple the tree in orchard outside Orsa. It would be a quick, sudden, and controlled explosion. It was also the same trick that made her such an excellent assassin when she worked for Baigen. She could touch a man, walk away, and moments later his heart would explode.

She swore she would never use it again on a living creature, not even on the Avidan, had she even been given the opportunity. But she needed to do it one more time. Just one more time, she said to herself and started forming the miniscule ball of flame inside Chilali. It had to be fed carefully and the Fire King's power wound in just the right way to not immediately fly apart. Though she was unpracticed, it came back to her quickly. But something felt off, skewed perhaps. She never experienced it before; it was a draining of sorts, like her power was running out of Chilali. More of the Fire King's power poured out of her and into Chilali, too much perhaps, but still she felt like it was ebbing out. She shook the sensation away and focused on finishing the deed.

She pulled back and fell into Falcon's arms, wailing. Only the knight's strength kept her on her feet as he shed tears himself, silently.

Olin's eyebrows shot up in alarm.

"The enchantment has exhausted itself. The damage her armor sustained reduced its lifespan."

"How much longer?" Falcon asked, grasping Jerle roughly.

She shook her head, her face in her hands.

"Soon," she sobbed.

The silver metal shrieked as Chilali started to move. Slowly at first, but she picked up speed as it fatigued. The enchantment's power diminished with each new second. She shook off some pieces as they cracked and tore around her body. Her skin bled from fresh cuts, and she exuded violence. Her mind was lost to madness generated by fear.

Falcon moved Jerle aside and drew his blade to face the metal clad Divergent. She took a step toward him, and he raised his shield. Jerle leaned against the rock wall, shaking her head and mouthing how sorry she was over and over.

A loud crack, sharp and piercing like a lightning strike, echoed off the rock walls. The metal covering Chilali's torso blew off and crashed into Falcon shield, bending it around his arm. The explosion slapped the Divergent backward into the hole in the mountain and left a puff of bloody frost momentarily hanging in the air where she once stood.

Falcon dashed to the hole and looked over the edge as he freed his arm from the shield's strapping. He held it to his stomach, the limb broken again. Jerle held her ringing ears and shuffled to the hole on her knees. Astra curled into a ball by Olin, who held his hand over a shrapnel-caused wound on the side of his neck.

The knight and the fire elemental user could only see so far into the darkness below and Chilali was nowhere to be seen.

"I cannot tell. It is too deep," Falcon said, looking at Olin for some determination.

Jerle wondered if the knight was truly that paranoid.

The explosion was much stronger and larger than she intended. Something tried to swallow her power and she overcompensated. The power she forced into Chilali would have split Beriszl in two with ease. There was no way the Divergent survived. None ever survived it. None, she said to herself over and over, feeling the gravity of her deed.

The priest finally answered the knight, wincing.

"I sense her no more."

Falcon picked Jerle up, satisfied. He shook her.

"Enough, it is done. Regain yourself."

She couldn't calm herself down or stop hyperventilating. She couldn't look away from the hole.

He slapped her lightly, making her cheek rosy.

"Enough, this is the cost of victory. Accept it and embrace your purchase. Agraven's life is saved."

She held her cheek and swore then she would kill this True Silver Knight one day.

Strife's Journal: 11th Day, 4059, The Northeast Line

Snowflakes cling to strands of my blood-red hair. This winter remains gentle.

Sveta sleeps in my tent, warmed by my fire.

I sit outside on this rock looking at other rocks and the green-glowing horizon. The mold the Volitors spawn generates the sickly light.

In that light, the Volitors' Brute King (a term coined by Ren) lumbers, invincible.

I find myself contemplating my own mortal death. Suddenly, it frightens me, not like the living death continues to do so, but in a new and terrible way I have never experienced before.

I fault myself for having such thoughts on the eve of what should be the final battle in this horrible war. Allowing myself to experience a relationship with Sveta was a mistake.

Divergents should make no such attachments, because they represent the only weakness we truly have. Because of Sveta, I am now vulnerable. I see now that Sitara knew this; it is why she made us solitary creatures. If only I could make myself let go, I could become fierce and fearless once again. But I cannot, because I do not truly wish to do so.

Fool am I, but regretful I am not.

Tomorrow, I go alone to end the Brute King and this war. Tomorrow will be the beginning of a new age for us all. Tomorrow is a promise.

Sitara's light be with us, always.

—*Divergent Strife Ashwake*

Reward

Beriszl chugged down the mead the men gave him in celebration of their victory. He sat at a long stone table in the hall of what had been the main barracks for the Blackland Nation warriors. Surrounded by supposed comrades, he felt alone, even as they bumped him and slapped him on the back. He killed more than any of them but was still a Lesser and a slave, even if they were grateful and accepting of him for the moment.

Jerle left immediately after lighting the mass pyre in the mountains to honor the fallen. She took Astra, Teth, Lea, and Marcus with her, as well as some of the surviving horses. Falcon and Raife did not agree with her decision, but she was adamant enough. And they would not travel through the Southern Wilds alone. A small contingent of men from different houses would go with them to secure the mining tools they left behind. Falcon and Olin planned to leave with the next sunrise to report to the emperor.

Raife intended to remain for a while and assist with setting up the mine. He was one of the few survivors with the knowledge to conduct such an operation. But he was not at the celebration. The pain his missing arm caused left him bedridden.

Falcon and Olin sat at the head of the table, taking part in the merriment. The knight smiled on the outside, but the old Ragebourne could see in the man's cold blue eyes just how tormented by his deeds he truly was. The dead still burned outside, high in the mountains so the smoke would not blow into the settlement. And deep inside the mountain, Chilali's corpse rotted. Jerle confessed the truth of what occurred, and it did not surprise the old Ragebourne. He suspected the plot from the very start but could say nothing directly. He pitied the fire elemental user for what she did and what she would continue to do to herself. She would never find forgiveness from herself.

Chilali was the hero swept aside too early, another that would be forgotten by history. The explanation for her disappearance was that she simply left. Some men believed this and hoped she would return. Others drank away their disappointment. There would be no new age for the Empire, no savior like Strife. This was just another disheartening reality for them.

Beriszl set his stein down and stood from the table. With his large size he could not help but to draw attention to his leaving.

"Honorable Ragebourne, why not stay longer?" Falcon shouted to him.

His heavy shoulders rose and fell.

"I will return. Mead passes through me as it does you," he answered.

Falcon toasted him and he left, receiving more adulation. Outside the air was uncomfortably hot, even as twilight drew near. He did not enjoy being this far south, but this was to be his new post. His mission had always been to see to the security of the mine. Duke Medwin had many plans for it. Beriszl cared not what they were.

He relieved himself on the short wall, watching the Briam make steady trips in small groups up and down the mountain for ice. Because of them, food, instead of water, was actually harder to find, but losing so many in battle meant their diminished rations were no longer so diminished.

The Ragebourne shook himself dry and passed a lit bunkhouse where the Talarians were kept. Men moved in and out of the structure, appearing more relaxed after leaving, it seemed. He sighed and sighed again. This was all there was for him, he thought, wishing for a moment that just one of those spears had pierced him a bit deeper in battle, while he absentmindedly scratched the tops of his feet. Perhaps he developed a rash, he wondered. He scratched a bit harder and sighed one last time.

* * *

Alden moved the meat and vegetables around his plate to pass the time. His uncle sat next to him at the dining table, watching him intently and in silence. Both were dressed casually and in private quarters high in the palace, but it was all steeped in formality. Portraits of the late Empress Saveria hung around the room, always with her beautiful hair blowing in the wind and her armor shining like a black sun. The whole scene was lit by a pair of low-hanging candle chandeliers. The room, itself, was interior to the palace tower and had no windows.

Knights kept guard outside the room and only the most trusted Talarian servants brought in the meals and took them away. The palace taster, a small priest with beady eyes, sat quietly in the corner with a napkin and silverware in his lap. Alden cared not for the little man and tried to ignore him whenever he came in the room.

"Your brother-in-arms will be here shortly. Do try to relax," Adelphos assured.

Alden set his knife and fork evenly apart on his plate and rested the edges of his palms on the table. While captive, his uncle treated him with more comforts and luxuries than he himself had at his own estate. The ruby-colored jacket he wore was made of the finest cloth in the Empire and ornamented with polished obsidian stones. His cufflinks were a swirl of precious, refined metals and not the usual silver, which was the fashion in the Empire.

But he was told nothing of Chilali's efforts and forced to focus on refining strategies for future conflicts in the north for when the truce would inevitably be broken.

"It is hard to relax when one's life is at stake," he sighed.

The emperor smiled and took a sip from his goblet. Plain water, Alden observed.

"Did you really think I would put you to the wall?"

"Yes," Alden answered with a blank expression.

Adelphos chuckled, unsettling his nephew.

"It is not that it didn't cross my mind, given how much you infuriate me. But the truth is, you are simply too valuable to the Empire. And you are the only man I may speak to as an equal."

"Chilali could be invaluable as well," Alden postured, hoping to irritate his uncle a bit, but failing.

"The Divergent was little more than a symbol of our misguided hopes, our fantasy of our ill-remembered history. We must look beyond our past and stop hoping for another great hero to save us from all our ills," he grabbed Alden's shoulder and leaned close to them. "We must be responsible for ourselves and our own futures. That is the path Sitara has put before us."

Alden smiled at the old man and relaxed a bit. His uncle leaned back in his seat and directed Alden with his eyes to look behind.

Falcon stood in the doorway, cleanly shaven and dressed in a rich green tunic embroidered with silver thread. Battle had hardened his body, building and toning his figure and making it startlingly more impressive than Alden remembered. New scars also marked his exposed flesh.

He was joyful to see his friend and rose quickly to shake hands with him, but he chided himself for being disappointed at not seeing Chilali peeking out from the doorway behind the knight.

"It seems you were victorious," Alden fished for information.

Falcon slapped him on the shoulder.

"There is much to tell you," was all his friend would offer.

Falcon took a moment to salute the emperor and bow slightly. Adelphos waved his fingers, signaling the True

Silver Knight to be at ease and to have a seat. Both men joined the emperor at the table and a Talarian obediently came in and served Falcon a plate of food and poured him a goblet of wine.

Alden leaned forward, desperate to know.

"What happened? Where is Chilali? Tell me everything."

Adelphos's eyes shifted sternly to Falcon, who sat up straight in his chair.

"We were victorious, but not without cost."

"Cost?" Alden urged.

"Orsa is no more. A raiding party ravaged it and its people."

Alden took a moment to collect his thoughts as the joy he felt at finally seeing his friend and an end to his imprisonment drained out of him.

"By Sitara …"

"We sent the handful of survivors, women, back to the capital and took the Lessers with us at Chilali's insistence."

Alden's brow furrowed as he thought Falcon's words through.

"That could not have been easy, but does it mean there are Lessers at the settlement?"

Falcon nodded and continued.

"Many were slain in the final battle, but enough lived to service the men who remained behind. And even now the Briam make trips into the mountains to recover snow and ice for water."

"Clever. And Chilali?"

Falcon looked to Adelphos, and the emperor signaled him to continue with a wave of his fingers.

"She merely left, wandered off into the wilderness."

"As my pet bird did so long ago?" Alden asked with an accusatory tone.

Adelphos intertwined his fingers and set his hands on the table. Falcon reached into his pocket and withdrew

Alden's amulet. He put it on the table between them. Alden took it with a shaky hand.

"The Divergent is dead," the emperor confirmed what he feared.

Alden switched between them, not believing and trying to see deception in their faces.

"How?" he demanded, slamming his fists on the table.

Adelphos rose, indignant.

"How else, you fool? I ordered it and Falcon carried it out."

Alden sat in silence, staring at his friend across the table.

"And for the difficulty of all that he accomplished, I will formally promote him to the position of True Silver Knight Captain."

Falcon crossed his arms, watching Alden's reaction. The merchant's fists balled up on the tabletop and he stood, pushing his chair out with enough force to knock it over backwards.

"Am I free to go now?" he asked his uncle coolly.

Adelphos crossed his arms, taking measure of the man before him. He did not think he misjudged his nephew as much as he had. He believed the time spent at the palace, working at his side, would have shifted his opinion and opened his eyes to the Empire's true priorities. He expected him to be shocked and angry upon hearing the Divergent's fate, but this was different. He was genuinely upset, but there was still a glimmer in his eyes, the same glimmer the emperor hoped to cut from his heart. That light of dreams and ideals did not belong in the eyes of a true leader.

His nephew was a man who believed he could change the world on his own through deed alone. Adelphos intended to teach him otherwise. The world was not such a simple place, and such archaic thinking did not befit one of his nephew's intelligence. The rule of law, the sacrifices of many, carefully won victories, and faith in the Silver

Goddess—these things would change the world for better, not a single man and not a single dream.

With Eos missing, he needed to groom a new heir. He believed it would be Alden, but now he was terribly disappointed. There was still time to reevaluate the situation, to let Alden reevaluate the situation. Perhaps not all hope was lost.

"Go for now and do what you will. But know I will seek you out again in time."

Alden excused himself with a bow and left the room.

Adelphos turned to Falcon and the knight stood.

"Do not become too comfortable. The war in the south lands has just begun. You will lead the Imperial forces to the settlement-"

"Nesma, my Lord."

"Pardon?"

Falcon leaned to extend his line of sight through the doorway to make sure Alden was gone.

"If it pleases you, I wish the settlement to be named, 'Nesma.'"

"After my sister?"

"Yes, after Alden's mother."

"That is good," Adelphos marveled, rubbing his bearded chin. "You will lead the Imperial forces to secure *Nesma* or retake it from the Blackland Warriors, whichever. Now, enjoy your meal. I must have a word with another guest."

Adelphos turned to leave. Falcon stepped around him quickly.

"My apologies for trying your patience my Lord, but I have a question."

"Speak."

"Was Agraven truly a prisoner in all of this?"

The emperor patted him on the shoulder with a laugh.

"Why does it matter?"

"I used his captivity to push someone to do something

against their conscience."

Adelphos laughed harder.

"A brilliant stroke then, but it is no matter to you. The mission is past, and the fire elemental users will be happily reunited."

"Of course, my Lord."

Adelphos breezed past Falcon with a quick stride, his regal fur cape trailing in the air behind him. The knight sat again at the table, ill with his deeds and staring at the gravy-covered meat and assortment of vegetables on his plate. Without ceremony, he ate, watched by the small priest in the corner. He wished the small man would just go away.

* * *

Adelphos rounded a corner and passed another pair of his elite guards. They stood at attention as he walked by. He turned into an alcove in the hallway where a suit of battle worn armor stood proudly. It was the one he wore as a regular knight, tarnished and plain, but now historical. With a little pressure from his shoulder, he forced the wall behind the suit to turn with a slight grating hiss. He slipped inside the opening as silver crystals burst with white fire to light the passage and the wall closed up behind him with the same hissing sound. The shoulder-wide passage ahead spiraled up, circling twice to reach a higher floor.

The emperor reached a metal-banded wood door and passed through it into a small room with no windows and lit with more of the crystals in the passageway. Agraven lay on a bed with two Talarian girls on either side of him. They were all naked to the waist and cuddling. Adelphos's entrance startled the pair of Talarians, causing them to hurry out of the bed and onto their knees with their heads low to the floor in the presence of the emperor.

Agraven just lay there and drank from a wine bottle as Adelphos scrutinized him.

"Do you have no conscience?"

"Not when I have wine," he replied.

Adelphos paced.

"I don't understand. You were once so devoted."

Agraven sat up.

"These creatures do not count. There can be no love between us, no children."

"Like Jerle? Has her barrenness finally broken you after these few short years?"

Agraven waved the emperor's assumption away and grabbed a buttoned shirt from the sheets.

"I've done what you ask. I've sold myself to you. Now, I want to know the truth."

Adelphos crossed his arms.

"Your wife survived the ordeal, as promised."

"She is a capable woman, and I was never concerned for her much."

"Duke Medwin asked Baigen to have your daughter killed. It seems he always had an eye for her and hated your *relationship*."

Agraven's face went dark, and he finished buttoning his shirt in haste. He stood and went for his sword and hauberk, which were lying in the corner of the room.

"Oh no, not yet, not in the capital," Adelphos stopped the man, grabbing him by the shoulder.

Agraven spun out of his grip, furious.

"He will die tonight!" he shouted, then burped.

Adelphos raised his hand and pointed his finger right in Agraven's face.

"He will perish when I say he does. Or I will destroy you and everything you love in this world. Go home to your wife."

The words sobered Agraven a bit and he shrugged past Adelphos to go to the secret passage. The emperor smiled, thankful not all men were as complex as his nephew. This one was chaotic but as easy to direct as the element he controlled. Baigen did well this time, Adelphos thought, by shaping the fire elemental user into a man the Empire could use, one that could be directed.

* * *

Jerle didn't cry anymore at night about Saveria. She just lay in Agraven's arms, staring into the darkness of their room. He told her he had been kept in a palace room under guard and not the dungeon and it hadn't been an unpleasant experience, except for the potential execution.

He told her all the things a husband should: how much he worried for her, how much he missed her, and how he never wanted to let her go, again. And she confessed almost her entire journey to him. He was saddened over Raife and vowed to visit his brother as soon as she was ready to brave another trip south. That would be a long time, she thought to herself.

When they were alone, he kissed her new scars, the ones that were visible. What she did to Chilali would not leave her, not even when he held her and not even when she explained what she did and why—to save his life. He simply said he understood, he loved her, and she was forgiven.

She would never be forgiven. Blood like that doesn't wash away, they both knew. It seeped deep inside with the rest.

She climbed out of bed and wrapped herself in a blanket. In the dark she found her way to the lavatory just in time. She was sick again, even at this odd hour. It was just one more thing she kept from Agraven. She rinsed and cleaned up and walked through the halls of her house, feeling like a memory of her old self.

She passed Astra's room. The Talarian slept soundly and deep beneath the covers. Agraven objected to giving the Lesser her own room, but Jerle didn't care. Astra was important to her now and she would protect her and treat her well. Isolating her was also the best way to watch her and make sure she never made the grave mistake of using Sitara's light again—one more thing she kept from her loving husband.

She stopped in front of the cold hearth where Falcon first began to coerce her into carrying out Chilali's murder. She chose to keep secrets from Agraven now, because of what she learned from Falcon. The men she trusts most are capable of lying to her and manipulating her. Beriszl's words stayed with her, and she heard them each time her husband touched her in a slightly unfamiliar way. Agraven served the emperor; she was almost completely certain and intended to learn the truth about his captivity before birthing another of his children.

Divergent Chill

Chilali felt as if she had been ejected from her body but remained anchored to it with millions of white-hot threads. She couldn't make it move, couldn't think about anything other than her own suffering, and was completely numb to the world outside herself. She didn't even know she was falling or could even remember why.

But she did, building speed the deeper she dropped into the mountain until the wind howling in her ears stirred her awareness. There was a crack, she thought her hip struck something, but she wasn't sure. She just felt the power of the centrifugal force on her limbs as she spun from the blow. Another hard crash followed. It rocked her whole frame and clacked her teeth together. From there, she distinctly remembered rolling, tumbling over her jumbled, lifeless limbs.

It ended with cold swallowing her, thick and black. She didn't even realize she had been breathing at all until the cold shocked the air from her lungs. But only masses of warm bubbles came out as the pressure squeezing her and pressing against her ears became overwhelming.

She tried to fight against it, the impossibly strong frozen hand crushing her and pulling her ever deeper, but she couldn't move. And the metal still wrapped around her body only helped to drag her down more.

But it was in the cold she noticed a light, but not with her blind eyes. The light was inside her, gentle and small like a tiny candle burning in a far-off window, but blue like the cerulean leaves of her forest when sunrays would make them glow. She reached for this light, despite the thousands of searing knives poking into her skin and the thousands more inside of her trying to pierce their way out. The light had its own coldness to it, like a frail melting icicle in her hand. She grasped it and the cold engulfing her went away. The black hand pulling her down relaxed its grip and after a time, she could breathe again, even if breathing were like imbibing fire itself.

Her mouth and nose barely bobbed above the water's surface as ice encased her entire right arm, spreading across her chest and back and down to her waist and both her legs. Her left arm was broken in many places and drifted loose like bound driftwood, circling around her head on top of more ice. Beneath the ice, the explosion burned most of the skin on her chest away, exposing the raw meat and bone and a pair of cracks in her sternum. She was too hurt to even know she was still alive, floating in pitch beneath thousands of feet of rock.

She was only aware of the icicle like cold spot she grasped. It slipped from her hands for the moment, but she could feel its cold bleeding into her from a place just behind her eyes. It was as familiar to her as her five senses, but she never noticed it before. And she floated, thinking that was odd of her not to notice.

Much time passed as she slept beneath the mountain, held aloft by ice that never seemed to melt. Her awareness returned slowly and usually with more pain. With great effort, she straightened her battered left arm so it would heal properly. She struggled to free herself from the ice but didn't have the strength yet to break it. But her strength did return in time, and she was able to tear herself free.

When she did, she immediately sank, pulled down by her own body's mass and that of the metal still frozen and clinging to her. She wrenched it free and fought her way back to the surface. Her wounds healed some but left her in dazed agony for just trying to tread water.

Swimming in an unknown direction, she found a shore of sorts, a flat slab of rock. She crawled on top of it and slept more. Small creatures that had no recognizable scent and moved with impressive silence often skittered for her to try to make a meal. But she ate them instead, crunching on their thick carapaces and fine, hairy legs. Their insides were spicy and bitter, but warm. Their actual shape, however, she wasn't able to discern.

She slept much more peacefully on the damp rock with sustenance in her belly. And she dreamed of the cold spot behind her eyes. Suddenly aware of it, she found it annoyed her, like an eyelash dangling in front of one of her eyes or an odor that clung to her and would not leave.

She woke from such a dream and sat up. Her eyes were completely adjusted to the darkness, but even she was only able to make out the barest of shapes. It was more like trying to tell the difference between the darkness of shadows and served little purpose. High above, like a dim star in the night sky, she believed she could see the hole through which she fell but could not see the walls to try to climb out. And she wasn't sure that she wanted to do so anyway.

The reality of why she fell into this pit lingered at the edge of her consciousness. For so long she was preoccupied with her physical pain and now those hurtful memories returned. She sobbed to herself in the cool dark, where no one could see or hear. Jerle's words wouldn't leave her and stuck in her throat like a swallowed hair. She didn't want to believe her mother was gone, that she would never see her again. And yet, it felt so right and so easy to give into such despair beneath the world.

She couldn't quite understand their betrayal. She looked to herself and her actions for the cause. And she saw the little instances where they seemed afraid of her or disgusted by her actions. After the Avidan fell, she remembered letting herself go and wondered if that was the moment where Jerle and the others decided she was truly too dangerous to allow to walk in the kingdom of man. Violence came too naturally for her and with too much joy. She wanted to make herself angry over it and to blame them and not herself. But she was alone and even Jerle turned against her.

The fire elemental user learned of her treachery; the secret Falcon asked her to keep. She wanted to tell Jerle from the beginning and did not like the lie she told. All she needed to do was return to the forest and none of this would have happened. Minnie would be alive.

Should she just stay in the dark forever, she wondered. Trying to escape didn't seem to serve any purpose. She could not go back to them, Alden and the others, even if she wanted to. Falcon, Olin, and their emperor made it clear what her role in their world would be—servant or corpse. She could find her way back to her forest, however, and return to the silent, violent existence she first knew. But she felt no real nostalgia for it.

She began to shiver, and the sensation surprised her. Since the fall, she hadn't felt the cold, but the entire time she had been captivated by the newly realized sensation inside of her, that little cold spot. She mentally grasped for it in reflex to not have to suffer the cold. But she pulled at it harder than she intended, and its freezing power jolted into her, rolling down her arm with a numbing tingle, and manifested in her right hand. The gentle blue flames undulated along her fingers and danced on their tips, casting soft illumination.

Her eyes widened with elation, and she held her breath in disbelief. She was an elemental user like Jerle, Agraven, and the Avidan. But her element was not fire, she understood, as she dipped her burning hand in the water and watched a patch of it freeze. It smoked and cracked as it floated away from her and her island, and the light generated by her flames died.

Possibility and the hope it brings came to her as she began to shiver again. With enough time to really learn how to use this new power, she could match anyone in the Empire. But Jerle and Agraven told it was a dangerous power, so she would have to be cautious. And she would have to escape this mountain.

She grasped at the cold spot, again, drawing the flames to her hand so she could see her surroundings. She sat in a narrow cavern that tunneled in a few different directions. The walls were smooth and sloped outward and seemed impossible to climb. Though, several stalactites and stalagmites met each other with some crisscrossing and other meeting point to point. She could scale those to reach the cavern ceiling and then the edge of the shaft. Those walls were too far away to be seen clearly, but she was determined now to leave this place.

The night turned to day by the time she finally climbed out. Her fingers and toes were raw and bloody, and she laid at the edge of the shaft for a moment to catch her breath. The glare from Sitara's star felt blinding, but she was relieved to see it once more. The air was as chilly as she remembered, and the wind blew more strongly with a low growl.

She stood and took measure of herself. Nothing of her armor remained and the clothes beneath were less than mildewed rags. She stripped them away and tossed them below and then scaled the mountain to the point where snow and ice collected. She scrubbed herself clean with the cold powder, using her new power to not feel its bite.

She stood in the crisp air with the wind teasing her lips with strands of her wild hair. Her bare feet sank down to her ankles in the snow. From so high and with such vision, she felt she could see everything, but only focused on one thing in particular. The settlement she bled to take for the Empire to free Alden and Agraven no longer belonged to the Empire. Like a pile of angry ants, Blackland Nation warriors dotted the landscape in numbers many times greater than what she and her supposed army faced.

Thousands, she was certain. They had many, many wagons, stacks of supplies, and were busy scavenging the surrounding lands for building materials. They were building an even higher wall that would encompass the original one several hundred feet out with new towers.

She had many questions about her former companions, including whether or not Alden's life was really spared. But upon seeing such a massive number of warriors swarming the settlement, she had many more. Beriszl and Astra could have been overtaken and killed. She had no sense of how long she was beneath the mountain. Did even Falcon and Olin escape before this force arrived? She sincerely hoped they did, finally finding the rage she was searching for in the dark.

The knight was to blame for all of this, she began to understand. He asked her to lie to Jerle. And he ordered Jerle to kill her. She quaked for the day they would meet again.

Her lips curled in a slight smile, as she noticed Blackland Warriors, six, hiking up the mountain along a slope certain to cross her. She could force information from them, take their clothes and supplies, and make a weapon of one of their spears as Beriszl had done.

Murder and starlight glimmered in her eyes, and she no longer cared that this world of man had no place for her. If necessary, she would hollow out a place inside of it and eat its heart and liver for sustenance. Its carcass would become her new home. No one would stop her from achieving this, not Falcon, not the emperor, and not even the pursuit of her mother.

She grew tired of always hurting over that old wound. And wished she could just let it slip away from her, but it would always be with her, altering her perception of this world and motivating her toward one course of action over another. Her new power provided her with more than just a distraction from this pain; it gave her a new way to define herself. She was grateful for this most of all, but also acknowledged she would never give up her search. Jerle be damned.

With her element and her new understanding of this

world and its machinations, she felt more than just empowered—she felt reborn. She became something even more deadly than the wild beast that was taken from the forest and was given a pet's name.

"I'm not your pet," she hissed into the wind. "I'm not Chilali."

She let the wind carry her words into the sky, her eyes clouded in thought.

"You will call me, Chill," she growled at the world and the wind seemed to settle at her words.

The memory of the ribbon and its enchantment remained clear in her mind. The ruby color in her hair drained away with the emerald in her eyes, as she took the guise of an ordinary girl of the Empire. She would have a much easier time ambushing the Blackland Warriors below this way and if any others saw her, word would not spread of a Divergent roaming the mountains. This time she would be more careful and respect the danger the men of the Empire posed to her. As Alden suggested to her in the capital, she would be more discreet and vowed she would see the merchant, again.

She licked her lips, reveling in the moment and knowing it was a new beginning for her. She dashed down the mountain with snowflakes in her hair.

Epilogue

315th Day, 4254, Nowhere

Strife's last known journal was dated the 11th Day, 4059. He died on the 12th Day, 4059, while destroying the Volitors' Brute King (the descriptions of which are inconsistent). But it is generally accepted knowledge that the Brute King wiped out roughly one-third of the Empire's entire force of 22,000 before Strife intervened, alone.

The Order preaches Strife was consumed by his own elemental power, because of the curse of the amulet he wore (an amulet that supposedly held a fragment of the Time King inside of it and radically increased his element powers). But none in the Order dare to say he suffered a living death or became an elemental. They would not tarnish his memory.

I head southeast. I do not know where, perhaps the coast. I thought to pay Orsa's ruins a visit. I thought to take up my hunt of Shank, again. And then I thought better of it all.

Feeling as I do, I am reminded of the story of the first ice element user as told by my father. She was a beautiful, yet solemn woman who lived thousands of years ago. She discovered her unusual element at an early age, but its power was pitifully weak, despite its uniqueness. But it drew the attention of a powerful chieftain who thought to add her to his harem for the novelty of her power. She continually refused his advances, however, angering him. He thought to shame her for her arrogance by marking her face with searing metal, which would forbid any man from marrying her.

But in his attempt to shame her, he woke the true extent of her power. In her fury, she turned the sky itself to freezing liquid and made the Blackland Mountains as jagged as they are today.

She became the first matriarch of the Blackland Nation and was known as the Ice Queen, the mortal wife of the Ice King. She could freeze all things, crack metal as it if were glass, and blanket the land in snow for a day's travel in any direction. More importantly, she was loved, revered, praised, and worshipped.

But her first and only child took ill and was destined to die. She thought to freeze the passage of time, to hold everything just as it was to keep her child forever.

Once again, her ice cracked the mountains and turned the sky into freezing fluid. Many, many thousands died, but it was still not enough. Whether she succumbed to the living death or became an elemental, no one knows. But I believe she learned some difficult lessons in her final moments. Time will always move forward. Loss is inevitable. Change forever and always occurs.

Sitara and Shyamon saw to this long ago when they shattered the Time King, the only being capable of holding the world still. But they could not destroy the temptation to want to preserve all that we love. And they could not remedy the foolishness that leads us to believe we can succeed in doing so.

The Empire I love is destined to fall, not to just the eventuality of time, but to its enemies, because we have not learned the lesson of the first ice element user. We were not willing to accept Chilali and the change she represented.

In my weaker moments, I pray to Sitara to give me the power to accept her loss. I still dream of her riding at the front of a silver army, even though I know it has more to do with desire than prophecy. I still hope for the impossible.

This is why I am and always will be a fool. No amount of knowledge or experience will change this. Even Sitara must accept this one thing as eternal.

—Alden Amos

Author's Note

    Thanks for reading Divergent Chill: Battle of Nesma. I hope you enjoyed it and are looking forward to reading the sequel, Divergent Chill: Fall of Night.

    For more information on the Divergent Chill series and other upcoming books by me, visit my website: www.DivergentZen.com.